FINANCE BROS

BAY AREA BROS
BOOK 1

AUGUST JONES

Copyright © 2025 by August Jones

Ryan and Malcolm Illustration:@pro_art_digital

Cover Design: RavenRed Designs

All rights reserved.

No part of this book may be reproduced in any form or by any electronic or mechanical means, including information storage and retrieval systems, without written permission from the author, except for the use of brief quotations in a book review.

The author does not consent to any Artificial Intelligence (AI), generative AI, large language model, machine learning, chatbot or other automated analysis, generative process or replication program to reproduce, mimic, remix, summarize or otherwise replicate any part of this creative work via any means: print, graphic, sculpture, multi-media, audio, or other medium.

To what could have been.

FINANCE BROS

CONTENT AND TRIGGERS

Thank you so much for picking up the illustrated paperback of *Finance Bros*! The Bay Area Bros are sooo much fun. And hot!

For new to me readers, welcome, and thanks for giving me a chance to impress!

That all being said, this is where I give you the content and trigger warnings, so if you're cool with not knowing, feel free to skip ahead.

Content: Finance Bros is an MM stepbrother hate to love romance meant for adults. It contains explicit sex scenes and a few soft kinks such as feminization, watersports (don't be scared, I think you'll be surprised how much you like it), first times, and flesh lights.

Triggers include homophobia, both internalized and not. A potentially disturbing childhood memory involving sex (no abuse or inappropriate behavior with minors), past deaths of parents (not described), and a history of bullying behavior.

Should you notice a trigger I did not mention here that you feel is worth listing, please don't hesitate to reach out to me about it. I can update the content of the book at any time.

If you're ready to meet my finance bros, please do carry on.

CHAPTER ONE

RYAN

I have the worst song stuck in my head. I blame my former stepdad. He had terrible taste in music. Eighties hair bands. And I'm not talking Guns N' Roses or Metallica—nothing that stood the test of time. I mean Slaughter. Cinderella. Faster Pussycat. Shit no one my age has heard of but serves as a default soundtrack to my life whether I like it or not.

Tonight, the band is Poison. The song, "Every Rose Has Its Thorn." The reason—I'm on a date, and I'm hoping to get laid. The date is the thorn, the rose—self-explanatory. The problem? I only know the chorus, so that one part is playing on a loop in the lead singer's stupid twang, and I can't shake it.

The law student sitting across from me must have seen something on my dating profile that appealed, so here I am, rolling through the thorns of social interaction in order to lie down in a bed of roses—*Bon Jovi*. She's pretty. Her long, dark blond hair has lighter highlights around her face. She's got a few freckles across her cheeks beneath bright blue eyes. She's tiny, though. Like super petite. Short and skinny. I'm no giant, but she makes me feel like one. Her name is Ruby, which is maybe where the idea of roses came from.

We've been quietly studying our menus since the waitress dropped off our wine, which means it's time for me to ask a thoughtful question in order to seem like I can hold a conversation. "So...law school..."

Ruby smiles, nodding encouragingly.

"What's that like?" I ask.

"I mean, it's competitive. Really busy. Tons of writing, even more reading."

"But you like it?" I ask, drawing on my rudimentary communication skills.

"It's a love-hate relationship for sure," she says.

I set my menu down. "Thanks for taking the time out."

Ruby smiles as she picks up her glass of wine. "Thanks for asking me out on an actual date. Most guys just invite me to their apartments."

"Oh yeah?"

She shrugs like *dating, am I right?* "Usually it's fine, but my ex was the last person to take me to dinner."

"Oh." Did I miss a memo? Am I fucking up *dating*?

"Seriously, Ryan—it's a good thing."

She says that like I'm a damn unicorn, and I'm forced to wonder whether all the other women I've taken out think dinner is—what? Weird? Extra? Old-fashioned? Should I be skipping all this expensive shit—the whole getting to know you song and dance—and inviting them back to my place to get drunk and go to bed? It'd save time and money, and if that's how the rest of guys in the Bay Area do it, who the fuck am I to buck the system?

"It doesn't mean anything," I blurt out, suddenly defensive.

She jerks her head.

I could have phrased that better. Way better. "I mean everybody has to eat, right?"

"Right." She averts her gaze and takes a sip of wine. After

swallowing, she says, "So you said you're starting a new job Monday?"

"It's an internship."

"Oh."

"But it could lead to a job—a really good job."

"You've got your MBA, right?"

That's on my dating profile. "Yes." I might not look like the type, but I'm good at school. My whole life, I've wanted to be rich. I don't believe in the saying money can't buy everything. Of course it can. Maybe it can't technically buy happiness, but it can sure as hell get me a ton of distractions.

"What's the job?"

"Investment banking."

"Nice. I've heard that's a good gig. Great work if you can get it, right?"

"Right."

A glint in her eyes accompanies a small smile I interpret as flirtatious. Thank God. I'm not completely blowing this.

"You don't look like an investment banker," she says.

"No?" I already know this. "What do I look like?"

She laughs, covering her mouth with one of her tiny hands. "When I saw your profile pic, I thought you might be in a band or something. Maybe a bartender? But I mean that in the best possible way."

"That's a terrible picture of me. I've had multiple haircuts since. I should update it."

"It's a great picture," she argues. "And who doesn't like a bartender?"

"Why would you want to go on a date with a bartender?"

"Ouch." Her next laugh is less amused, more cautious. "What's wrong with bartenders?"

I shrug and swallow the dregs of my wine. As usual, my baseline personality is getting in the way of maintaining a decent impression. My mom calls it "caustic." Occasionally, someone will like me despite all my rough outer layers, but I'm an acquired taste. I refill Ruby's wine, hoping more alcohol will help blur my sharper edges.

I don't hate the idea of skipping dinner in the future. A meal with me rarely ends well, usually goes a hell of a lot like this, and only sometimes winds up in someone's apartment. "Nothing," I say. "Bartenders are great. Me personally, I'm really looking forward to the internship. If it goes well it could mean getting my dream job." Dream life. Dream everything.

"You're peaking early," she says.

I shake my head. "The job's just the beginning."

"Then what?"

My microeconomics professor Norah comes to mind. She was an adjunct at PSU before going back to work at her firm in Seattle—a satellite office of Marks & Baker. Norah swears she had nothing to do with my getting the internship at the flagship offices here, but I don't care whether she did or didn't put in a good word for me. The opportunity at Marks & Baker is all that matters.

Norah was married while I was taking her class, but she isn't anymore, and she's somehow worked her way into these visions I have of my dream life. She's gorgeous. Single. No kids. And, more importantly, she's one of the aforementioned people who likes my personality. I like hers, too. So much that I actively picture her with me when I say to Ruby, "Dream home, dream yacht, dream vacations."

"Sounds like you have a whole plan."

Damn right. "What's yours?"

"Pass the bar exam."

"Amen." I lift my glass for a toast.

The rest of the conversation goes well enough that Ruby invites me back to her place. We have sex with her on top because I'm scared I'll crush her, and afterward, I crash hard, exhausted from all of it—the wine, the talking, the orgasm. The effort the whole night took.

I'd take a fucked up stock portfolio to sort out over *that* any damn day. No offense to Ruby. She's great, but dating wears me the fuck out.

My Apple watch wakes me before dawn, and I slip out of Ruby's bed in a maneuver I've perfected—guaranteed not to wake even the lightest of sleepers. On my way out of her building, I send her a text, thanking her for the night and apologizing for having to leave early.

Once I'm home, I intend to go straight back to bed, but when I arrive, my roommate is already at it, working out in the living room he's turned into his home gym.

Deacon is a friend of a guy I knew at PSU. I wound up in his apartment because he was looking for a sublet after his previous roommate moved out to live with his girlfriend. I've been here almost a month, which more or less makes this living situation the world's longest blind date, which is to say, he and I are still feeling each other out.

From what little conversation we've had, I know he writes code for some big tech company, but I only ever see him working out. It's six in the morning, and he's already dripping sweat, his corded muscles shiny and defined as hell. The dude's got zero body fat. And I know because I've watched him check it. With calipers.

It's not all for looks—he's literally training for an Iron Man. He's got goals, but in terms of looks, in my humble opinion, there's no room for improvement. He's out most weekends, where I assume he's putting his looks to good use. I guess it's possible he's got a girlfriend, but I haven't seen one yet.

"How was the date?" Deacon asks, out of breath.

I look blankly at him, like the fact that I'm just now coming home speaks for itself.

He grins. "Right. Cool. I got um...fresh bananas."

I continue staring at him.

"In case you're hungry."

"No."

"Yeah, okay."

"Have a good workout." I slip out of the living room and lock myself in my bedroom. I need to hit the gym at some point today, too, but I'm trying to chill my brain out before Monday. Step one was the date, which—while I won't be marrying Ruby or anything—ended as well as it could have. Step two is to bank some sleep before my first day at work so I don't look like some burnout they dragged off the street and put into a nice suit. Step three is to memorize some talking points, which I figure I can do on a treadmill.

I suck at small talk *and* strangers. I'm awkward and sour on a good day and rude as fuck on a bad one. I have this issue with keeping my mouth shut when I don't agree with something. It's a byproduct of deciding a while back that I needed to stop giving a shit what anyone thinks of me. The problem is I need to make a good impression Monday. I need to build a filter, put it in place, and make it work.

Using my small shaving mirror, I practice facial expressions in the shower. A huge smile looks terrifying, but it's a starting point. I'm going for bland but interested. Even that, though, is a stretch. It feels like smiling, too. In its resting position, my mouth is moody and pouty, like I just got grounded for three weeks. In order to make it not look like that, I have to activate my cheek muscles, which not only feels unnatural, it makes me look like an idiot.

Even when I smile small, it looks like I'm disapproving of something.

Fuck my mouth, Jesus. I'm gonna have to make this work with my eyes and forehead. A slight widening of my eyes smooths out the perma-line between my brows and opens up my expression a little. The muscle strain is minimal, and I look sort of pleasant that way.

I try to build some muscle memory by forcing myself to maintain the expression while I finish up in the shower. It's not easy. My mouth keeps wanting to get involved, and every time I catch a glimpse of myself, it feels fucking hopeless.

Afterward, I lotion up my two sleeves of tattoos, the ink on my torso, and the intricate design on my thigh. It's been about six months since I got a tattoo, and I'm feeling the itch again. I've been wanting to get started on my back, but until I'm making some serious coin, it seems dumb to spend so much money on something I'll only see when I twist around to look in the mirror. Still, the burn of the needle is a craving—an addiction I can't quit.

My stomach growls as I'm getting into bed, and I think about Deacon's bananas, but in the end, I don't have the energy to get up and grab one.

I'M LIKE—COMPLETELY in love with you.

I wake up coughing, like I'm trying to choke the words back into my throat the way I wasn't able to when I said them ten years ago. The worst fucking mistake I ever made and not—I repeat—*not*—the thing I need to be thinking about when I'm headed to the most important opportunity of my life. But that's the problem with recurring dreams—they tend to pop up in times of stress.

It doesn't take a psychoanalyst to decipher what the dream

means. It was my most embarrassing moment, and I'm afraid of embarrassing myself today. It makes sense, but still, I have to pat my body down to remind myself I'm not fourteen anymore. Kids are stupid, and they fuck up bad sometimes, and I'm not that kid. The hair on my legs proves it. I didn't get that until I was sixteen and had already learned my lesson. Over and over again, I learned the damn lesson.

I get out of bed as quick as I can in case I start to dwell on stupid shit I can't change, and head for the shower. After an hour of painstaking self-care—hair styling, a close shave, a nail trim, and a lot of expression training, I'm on my way to the Marks & Baker building in downtown San Francisco. I'm wearing my nicest gray suit, brown leather shoes polished to a fine gleam, and my late father's watch fit snugly over my wrist.

My phone rings, and a small smile makes its way onto my face when I see it's *her*. She can say what she wants about boundaries and student-teacher relationships, but she and I both know we'd work. "Hey," I answer.

"Hey! Are you excited? Nervous?" Norah's voice is on the lower side of feminine without being husky.

"Yes," I tell her, catching a reflection of myself in the window of a building I pass.

"It'll be great. You'll see. I'm *still* friends with the people who were in my internship."

"Did you forget I don't have friends?"

"You have me, don't you?"

"Ouch," I say, smiling again.

"Ugh...you're *killing me*, Ryan."

"Me? I'm not the one with all the prissy rules."

"Prissy? You could have just as easily gotten a job in Seattle."

"You told me not to," I don't hesitate to remind her.

"Well, I was stupid."

I laugh, and she does, too. Then, with a sigh, she says, "One day..."

"Maybe..."

"Wanna tell me about what you're wearing?" she asks.

I shake my head. "No. But you're welcome to tell me what you've got on."

"I'm still in bed..."

"Must be nice."

"Just a tank and panties."

"Okay, that's enough," I cut her off. "I can't be thinking about that right now. I have to practice being friendly."

She laughs, and I picture her rolling onto her stomach, her ass covered in black satin underwear. "Bye Ryan, have an amazing day."

"Bye. *Norah*."

She groans again and hangs up.

I grin as I pocket my phone. She and I were never like this in person, but since she moved to Seattle and decided she wanted to keep in touch with me, things have shifted. I don't hate it.

What I do hate is being this nervous. The Marks & Baker skyscraper is all white concrete and glass, glittering despite the fog rolling over the bay. It's windy, cloudy, and cold as usual. I heard the sun is planning to make an appearance later this morning, which I have to admit makes today feel auspicious and promising.

I had my appointment with building security last week, so the man at the front desk has my new badge waiting for me. It's only my fourth time in the building—two interviews and the background check, but I know where I'm headed. Tenth floor—progressive investments.

The elevator is loaded with a wide array of people encompassing various ages, genders and ethnicities. I'm the young white guy with the nearly black hair and disappointed smile.

Marks & Baker is a top ten company, known for the diversity of its work force, which it's not shy about crediting for its massive success in the investment world. They hire from everywhere on the planet, and it doesn't matter where you went to school. They look at your transcripts and grades, but they're more interested in what you did while you were there—the ideas you had, and the mark you want to make on the world.

While I do want to be rich beyond reproach, I also want regular people to stop suffering over money so much the way my parents always seemed to. Wealth should be accessible to anyone who wants it.

In college, I started a club to help demystify the stock market for people who wanted to make some extra money. If anyone thought "this guy doesn't act like someone who'd start a club," they'd underestimate my desire for this internship in particular. I'm capable of coming out of my comfort zone in pursuit of a goal—especially one I want this much.

This internship is my ticket to some of the best jobs in the country. Wall Street...or Seattle.

I grew up in a suburb of San Francisco, so Marks & Baker has been on my radar since my teens. I've known what it takes to get hired here since I was signing up for classes my junior year of high school. AP Econ, Calculus, fucking golf, which I have a stupid knack for. Whacking a tiny ball with a metal club turns out to be directly in my internalized rage wheelhouse. The only reason I don't play anymore is because the sun is bad for my tattoos, but I have no doubt that with enough sunscreen and motivation, I could pick it back up and not make a fool of myself.

Three other people get out with me on the tenth floor. They disperse while I approach the receptionist.

Her large, dark eyes take me in from head to toe. Her thick black hair is styled in long waves. Makeup is precisely applied, and her white, sleeveless dress sets off her rosy brown, South

Asian skin. She notes my badge and smiles, crimson painted lips revealing dazzling teeth.

"Ryan Vale?"

"Yes ma'am."

"You'll be in the east conference room." She points east, I guess. "Second door on the left."

The progressive investments offices are open and collaborative. There aren't any cubicles. It's set up more like a community coffee shop with one long wooden table where people are working on their laptops and sipping lattes. In another area, couches circle low tables, but there are no individual desks in the primary workspace. All the actual offices are enclosed with glass, reserved for the senior investors. They line the back wall and feature a broad view of the Bay.

The hallway I'm being pointed toward has a chic, rustic sign signaling there are restrooms, conference rooms, and "The Lounge," which is half coffee bar manned by a barista with basketfuls of free snacks and half break room equipped with refrigerators for employees next to a countertop covered with microwaves.

I was told lunch would be provided today, so all I have in my messenger back is my laptop, a notebook, and an aluminum water bottle.

I fix my face as I approach the conference room where the door is already open. Low chatter comes from inside, and I have a brief moment of panic that I'm somehow late.

I step into the doorway, and four pairs of eyes land on me. I force my mouth into a smile with no teeth, which I remember too late is the one that makes me look annoyed, so I stretch harder to show teeth.

A curvy Black woman rises from the head of the table. She's a head shorter than I am and wears an amethyst-colored pantsuit that's doing its level best to contain her ample bust. She holds out a hand, and a woven Pride bracelet slides out from under her sleeve. "Georgie King," she says. "Pronouns they/them."

I mentally correct myself for misgendering them in my brain and apply the new filter layer to the shaky, newly assembled one I worked hard to put in place this weekend.

I shake their hand. "Ryan Vale. He/him."

"Pleasure. We'll introduce ourselves again once everyone arrives, but this is Piper, Miguel, and Bailey." Georgie points out the three others seated at the table.

Piper is a young white woman in the lethally good looking blonde category with high cheekbones, and an oval face. She's wearing a pale silk blouse buttoned all the way to the neck. Miguel looks to be on the shorter side. He's thin with bronze, hairless skin. He's sporting a sleek man bun over tender brown eyes. He's dressed as I am, in a well-tailored suit, though his is a deep forest green with a floral pocket square. A statement.

For me, Bailey stands out the most mainly because she doesn't stand out at all. She's also white with dark, frizzy hair pulled into a bun, thick eyebrows and no makeup. She's wearing a suit jacket, but I get the immediate impression she'd rather be working from home in sweatpants. Her expression is as sour as I'm afraid mine is.

There aren't any more pronoun surprises—Bailey's a she/her who I don't think cares much for he/hims. I sit next to Miguel, opposite the women and a seat away from Georgie, who says, "We're expecting four more. Feel free to be thinking of any questions you all might have for me or Jonathan."

Normally, I'd use this time to scroll my phone. I'm not here to ask questions. I'm here to listen and learn, but instead, I take out my notebook and pen. Next into the room is Jia pronounced with a long I. She looks mixed to me, Black and white with pale brown skin and natural curls piled high on her head. She's pretty with minimal makeup—her eyes are fringed with long, dark lashes. She has a bubbly laugh and a big smile. Her slender body makes her seem taller than she is when she sits next to me and gives me an excited grin. I do my best to smile without looking like a serial killer.

I'm writing down names, and it helps that everyone else comes in one at a time. Nathan is next. He's gotta be at least six-five. His suit is off-white, which I could never pull off, but he's a Black man with a shaved head, and so it works. He seems a little thrown off by Georgie's pronoun intro, which makes me wonder what part of the country he's from, but he's a good sport about it when Georgie laughs and tells him he'll get used to it.

The last two people to enter the conference room come in together.

It's rarely a relief when I see someone I know. I burn bridges like they're meant for kindling. But it's not the cute redhead Lisette who's got me immediately turning my head back to my paper and pressing a thumb beneath my watch on the pulse point of my wrist in an effort to will myself to remain seated and show no fear—no emotion of any kind.

Because it's *him*. The golden boy of Thousand Oaks High. The best friend I couldn't keep. The bully of my worst nightmares.

The man I swore I'd move heaven and earth never to see again. Definitely *not* the love of my fucking life.

My former stepbrother.

CHAPTER TWO

MALCOLM

Professional. Stay professional. Act like you've got no idea who he is because it's not like he looks anything like someone you'd ever associate with anyway.

I'm sitting next to a butch lady named Bailey who smells like she bathed in coffee grounds, which puts me out of Ryan's direct line of sight. If he looks at me, I'll notice, and I'll shut it down right then and there. For the purposes of getting through the next three months and landing a job at this firm, I don't fucking know him. Never have, don't plan to.

This is fucking unbelievable. The horoscope Kaylin read to me this morning over FaceTime should have been my first clue to brace myself for something like this. It sounded like all the bad ones do—the position of the planets would be clouding a "certain issue", and I might have to make "difficult decisions." I told her I didn't need that kind of negativity, and she argued that it wasn't bad—like how getting the Death card in a tarot reading is supposedly a good thing?

I was already nervous enough about today. I felt better when I ran into Lisette in the elevator—she and I were in grad school together. I also know Nathan. We played basketball in an informal summer league I joined last year before quitting after two weeks.

Ryan is a major blindside, though. The last time I saw him, he looked like he was preparing for a long career ringing up groceries at a Trader Joe's—not like a Tom Ford model at one of the most prestigious internships in California.

I'm not thinking about it. As far as I'm concerned, he's not here.

When the roundtable introductions begin, I'm less listening to anyone else, more practicing my own in my head. I'm Malcolm Walsh. I went to Stanford where I also got my MBA. I want to get rich by making other people richer. No, not that—I'm here to learn from the best and build a career that's not boring—no—*a career that challenges me.*

Ryan's melodious tenor of a voice knocks my thoughts clean off the rails.

"I'm Ryan Vale. I'm twenty-four. I grew up around here, but I went to school at Portland State. I helped run a club where I taught other students to build out their savings accounts by investing in stocks, 401K style. Mixed risk, mixed yield. Talked a bunch of people out of crypto. I like the idea of making wealth possible for anybody no matter what their income or education is."

I find my mouth hanging open slightly, and I close it immediately. As he spoke, memories surged. The way my dad and his mom had their worst fights about money, and the look of terror when I told my father I wanted to go to Stanford. And further back to the minimalist birthday parties with homemade cakes, totally unlike the parties the other kids would have at indoor play areas with bowling and rock climbing and laser tag—all-you-could-eat pizza and huge, pretty cakes.

Our parents weren't broke or anything—there was always food on the table, and the lights only went out during storms, but my dad's an economics teacher, and his mom's a nurse, so we weren't rolling in it either.

Georgie responds to Ryan's introduction. "You'll enjoy this summer then. Nathan?"

I stare at my former stepbrother while he's looking down at his notebook. I can't get over how different he looks from three Christmases ago. That dude was tatted, shaggy, skinny, and reeked of weed. He looked *exactly* like what anyone would picture when they hear someone goes to Portland State. Today, his nearly black hair is in a slick, expensive cut styled away from his face. All his tattoos are covered by his perfectly cut suit, and he looks almost—normal. He's not skinny anymore, either. He's not bulked up like my friend Jake who looks ridiculous, but Ryan's filled out his six-foot frame like his weight finally caught up to his height.

He glances up, and the flash of his dark hazel eyes startles me into looking quickly away, even though he isn't looking at me. Given the fact that he didn't mention me in his intro, I'm gonna take that as permission to proceed as if he and I are total strangers and didn't share parents for more than a decade.

Nathan makes a joke that has everyone but me and Ryan laughing. Too late, I add my laugh, too, but it comes out sounding awkward and fake. I need to sharpen up.

My intro goes about how I planned. I manage to only "um" once, and I don't sound like a totally mediocre white guy, although I don't think Bailey is convinced. I can feel her judgmental side-eye as much as I would be able to feel if she suddenly leaned over and started licking my face. I want to tell her she's not my type either, but I know how well that would go over at this firm.

I've lived in the Bay Area my whole life, and I get how people are around here. You can't go anywhere without seeing a Pride flag, same sex couples, or gender nonbinary *folx*. My first roommate at Stanford was gay, and he had more than a thing or two to say to me Freshman year about my supposed "homophobia," which mostly consisted of my sneering at his guests before I left the room.

It's not like I ever said anything. I just didn't need to see that shit. And I wouldn't call myself homophobic in general—my homophobia is extremely specific—but I did learn what triggers people of that particular persuasion, so I learned to school my expression and use my words more judiciously, which is a useful skill to have in a place like San Francisco where being a cis-straight-white man puts me in a minority. Even at this table, I'm outnumbered. Three women, two gay guys—Ryan and Miguel, a they/them, and Nathan, the Black dude. At least *he's* straight. I think.

I'm all for diversity in the workplace, but my life outside school and work is likely something this lady Bailey would roll her eyes at. I've had the same girlfriend since high school, and all our friends are straight couples—all white. My gym is kinda gay, but there are plenty of women there, too. I believe in live and let live, but that shit goes both ways. I don't need people questioning my identity or my sex life either.

We take a ten minute break before one of the partners is set to come greet us and answer questions. I immediately go to the bathroom to check my hair, which is fine and will stay fine if I manage to keep from touching it.

When I get back to the conference room, it looks like Ryan hasn't moved except to scoot his chair back from the table to give himself room to look up at Miguel who's standing and leaning back on the conference table, smiling down at him and speaking with elaborate hand gestures.

When Miguel hands Ryan his phone, it looks very much like Ryan puts his number in it. It could be an intern thing—we'll probably all have each other in a group text by the end of the week. Or it could be that gay dudes just move *that fast*. I fight the sneer that wants to twist my mouth. It's none of my business. *Stay professional.*

I clear my throat, and Ryan's shoulders stiffen, but he doesn't turn. Miguel smiles brightly at me. "I was just telling Ryan that I have a friend who did this internship six years ago—apparently there's a big team project involved."

Awesome. I love team projects. Kidding. I fucking hate them. "What was the project?" I ask.

"They had to take on a failing business in the neighborhood and make it profitable, but they said the project changes every year."

"Sounds fun," I say, in terms of resurrecting a business. I love a good project. Just not teams. I've always been told I'm not a team player, hence leaving the basketball league after only a couple of weeks. But I also hate losing.

Georgie returns, accompanied by one of the partners, Jonathan Baker. He's a good-looking white dude in his forties with a diamond earring and a few stray silver hairs in his otherwise thick, dark hair and beard. His wire-rimmed glasses make him look intelligent and approachable, but he's one of the richest men in this city, and he's got the future of everyone in this room in his hands.

He pulls up a seat next to Georgie's at the head of the table and introduces himself. "I'm excited for this group," he says. "We're expecting great things. You'll each be paired with either one of our junior advisors or analysts. They'll work with you one-on-one to show you the ropes and expand your knowledge of the field. At the end of this meeting, Georgie will take you around the office, and you'll meet your summer mentors. Sound good?"

We all murmur that it does. But I hear the leading edge in the question, like he's not finished with us yet.

"In addition, we like out of the box thinkers here. When an intern impresses us, we're more likely than not to offer them a job at the end of summer, provided we have positions available. We like to give you opportunities to distinguish yourselves, which is where the summer project comes in."

I tense internally, the shitty horoscope sounding more like a curse than one of Kaylin's tired daily rituals.

Jonathan continues. "The only rule in this summer's challenge is there are no rules."

In an overly dramatic pause, he lets his words sink in, and I get the sense we're all collectively holding our breaths.

"I'm giving you each one hundred dollars. Whoever turns that hundred dollars into the most money by the end of the summer wins. I want to see your work at the end. If you lose your money in a week, you're out, but I expect you'll invest wisely."

"They have to be investments?" Bailey asks with a slightly raised hand.

"What was the first rule, Bailey?" Jonathan responds.

"No rules," she says.

"Any other questions?"

I don't have any. It seems straightforward enough. While I do tend to think in terms of investments, those are slow to yield, so it'll have to be something besides stocks. I backburner it for now. Since I'm not the most creative person in the world, trying to force an idea will only frustrate me.

"Great," Jonathan says. "I'll leave you to Georgie and welcome you all again to Marks & Baker. I hope you enjoy your time here."

No teams? Fuck yes. I'm so relieved, I'm tempted to turn and smile at Bailey, but she's busy scribbling in her notebook. Without thinking, I glance across the table at Ryan. He's looking directly at me. His hazel eyes are subzero cold, and his jaw is set in a perfect square. I perceive the implied threat—the challenge —the *hate*. It lasts all of one second, and I feel like he's got me on my back ready to pound my face with his elbow.

Okay, so the last time I saw him, I wasn't exactly on my best behavior. Or the time before that. But you don't train a dog by telling them no once. You have to reinforce that shit, or they'll test you whenever they get the chance.

It's his fault how things turned out. He was the one who fucked everything up. If he could have kept his stupid mouth shut, we might still be friends even if we're not stepbrothers anymore.

But here we are.

The break I was planning to ask Kaylin for this summer might have to wait. It's not like I can be single *now*. Between this internship and the trips she's planning with her friends, it would have been a perfect opportunity to hit pause on our stale relationship. I figured it would either make us realize we really do belong together or give us each a chance to accept that we don't. There's another couple in our friend group who've also been together since high school. They're engaged, and they seem way more into each other than Kaylin and I do.

But they also live together. They play pickleball and go hiking on weekends. They have date nights and plan fun vacations. Kaylin and I don't do any of that. If she goes out or travels, it's with the girls. If I go on a hike, it's because I want to be by myself. She's not a fan of the great outdoors, and I for one, enjoy jerking off in a tent in the middle of the woods where I can be as loud as I want.

We did try pickleball last spring, but since it required working as a team and losing to better players, I decided pretty fast I wasn't into it.

To be clear—I'm not looking to date or fuck other women. Not that I'm saying if we took a break I wouldn't, but I really do want to focus on this internship. Sex with Kaylin is fine. Or as fine as it can be after ten years together. We still do it a few times a month and know what to do with each other to make it work, so I'm not unsatisfied exactly. It's just that I don't feel any closer to end game if that makes sense.

I do have a sense the clock is ticking for her, though. Last year, I considered taking the plunge and proposing, but the more we talked about being together long term and having kids, the more I chickened out. A break might help clarify whether I actually want to marry her, or I'm just used to her.

And maybe this internship will lead to a job and help me feel more settled in general. Or at least, that's what I thought might happen before Ryan plopped his ass into it.

Just when I thought I'd gotten away from him for good.

I hate how all the severely uncomfortable shit I've spent most of my life pushing to the back of my head is suddenly clamoring to be dealt with. I hate that he's glaring at me like I was the one who fucked everything up. I hate that *I'm* the asshole, when he so obviously is, too.

Georgie introduces me to my mentor—a financial analyst named Isla Dennis. She's a curvy thirty-something with long, nondescript brown hair and vivid blue eyes. Her skin is extremely pale, but she lights up when she stands to greet me. I get a head to toe once-over and a "Wow. Is this my summer bonus?"

I don't know whether to laugh or file a complaint.

Georgie ignores this and leaves me with Isla. There's an immediate vibe—one I immediately dislike. "You're my first intern," she says. "Malcolm, huh? Is that what people call you?"

"Yes," I say, though most people call me Mal.

She says my name several times like a chant as she pulls another chair toward hers and gestures for me to take a seat. When I do, she scoots in. Her knee bumps mine, and she makes no effort to adjust it. To be fair, she's got a large laptop, but it's not gigantic. For both of us to see the screen, we do need to be next to each other, but could she cross her legs?

"So...tell me about you," she says.

I give her the brief bio I gave the other interns.

"I went to Stanford, too! Did you play sports?"

"No. I mostly just hung out and went to class."

"You're so tall. You look like you would've played baseball or basketball or something."

"Yeah. No."

"What do you do to stay in such great shape?" she asks.

"Go to the gym..."

"Which gym?"

I look longingly at the spreadsheet pulled up on her computer screen as I tell her the name of my neighborhood gym, which leads down a rabbit hole about where I live, how many days of the week I work out, and whether I live alone or not.

I'm a terrible liar, so I tell her the unfortunate truth. "Yeah." I'm careful not to ask any reciprocal questions because she's playing with her hair and touching her face too much. She's flirting with me, and it's about as subtle as a brick to the face.

At my first opening, I clear my throat and ask what she's working on.

"Oh! Yeah, I guess we should talk about that. How are you with Excel?"

"Not bad."

"Good. Maybe we can learn from each other, then."

At last, she puts me to work, pointing me in the direction of some cluttered spreadsheets that aren't the easiest to decipher, especially with her constant questions. My concentration is also jacked because I'm thinking about that hundred dollars, and obviously Ryan, who's two tables down with his own mentor, a young, very good-looking white guy in a fully motorized wheelchair.

Ryan's got *glasses* on now—I don't remember him ever wearing glasses—and it shouldn't distract me even worse, but it does. They've gotta be fake. Or like blue light glasses or something. He just looks so...grown up and *normal*. So well put together—I shake my head and look away. It's annoying is all. That he's here. But it doesn't need to ruin my summer or this opportunity.

"Oh—" Isla cuts off my disconcerting train of thought. "That's a tricky one—let me walk you through a few things."

She scoots in close enough that her thigh is fully flush with mine, and I can smell her floral-scented hair. Needless to say, it's a long morning. I finally get a break from her after lunch when she goes to a team meeting, and I insist I'd rather keep looking through the spreadsheets.

She looks disappointed but eventually leaves me alone. I manage my first deep breath of the day. It's not that she's unattractive, but she *is* overwhelming, and there's something slightly wild behind her eyes whenever I look directly into them. Like she's not entirely tethered to reality.

However, she's smart, she knows her shit, and I'm here to learn. Also, I'm not the only new meat in the office. Nathan could be single. Ryan may or may not be, but I know full well he's not into girls. I wonder what he's thinking about his own mentor, who, despite his mobility challenges, is a young, handsome man with no wedding ring. They sure seem to have a lot to talk about. I have yet to look over at them and not see them deep in conversation with full eye-contact and everything.

Why doesn't he just sit on the dude's lap for fuck's sake?

Why the fuck am I picturing that? And why does the image of it make me have to forcibly unclench my fists?

Just before four-thirty, Isla returns from her meeting, a

fresh coating of lip gloss on her full lips. "Want to grab drinks after you're done with your debrief? I can tell you all the office tea."

Here's my best opportunity to reverse this tide, and I jump for it. "Can't. I have plans with my girlfriend after work." Not a lie. "But I look forward to tomorrow. Thanks so much for a great start."

Her smile wobbles, but it doesn't fall. "Girlfriend, huh? What's her name?"

Does she think I'm lying? "Kaylin."

"Hm." She looks me up and down again. "All right. Well, enjoy your evening."

"Thanks," I say, rising from my chair. "You, too."

Making my way to the conference room, I find myself walking next to Nathan. "Heard a few things about your mentor," he says in a low voice.

"Yeah?"

He gives me half a mischievous grin. "You like 'em freaky?"

I sigh. "Shut the fuck up."

The interns meet with Georgie for a half-hour debrief of our days and we're allowed to ask questions and give observations. Ryan is characteristically quiet, and I'm uncharacteristically so. Everyone else wants to know more about the challenge and past challenges. It's enough to hold my attention and distract me from the fact that I'll be stuck in rooms with my ex-stepbrother for the entire summer.

About half of us make it onto the same elevator after the meeting.

Ryan stands in a corner, eyes trained on his phone. Jia, Nathan, and Miguel are also on board. Nathan gives me a nod. "What do you think about the challenge?"

I think it's already stressing me the fuck out. "Sounds fun. I've got a few ideas popping." I don't. I've got nothing.

Miguel says, "Since there aren't any rules, we could pool our cash and have a better start."

"*Yes...*" Nathan says, his dark eyes calculating. "I'd absolutely be down for that."

Miguel brightens, looking to me and Jia. Ryan might as well not be on the elevator. He's got all his walls up. Typical.

I hedge. Like I said—teamwork isn't my strong suit. Every group project I've ever been part of ended with me doing way more work and micromanaging people to the point of visceral hatred on all sides. "I'll think about it."

Miguel cocks his head in Ryan's direction. "Ry?"

Ry? He's got a fucking *nickname* for him already? Just hearing it grates on my nerves. The hairs on my arms stand straight up.

But *Ry* shakes his head without looking up from his phone. "I've been told I don't work well with others."

Miguel laughs like Ryan just said something hilarious and isn't being a complete dick.

I glare at him, not that he notices. Same old asshole.

His eyes flick up and meet mine. Nausea—instant nausea— makes me nearly double over. I don't look away because fuck him. His pale cheeks flush just as fast as bile rises up my throat. The strong physical reaction to what amounts to maybe two seconds of eye contact makes me sick and dizzy. I don't know why I let him get to me like this. I don't know why I keep looking at him, period. He doesn't look *that* different.

When he dips his head down to study his phone screen, I let out my breath and force a grin for the other three interns. This is shaping up to be the worst summer ever.

CHAPTER THREE

RYAN

After sixteen miles on the treadmill, I'm not nearly finished. Sweat is pouring off me, creating a mess of the machine. My body is screaming at me to stop. My lungs burn. My heart is begging me to give it a rest, but I can't.

I can't.

One hundred dollars. Malcolm. One hundred dollars. Malcolm. Malcolm. *Malcolm.*

Fuck.

I grunt with effort and increase the incline, charging forward, going nowhere.

The existence of him hurts like a twisting knife in my side. The sight of him was a swift slash to the gut from which I'll likely bleed out slowly. How did that fucking asshole wind up in one of the best internships in the business? I'm still struggling with the fact that he graduated from Stanford, much less stuck around for an MBA. When did he manage to crack open a textbook in between fucking my ex-girlfriend and going to his fraternity parties? Color me fucking shocked.

It's not like I wish bad things for him. I wish I could, but that's not how I work when it comes to Malcolm Walsh. I merely need him to exist outside my sphere in order to pretend he *doesn't* exist. Is that so much to ask? Because for the purposes of me being a functional human, Malcolm needs to have never happened—as a person or my stepbrother or an embryo even. He should have never been born. Then I'd have been fine. I wouldn't be this sweaty fucking mess who can't punish myself enough.

The most beautiful person to ever grace the earth steps up to my treadmill and strikes a seductive pose. Long, smooth legs, golden blonde beach waves and lips photographers pay to photograph in the Maldives all belong to my new gym friend Calyx. He always brings me up short just because how can he look like that and be real?

At first glance, he's the most gorgeous woman you've ever seen, but Calyx is all boy. Sort of. I don't know. He's hard to describe. "An hour and a half is plenty," he says over the noise of the machine.

"You're not my trainer."

"No, but this much cardio is gonna make you skinny."

I glare at him and keep pounding the tread. He wipes a drop of my sweat off his face and examines his fingertips calmly, then levels his soft brown eyes at me. "You told me if I ever see you going for twenty miles again to save you from yourself."

"I don't remember saying that."

He presses some buttons, lowering my incline and pace.

"Hey!"

"You need a shower."

Calyx and I know each other because he guest teaches yoga classes here, and I took one of them a couple of weeks ago. I was hopelessly inflexible, and he felt sorry for me. We sort of clicked, I guess, but we're strictly gym friends. Our relationship has not reached beyond these walls, and I don't know how we got to this point where he feels comfortable enough to control my workout.

Calling him a friend might be a stretch. Really, he's an extremely pretty person who sometimes interacts with me and tells me what I'm doing wrong. I consider that friendly. Over about a minute, I slow to a stop and step off the treadmill. That's when the sweat really starts to pour.

I push my hair back, grab my towel, and wipe my face and chest. Calyx looks me up and down from his slightly shorter vantage point. He's dressed in tight, gray gym shorts and a tank, revealing his boyishly feminine figure and every toned muscle he's got. He confuses the fuck out of my sexuality. If he were a woman, I'd be all over it, but the straight guy in me can't reconcile how beautiful he is with his flat chest and the fact of his dick. Still, he's impossible not to stare at. He's kinda mesmerizing.

"Training for Everest?" he asks.

"Maybe," I mumble.

"What's your problem?"

"I'm trying not to think about it."

"Which means you definitely won't want to talk about it," he surmises.

"So, you *can* take a hint..."

He peeks at the numbers on the treadmill. "Seventeen point nine? Seriously? Who hurt you?"

Malcolm.

"No one," I say. "Just didn't feel like stopping."

"What's next? Hair shirt? You have a rack to stretch yourself out on at home? I could show you one of the Pilates reformers."

"I'm good, thanks. I have work tomorrow."

"How was your first day? Or should I ask?"

We walk toward the locker room together. Avoiding talking about the reason for my shitty attitude, I ask, "If you had to make a hundred dollars turn into a huge pile of cash by the end of summer where would you start?"

"Hm." He takes a few steps and seems to be putting some thought into it. "I'd come up with a genius catch phrase, trademark it, print it on a few t-shirts and make them the next must have fashion item by forcing everyone I know to wear them and plastering them all over my social media."

"That's not terrible," I say. "Got a good catch phrase?"

"Nothing PG, but I'll think about it. I'd absolutely want a cut if you use my idea."

"Your idea's better than anything I've come up with so far."

"This is your job?" he asks.

"It's like a competition at my job. A side project."

"What's your idea?"

"I don't have one," I admit. "What's worse is I think some of the other interns are teaming up so they start out with more cash, which opens up the possibilities a lot."

"Why don't you join up with them?" he asks innocently.

I glare at him in response.

He laughs, showing his perfect teeth as he throws his head back—all hair, neck, smooth skin. *If I were that pretty, would Malcolm...?*

No. I'm not going there. The answer is no. It's no, it's no way, it's always been no.

$$\$\$\$$$

CALYX WAS A HUNDRED PERCENT RIGHT, of course. I pushed myself way too hard on the treadmill last night, and this morning I feel it in every limb. My legs are wobbly. My arms are heavy with fatigue. My heart rate is so low, I nearly pass out in the shower. Once I've had some coffee, I'm a little better, but I'll need to pick up some breakfast and more caffeine before I get to the office.

There's a dine-in deli called Big Bites a few doors down from the Marks & Baker building. It's got a grab and go counter, so that's where I stop in twenty minutes before I need to be in the morning huddle. My mentor Charlie wants me doing client calls today, and I need my brain firing on all cylinders. Another terrible song is in my head. Thematically it fits—"Don't Close Your Eyes" by the band Kix. Again, I'm only familiar with the whiny chorus. It's two lines: *Don't close your eyes. Don't sing your last lullaby.* Over and over.

While I'm waiting in line to check out with my egg sandwich and energy drink, I feel a tap on my shoulder. I give a sharp glance back, pissed off on principle—no one should touch anyone in public period—but my eyes open wide when I see it's not a stranger. It's my ex stepbrother. "What?" I snap because he doesn't get whatever shred of kindness lurks somewhere in my soul.

"We should probably talk," he says, a grim expression on his annoyingly handsome face.

"I don't think so," I say as my heart leaps forward in my chest desperate for any words he's got for me, no matter how bad they slice or how deep they burrow.

"Maybe you don't, but I do," he says through a tight jaw and tighter lips.

To the outside observer, Malcolm Walsh is your basic golden boy. It's not until you get up close that you see how thick his dark golden hair is—the way it's the prefect shade for his lightly olive skin tone. You wouldn't get the full effect of his heavy-lidded blue-green eyes, and unless he smiles, you might not notice how bright they shine. The way I crave the sight of him is fucking pathological. His face is etched into me far deeper than any tattoo I've suffered through.

"No thanks," I tell him. I turn back to the counter, cutting myself off from the source before he sees it on me—the one way I *haven't* changed.

"Ryan..."

I stiffen—every muscle, every joint. My heart feels like it has to beat harder to overcome the sudden resistance.

"Look," he says, his deep voice taking a grim turn and giving me chills. "This internship is only three months. I don't want any drama. That's it. The only thing I wanted to say."

I shake my head, mostly at the situation.

"No one needs to know we know each other," he adds.

"They're not gonna hear it from me," I assure him.

"Not that it matters," he says. "Or... It's not like I mind."

I scoff at that. He minds. He minds a lot. If he didn't, he wouldn't be speaking to me. It's gotta be pretty fucking inconvenient for him that my PSU degree got me the same place his fancy Stanford one did. "Not my problem," I say, which couldn't be more of a lie if I tried, but since I want it to be the truth, I figure it doesn't hurt to speak it into the universe.

"Still an asshole," he mutters like this comes as no surprise.

I shut my eyes and make myself breathe. I need the line to move and not because he's wrong. He's *right*, and I don't need to hear it from him. Obviously I'm not going to be able to avoid the constant reminder this summer, but I *can* pretend it isn't already breaking me. At least he doesn't have to worry about keeping his shit together the way I do. He broke a long time ago, and I know because I was the one who took a perfectly nice guy and turned him into a raging dick.

To say regret is the defining pillar of my existence doesn't begin to cover it. I have the word tattooed on my left inner forearm in bold, block letters—a visual representation of what I carry with me along with a warning for anyone who gets too close.

"I fuckin' hate you, man." Malcolm says in a low voice behind me.

I fucking wish I did, too. But I do get where he's coming from. I always have. I stop short of apologizing for my existence. I've tried that before. It doesn't work on him.

I think crucifying myself *could* work, but I don't know anyone who would help me out with that.

"Fine," he goes on talking to himself. "We don't know each other. If that's how you want it, fine with me."

I don't say anything. I pretend he's speaking to someone else. When it's finally my turn to pay, I quickly do and get the fuck out of there.

$$\$\$\$$$

DESPITE A RELATIVELY GREAT day at work with Charlie, I'm still in suffering mode when I leave the building. I manage nineteen miles tonight before Calyx stops me. I was trying so hard to clear my head of Malcolm and make magic happen with a hundred bucks in my usually very quick and reliable brain—I didn't realize how far I ran. And after all that—*nothing*. No ideas. Not even a glimmer of one. Just Kix.

Over our lunch break today, Miguel mentioned to me that he, Nathan, Jia, Piper, *and* Lisette are pooling their cash and working together. Evidently they already have a plan, but he said he could only let me in on it if I teamed up with them, too. I highly doubt Bailey wants anything to do with working with a partner, and I already heard Mal turn the group down, so it looks like it's just the three of us going it alone, which sucks. I should have put more thought into joining them. I don't hate Miguel. He seems cool.

Still, I'm about as good at teamwork as a barn cat. I need full control of my own destiny to survive. No one would want to work with me for any amount of time, much less a summer. I'm glad Charlie has me talking to clients on the phone. I don't enjoy it, but it's letting me play with different personas, experiment with what works and what doesn't. Communication is one of my weaker spots, which he and I went over extensively before we started working together.

If I want to be a grown ass adult working in finance, I'm gonna need more than a good golf swing. I need people skills. Charlie has amazing people skills. I, on the other hand, have to pretend I'm some smooth-talking character from a movie and do my best impression. Today I tried to channel Matt Damon. It went okay. Maybe I'll try McConauhgey tomorrow. Not the accent. Just the laid-back attitude.

Currently, I'm home, sitting at my desk, staring at financial news, reading any article I can find about successful startups, and trying to figure out a way to shorten the timeline on turning a profit. I'm on the phone with Norah, and she's trying to assure me the summer project isn't that big of a deal while also telling me about the one her internship had to do, very much romanticizing it. She'd been at the Seattle firm, and it was a team challenge—thank fuck ours isn't—but I'm only half listening to her.

To be clear, Norah and I never officially dated. The last time I saw her, I did kiss her because it was her last day in Portland, but that was it. I've very much romanticized this idea I have about winding up with her. It's a vision, but it's a hazy vision. Still, I've managed to keep our tiny spark alive for the last year, and I really do intend to move to Seattle at the end of summer. We'll see what happens when I get there.

For now, we talk a few nights a week. Sometimes our conversations are more personal and needier than others. Sometimes we talk about how great it would be if we could go grab a drink together, or—if it's sunny in Seattle, she'll say how nice it would be to take a walk with me and show me around. It's the phone call equivalent of holding hands, but I like it. In some ways it feels more real than any of the dates I've been on or other relationships I have—besides Calyx. He's very much in my face, but only at the gym.

Other than my mom, Norah knows the most about me, but even that isn't all that much. I don't like to talk much about my life before I got to Portland, whereas Norah will talk about anything except her marriage.

Like she senses she's losing my attention, she says, "You could start an Only Fans. I might know someone who would be your first subscriber."

"Do you?" I ask, biting the tip of my pen. She's got my attention. "And how would you recommend I scale that?"

"Um...well..easy, right? You start off with yourself and end with a harem?"

I laugh. "You'd sign up for that?"

"I didn't say *me*."

"How would I know if I'm any good at being on camera?"

"Ah...well...you could always record a demo and send it my way. I promise to give you an honest opinion."

I nearly snort. We've sent sleepy selfies, but we have not graduated to dick and tit pics. "I think I better let you go. But if I don't think of anything, OF might be where I wind up."

"Remember me when you're famous?"

"Obviously," I tell her.

We say goodnight, and I go back to my less than productive brainstorming, only halfway thinking about sending Norah a picture of my tenting pants.

I'm not sure I'm ready for that level of intimacy with her yet—not with this project looming and *fucking Malcolm*.

Another useless hour later, in a moment of desperation for any idea to click, I turn to ChatGPT. The smart fucker steals three ideas after a five second scrape of the internet. One involves buying and selling vintage t-shirts, another has to do with going viral—not unlike Calyx's idea, and the third is a dog walking business. The only issue with all of them is that the yield over twelve weeks is only in the low thousands, not tens of thousands.

Still—if I look at the vintage t-shirt idea and scale it to include other rare thrift finds, maybe...

No. No way. I get it now—it's an impossible challenge. I'd be better off putting the money into my savings account. Not thinking about it anymore would probably help, but if I stop, I know exactly what I'll start thinking about, and I'm not going there tonight.

Instead, I put on a song I actually like and ask ChatGPT to make me more money.

CHAPTER FOUR

MALCOLM

"You're being weird."

Kaylin says this Friday night as I'm literally pulling off my full condom and still breathing heavy. Definitely not what a guy wants to hear after coming. "Did you not...?"

"No. I did."

"Then what?"

"You just seem pre-occupied. That's all I meant."

She's still wearing her bra, and she sits up in bed against the headboard while I get rid of the condom. When I turn back to her, she pats the mattress in front of her crisscrossed legs. "Talk to me."

I sigh, plopping my naked ass down. She gives my arm a stroke, and I glance at her briefly. She's a cute girl. Always has been. Petite. Curvy. Soft. Her brown hair was in a perfectly fine bun before we had sex, and now it's mussed and crooked. Her large, dark eyes are sincere and concerned. Because we've been together since freshman year of high school, she's my best friend as well as my girlfriend. She reads me with laser accuracy most of the time, so I never bother with my bad lying.

"One—I can't think of a fucking way to make a single dollar out of a hundred dollars. Two—Ryan's in the internship."

"Whoa—*what*?"

I squeeze my eyes shut. There's a reason I didn't mention this earlier in the week, but ever since he and I "talked" and we're dealing with it by not dealing with it—or he is—I realize I've gotta figure my end out somehow.

"*Our* Ryan?" she asks in a way that makes me flinch.

"You know what I mean," she adds.

She means the only Ryan we both know. She means the guy she was sort of dating before I kissed her at a party and plastered her to me like a shield. She means the stepbrother I used to have who had me dreading every family function for years until his mom divorced my dad. She also means—because she knows everything there is to know about me—the Ryan who used to be my best friend before he ruined everything by telling me he was in love with me.

Normally, I wouldn't have told her or anyone about that day because it was so fucking embarrassing, but I'd desperately wanted to get into her pants at the time, and since she was sort of hung up on him, I had to give her a reason to look my way.

"Yeah. That Ryan."

"How is he?"

"I don't fucking know," I grumble. "Still an asshole."

Kaylin sighs, her hand slipping down my forearm to encircle my wrist. "Have you talked to him?"

"You know, I actually tried. The first day we ignored each other, but I ran into him at a deli Tuesday morning, and I made an effort. He wasn't having it."

"Do you think he still..."

"How could he possibly?" I have given Ryan zero reasons to love me in any capacity for the better part of a decade while giving him infinite reasons to hate me with his whole chest. It appears to have worked.

She studies my face, my eyes in particular. "Yeah. I guess. Do you have to work with him?"

"Not really. We huddle in the mornings and have these intern debriefs at the end of the day where we sit in the conference room for twenty minutes with our supervisor, but other than that, no."

"So, what's bugging you?"

I fucking *wish* I could articulate the answer to that. "You tell me."

She perks up, loving the chance to play therapist. "Any guilt in there anywhere?"

I scowl. "Guilt? For what?"

"I don't know. For being a douche to him every chance you got. For *me*. For trying to out him in front of your stepmom?"

I roll my eyes. "I didn't realize it was some huge secret."

"You said yourself you never saw him with a guy."

"That doesn't mean he isn't off doing it with dudes." Miguel immediately comes to mind, but I shove the thought away. "He's close with his mom—why wouldn't she know?"

"Because maybe *he isn't gay*."

I laugh. "I wasn't the one out of my mind on cough medicine that day. I heard exactly what he said."

"And you majorly over-reacted."

Yes, I know that. I wasn't exactly cool with the concept of my *stepbrother*—the guy who'd been my favorite person ever—who I *trusted*—flipping the tables on me and making it *sexual*. Not that he tried anything. He had the flu. The cough syrup was strong, and he was running his mouth. Still, he never took it back. He tried to apologize, but he didn't take back what he said.

After I shut down his apology, he tried to act like it never happened—like maybe I would forget about it. But how could I?

It changed *everything*. "I just didn't want him to get the wrong idea—obviously he got it from somewhere."

Jesus, shut the fuck up, Malcolm. The last thing I need is Kaylin asking questions about the why of everything, which would force me to think about it, too, and I am *not* going there. I've moved on.

"I'm sure the message has been received by now," she says. "Don't you?"

"I should certainly fucking hope so."

"God," she groans. "I could really do with you being less of a classic homophobe."

"I am not!"

"You completely are. I hear you and the guys talking. I've seen how you act when you see two men on a date."

I genuinely don't want to know what she sees in me when that happens.

Latching onto the rest of her statement about our friends, I say, "Look, Jake, Evan, and Henry are way worse than me. Sue us for being straight."

"I've got no problem with you being straight, Mal, but do you have to be so disgusted by queer people?"

"I'm *not*," I say emphatically.

She gives me a glare, and I guess it withers a critical part of my guard.

"Okay—fine—when I see two guys together in public, and I start thinking about it too hard, it freaks me out a little, but that's just because..." *Whoa there, she doesn't need to know everything.*

"You don't get how a man could find another man attractive?" she asks.

I am *not* answering that question. We're not going there. I have an actual therapist if I ever want to talk about *that*, which I don't. Finally, I manage to gather myself and shut the fuck up. I get up and pull on my sweatpants. "You know, if you really want to help me with something, think of how I can turn a hundred dollars into ten grand in three months. That would be useful."

"Gambling?"

I snort. "Yeah?"

"Sure. Start off small, then increase your risk as your winnings improve. People make whole careers out of gambling."

"I don't know anything about gambling," I say while I look for a clean t-shirt.

"YouTube knows all."

"Yeah, all right. It's not the worst idea. If I can pass microeconomics, I'm sure I can figure out how to play blackjack and not lose my shirt."

"I'll help, I just have to pee first."

I leave her to it and go to the living room. If she's staying, I should order dinner. Having sex took the edge off my restlessness, but it's still there. I pace behind the couch while I scroll for food delivery. Kaylin reappears, sitting on the couch and pulling up YouTube on the flat screen. "Thai," she tells me, and I focus my search. I put in her order for soup and fried rice then drunken noodles for me.

"Five of the other interns are pooling their money and teaming up," I inform her.

"They can do that?"

I shrug. "The only rule was no rules."

"So, are you gonna get with the other two?"

"The other two are Ryan and this woman Bailey who I'm pretty sure wants me to burn slowly in hell for having a Y chromosome."

"Mal, Jesus."

"What? Is that homophobic, too?"

"It's a lot of things, babe. Judgmental being the main one. You only met her a few days ago."

"Sorry," I huff, sitting next to her.

"I'm assuming you don't want to work with anyone else on this."

"You know how I get."

"Competitive?"

"Teamwork brings out the worst in me," I say.

"No. *Losing* brings out the worst in you. You're not really setting yourself up for success here. I know you want to work at that place."

I do want to work at Marks & Baker. I worked hard for this internship, and I love San Francisco. I want to have a life here, and I can't do that earning the industry minimum at a bank branch. So yes, I want to win, and no, I'm not ruling anything out, but being on a team of six? How am I supposed to stand out that way? And regardless of whether Kaylin thinks I'm being too judgmental of Bailey—*I'm* the one on the receiving end of her fuck off vibes every day—I know she's going this alone no matter what. Ryan's just—I shake my head as a full body shudder rattles through me.

"You're not ruling it out," Kaylin notes.

"I..." I feel like I'm missing something. It's a frustrating feeling, and it makes me restless. But I also feel something else—something I haven't let myself feel in a long time—and it's making me equally restless and impatient—like all the answers are right there, waiting for me to stumble on them, and then I'll be settled. Then I'll know what to do. Then I'll be still.

"Wait—do you think you *could* work with Ryan on this?"

I shake my head, the stone in my stomach asserting itself heavily.

She goes on. "I mean, I know *he* wouldn't want to, but you think *you* could? Babe..."

"I didn't say that."

"Mal. Do you feel bad?"

"No," I say firmly.

"Are you sure?" she presses, forcing me to actually consider the question. *Do I feel bad?*

I guess seeing how Ryan turned out after everything—all my rejection and hateful bullying—is sort of a relief. Like I said, the last time I saw him, he looked like a burned out stoner —a loser. To know he got his MBA and is all cleaned up—or looks cleaned up anyway—reminds me we all grow up eventually. The beef I've got with him is legit, but if there's a chance he and I both get jobs at Marks & Baker, do I really want to spend the rest of my career avoiding someone I lost the ability to get along with over something that happened when we were kids?

"He looks different," I say, annoyed that those are the words I choose. I have no business thinking about what Ryan *looks like.*

"Yeah?"

"You know," I mumble. "Like he gets haircuts and works out."

"Uh-huh."

I don't say anything else. I shouldn't have brought it up. I take the remote from Kaylin and start flipping through video thumbnails on the screen. She was right. There's no shortage of people who want to teach me how to gamble and win big. It's probably not much different than investing in the stock market, and I'm not too bad at that.

"So, you're saying he grew up."

"We've all grown up," I mumble.

"Have we though?"

I drop the remote and look at her. "What do you want me to do?"

She holds up both hands. "Nothing. I'm just throwing out ideas. If you're okay with having bad blood, I totally support that."

"Thanks, Kay. Really appreciate you putting it that way."

"But I mean, for real—after all this time, don't you forgive him?"

Forgive Ryan? Have I ever thought of it like that? I mean, he *was* basically a kid. A dumb teenager fucked up on narcotics. Forgiveness isn't really the issue. Back then, it was more like I couldn't hang with him if that was the way he really felt about me—about *guys*. Not when all my friends thought queer people were sexual deviants—aberrations—freaks.

What would I be forgiving him for? Lying to me? Betraying me? Manipulating me? No, that doesn't sound right. Maybe what really upset me was discovering he wasn't who I thought he was. And then...what would that say about me?

"Like you said, it was a long time ago."

"And he was a kid..." she reminds me.

"So was I," I argue.

"Oh my God, never mind, I don't want to talk about this with you anymore. You brought it up, you know?"

"Sorry," I mumble.

"Why? It's not like you ever make up your mind about anything. I'm sure avoiding Ryan for the rest of the summer is by far the easiest thing you can do. You won't even have to think. You just have to not be an asshole."

Whoa. "You sure you want to stay for dinner?"

She doesn't say anything, just selects a video and presses play.

BY MIDNIGHT, I'm down to fifty bucks, and I'm getting desperate. Gambling is fun, and I was doing well for a few hours, but I have to call it quits. I've still got a shot at turning this challenge around with fifty dollars, but if I lose that, I'm out in one night. Yeah, I get that I'm fucked.

Logging into ChatGPT, hoping for some inspiration at a minimum, if not a fantastic idea, I ask the internet to give me three ways to turn fifty dollars into ten grand in three months.

"Buy vintage t-shirts?" I say to the computer screen like it's personally offended me. Would I know a vintage t-shirt if I saw one? Do I know someone who would? My friends are more mid-century modern. Maybe Jake's girlfriend? She dresses kind of quirky.

The escalation of the t-shirt scheme is extreme, too. It's got me turning over refurbished computer parts in two weeks and then rapidly scaling up to limited edition sneakers—like I have time to look for those. As if. But it's either that or dog walking. I might consider dog-*sitting* since I can do that in my time off, but when I plug that in as an option, the yield isn't more than a couple hundred a week—once I start getting clients, which fifty dollars wouldn't help much with.

I go to bed alone and stressed, thinking about everything Kaylin said before the food got here, especially this whole concept of forgiving Ryan for a dumb feeling he had when we were fourteen. I really thought she was going to tell me I owe him an apology for how shitty I've been with him ever since, and I think if she had, I wouldn't necessarily be tossing and turning now.

I probably would have agreed under protest—no harm, no foul. If an apology would smooth the waters for any future interactions, it might be worth it, but forgiveness is like—way different for some reason. Do I just walk up to him and say, hey, asshole. I forgive you? *Would he want that?*

But truly—*do I forgive him*? I'm decently bent out of shape for someone who supposedly got over something years ago.

I don't know. Now that he doesn't look like someone who

washed up on the shore of Venice Beach, I don't really see him as the kid I used to know. The one I spent most of my childhood with as best friends and then bitter enemies. Is enemy the right word for it? For the way I hate him?

Do I still *hate* him? It's obvious there are strong feelings there, otherwise it wouldn't be keeping me up.

Why *the fuck* is Ryan Vale still keeping me up at night? Is seeing me at work every day fucking him up, too? Is he lying in bed right now somewhere with the sheets thrown off running his hand down his bare chest and stressing? Are his abs super cut now, too? I feel my way past mine, which could use some work and fewer carbs.

My fingers swirl through the hair beneath my navel, and I picture what his happy trail might look like—dark...silky maybe?

Goddamnit. *Stop.* What the *fuck*? I take my hand off my stomach and flip to my side. Do people need midnight dog walkers? Surely there's a market for that. Night shifters? I could put up whatever small stack of flyers I can afford to print for fifty bucks in hospitals, I guess.

Okay. I'm spiraling. According to my therapist, the best way to manage a spiral is to take an action. So fuck it. I pick up the phone and call my stepmom.

Jill answers the call, breathless, panicked. "Mal? What happened?"

Oh wow. I totally just called my mom after midnight. Not cool.

"Nothing, I'm so sorry. I didn't realize what time it was."

"You're okay?" she asks.

"I'm fine. I just wanted to see if I could get Ryan's number."

"My Ryan?" Now she *really* sounds alarmed.

"Yeah. Ryan. I don't have his number, and we're in an internship together. I had a work question I wanted to ask him."

"You're in the Marks & Baker internship?" she asks, like it's the first she's heard about it. Granted, I do consider her my mother, but in a distant way, especially since she ditched my dad. Not that I'm mad at her. I'm just not the best about keeping in touch.

"Yes."

"With *Ryan*?"

Now I'm getting nervous. "Uh-huh."

"Why didn't I know about that?"

I dodge that question, not wanting to think about all the reasons *he* wouldn't want to tell her. "Did I wake you?"

"Yes. Do you have a pen?"

I put her on speaker and open up my notes app. "Yeah."

She gives me his phone number and asks again if I'm all right. I assure her I am.

"You're not going to upset him when you call, are you, Malcolm?"

"I...I'm not gonna try to."

"Because you know it doesn't take much between you two."

"I really just have a quick question for him."

"Well, can it wait until Monday? Won't you see him?"

"Maybe," I admit. "I'm sorry I woke you."

"I'm just glad you're okay. You scared me."

"Sorry," I say again.

"All right, good night. Good luck with the internship. And don't be such a stranger."

"I won't. Let's catch up soon."

"In the daytime," she says.

"Of course. Sorry again. Good night," I tell her, and hang up. Exhaling, I stare at the digits I typed. Talking to Jill was like dunking my head into a bucket of ice water. Sanity has temporarily returned. I guess my therapist knows what she's talking about.

Closing my phone, I try to go to sleep again. A phone call doesn't need to wait until Monday—it doesn't need to happen at all.

I don't need to talk to Ryan. Rebuilding the bridge I burned between us is a terrible idea. It brings up way too many memories I'd just as soon put behind me for good. The bottom line is, I don't know him anymore. In fact, there's an argument to be made for whether I ever knew him at all.

I don't delete his number or anything, but I don't add him to my contacts list, either. I need to calm the fuck down. Anyway, it's Friday night. I don't have to lie here and dwell on this.

I send Henry a text in case he's up to something fun.

Turns out he and the guys are out. I put on a fresh pair of jeans, run some gel through my hair, and get the hell out of my apartment.

$$\$\$\$$$

RYAN'S LAUGH IS SUDDEN, unexpected, and makes every hair on my arms stand on end. Isla startles when I whip my head around to the couch where my ex-stepbrother has been camped out with his mentor since we got out of our intern huddle this morning.

Isla's hand lands on my forearm, and I jerk away without thinking.

"Sorry," she says without regret. "Let's go to the coffee bar. You look like you need a break."

"I'm fine," I grumble, turning to look back down at one of her client's most recent financial statements. I've been studying it for half an hour, but it's like that one time sophomore year when I tried to read *A Clockwork Orange* because I thought it would impress Kaylin. Except half the first page wasn't written with real words, and it took me four reads through it to realize I didn't have an attention problem—the book literally wasn't written in normal English. Likewise, none of the words and numbers on my screen are making any sense, and I wonder what the fuck I went to Stanford for.

"My treat," Isla tries again.

It's a free coffee bar, so I get that I'm supposed to smile at her joke or something, but I'm not in the mood.

Ryan laughs again, harder this time. Longer. I can't hear what Charlie is saying from here, but it must be really fucking funny *or* Ryan's acting like he thinks it is. It's the same way Isla treats everything I spontaneously say like the cleverest or wittiest thing to ever come from a human mouth. Are they *flirting*?

In the middle of the office on a Monday morning?

We've been in the internship for two weeks now, and Ryan and I haven't spoken since that second morning at the deli. I haven't gone a single day without having to tell Isla no multiple times, whether it's an offer to grab lunch, coffee, drinks after work—I even turned down concert tickets. I'm not sure which part of "I have a girlfriend" she's not understanding, but I feel the mask of politeness I wear around her slipping.

There's this other annoying fact nagging at me that I might not be cut out for this kind of work. While I've listened to the other interns rattle on about how much they're learning or gushing over a compliment from their mentors about some idea they had, I have to acknowledge I don't feel prepared, and Isla's constant personal questions and comments truly mess with my concentration.

Let's also forget for a moment that if someone asked me to list them, I could write down all of Ryan's outfits from the day we started the internship to the brand of shoe he's got on today. I could also rate how well he wore each one on a scale of one to ten. He's not flashy like Miguel, but clothes look good on him. It's the only excuse I've got for noticing his ass on a daily basis. Well-cut pants.

I probably only pay attention because his jeans used to practically fall off of him, and I assumed he didn't have the equipment to fill them out. But in retrospect, maybe they were just too big for him, and he didn't care. Now that it matters what he looks like, he's dressing the part.

I pinch my eyes shut and nearly take Isla up on her offer. This fixation I have on Ryan's outfits and his body isn't like me. I'm going fucking nuts in this place. I blame the failure of my brain to make sense of the spreadsheets and the absolute lack of ideas I've had on what to do with my remaining fifty dollars. Meanwhile, the group of five leaves work together half the days of the week, and more than once I've watched them all go into a nearby bar for happy hour while I feel fucking lost.

I wish I would have just gotten over myself and said yes to Miguel that day in the elevator, but at the same time, I feel useless and stupid. What good would I do the project they're working on?

It's annoying how every single one of them seems to be thriving in this environment. Even Ryan—a guy who's never fit in anywhere that I know of—seems to have made himself at home with his new bestie Charlie.

I hate them. I hate listening to him laugh and the way he keeps turning my head. It's fucked up.

I think I might also hate this job. Worse, I might not *get* it. So far, I've kept those thoughts to myself, but it might be time to sit down and have a talk with Georgie. Not necessarily about whether I'm a good fit or that I'm having trouble finding my footing, but maybe about Isla. It could be that her desire to get me alone is interfering with her ability to be a good mentor.

Fuck, when did I turn into such a pussy? I should be able to do this. It's driving me nuts that I apparently *can't*.

"Are you beefing with that other intern? Ryan?" Isla asks. "I've never seen you talk to him."

"No," I mutter.

"It's just…" Here, she reaches out and gives my shoulder a squeeze without letting go. "You seem tense."

I shrug away from her and excuse myself from our workspace. "Be back in a few," I tell her, unable to tolerate her suffocating presence a moment longer.

I take the elevators to the lobby and step outside. The smog is thick today, so I can't say I'm getting fresh air, but I need out of the office. Away from Isla and her gardenia perfume. When I told my buddy Jake about her, he'd asked if she was hot.

I told him that wasn't the point, but the truth is, Isla is sort of hot. Under different circumstances, I might be attracted to her, if not her personality, at least physically. She's nothing if not extremely physical. I've never been with anyone other than Kaylin, and I do feel a certain sense of loyalty to my longtime girlfriend, but she's seen other people since we've been together. While I was at Stanford, she was at UCLA, and we were sort of "open."

I made do with meeting up with her once or twice a month, but I know she saw other guys while she was in school—nothing serious. I wasn't jealous exactly. It felt like a natural evolution—like what would normally happen when high school sweethearts go their separate ways for college. The fact that we wound up back together also felt normal and easy. We never even fight. We're really fucking boring.

My point is, there's a reality in which I could be excited that Isla seems to want in my pants so bad. Like I said, I've been considering asking Kaylin for a break. On the break, or if we broke up—a messy affair with my mentor would probably appeal to my chaotic side, but in this case—*this* reality—I feel like I'm spinning out, and I don't know what my fucking problem is.

As I sit on a bench across the street from the Marks & Baker building, a thought occurs, as clear as today isn't. The only thing that's changed—besides starting a new job—is the reemergence of Ryan in my day to day life. If history is any indicator—*he's* my fucking problem. As much as I try to avoid looking at him or thinking about him, the urge to mess him up lies just beneath the surface of my skin. Hearing him laugh, seeing him *thrive* while I'm barely treading water must be some kind of trigger.

Embers of an old rage flare hot in my chest. It's the urge to prove him wrong. The urge to make his words meaningless. It's enough to push my ass up off the bench and charge across the street, determined to take action.

When I pass him and Charlie on the couches, I look down at Ryan only to see his slightly dimpled smile fade from his face. I need to shove him the fuck out of my head. My rage burns bright enough for me to slide my thigh alongside Isla's as I take my seat next to her.

She glances at me with an intrigued smile. "Feeling better?"

"Yep," I say, double clicking my screen to bring the financial report back up.

"Then maybe you'll finally let me buy you a drink tonight."

"I think I might."

Because fuck *him*.

CHAPTER FIVE

RYAN

On the one hand, the internship is incredible. Charlie is a fucking genius. He's funny, a good teacher, and he's great about encouraging me to ask questions. I tend to clam up and try to figure things out on my own, and he saw right through it day one. "I can't teach you shit if I don't know how you think."

So now he knows, and working with him feels like I won the mentor lottery.

On the other hand, I have a hundred dollars and no fucking clue what to do with it. I'm about a week away from asking Calyx to go thrifting for vintage t-shirts with me. I'm currently considering re-formatting some of my college essays, putting them into a book, giving it a catchy title and self-publishing it online.

The more I look into publishing a book, however, the more bogged down I get with the marketing end. That alone looks like a full time job, and I have zero social media presence. A hundred dollars would barely make a dent in a marketing budget, and it takes some authors years to break even on a single book. Still, it's the best idea I've had that uses a skill set that seems manageable.

The t-shirt thing? I'd need help with that. Between work and the gym—working out isn't optional for me—I don't know how the hell I'd find the kind of inventory I'd need to get started, much less scale up.

The good news is Malcolm is occupying at least twenty-five percent less of my brain space. I have noticed how miserable he looks every morning in our huddle and how much he's itching to get the hell out of the office in our debriefs, but while I'm working with Charlie, it's heads down, total focus. Next week, Charlie's planning to give me two of his accounts to start managing on my own. One small business, one personal. I've been brushing up on risk assessments in my spare time, hoping if I don't think about the challenge so hard, an idea will suddenly come to me in the shower or something.

But I won't lie—the group of interns who teamed up together are starting to look pretty fucking smug when they leave work together and file into the bar across the street for happy hour.

Miguel texted one last time to convince me to join their team, but I declined without putting a lot of thought into it. Piper and Lisette rub me the wrong way. I don't know if they were both cheerleaders or prom queens or what, but they give mean girl energy, and while Jia might be able to tolerate it, and guys like Nathan likely dig it because it's their crowd, too, I don't like it.

Piper, whose mentor is probably the best investment banker in the firm—a woman named Sadia—is already acting like she's head intern or something, which is plainly ridiculous. There's no way I could take direction from Piper, even if their group has the best idea in the world.

Jia's cool, though. We realized we live in the same neighborhood, so we walk to work together, and home if she's not going to happy hour. At first, I wasn't a fan of the company. It's a lot of pressure. But she talks enough that I barely have to. She surprised me on the walk home last evening though by asking me out.

Our date started at my gym where I got her in with a guest pass. She kept pace with me on the treadmill for six miles. It ended in her apartment with both of us proclaiming we weren't looking for anything serious and then having sex on her couch. I had to use my wallet condom. I didn't sleep over, and our walk to work this morning was more relaxed—joking about how strong the wine was, among other things.

Without going into too much detail, she's not planning to have sex with me again, but there are no hard feelings.

It's been an unexpectedly good two weeks, and I'm lowkey proud of myself for being able to rise above the fact that I have to see Malcolm five days a week.

It's not that I don't think about him. That'd be impossible. But I'm not miserable around him, and that's an improvement. If anything, he's the one who looks miserable. I try not to think too much about how that makes me feel, but it always seems to happen when I'm closing my eyes to go to sleep. It's this stupid yet totally familiar desire to ask him if he's okay.

I end up dreaming about how the conversation might go more nights than not. Sometimes it's a fistfight. Sometimes, it ends in a long, endlessly confusing hug where the words I said to him on accident the one time build up in my chest until I feel like a volcano about to burst.

Once—Wednesday night—the dream turned into one of *those* dreams where I woke up with cum-stained underwear. I was physically unable to look at him on Thursday, certain he would know if he took one look at me and then announce to the whole office that I'm a pervert.

On Friday, though, he looks particularly messed up. There's a look in his eyes I recognize. The kind of look he used to get when he was about to do something reckless—like get blitzed drunk, start a fight, or fuck his girlfriend in the laundry room. But that particular look of his isn't wild or desperate. It's calculating. Devious. It also means he's hanging on by a thread.

Now I'm up late again, thinking about it. Weighing a scenario where I casually sit next to him Monday morning and ask how things are going with the internship. Let him know if he wants to talk, I'm around.

And how fucking pathetic would that sound? How quickly would he shut me down?

Jesus, I hate the way I feel about him. This is the problem with imprinting on someone at an early age because your dad is dead, and your mom is too busy with her new husband to give you the kind of attention you need. It makes you stupid for someone you've got no business being stupid about.

Since it's Friday night, and I can't sleep, I think about firing up my computer and trying to make an ad for the book I haven't put together yet, but I can't make myself get up. I went hard on the treadmill today and even harder on the leg press. Also, my cat is snuggled into my side, purring comfortably, and I'd hate to disturb him at this late hour.

When my phone buzzes, my eyes pop open. I might not be able to get up to make a graphic, but a booty call... I could be motivated to do that.

There's no name on the screen—only a number. I recognize it immediately. It's Malcolm. I deleted his contact years ago, but his number is one of the few I know by heart.

I swipe to answer, guard up. "Hello?"

"Hey. It's me. Sorry to call so late—"

I got a new number after high school graduation. He shouldn't have it. "How did you—"

"Your mom gave it to me," he says, like there's no need to complete my sentence. There never really was with him. We were always creepy like twins that way. Until we weren't.

"You called her at—"

"I called her a while back. Look, I just need to ask one question." His tone is brusque, direct, and puts me on edge.

I rest a hand on my cat to ground myself. Bud's purrs intensify. "What's the question?"

"Do you still have your hundred dollars?"

I scowl. Is he calling after midnight to ask me about the stupid challenge? I mean, obviously he is, but why me? Why now? "Do you not?"

"I don't know what you're planning to do with it, but with the rest of them all working together, are you worried about not being able to compete?"

Of course I am. He should be, too, but I have a feeling I know where this line of questioning is headed.

"Ryan?"

The sound of my name in his low voice scrapes my ear. It makes my neck break out in chills. "Uh-huh."

"I forgive you all right? For the thing that happened when we were kids. I forgive you."

My first thought? *Bullshit.* One, because I don't believe it for a second, and also because what the fuck? "You *forgive* me?"

"I mean..." He's already hedging. I knew he didn't mean it. He's so full of shit.

"I never asked for that," I say firmly.

His response is as ice cold as ever. "Fine. I take it back."

I'm shocked. *Shocked.*

"About the challenge—"

"You've gotta be fucking kidding me," I sigh.

"Yeah, well, I'm not. If it's a no, just tell me to fuck off."

It's tempting. *Really* tempting. But then I think about Piper and goddamn Nathan and their smug looks like they've got this in the bag. Still—teaming up with Malcolm? I may be in a bad mood more often than not, but I'm not suicidal. However, as the fuck off readies itself to fly from the tip of my tongue, there's a deafening crack in my guard. Bud twitches beneath my palm like he *heard* it.

"Fine," I hear myself saying. "I'll work with you on it, but only if you want to win."

"I do," he says, not sounding nearly as confident. He almost sounds—*shaky.*

"Then come with ideas on Monday. I'm going back to bed." I'm also frozen in place. "Good night," I tack on, rushing to hang up.

"Good—"

His voice cuts off. I drop my phone onto the mattress and let my head fall back on my pillow. My heart—*goddamn.* It feels like I just ran nineteen miles.

$$\$\$\$$$

MONDAY IS STARTING off as one of those mornings where my hands won't work right. It's not because I have some hand disorder—I just keep dropping things. My hair gel. My toothbrush. The coffee pod. And it's not like they're shaking—more like they won't close all the way—or they forget what they're trying to do the second they touch the thing I'm trying to hold. One thing after another slips from my grasp.

"Up All Night" by Slaughter is stuck in my head. It's got the most repetitive chorus next to "Shout" by Tears for Fears. I don't know which would be worse right now, but "up all night, sleep all day" on repeat is not cool, especially when sleeping all day isn't an option I've got this morning. What's more annoying is I wasn't up all night. I slept. Some.

Deacon is watching me, silently noting my chaotic state while he pulses through some stationary lunges in the living room. I still want to text my mom to ask her what the fuck she was thinking giving Malcolm my phone number, but my damn hands haven't been functioning properly since I hung up with him Friday night.

There's this other thought I'm having—that I've been having since I woke up—that I dreamed it. Whenever I fell back asleep, it was deep and hard and the kind of disorienting that makes me doubt my memory. It's that bizarre uncertainty making me bumble through my morning routine.

It's very difficult to believe he called me. It's harder to believe he asked me to partner up with him for the challenge. Because that would *never* happen. And the whole forgiveness spiel? I had to have made that up in my imagination.

And yet...Malcolm's waiting for me at the elevator bank when Jia and I arrive at work. I spot him the second I come through the glass doors, and he keeps his eyes on me while other elevators open and close without him getting on. My mouth is bone dry, and my heart is a jackhammer in my chest.

I hate how perfect he looks. Tall and broad and golden like a god. He's always been larger than life. A sun I once orbited, rarely feeling worthy of his light. Deserving of being put into his shadow when he turned on me.

His ruthless cruelty was also perfect in its precision. Like the careful cuts of a master chef meant to carve me down to size. Kaylin was only his first slice. She was the closest I ever got to having an official girlfriend. We shared a science class, studied together, ate lunch with each other for more than a month before I got the flu that changed the course of my life.

What fucking doctor prescribes narcotic cough syrup to a teenager with the flu? And my mom—*a nurse*—just left it in my room. I loved the stuff. It made me feel amazing. Euphoric and hazy and a shit ton better than the virus fucking me over at the time. I never *ever* would have said what I said to Malcolm if it weren't for that medicine.

Like any teenage boy, I was all over the place emotionally, but I wasn't self-destructive. I'd gone a whole year without telling Mal how I felt, and I would have gone the rest of my fucking life not saying it, but he'd been snuggled up next to me watching our favorite movie, and for a minute it felt so good and perfect, I couldn't conceive of the possibility that those feelings were anything but mutual, so I said it. *"You know I'm like completely in love with you."*

And no—no he *hadn't* known that. And he was never *supposed* to know that. And I was perfectly fine with him being forever *unaware* of that.

It's just that we'd had a few moments—before the cough syrup—where I felt like he might feel the same way. For example—he never pulled away from a hug first. Believe it or not, I used to be a hugger because of *him*. He was the one who started the whole hugging thing in the first place.

One time in particular—the time that really got my hopes up—was a hug goodnight. Our parents had been fighting about money—a credit card bill. They didn't often fight in those years, but since Malcolm and I were best friends, when they did fight, it sucked a little bit extra to think they might get a divorce. We'd been in my room, lying silently side by side on my bed listening to yelling we weren't bothering to drown out with the TV or music.

Our shoulders were touching, and I remember thinking that if he and his dad moved out, I'd have to work to keep him in my life. I could easily see us drifting apart in high school. We were already on separate tracks—him planning to try out for all the sports and me doing the nerdy mathlete thing. Chess club and shit like that. We didn't have much in common even then other than both having a dead parent, but what tied us together most was home where we were more or less inseparable.

If we lost that, I would have to make an effort to stay his friend. And it was an effort I wasn't sure he'd make in return because Malcolm didn't really worry about stuff like that. It was easy for him to fit in, while I had a harder time with it.

That night, because I couldn't verbalize any of that—my fears or my concerns if things with our parents didn't work out —I walked him to my door once the yelling stopped. He'd had his hand on my back, and he was rubbing a reassuring circle between my shoulder blades. He hugged me, and I hugged him back.

I held on a long time. Both of us were breathing heavy, relieved that the fight downstairs had dropped in intensity, but still worried that it might be the beginning of the end. His hand moved from my back into my hair as he held me against him. It felt so good, I'd done the same to him, and he didn't pull away.

It was the closest I'd ever been held. It aroused me in a way holding him never had before. I considered pulling away but didn't. On a shared breath, we'd looked each other in the eyes, and whatever I saw lingering in his gaze made me wonder— maybe—*maybe* he felt it too? This thing I've never felt for anyone else? Love that hits a little harder, weighs a little heavier, invades me a little deeper than any other love in my life.

It was the kind of moment I've shared with women since— the moment before the first kiss. I remember wanting it and being terrified of it at the same time. He was my stepbrother. He was my best friend. He was a guy. And I didn't like guys—or I never had before him. Never thought of them *that way*. But I'd been thinking of Mal *that way* since he turned thirteen and started wearing cologne. So, my thoughts slipped through the gears pretty quickly as we stared at each other before fisting each other's hair and embracing again.

Obviously I read too much into it. I saw what I wanted to see, and didn't recognize it for what it was. He just needed a hug, and he took it. My mind ran away with it, and in the days before I got sick, my mind ran away with it constantly. I started trying to put us into situations where he'd hug me like that again. I approached it like a science experiment to see if close proximity yielded the same results as the first time. Whether if more heat was applied, the reaction would intensify, or if the conditions were too different to replicate the outcome.

That day—the day I'm now forgiven/not forgiven for—he'd had his head on my shoulder, a leg draped over mine, and his hand on my rattling chest. I don't know why we were wrapped up like that other than that was how we watched TV sometimes. I'll probably never know why he was that close on that particular day since I was a flu factory at the time.

But anyway, I said it. I told him what I'd been tossing around in my head ever since I saw him flirting with a girl at the pool the previous summer and got irrationally jealous. At first I thought I was jealous because the girl was cute, and I'd never be able to flirt with someone the way he did so effortlessly. But it wasn't the girl. Or it was—because she was the one I was jealous of.

And of course, at first I thought it was because if he got a girlfriend, he wouldn't have time to be friends with me. But then I started noticing *him*. And more specifically my reactions to noticing him. The feelings were hard to swallow at first. But as I tested them, poked and prodded at them, I started having fantasies. Daydreams at first—experimental thought exercises, and then soon enough, I was masturbating to thoughts of my own damn stepbrother—experimentally, and then when I realized how fast I got off when he entered the scene in my head, he became the unmoving center of my universe.

By the time I told him I was in love with him, I meant it with my whole chest. I just never would have said it if it hadn't been for the drugs.

I completely understand that it was a dick move. I overdid it with the cough syrup. My lack of control—my irresponsibility—was on me—my fault. I didn't blame him for pulling away. For wanting nothing to do with me. The real issue—other than being rejected—was how far he took it—the lengths he went to in order to prove he wanted no fucking part of me. It most definitely changed me for the worse.

For the record, I've never looked at another man that way. I'd like to say lesson learned, but the problem I had then is the same problem I have now. I may hate him, but I'm also still sort of in love with him. He's a foundational part of me. Loving Malcolm is part of who I am.

I don't think it means I can't love anyone else. I don't think love is finite. But I don't think I'll ever love anyone else in the all-consuming way I once loved him. It doesn't matter how he treats me—how many years go by without seeing him. Nothing changes the fact that some part of me is still deeply in love with the stepbrother I used to have.

It's the most hateful thing about me, and I'd very much like to put it in the past. Being around him isn't easy, and yet, I can't say no to the offer either. If there actually is an offer.

Today, he's wearing a navy suit over a white shirt. His tie is the color of his eyes. Aquamarine. They pop vividly within the already attractive lines of his face. The reddened rims prove he lost some sleep last night, too. I prepare myself for him to tell me to forget it.

I nod as I approach him. "Good morning." We both turn to face the elevators.

"Morning."

Jia pipes up with her own greeting.

I lapse into my usual awkward silence, edgy and agitated, not sure what's real or a product of my historically over-active imagination when it comes to him.

An elevator opens. The three of us and a number of other people crowd on. Malcolm and I wind up shoulder to shoulder, packed in like sardines.

"I don't have many ideas," he says to me in a quiet voice. "Sorry."

"I've got a couple," I lie, thinking about vintage t-shirts. Vintage *anything*.

"I tried gambling," he says. "It didn't go well."

I snort.

"What?" he says. "Are *you* any good at it?"

"I'm not gambling to win this," I tell him.

"Why not? It's just like the stock market."

"Uh, no. It isn't. Stocks have histories and certain ways of behaving. Gambling is a little strategy, but it's mostly luck."

"Yeah…like the fucking stock market," he mumbles.

I scoff at that. "You went to Stanford?"

He stiffens. The air between us might as well have just frosted over. "You goddamn well know I went to Stanford. You were in the same room when I got my acceptance letter."

"I was probably stoned."

It's his turn to snort. "You were definitely stoned."

The doors open on ten, and I shove my way out, needing not to be so close to him anymore. He's got a nasty temper not many people know about, but it isn't hard for me to tell when he's working himself up. I'd rather not be in the blast zone this morning. I'm already a scattered, emotional mess with all the shit his unexpected phone call dragged up.

"Should we see if Bailey wants to partner up, too?" he asks, easily matching my stride.

"Sure, go for it." I'd *love* to watch that conversation.

"You should be the one to ask. She can't stand me."

"No?" I ask. "What gave you that idea? I thought everyone liked you."

His voice is a low grumble. "I just think you might have better luck."

"I'm as straight and white as you are, bro."

At that, he gives a short, barking laugh. "Yeah, okay."

Excuse me?

I stop walking, and he does the same. We're a few feet from the conference room where we huddle with the other interns in the morning. Jia goes inside leaving Malcolm and me in the hall together.

Which is just as well because what he said pissed me the fuck off. "You can think whatever the fuck you want about me, but don't pretend you know more than you do. You haven't known me since we were fourteen. I know who the fuck I am. Do you want to do this or not?"

He swallows hard. "I don't have a choice."

"Sure you do. You can *lose*. I'm not the one who called my mom in the middle of the night begging for help."

His cheeks twitch, and his tone turns nasty. "I didn't *beg*."

"Correct me if I'm wrong, but you need me more than I need you." I'm not sure that's true, but he doesn't need to know that having no ideas for how to tackle this challenge is eating me alive.

His expression remains grim. He nods once.

"Then *you* ask Bailey if you want her on the team. Don't assume you know who she is either."

"Do I need to apologize?" he asks.

"To Bailey?"

"No, asshole." He gives me another intense look.

"I'm not getting into this right now," I say. We need to focus on work. Malcolm's a big enough distraction already. I've learned to cope with having him around—the masochist in me gets a sick thrill from it, but what I have no time for is hope. Forgiveness? Great. What the fuck ever. But this stupid hope that I could ever get my brother back is the *worst*.

No—not my brother. My friend.

"Ryan, dammit," he begins, but shuts up when all eyes are on us as we enter the conference room.

I plaster on my fake smile and take my seat. Murmured good mornings pass across the table. Mal takes his usual seat next to Bailey, and she visibly shifts away from him like he stinks or something.

He smells fucking incredible. She's clearly not a fan.

This is going to end up being him and me. Ergo, a nightmare.

I make a rule for myself as Georgie touches base with everyone. If Malcolm and I actually team up, there will be no drinking. No mind-altering substances of any kind for as long as he and I work in the same building. I will never speak to him without thinking first again.

I can't risk it. Of all the things to come out of that phone call other than my hands deciding to up and quit on me is the realization that missing him *hurts*.

Part of me must enjoy the pain, though, because I've also come to the conclusion that I'd rather have the opportunity to see and not touch, have and not hold because his existence reminds me who I am. After this summer, I may never see him again, and that's healthy. It's right for me. But there's a sweet and only slightly depressing nostalgia at the chance of having him talk to me like a peer again. He's like a song that changed my life —a part of me crystalized in space and time. He's a memory of me when I was happy, and I don't want to let this chance to remember go. If it hurts, it hurts. It's just for the summer.

It's closure. And who knows? Maybe I'll be less of an asshole afterward. Or maybe I'm the same idiot for him I've always been, but at least I won't live in the same town with him much longer. Distance worked well enough while I was in Portland.

The morning goes smoothly with me and Charlie. He gives me the two client files and talks me through an overview of them while I take handwritten notes. My handwriting is shit, but otherwise I'm focused. That he's trusting me with this is a big deal, and I'm excited to get to work.

I spend an hour taking my own notes on each file before calling to introduce myself to the clients. I'm getting better on the phone, mostly copying Charlie now. He has a kind, confident way about him that isn't shy about cutting someone off when they're on the wrong track or stressing about something. He's also good at listening.

When I hang up with the business owner, Charlie's arching an eyebrow at me with a half grin. "Nice," he says.

I blow out a breath. "Thanks," I tell him. "Felt good."

"Take a break and bring me back a latte, will you?"

"Sure thing."

Bailey corners me at the coffee bar, standing way too close, her neck craned back to look up at me. Her hair is down today, a slightly frizzy mop. She's stopped wearing suits and started wearing loose-fitting dresses I assume are more comfortable. Today's dress is black with small red flowers on it, the same color as the cardigan she's got on. Overall, Bailey is unremarkable to look at, but it seems intentional.

"Do you want me on your team, too?" She asks it like she's daring me to say no. Or yes. I can't tell.

Her right earlobe has more piercings than it should technically be able to have, and this is what catches my attention as I decide how to answer her question. I wouldn't mind having Malcolm all to myself, but that's the stupid part of me. Someone absolutely needs to be in the room with us. He's much more likely to not act like a total shit, and I'm more likely to keep my brain in reality where it belongs.

"Yes," I say.

"Why?"

Jesus. "Level the playing field?"

"Five against three? Hardly level," she says in that no-bull-shit way she's got.

"Better than seven against one," I say.

She narrows her relatively small eyes. "How do we decide who wins? What if only one person can win?"

"How do you think we should decide?" I ask.

"We could write reports on our contributions—decide who's responsible for how much money. It has to be fair. And I won't be side-lined."

Believe it or not, I get where she's coming from. "Look, it's a legit offer to team up. You don't like working on teams?"

"Do you?" she asks.

"Not particularly. But I want to win."

"Really?"

I nod.

"And you don't have a problem working with women?" she asks.

What? "No."

"Because that *will* go into my report if I even get a whiff that I'm being marginalized."

"It's totally up to you," I tell her.

"What's your best idea?" she asks.

"What's yours?"

I get a definite glare for that. "We'll need to have a planning session ASAP."

"Okay."

"I'm free tonight," she says. "What about you?"

"Yeah, sure."

"I'll talk to Walsh. Plan for tonight. Location TBD." With that, she backs off and walks away.

I set my coffee down on the counter and will my balls to drop back into their sac. Bailey is terrifying. I think I might like her, but there's not a chance in hell I'd ever try to marginalize her. She'd have me for lunch.

As I return to Charlie's workspace, I think about getting together with her and Malcolm tonight and how that's going to look. The three of us all sitting down somewhere brainstorming quick money-making schemes. Actually, this is going to be much better—having her there. Just him and me? I won't be at my sharpest. I'll go along with whatever stupid idea he might come up with just to be agreeable. Like I said—he's the sun, and I orbit it. It's always been that way. Even this bonkers idea of teaming up was because *he* asked. I never would have had the courage to do that. I get that I should have said no, but I'm not sure I'm physically capable.

I haven't felt this pathetic since high school.

Charlie grins up at me from his wheelchair like he's got something evil planned for me. "Good. You're back."

I happen to notice one of the lights on the phone blinking, like someone's on hold. "Should I be scared?" I ask as I take my seat.

"What did I tell you day one?"

"Show no fear?"

He nods. "Mr. Estrada is on line one. Make him happy, and I'll buy you lunch."

Long story short, I have to pay for my own lunch today.

CHAPTER SIX

MALCOLM

Kaylin is sketchy about the idea of taking a break. She's going on a trip to Europe for three weeks with some of her college girlfriends in a few days, so I thought it'd be good timing for her, which is why I don't get why she's pushing back. I thought she'd be relieved.

But maybe it's the "date" I went on with Isla that's got her looking at me funny. Admittedly, I'm not proud of caving to Isla's relentless flirting either. I wanted to prove something to myself, I guess, but I only ended up making a bigger mess.

When I tell Kaylin about it, she stares at me like I just struck her. "Your mentor? Are you fucking kidding me?"

"I told you—nothing happened."

Kaylin crosses her arms and breathes heavily, facing off with me in the kitchen. "I'm not the one asking for a break all of a sudden."

Is it all of a sudden, though? She's gotta feel this relationship malaise, too. Right? Is it just me? "I'm not the one going to Europe for three weeks," I mumble.

Her gaze narrows, but with a little less heat, she asks, "Nothing happened? Really?"

I sigh, remembering Isla's hands all over me at happy hour. I'd tolerated it, tried not care about the fact that I was putting myself in a compromising situation, but the second she started sliding her hand down my abs, I'd balked, asked for the tab, backed away from her, and left the bar. I didn't even jerk off when I got home, which is as much a part of my routine as brushing my teeth.

"Really," I assure her. "But I feel like the fact that I even considered it is enough reason to take a step back here. I'm obviously a fucking mess right now."

Her lips press together as she studies my face. "Why is that?"

"The internship I guess. This stupid challenge," I say. *Ryan.*

She drops her arms and sighs before taking a look around the kitchen. "Right. Well, if they're on their way, we should..." She gestures at the cluttered kitchen like she's run out of words for how much of a disaster I am.

"You don't have to help," I tell her. "I'd understand if you want to go."

She inhales deeply through her nose and gives her head a small shake, her disappointment in me evident. "No. I'm okay. I wanna see Ryan anyway."

Ouch.

He and Bailey are going to be here soon, and my apartment is a mess from a chaotic weekend spent ordering takeout, letting dishes pile up, and leaving things wherever.

Kaylin grabs a sponge and some cleaning spray from under the sink, getting to work on the kitchen island.

As I do the dishes, I let her go on about what a screw-up I am.

"Did you decide to take this break before or after you reached out to Ryan?" she asks.

"Before. Why?"

"Because you're right. You've been a hot mess since you started that internship."

"It's fucking hard," I say.

"Being around him?" she asks leadingly.

The question makes me clench my jaw. *What is she implying?* "No," I say, annoyed. "The internship. I'm not sure finance is for me."

"Oh my God. *Mal.*"

"*What?*" I snap, already knowing what she's going to say.

"Please tell me you're not gonna quit this, too."

"I didn't say that." I've thought about it, though. I've been thinking about it all weekend.

"Can you ask for a new mentor? It sounds like Isla is more interested in getting laid than teaching you anything."

Kaylin's not wrong about that. I have no idea what I'm in for the next time I see Isla. "I'm considering asking."

"If you think fucking her is gonna make it better—I've got news for you—"

"I am *not* going to fuck her," I say definitively.

"But if she's the problem..." She trails off leaving me to think things through, which is never a good idea.

I'm not sure Isla *is* the problem. She's not making life any easier, but at least I know where I stand with her.

"It's more like I feel like a loser," I tell Kaylin as I close the dishwasher and start the wash cycle. "Everybody else seems like they're doing great, and I'm over here flailing."

"Flailing is one word for it."

"Do you have a better one?" I ask.

"I'm interested to see how you interact with Ryan."

I groan. "It's not even about him."

"Are you sure?"

No. I'm not, and I hate that she can see right through me. "It's not *only* about him."

"Is there something in particular you're hoping will happen with him?" she asks.

My shoulders stiffen as I turn to face her. "What does that mean?"

She also turns, a shockingly dirty sponge in hand.

I asked Kaylin to be here for three reasons. To tell her about what happened with Isla and how I needed to take a break. To help me clean up my apartment, and for moral support. She knows the history between Ryan and me, and she can help pull me back from the edge if I find myself too close to going over. This all presupposed the theory that she'd be okay with taking a break, but since she's not a hundred percent agreeing to it, I'm leaning into the other reasons.

The other problem is she brought her dog. It's a Yorkie—a tiny blue and tan ball of nervous energy who's clingy as fuck—and not with Kaylin like she should be. With *me*. The dog is like velcro when I'm around. Like we're bonded mates or something. She's currently circling my feet, and I pick her up, tucking her under my arm so I don't accidentally step on her. Her name is Stephanie, which is a ridiculous name for a dog, but suits her.

Today, Stephanie is dressed for a night out with a crystal collar and a little black satin bow over her right eye. Kaylin is a pretty normal person except when it comes to her dog, who has the bigger wardrobe and far more accessories.

"I mean—are you ready to clear the air and put the past in the past?" she asks.

"I told him I forgive him."

She lifts her brows. "How'd that go over?"

"He made me feel like I'm the one who needs forgiveness."

"He's not wrong..."

"You always take his side," I complain.

"We haven't talked about him in years," she argues.

"It's fucking complicated, okay? Do you think I should

mop?" I stare down at my kitchen floor. If the counter's that dirty...

"Do you own a mop?"

"I have a Swiffer, but I never feel like I'm using it right."

"How can—? Never mind. Just sweep. I'll get the stovetop since you've got your hands full."

"Thanks," I say, very grateful. Before Kaylin arrived, I cleaned the bathroom and vacuumed the living room rug. After that, I suctioned out all the crumbs between the couch cushions and wiped down the coffee table. Now, with the dog tucked under my arm, I sweep the kitchen one-handed then take a bottle of spray cleaner over to the dining area, figuring we'll work there whenever Ryan and Bailey get here.

I offered my place to meet since I don't have a roommate, although I realize it's gonna look like Kaylin lives with me with her dog here and all.

"Are you nervous?" she calls from the kitchen.

"No. Sort of."

"Who scares you more? This Bailey person or Ryan?"

"They scare me equally," I say, but I'm far more nervous about being around Ryan and keeping my cool. The effect he has on me is unpredictable. Sometimes I manage complete indifference, and other times I feel a rage so primal, I could literally kill him and get off with the insanity defense—it's that irrational.

"Sorry you suck at blackjack," Kaylin says.

"Yeah. Well. Thanks for staying."

She walks over to me and rubs her hands on my arms before leaning in to peck Stephanie's forehead. Then she looks up at me. "For better or worse, you're stuck with me. Break or no break."

"So the break...are you okay with it?"

Her mouth flattens into a grim line. "If that's what you need."

"I thought you'd be more receptive," I admit.

She sighs. "Look, I get that this might not feel like mad, passionate love anymore, but I *do* love you."

"Like—*in love*?" Because it hasn't felt like that since we graduated high school.

"More like solid, I want you to be happy love," she concedes. "So if this is what you need…"

"I want you to be happy, too," I tell her.

"I appreciate that. And I get that we're both creatures of habit," she says. "What we have is easy. You're still my best friend, Mal."

"You're mine, too," I tell her.

"Is this just a prelude to a break up, though?" she asks.

"I'm honestly not sure."

She breaks eye contact and takes another deep breath. "Wow. Okay."

"Please don't," I nearly beg. The last thing I want is for her to be sad. "I only mean I don't want to waste any more of your time if I'm not sure."

"What are you not sure about, Mal?"

The question is too direct. It causes a pressure drop in my stomach.

I dodge. "Maybe we can table this until after you come back from Europe."

She returns her gaze to my eyes and squints like she's trying to read the fine print. "Okay," she says carefully. "Any plans?"

I shake my head. My mind is literally a blank space. This is the right move—I know that for sure. What I don't know is why I'm so sure about *that* but absolutely nothing else.

"Steer clear of Isla."

"Have fun in Europe, okay?" I say in return.

Her expression is grim. "I feel like you want me to thank you or something."

"It's not that, I promise."

"When you figure out what it is, you'll tell me?"

That, I can do. "Yes."

A knock at the door causes Stephanie to yip, and I nearly come out of my skin.

Kaylin asks, "You want me to get it?"

"No," I say weakly, then clear my throat and try it again. "No. I got it."

I take a deep breath that doesn't quite reach the bottom of my lungs and open the door. It's just Bailey. She's wearing olive green denim overalls over a white tank top. She's got a half sleeve tattoo on her right arm of the Lovers tarot card, but in this case, both lovers are women. It's a really nice piece of ink, fully saturated color and fine details. "That's really pretty," I tell her, nodding at her arm.

I get the glare I expect for that, but then a grudging, "Thanks. Cute dog."

"She's my girlfriend's." Should I still be calling Kaylin that? Fuck it, I don't know anything right now. "This is Stephanie."

Bailey snorts, which is the appropriate reaction to meeting Stephanie and learning her name.

"Come on in."

"Can I hold her?"

"I'm kind of her person, so it usually doesn't work out when I hand her over to someone and she can still see me."

"*Okay...*" Bailey says like I'm a complete weirdo. She comes into my apartment and spots Kaylin. "Hi."

"Hi," my ex? girlfriend says, with a smile and a wave. "I'm Kaylin."

"Bailey," my fellow intern says as she takes in the surroundings. My apartment is a one bedroom, one bathroom box with an open floor plan. It's literally nothing special down to the boring windows and wood laminate flooring. It's one of those places that was slapped together fast to make a quick buck on people with mid incomes wanting to live in the city. It verges on depressing. "How long have you lived here?" Bailey asks.

"About a year," I say, closing the door and switching Stephanie to my other arm.

"Seriously? It looks like you just moved in."

"How's that?"

"For one thing, you don't have anything on the walls."

"I can't ever decide what to put up."

"You know, if you don't like it you can take it down."

All that makes me think about is putting holes in the wall for no reason if I change my mind. Reason number a million why I could never get a tattoo. I check my watch, and it's seven on the dot. I'm less surprised when the next knock and yip come.

Opening the door for my stepbrother, it's like coming face to face with yet another stranger. Yes, in terms of how he's dressed, he looks more like how I remember him, but also like if that version were airbrushed, run through AI and perfected. Or one of those *what would I look like as a Disney hero* filters.

He's in a black t-shirt that hugs his ridiculously sculpted chest and dark-washed jeans with a slit of a hole in one knee. Both his sleeves of tats are on nearly full display. His hair isn't slicked back. It's falling around his forehead in thick, dark waves —longer than it looks at work. He's got his messenger bag strapped across his body in a way that makes me notice his shoulders, collarbones and pecs.

My fingers twitch, an urge to trace the lines of him as compelling as the desire to stroke velvet. And *what the fuck*? This is *Ryan*. We're not friends. I'm not—*attracted* to him. It's probably more like jealousy. Like I wish my body looked like that. If my muscles were that defined, then I could feel all those ridges and dips when I touched myself.

Okay. Fuck. No. Jesus, I'm an hour into my break with Kaylin and I'm already all over the damn place. I don't *want* to touch Ryan—or—I mean—touch myself thinking of Ryan—or wait. No. Jesus, he's a *guy*. I don't do that. That's not—it can't be—this is nothing.

Still, I can't look at his body. I can't look at his face, either, so I look at the dog as I step aside and let him in.

One of the many, many problems I have with what he said to me so many years ago was it put me in an impossible position because he'd been my stepbrother since we were eight. On top of that, he was my best friend in the universe. The pressure his confession put on me felt like he was shitting all over everything.

Granted, I didn't immediately recoil. I knew he was out of it, but I also knew he was telling the truth, and I wrestled with it. I didn't want our friendship to be over. I was fourteen, we were in high school. Everything was changing—he was going one way, and I was going another, so I actually *did* think about it. I thought about whether how close we were meant I had feelings like that for him, too. But very quickly, I realized what it would mean if I did, and how it would change not only everything at home but also at school, and I couldn't let myself go there. In short, I freaked the fuck out.

Literally overnight everything that attracted me to him—his wit, his patience with me, the way it felt to hold him or be close to him—morphed solidly into a deep revulsion that only picked up steam over the years as we completed puberty, and he started getting stoned all the time.

But he's all respectable man now. Angry respectable man.

His gaze is flinty and hard, guarded as he looks between me and the dog. His dark hazel eyes are mostly a pale brown with bold flecks of emerald green. It makes him look a little unreal, to be honest, in a way that's hard not to stare at.

"Hi, Ryan," Kaylin calls out.

Those eyes widen slightly at the sound of her voice. He gives me a look like *what the fuck*? About three feet into the dining area, he stops and stares at Kaylin approaching. "Hi," he says flatly.

She's going to hug him. Of course she is. She's always felt bad for him and guilty and whatever else her big heart can hold. Because she was an asshole to him, too. She's just allowed to feel bad about it, while I've had to convince her that she and I didn't do anything wrong. Apparently, it worked.

She slings both arms around him, and I want to put my hands between them and push her off. If I don't get a goddamn hug, then she shouldn't either.

He keeps it brief as she gushes. "Mal said you looked different, but damn, you look *amazing*." When she pulls away, she doesn't stop touching him, running her hands up and down his arms like she did with me, both the parts covered with his shirt and his bare skin. I have an insane urge to slap her hands away. He's my—I mean, she's my girlfriend. Or...*fuck*.

I don't know what any of us are anymore.

"It's great to see you," she says giving his biceps a squeeze before catching the look I'm giving her and stepping back.

"Yeah," he says.

I blow out a breath. We need to get this over with, and I say as much.

"I'll order pizza," Kaylin says, heading toward the kitchen.

Bailey and Ryan nod their greetings at each other, and I ask if anyone needs a drink.

Bailey holds up her refillable water jug, and Ryan shakes his head. He looks disconcerted, the line between his eyes more prominent. As he glances around the room like he's not sure where to put himself, I use my free hand to gesture to the table.

Bailey takes her phone out of the front pocket of her overalls and Ryan sets down his bag to pull out his laptop. I grab mine from the coffee table and put Stephanie on the couch. She protests, immediately racing after me, but I try to ignore her as she scratches at my leg to get on my lap.

"Anybody have a great idea since we last talked?" I ask in an attempt to both break the ice and get my wayward thoughts on track.

"Does anybody have a book they wrote lying around that we can self-publish? Put the money toward a nice cover and a few well-placed ads?" Bailey asks.

Ryan shifts in his seat, eyes on his laptop. He glances up at her with his brows raised. "I had the same idea."

"How long would it take to write a book?" I ask.

Bailey shrugs. "I figure it doesn't have to be good. Just really hyped."

I don't get it. "How do you hype a book that sucks?"

"What makes you think it would suck?" Ryan asks, like he's already written one, and I've offended him.

I didn't mean anything like that, though. "I'm just saying if we don't have one, maybe we can find a book that doesn't suck and offer to hype it for a cut of the royalties."

"Like—start a small PR business?" Bailey asks.

"You're just pulling this out of your ass, aren't you?" Ryan says. "Did you come up with an actual idea?"

Stephanie nips at my pants leg. "What about a dog walking business?"

I feel Ryan's gaze creeping on me.

"For night shifters," I add. "Midnight dog walking. We recruit some college kids or whatever, run some online ads, then scale up."

"Dog walking, huh? Where'd you come up with that?" he asks, his voice low and suspicious.

I give him a flat stare. "Why?"

"Sounds like something I've heard before. Let me ask you

this: what would you say to turning over some vintage t-shirts and scaling up into limited edition sneakers?"

I'd say I don't usually blush, but I might now. Fucking ChatGPT.

Bailey speaks up, "How much could we make doing that? And how fast?"

"We're not doing that," Ryan says. "It was a joke."

Haha.

"It doesn't suck," she says.

"No, but unless you have a ton of time to go thrifting and manage online sales, it's not viable for our timetable."

I've gotta say, I remember Ryan being smart and good at math, but I don't remember him being this quick. It's...impressive. Cynical, but still impressive.

"Well, what's your best idea?" Bailey asks, leaning back in her chair and folding her arms over her chest to look at him.

"I'm not sure it's the best I've had, and I haven't put much thought into it, but at the gym tonight, I thought about maybe like a financial advice YouTube channel? We do a small ad buy and once we have a following we start a subscription tier?"

"Is that how YouTube works?" she asks.

"I think so," he says. "I'm not sure. I didn't say it was a good idea."

"I'm not doing videos," she says.

Ryan sighs. "We've got three hundred dollars—"

"Two fifty," I interrupt him.

He glares at me. "Great. Perfect. Two hundred and fifty dollars. We need something scaleable at a rapid rate, and I think the cheapest, easiest way to do that is by utilizing social media. It would take some luck, though."

"I'm not sure about that," Bailey says. "Influencing is a business—it can't be *all* luck."

A moment of silence passes while we digest this. Neither of

them are wrong, but I'm running a little short on luck these days. Bailey asks, "How would we stand out? There's literally millions of people trying and failing at going viral daily. What do we have that they don't?"

Stephanie finally manages to find her courage and leaps onto my lap. Once she's on firm footing, she keeps climbing. She lands on my laptop and raises herself up on her hind legs, her little paws clawing the air for my attention—the signal that she wants to be held—not that it's subtle. I grab her and tuck her under my arm before she gets any more embarrassing.

"Is she always like that?" Bailey asks, clearly amused.

"I told you," I mumble.

She sits back and appraises me. While she's doing that, I glance at Ryan, and he looks away, turning to look at Bailey.

"You know," she says to Ryan like I'm not here. "If he took off his shirt..."

"He's not interesting enough," Ryan says shortly.

I whip my head over to look at him. "Not—*what*? I'm not enough *what*?"

"No offense, *Malcolm*, but you're too uptight to be a TikTok thirst trap."

"Aw, give him a chance," Bailey says then gestures. "The dog? Come on. You've gotta see it."

See what, exactly? "Wait," I say. "What are you guys talking about?"

Ryan sighs heavily. "She wants you and the dog to give financial advice on TikTok. Shirtless."

I laugh awkwardly. "No, she doesn't." I look at Bailey.

"The dog kinda seals it. I can write the content. All you have to do is say it and post it."

Hold on. "Did you call me uptight?" I ask Ryan, still stuck on that, and just generally not keeping up with their apparent mind meld.

"Yes." He looks at me directly. Well, me and Stephanie. "I said you're not interesting enough to pull together a big following in a hurry. Maybe if we had six months—"

"Excuse me? First, I'm uptight, and now I'm not interesting? Why don't you take *your* shirt off?"

His face goes red so fast, it's like someone threw paint on it. "She's not my dog, bro."

My rage flares at the "bro." "She's not *my dog* either."

"Tell *her* that."

"Boys..." I hear Kaylin say from the living room couch. Her tone is motherly with a note of warning.

"Maybe he's insecure about his body," Bailey says to Ryan. "Do you have a dog?"

"I've got—"

"I'm not *insecure*," I argue, cutting him off, then to Bailey I say, "You love this, don't you? Objectifying a guy?"

"Kinda, yeah. Look, you're not my type, but you've got a good tan. I assume there's a set of muscles under there." She waves a hand vaguely at my shirt. "We'd need a great handle," she says, like this is the idea, and we're running with it.

"He can't do it," Ryan insists.

"Why do you keep saying that?" I ask, growing more offended by the second.

"Because you'd have to remove the rod from your ass first."

Never in my life have I been accused—

"At least I don't let people put—"

"Hey!" Kaylin's voice rings out sharply, and suddenly she's behind me, taking the dog away and flicking my earlobe. I shut my mouth.

Bailey leans forward. "Are you guys beefing?"

Why do people keep asking that?

"They used to be stepbrothers," Kaylin says, telling my business to a total stranger.

"No shit?" Bailey eyes us both. "That explains the lack of manners. It doesn't explain why you don't think he can pull off a TikTok video without even giving him an audition." She aims this last part at Ryan.

He's still glaring ominously at me, knowing exactly what I'd been about to say. I'm so fucking glad Kaylin stopped me, grateful all over again that she stayed after I told her I needed a break. I do *not* deserve her.

"Fine," Ryan says to Bailey, sliding his attention to his laptop screen. "Give him something to say and see how it goes."

"I didn't agree to this," I tell him specifically.

"You'll probably suck at it anyway, so I understand why you wouldn't want to, golden boy."

Low fucking blow.

"Asshole." I stand up and rip my shirt off over my head. I'd tell him he can suck my dick, but he might actually take me up on it. I shudder. *Ugh.* Why does he *get to me* like this? I refuse to give him the satisfaction of being right. I am *not* uptight.

"Okay, okay," Bailey says appreciatively, checking out my abs and somehow managing to ignore the tension. "This works." She gestures at me and looks at Ryan who is very deliberately *not* looking at me.

"Give him something to say," he mumbles. "You'll see."

I cannot wait to prove him wrong. My competitive streak has come online, and I refuse to back down.

Bailey types something into her phone and hands it to me. It's an AI answer to the question "What's a great stock market tip?"

"Are we planning to use AI for this?"

"It's an audition," she says. "And don't disrespect Google. I learned everything I know from the internet."

"Are you gonna film it?" I challenge Ryan who still hasn't looked at me.

"Um...I can," Kaylin says. "You need the dog, right?"

I watch her approach with Stephanie. She looks very unhappy with me. Not the dog. Kaylin. She hands me her Yorkie, though, and takes her phone out of her back pocket. All of a sudden I realize I've never done anything like this before. I get an instant case of stage fright.

"What do I do?" I ask anyone who'll answer.

"Just read the top paragraph and look like a hot guy holding a dog," Bailey says.

Ryan snorts but hides his mouth behind his hand.

Doing my best to ignore him, I look down at the phone. It says: *A great stock market tip for long term success is to invest in a diversified portfolio and stay committed to your long-term goals, avoiding emotional and short-term trading.*

"We're gonna need better material," I say. "Everyone knows this."

"Not everyone," Bailey argues because I can't say anything right apparently. "And this is practice. Make it sexy."

I gape at her. "What?"

"I told you," Ryan says to her.

"I heard that," I snap.

"I figured since you're five feet away, but go ahead," he taunts. "Show us what you got. Be sure to incorporate the dog, or it's pointless."

"This is ridiculous," I say. "What does Stephanie have to do with anything?"

Bailey laughs. It's the first time I've heard the sound come out of her, and the way she giggles would be endearing if I weren't standing in the middle of my living room shirtless with three people staring at me waiting for me to read the most boring line of text ever written and "make it sexy."

I look at Kaylin who's got her phone aimed at me. "Are you filming already?"

She nods.

"Great." I run a hand through my hair and reposition the dog to make her more visible. In a deep, slow voice, which I guess could be sexy in the right context, I read the stupid line of advice.

Bailey is wrinkling her nose at Ryan when I look over at them.

"What?" I bark.

"Maybe you could lean against the wall or something?" she says.

"What was wrong with that?"

She shrugs. "It was...uptight."

Ryan takes a breath I swear to God is a preface to I told you so, and I stop him. "Don't say it."

He bites his cheeks and gives me a look I'll probably never understand except it's shitty.

Bailey stands up like she's going to direct me. "Lean on the wall and give the advice to the dog."

"That's gross," I argue.

"It's cute!" she says.

"I'm not sure," Kaylin says, backing me up. "It could be kinda weird."

Thank God.

"But I agree about leaning on the wall," she adds.

"Lean how?" I ask her.

"For fuck's sake." Ryan sighs. "It's like you've never seen a fucking TikTok video."

"Give him a minute," Bailey chides.

Ryan does not, in fact, give me a minute. Instead, he pushes his chair back from the table and walks past me. I watch as he lifts an arm, exposing his inked triceps, and presses his upper arm to the wall. Meanwhile, he shoves his other hand in his pocket and does something with his body that stretches him out like an unwound snake. It's—

Something.

"Lean on a wall," he says slowly like I'm new to English. "It's not financial analysis."

I could punch him. I really could. I could punch him in his pretty fucking face and break his stupid perfect nose and give him two black eyes. I get that he's smarter than I am. I know I got into Stanford because my father went there and knows people. But now all I can think of is that financial statement I couldn't make heads or tails of.

Glaring hotly at him, I fume, but because I also need to prove I'm not a fucking moron, I lean on the exact same wall, mirroring his position, hip out and everything, except while holding the dog. When I meet his eyes, his lips twitch as my arm flexes on the flat surface.

His gaze falls down my face, then my chest. As I warm all over, he pushes away from the wall. He nods to Kaylin. "Stand where I was," he says to her.

What does that mean? Did he like what he saw? Should that be making me feel better? Because it is.

Thank God I don't have time to think about it because a second later, I'm looking into the camera lens of Kaylin's phone. She raises her eyebrows and smiles. "Mmm...much better. Now what was that you were saying about diversifying my portfolio?"

CHAPTER SEVEN

RYAN

Calyx stares down at my phone, watching the video Kaylin sent me of the disastrous audition Malcolm attempted last night. His eyes bug out at a certain point, and I lean over to see what he's seeing. It's when Malcolm leaned on the wall, copying me.

I can't watch that part without sweating, so I sit back and wait. Calyx has the volume up loud enough that I can hear what he's watching anyway. The lean effect is real, and now I know. Not the way I wanted to find out, though.

"Okay, being honest," Calyx says, "It's better with you both."

"Okay, but let me be honest and say the dog is the point."

"I *love* the dog."

"If I give you fifty bucks, can you come up with a handle for this and tell me what hashtags to use if we're gonna post more of him doing this?"

"If you give me fifty-one dollars, I'll even give you some advice to make it better."

"Deal."

"You should create a competition—like a rivalry. Like he

gives a piece of advice, and then you stitch it to a better piece of advice, but you have to be just as sexy. Do you have a cat?"

"Yeah."

"Oh my god, perfect."

"Is that your best advice?"

"For a dollar? Yes."

"I said fifty."

"Fifty for all the work I still have to do." He slides the round lollipop he's been intermittently sucking between his lips and holds it in his cheek. It's almost obscene to see him like that. He's like fucking Lolita or something.

"Can you have some ideas for me by this weekend?" I ask, snapping out of it.

"For sure."

"I'll run your stitch idea by our other partner, but it makes sense."

"The algorithm likes a stitch, and the kids love a battle. You'll be like the financial Kendrick and Drake. I love it already."

"And then we can do a YouTube, and people will watch it?"

"If you bring the dog." He sucks the lollipop and removes it from his mouth.

"It's not his dog. It's his girlfriend's."

"Well, if he's gotta compete with *you*, he needs the dog."

I snort. "Are you saying I'm hotter?"

"*Much* hotter."

"Right. Okay. I gotta run. I need to write some sexy financial takes."

"See you tomorrow?"

"Yep." I snatch back my phone and shove it in my pants pocket, then I grab my bag and go. I hate that I like this idea, but if it works—and I think it might, especially with Calyx's help, we could make real money. One month to build a following, two months to monetize—it could happen. I just hope that after a few videos, Malcolm will loosen up. Maybe if no one's watching him film, he can act more like himself. Because I don't know who the fuck that guy with the little dog was last night.

For the first time since we were kids, I felt like I had the upper hand. Like he was the one reacting, being knocked back on his heels and reeling. Where was the cocksure asshole who tormented me for years? I mean—I could tell he was in there somewhere, but the malice wasn't.

Is being around me still hard for him? Because it was nearly impossible for me.

I wasn't thrilled to see Kaylin there—nothing against her— well, a little bit against her, because she was supposed to be *my* first girlfriend, not his, and she certainly wasn't supposed to last. Bailey's presence saved it like I hoped it might. She made the evening bearable.

If I'm honest with myself, *she* was probably the one rattling Malcolm. I could almost laugh thinking about it, but laughing and Malcolm rarely go together. Still, he and I used to laugh all the time. I've never laughed more with anyone than I once did with him, but those days are long over.

After a shower, I get to work at my desk writing out some short scripts to send over to him to read on camera. They're quicker bites of easy to implement financial changes people can make, and per Calyx's advice, I jot down some possible responses to each point, either elaborating, educating, or offering a quicker, better hack for people with a little more cash to risk. I also make a list of counterpoints in case conflict is what gets people off.

We'll have to start testing this content sooner than later. I consider my cat who is lolling as usual with his cheek on the edge of my laptop and his body splayed belly up on the desk.

He's been with me since I took him in as a stray in Portland my first year there, hiding him in my dorm and annoying my roommate with the litter box. There is no cat lazier or more malleable than Bud, who—I'm not proud to say—is named after marijuana. He used to like lying on my chest while I smoked in bed, enjoying the contact high I gave him.

He's been stuck with catnip since I stopped smoking before grad school. He seems fine, but I'm convinced I destroyed half his brain. He's a big, handsome tuxedo cat with white paws and a sleek black coat that sheds constantly. I go through so many lint rollers, I have them on subscription shipping. Love the cat, can't stand the hair.

Once I've gotten a few short scripts written, I put them into a Google doc and share it with Bailey and Malcolm.

Bailey immediately enters the document and starts adding, editing, and moving things around. I have no arguments with any of her improvements. Mal's icon appears at the top of the document, his cursor, too, but he doesn't change a thing.

When Bailey begins communicating at the bottom of the document, however, there's a vibe shift.

Malcolm, you'll need to memorize the lines. No reading off a screen for the real thing.

Malcolm's pink cursor appears beneath Bailey's green text. *I don't need a script. I understand the concepts fine. What if I just talk?*

Bailey is quick to respond. *This is a group effort, and all our contributions need to be attributable.*

In pink: *So, no ad libbing? At all? Because if you want it to look natural, I don't talk like this.*

Green replies, *Practice makes perfect. This isn't meant to be you. It's acting. Like a persona.*

I don't want to add to this conversation, but I agree with Malcolm. He's gotta feel comfortable in order for this to work. I stay out of it, though, afraid if I stick up for him or take his side, it'll look like I'm trying to get back in his good graces, or worse, that I'm still in love with him. Never mind the fact that I kind of always will be. He doesn't need to know that.

As horrible and uncomfortable as it is to work with him and re-center him in my daily life, I don't hate having him there. Not that I love all the feelings coming back up, but they're as familiar as my heartbeat, and I can't help but welcome them back. The painful twists in my chest. The semi-obsessive thoughts. The overanalyzes of every word and gesture. Does he care? Does he not? Is there a future where we don't hate each other?

I'm not expecting to lie next to him in a bed, snuggled up watching a movie ever again, but one of those golden smiles aimed my way—for *me*—that wouldn't suck.

A question pops up in green. *You here, Ryan?*

My response is in blue. *Present.*

Green says, *Can we get together Saturday evening and try out this content?*

I don't have any concrete plans for the weekend, but now I have to say what needs to be said. *—Maybe Mal can film a few on his own and see if they come off more natural.*

I can sense pink's reluctance, but he types, *I can work on a few Saturday morning and we can look at them in the evening. Wanna meet here again?*

Bailey is fine with that.

Pink asks, *Should I use some of the money to buy a ring light and something to hold my phone with?*

Now I have to admit to using some of the money too, and I should have asked first. Shit. I type, *I spent fifty one today on a content creator to help us with handles and hashtags, and he had a decent idea too, but we can talk about that Saturday.*

Green in all caps: *FIFTY ONE?*

I reply: *Look, he's smart about social media and unless any of you are, I consider it money well spent.*

Anyway, pink cuts in, *ring light? Phone stand?*

Green: Keep it under fifty.

I write for the record, *These are all good investments if this is the route we're taking.*

Green: *with a hundred and forty-nine left, we're stuck with it, so we need to make it work.*

I reply, feeling fairly confident. *It's gonna work.*

THERE'S no sign of Kaylin or Stephanie at Malcolm's apartment Saturday night. I waited until I saw Bailey go in before I approached the door, not ready or willing to be alone with him. The awkwardness between us is worse than his cutting remarks, and I have no doubt he'd rather avoid it, too, the same way he's avoided me in the office all week like we're not working on a team together. I don't know where the hell he goes for lunch—I never see him in the break room anymore, and in the intern meetings, he's always hyper-focused on his phone or Georgie.

It's chilly this evening, even in my sweater. The concrete stairs shake slightly beneath my feet as I walk up to Malcolm's door. I really dislike his apartment. It's not like I think I have the greatest living situation in San Francisco, but at least the place I share with Deacon has character. It's in an older building of renovated townhomes, spliced into smaller apartments, but it has the classic San Francisco bay windows and warm wood flooring. There's even a fireplace. It's small and crowded with my roommate's workout equipment, but it's not half as depressing as this. This looks like stripped down corporate housing with its gray walls and cut-out windows. The kitchen has a fluorescent light for fuck's sake.

Okaying the ring light was a no brainer.

"I feel like we should make popcorn to watch the show," Bailey says once I'm inside, and we're seated on the couch.

"Not necessary. It's five minutes' worth at best," Malcolm tells her as he approaches the sofa with his phone in hand.

Tonight, he's wearing low-slung sweats and a long-sleeved t-shirt. His ankles and feet are covered with white socks. Bailey is almost as casual in yoga pants, a zip up UC Berkeley hoodie, and short Ugg boots. I feel overdressed in my black sweater and jeans. I'm not uncomfortable or anything, but no one told me it was a pajama party.

Malcolm takes a second to look me over. "Plans later?"

"No."

"You dress like this all the time?"

Why is he noticing? Why does he care? *Don't think about it.* "Sometimes I wear a suit."

He huffs. "Right."

I've come prepared to brainstorm after my noon gym session with Calyx. He had a ton of hashtags for me and a list of possible handles for both me and Malcolm. I already know which ones we're using, but I still need to pitch the stitch idea to the group.

First, we watch Malcolm's videos.

Leaving him alone was the right choice, much to my dick's apparent delight, forcing me to enter a state of cognitive dissonance while I watch the way he perfected the lean on the wall, complete with the occasional run of his hand through his thick hair, a rub of his morning stubble, or a stroke down his chest.

His voice is low and rough—like he just got laid and is about to crash—as he aims those aqua eyes at the camera lens and talks about 401ks and Roth IRAs. He gets particularly sexy when he mentions a website he uses to follow market trends—like he's trying to get the web developers into bed with him. I've got a semi by the time we get to the end of his content, and I want to say *works for me*, but I bite my lips together and wait for Bailey's assessment.

"The one where Stephanie licks your chin is priceless," she says.

A fucking dog named Stephanie. But she *does* look at Mal like he hung the damn moon and all the stars just for her, so Bailey's not wrong.

I need to change the subject, so I tell them about Calyx's idea.

Malcolm dismisses it with a scoff. "Like you would do that."

Excuse him? "Why wouldn't I?"

"Because you acted like you were allergic to being the one to do the videos before."

"I did not. I just didn't jump at the chance to rip off my shirt and show off my pecs quite as fast as you did. I don't mind making a few videos."

Bailey perks up. "Then show us the goods. Are you pasty? Because we can't have pasty."

"Then hire someone else," I tell her. "I don't look good with a tan."

She sighs. "There's always filters, I guess."

"I don't need a fucking filter," I say.

"You have tattoos any place besides your arms?"

I stare at her, and she holds my gaze in a challenge that feels a hell of a lot like a dare.

Fine. I stand up and peel off my sweater and the black t-shirt beneath it. I keep my eyes on Bailey, yet I'm fully aware of how Malcolm looks quickly away. With my sweater wrapped around my wrists, I let her examine my upper body. She squints at the tattoos, her gaze moving from one to the next. The crescent moon outlining my right pectoral muscle, the nautical compass above it and the phoenix on the left that extends to my shoulder.

Straight down the center of my torso is a sword with the handles beneath my collar bones and the tip stopping at my navel.

"Damn."

Malcolm looks up, and my muscles tighten involuntarily. "When the hell? Where'd you get the money for all that?"

It's a fair question. I easily have twenty grand worth of work on me, but the artist who tattooed me in Portland took a hefty amount off for alternate forms of compensation. She and I almost had a thing going, but school was always getting in the way for me to be more than anything but a casual hookup. Still, I'm half of her portfolio. "None of your business," I tell him. To Bailey I ask, "Can I put my shirt back on?"

She laughs and nods. "Please."

I do, smoothing back my hair once my sweater is covering me.

"And you said you have a cat?" she asks.

"Yeah."

"Please say it's a black cat."

"He's a tuxedo cat."

She literally squeals and claps her hands. "Yes! Oh my god, this is perfect. You're like total opposites, and the whole cat and dog thing is fucking gold. But you," she says to me. "You need to be dark. Can you do that thing with your eyes—like make them look kind of evil?"

"What?"

"Like..." She attempts to demonstrate, taking her eyes from normal resting to intense glare. "Smolder."

"I'll work on it."

"This total objectification doesn't bother you at all?" Mal asks me.

The conversation I had with Norah about making money comes back to me. This isn't the same thing. "It's not porn."

"I'll set up the accounts," Bailey says, phone already in hand. "Send me the licking one."

While Malcolm does that, I open my texts to find Calyx's list of handles. "Call him at justthetipfinancebro."

"No way," Malcolm says.

I sigh pointedly. "Are you gonna disagree with me about everything?"

"I should at least get to pick my own handle."

"What were you thinking then?" I ask.

"Mal's hot tips?"

I scoff. "That's gonna look like Mal shot tips. No. And it has to sound like money."

"Let's compromise on the fact that you both came up with the word tips in the handles and use Ryan's. It's objectively better. What's yours gonna be?" Bailey asks me.

"At billiondollarblackcat."

"Love it. Suits you."

Malcolm is glaring at me. Again. "What?" I snap.

"That's gotta be too many letters."

"The character limit is twenty four. Mine's twenty-one. Yours is twenty. We're fine."

"Do you need help writing responses, Ryan?" Bailey asks.

"I'll send them like I sent the last ones so you can do your thing with them."

"What else can I do?" she asks, sitting at attention, ready to be put to work.

"You know how to make a video go viral?" Malcolm asks.

Bailey reaches out her hand for my phone. "Show me your hashtags. I made a list, too."

I pass it over to her and she hums and nods as she reads. "Who's your friend?"

"Gym buddy of mine. He's a model, so he's always posting."

"What's his handle?" she asks.

Do I want to tell her that?

I decide it can't hurt. He's got something like thirty thousand followers on TikTok just for being so damn pretty while he talks about how cute he looks in the clothes people send him. That's his hook, trying on clothes and popping his ass out as he looks at himself in a mirror. His Instagram is more refined, mostly professional modeling photos, but he's a slutty little thing on TikTok.

"It's just his name. CalyxTeal. With an X."

"Calyx?"

"It's the outside of a flower," I say. "Did you take biology in school?"

She makes a pissy cat sound like I'm being rude.

I ignore it. If I tried to smooth out my rough edges all the time, I'd have no time to think about anything else. Anyway, Bailey doesn't take it personally.

"Whoa—this is a *guy*?"

"Pretty, right?" I ask.

Malcolm's scowl is visceral. I feel it in my soul.

"Yep, he's a real boy."

"Not trans?"

"Nope."

"Lemme see." Mal grabs the phone while Bailey is mid-scroll. His scowl deepens. "Who the fuck is this?"

"A guy at my gym," I tell him slowly like I'm explaining it to a child.

"Is this your—"

"I'm not fucking gay, Malcolm. Jesus Christ. Get the fuck over yourself."

Bailey jolts and looks from me to Malcolm.

He doesn't seem to notice her strong reaction. "Well, what am I supposed to think when you—"

I give him a harsh warning look and lift my hand off my leg, ready to shut him up with my fist if he brings that shit up in front of Bailey.

"Called him pretty," Malcolm self-corrects.

I pivot quickly and gesture at the screen. "Do you not think he's pretty?"

"Objectively," Bailey says, "He's beautiful."

"I mean if he's a model…" Malcolm mumbles, studying the screen where Calyx is showing himself off in a mint green swimsuit that barely covers his ass. Mal's cheeks are pink, and his breaths are heavy. He shoves the phone back into my hand, from which, Bailey promptly takes it back to keep scrolling.

I meet Mal's eyes, and the pit in my stomach doubles in size. "You're straight," he says bluntly, a clear challenge in the words.

I gesture at Bailey. "Do you fucking mind?"

"She doesn't care," he says.

"I'm actually listening very closely, so if you two need a minute…"

"We don't," I say.

He gives his head a small shake like I'm not getting off that easy.

"It's okay," Bailey says. "I wanna work on this from home. No offense, but this place is the worst. I also want to send a blast email out to everyone I went to college with to comment on the video so we get some early engagement."

"I should do that, too." I start to stand. My circle of contacts is likely much smaller than Bailey's, but Norah could probably help. Everybody likes *her*.

Meeting resistance, I look down to see Mal's fist furled in the fabric of my sweater. He shakes his head again.

Oh shit. "Can I go to the bathroom at least?" I ask quietly.

He lets me go. I smooth out the sweater and head for the depressing, fluorescently lit bathroom. My face, as expected, is too hot and too pink. I don't need the toilet because for whatever insane reason, the conversation we just had coupled with his hand wrapped up in my sweater got me rock-fucking hard, and that, more than anything, needs to settle itself before I go back out there.

Here's the thing: I'm a straight guy who would fuck Malcolm Walsh in a heartbeat. But my sexuality isn't that simple. The tattoo artist I used to hook up with called me demi who got really horny sometimes, and in terms of labels, it mostly fits.

My connection with Malcolm when we were kids resulted in a physical attraction. Simple.

It also explains why I prefer to take women on dates instead of just showing up at their apartments expecting to get laid. It's why I'm taking it slow with Norah. But I do get horny, and not sometimes, but often. I prefer a connection, though. It doesn't have to be incredibly deep. Like with Jia. It was enough that we talked casually and work together. I'm not the textbook defini-tion of anything, but I know what I'm attracted to, and Malcolm is my OG. Most men don't even tweak my radar.

Some—the ones who remind me most of Mal—same hair, same body type, similar nose or eyes—they'll get my attention, but no part of me wants to push them against the wall and start devouring them the way I apparently still want to do with *him*. It's a soul deep desire that doesn't understand it can never be fulfilled.

I run my hands under some cold water, hoping to tame my cock into something less noticeable. I think about the bond market and oil prices. I think about the other interns and what amazing plan for money making they're putting into action. Finally, I've got a deflating semi, and I flush the toilet for realism.

I've been in the bathroom embarrassingly long, and by the time I'm out, Bailey is gone. Malcolm is in the kitchen, stirring a spoon in a coffee mug.

"Coffee?" he asks. "It's decaf."

"No." I take a stool on the other side of the counter.

He doesn't look at me. "Explain what you said earlier."

"Which part?"

"When you said you're straight."

"I only fuck women." I say. "It's self-explanatory."

"Since when?" he asks.

"Since I started having sex."

"Which was when?"

I glare at him in case he happens to look up. "That's not your business."

"Humor me."

"Why would I do that?" I ask.

He glances at me, then looks back down at his mug.

Suddenly it hits me that I'm alone with him. Completely alone for the first time in more than a decade. I don't understand why he's allowing this.

"Because I want to understand," he says quietly.

"Since when?" I need to get my guard back up fast. I didn't come here prepared for a talk or whatever this is.

"Since forever. I just want to understand, Ryan. Why do you have to make it impossible?"

I'm impossible? "Your interest in my sex life is brand new to me."

"I'm not *interested*..." Malcolm sighs. "If you're straight, then why the fuck would you—" He cuts himself off, shaking his head.

I stare at him and don't answer the question I know he's asking. Instead, I say, "I wasn't trying to break anything."

He sighs heavily, shoulders sagging. "I know."

It doesn't matter, though. That's the truth between us that can't ever change. "Where's Kaylin?".

"I don't know. Out. At her place." He shrugs.

"I assumed she lived here."

"No," he says.

Did I misread something? "Are you not still together?" I ask.

"We're close, but we're on a break."

On second thought, I don't want to know about his relationship issues. I don't even like knowing he *has* relationship issues. Hope isn't an option here, and I can't allow it any oxygen. I can't believe I'm letting myself wonder. Maybe I *didn't* learn my fucking lesson which is so simple:

I can't make him be attracted to me.

It's weird enough that I'm attracted to him. Talk about fucking awkward. Our parents got married when we were *eight*. I should think of him like a brother, but I've been in awe of Malcolm since I met him. He was taller, cuter, sweeter, and better at everything. I wanted to attach myself to him. I wanted to *be* him. Do *everything* with him.

That explains why—way before I knew I was actually attracted to him—when I got my first boner while we were snuggled up watching a movie one day, I wanted him to touch it with me. Discover it together. I wanted to learn if his body was like mine, if it could feel the things mine felt. Obviously I didn't ask —I was too shy and embarrassed. Because what if my body was weird or something?

And then, later, when I understood boners and knew I'd fallen for him, I wanted to know what it would feel like to be naked with him while we cuddled with our legs tangled. I wanted to kiss him because, more than anything, I wanted to know he felt the same way.

I wanted to know what I meant to him.

And then, in a way I *never* wanted—I found out.

CHAPTER EIGHT

MALCOLM

Something happened last night.

It was an accident. Sort of.

Or I thought it was, but when Ryan peeled off his sweater to show Bailey his bare upper body, I realized something unshake-able about myself. *I want to touch him.*

In a way, this isn't anything new. We were very close when we were kids, and for as long as I've been with Kaylin, I've never felt as close to her as I used to feel with Ryan. He was my favorite place. My favorite person. He was the best and worst thing to ever happen to me.

Last night was a perfect storm. Work was insane this week. Not just dealing with Isla's cold shoulder or trying to decipher her terrible spreadsheets, but the mental effort I had to put in to stop my mind from wandering had me feeling like a hamster on a wheel—if the hamster was on crack. And the wheel was on fire.

Since Monday night when we started the TikTok project, I keep getting these mental flashes of Ryan at random moments—like of him leaning on the wall with his triceps flexed, his hazel eyes hooded, body positioned for maximum seduction. And then there are the daydreams. I'd see the perfect knot of his tie and think about his fingers undoing it at the end of the day. Same thing with his belt buckle. I've thought about whether he wears boxers, briefs, or boxer briefs.

I've thought about how flat his abs are and whether he's built enough to have that vee that leads down to his cock. *Cum gutters.* Fuck, I've thought about his cum gutters at least twice a day. And now I've seen them. They exist. They're as real and defined as the rest of him is.

When I found myself daydreaming at work, I stopped myself. I redirected my thoughts to my next TikTok video. I looked online for things Stephanie can wear so I didn't think about Ryan's body. But all bets were off last night when I got home from work to an empty apartment and went to jerk off.

It started in the usual way. A hot shower, some long, slow strokes to wake up my dick. A few squeezes of my balls. I don't typically fantasize when I masturbate. No porn. No spank bank. Just sensation. I have seven flesh lights that are currently in working order. With any one of them and the variety of different sensations they offer, I can get off efficiently with a clear mind.

The one I used last night has a mouth shaped insertion point, ribbing up and down the channel, *and* variable suction. I hardly have to do anything. Once it was lubed, I slid inside, braced my hand on the tile wall and thrust gently into the toy.

It felt good. I didn't need to do what I did, but I also needed to get it over with, or the idea was going to continue plaguing and distracting me for another endless week.

Closing my eyes, I gathered my courage, reminded myself no one had to know, and pictured Ryan untucking his shirt and unbuckling his belt. The idea was to give in to this one fantasy, figuring if I played it out, I'd get repulsed. I'd lose my erection, and that would put the question to rest for good.

Not that I would ever lose an erection in that particularly

well-conceived toy, but I could have puked and that would've told me something. Anyway, the fantasy went on once the belt buckle was open. In my imagination, he didn't open his pants, just put his hand down the front, and took hold of his own cock.

I hissed as my dick throbbed hard in the toy at the image of Ryan's fist moving behind wool fabric—at the idea of a light sheen of sweat on his lower abs exposed by his now open shirt.

Gritting my teeth, I'd shoved my impossibly thicker cock into the toy and pictured running my fingers through his happy trail, flattening the hairs to his skin. And then it was like he was in the shower with me, his hand was the flesh light, and my hand was moving up his chest, squeezing his firm pec. I imagined what his nipple would feel like against my tongue, and before I could get to the point where I might have grabbed his ass, my body lit up like a circus, nerve endings blasting, a cry bouncing off the tile as I came so fucking hard, so fucking fast it was like getting the wind punched out of me.

The massive load of cum I left in the flesh light took me five minutes to wash out. Five minutes where my thighs and hands were shaking and I could barely catch my breath.

So that happened. I went there. I jerked off to Ryan, and I came harder than I've come in my entire fucking life.

Tonight, when he pulled off his sweater, and I saw what I saw —cum gutters and happy trail in the flesh—the goddamn sword pointing straight to his cock—that very particular light bulb in that very particular place in my head that's been flickering all week blared bright. I can't ignore it. Or maybe it's truer to say, I don't want to ignore it anymore. It's too hard. Too exhausting. I give up. I tried.

I tried for ten fucking years, which is by far the longest I've ever done anything I didn't genuinely want to do.

So this is me—giving up. Admitting defeat because whatever

I've been telling myself is no match for what's underneath that sexy black sweater, which, I've decided, I want to touch.

"Kaylin's going to Europe next week and she'll be gone for the rest of the month," I say unprompted. "Don't worry, it won't affect having the dog. I was already gonna watch her, so she'll be here."

"What do you mean by a break?" Ryan asks.

"Yeah...it was in the works. I started thinking about it before the internship anyway. I wanted to be able to focus and figure out...you know...what's next."

Ryan plants his hands on the counter and pushes back on his stool. "I should go."

"Could you not?" I ask, annoyed. "We're talking."

"You're talking," he says. "I'm listening to shit I never asked to hear."

"Well, what do *you* want to talk about?"

"Dude—I don't. I want to go home."

I shake my head. He's not getting off that easy. I just told him something important about me. Matter of fact, I've said a lot since that forgiveness phone call, give or take. It's his turn. "I don't believe that. I also don't think you'd have agreed to team up with me if you wanted nothing to do with me, so here I am. Deal with me."

"Deal with—*what?*" he asks. "You're being fucking weird."

"Just say what you need to say." Or do what you need to do, I want to tell him. *Anything.*

"What?" he asks, looking disgusted. "That you're a total fucking asshole who punished me every single day for years over one mistake I made? That having to see you now reminds me of the worst fucking times of my life?"

I swallow hard. "Yeah." I guess that is partly what I meant. Not exactly something I love hearing, but I feel like it's important that he got that off his chest, even if it wasn't pleasant for either of us.

"Well…there you go," he says.

Pressing, I ask, "What else?"

He glares at me. "That's it."

"Is it?"

"What else would there be?" he asks warily.

Okay, here goes. Step one. "If I said I wanted to try being friends again—"

"No," he says firmly, shaking his head and standing up. "I know how you treat your friends. No fucking thanks."

"Ryan—Listen—"

"Nope."

Damn, he moves fast. I catch him by the arm before he gets to the door. The heat of his arm blazes against my palm. The sinew and muscle are as firm as stone beneath my touch just like I knew they would be. If I let go, which I should, he'll leave, and I don't want him to. Not yet. I'm ready to push through whatever this wall is and get to the other side. I might have trouble following through with pretty much everything, but I seriously hate what I did to him in high school and afterward. It was based on a lie I told him *and* myself.

Maybe I used to get off on making him jumpy and nervous around me, but it's not doing it for me anymore. There are better ways to get his attention. There have to be. I'd rather he just be honest. Then, maybe, for once, I can be honest, too.

"Do *you* have a girlfriend?" I ask.

He shoots me a glare over his shoulder. "Why the fuck would you ask that?"

It's what we were just talking about, isn't it? It's a normal question. "Has there been anyone serious for you?" Okay, maybe that's less normal. This must be what it feels like to be taken over by a parasite. Are these thoughts actually mine? They're familiar in a way, but also foreign enough that I'm not sure what to do with them.

Ryan moves with a hell of a lot more confidence than he used to. He puts his other hand on my wrist and physically removes my hand from his forearm. "Again, none of your business."

"Why can't I ask?" We have to figure this shit out. If we don't, I'll drive myself nuts. I'm halfway there already.

"Because..." He stops himself, then takes two long, deep breaths. Before I understand what's happening, he grabs me by the hips and slams me against the wall. It knocks the breath out of me, and heat instantly floods my face. Adrenaline spikes, my body ready to fight back.

But he doesn't hit me. He crowds me. First with his body, firmly pressing itself to mine, then his face. It's so close, his hair touches my forehead. His hands on my hips clamp down so tightly, it hurts. His harsh breath lands on my mouth as the world around us stills and quiets.

My heart slams frantically in my chest as he very deliberately grazes a line down my nose with the tip of his. I let out a delayed gasp that leaves me depleted and utterly empty.

"What the fuck are you doing?" I ask, breathless. My hands are on his shoulders, and I'm squirming. I need to get away from him, but if I wanted to, I could—couldn't I? I don't think I *do* want to. I mean—of course I don't. I'm getting exactly what I asked for.

"I'm showing you why you shouldn't ask so many fucking questions."

"Why?" I *need* to understand. Either nothing he's saying makes sense, or my brain broke when my head hit the wall.

"Because I'm not fourteen anymore, Mal."

He is *definitely* not fourteen. He's definitely a full grown man pinning me—another full grown man—to a wall, and I'm not fighting it. It's not like he's a stranger, or I haven't ever felt his body against mine. Or his legs, firm and hard pressed into mine. A flat chest smashed into me almost like we're hugging—one of those long hugs where I liked to...

Oh God...

I know why I'm not fighting him.

Before I let myself reconsider, my hand moves into his hair. I wrap my other arm around his shoulders, closing what little distance there is left between us. He lets out a tragic noise as his hands move from my hips to my mid back to hold me close, one fisting in my shirt. His cheek is rough against my neck. The texture is unfamiliar but the *heat*—I remember this.

Our breaths sync, deep and slow. I shut my eyes and inhale him. There's a hint of spice in his hair that stirs something deep inside me—a need that's as familiar as it is uncomfortable.

"I can't do this," he whispers, but makes no move to pull away.

"Why not?" I ask, wondering if this is as awkwardly arousing to him.

"Because this isn't us."

Isn't it? "It is right now," I say, grazing the edge of how I really feel.

"I don't like it."

He's lying. His dismissive words are in direct contrast to the tightness of his hands, the pressure his chest is exerting to keep me pinned to the wall.

"I do," I tell him. *I really like it.* Holding him makes sense. Way more than a financial analysis and certainly more than socializing with my mentor off the clock. His body might be different than it was when we were kids, but that heartbeat against mine feels exactly the same.

That same throaty whimper comes out of him again, and I tighten my own grip on him. I understand his objections, obviously. And I know I can't turn back the clock. But I'm sorry for how I treated him. I need him to know it wasn't him. It was me. It was my insecurity and my fear, and my confusion. I do forgive him, but I haven't managed to forgive myself.

"This isn't what I want," he complains again.

I swallow hard before I ask in a shaky voice, "What do you want?"

He doesn't answer me, still not giving up an inch between us.

"You used to like my hugs," I remind him.

His deep breath threatens to cave in my chest. "Please let go."

I don't want to. I get that hugs don't last forever, but this one doesn't feel finished. It's like there's this deep, empty well inside me that I never noticed until his presence started trickling into it again. Every second I'm holding him, there's another drop that hits the cold, hard bottom of it, and if I let him go, all I'll have is a dried up well I'm now fully aware of. "Can you forgive me?" I ask.

"Fine, yes, I forgive you. Jesus." He yanks on my shirt and bends his head until his forehead bangs against my collarbone. "Please let me go." He says pathetically like I'm gonna have to be the one to shove him off.

"Or what?" I press. I can't help it. For the first time in I don't know how fucking long I feel like I'm in the right place at the right time doing what I'm supposed to be doing. I'm not ready to move onto the next thing on my never-ending list of things to try hoping it might be a better fit—more "me." *This* is me. This is the me no one knows but him. The me only *he* could ever see.

"Mal..." He lets out another heavy breath before his hands settle once again on my hips, gripping them hard enough to put some distance between our lower bodies. "Don't," he chokes out.

The trickle stops as soon as our thighs aren't touching. He manages to peel himself away and take a full step back. When I get a look at his face, he's swiping his thumbs beneath his eyes—nearly green beneath wet lashes.

My heart, which hasn't felt much more than affection in years, is hit with an emotional blow so hard, I lose my breath again. "I'm sorry," I say, but the words don't make any sound.

He checks his pockets, and before I find my voice, he's got the door open and he's walking out.

In the final analysis, I'm not sure what that was—either from him or from me. I don't know what he was trying to tell me when he pushed me against the wall, and I don't know what I thought I could accomplish from hugging him like I used to when we were kids.

What I do know—more acutely than I've ever let myself acknowledge—is that I miss him. Somewhere behind all those walls is the best friend I've ever had. I could *feel* him. He was the water in the well. He *is* the well. And I'm so fucking thirsty I feel like I'm moments away from dying of it.

ON SUNDAY MORNING, the video on the new account @justthetipfinancebro has 2,172 views and thirty five comments. Some are appreciative of my looks or Kaylin's dog, and others are questions about the actual tip I gave.

I lie in bed and respond to all of the comments in an effort not to dwell too much more on last night. I spent way too many hours doing that after Ryan left, going so far as playing some of our favorite songs from when we were young and full-on wallowing in my butt hurt feelings. What still sucks today is I want to text him screen shots of some of these comments and see what he has to say about them. Where *that* urge resurfaced from, I've got no clue, but it's not like Jake, Evan, Henry or any of my friends now would get it—or even think it's funny.

When Kaylin comes by to drop off Stephanie, she mentions she saw the video and thought it was great. She also tells me not to be afraid of dropping my waistband, which she reaches out and does, pulling my sweats past my hip bones. When she pats the newly exposed skin with her hands, I remember Ryan's hands on them last night, and I get a *feeling*.

It's a weird, something's crawling under my skin feeling I want to both twist away from and also curl up in. The only better way to describe it is the way it feels to get your first orgasm—like something's wrong—it's not okay—oh holy shit what happens if I keep doing that—I might die—*that* kind of thing. But it's also *familiar*.

I'm not an idiot. I get what's happening here. The reason I wanted that hug last night wasn't *only* about missing him. I've been thinking of him in a way I told myself I never could—in a way I shouldn't and therefore wouldn't. To be honest, it's still got me a little nauseous, and once Kaylin pecks me on the cheek and leaves Stephanie in my arms, I curl up with her in bed and start the *Lord of the Rings* trilogy. The trilogy of last resort. It's either that or pull out one of my flesh lights, and that just feels wrong now that Stephanie's here.

When *The Two Towers* is just getting started, I get a ping on my phone.

@Billiondollarblackcat stitched your video.

Stephanie sniffs the screen when I try to open the video, and I pull her against my chest to get her out of the way.

It starts with me—shirtless—holding the dog while I lean on the wall outside my bathroom because it was the best place to set up the light and phone stand. I say, "Mal and Stephanie here with today's hot tip to get rich and stay that way."

My image is replaced with Ryan—leaning against a window

with his face bathed in golden sunlight. His tattoos stand out starkly on his pale skin, and his black hair looks thick and lush. The overweight tuxedo cat on his shoulder has bright green eyes and a white nose. It's purring loud enough to hear. "Here's a tip, Justthetip," he says, voice deep and eyes smoldering so hard Bailey would give him ten gold stars. "Think real estate."

He goes on, giving a quick piece of advice about how to determine city areas slated for growth by following infrastructure trends, but I can't get over how *good* he looks. I'm okay on screen, but Ryan's coloring—his angles—his goddamn pouty lips—his *edge*—the camera loves him. He has zero bad angles. No unflattering shadows. No flaws.

I had him in my arms last night.

"Stephanie, what the fuck is happening?"

I toss the phone aside and bury my face in her fur, feeling the heat inside me everywhere.

I guess it really could be that I just miss him—that having him back in my life is playing games with my head, crossing wires and desires, confusing one need with another.

I wasn't oblivious to him as a teen or even before that. I know normal brothers and friends don't snuggle to watch movies like we did or sleep with their heads together and their legs tangled under the sheets. I always liked the feel of him. I liked knowing he was nearby. I never *had* to hug him for as long as I used to, but it felt good.

But when he threw down a gauntlet that day while he was high on cough syrup, I took one look at it and ran. I freaked the fuck out because whatever he thought I was—I couldn't be *that*. I couldn't want him *that way*. It would mean things I didn't want it to mean, and I was exactly young and stupid and confused enough to be scared shitless.

I also blamed myself for leading him on and taking too

much and confusing *him* with my own needy ass, but fuck—my mom was dead, and I was still processing that. My dad had someone new, and all I had for myself was Ryan and a compulsive need to be held. That's what I told myself. Or tried to.

I've been staring down at that gauntlet ever since, wondering not if I made a mistake, because he was my stepbrother so obviously I couldn't return feelings like that, but whether my innocent touches weren't so innocent after all. Whether it was my fault for leading him on. Whether I was damaged.

He was such a mess after I rejected him, though, it was easy to believe I did the right thing by convincing myself that he was disgusting and wrong and an asshole. I fucking *reviled* him.

But something's different. He's still the asshole I turned him into, but my disgust, my revulsion—all that's gone.

That hug last night was intense as hell. The heavy breathing. The agonized sound he made. The scent and heat of him. That vast empty space inside me that felt slightly less empty with him up close and his breath on my neck.

So what do I do now? Do I say something? Do I try fantasizing about it again and see if it's as potent as last time? Picture undoing his tie... his mouth on my neck.

My cock stirs, and that same sickness from before pools in my belly, stirring, twisting...

I don't know. I don't want to lie to myself, but this is major. This is a decision I can't make on one impulse, based on *one* hug. "*I don't know how to do this,*" I groan out loud to the dog and the room.

Stephanie gets up, makes a circle in front of me and snuggles hard against my chest. She weighs four pounds normally, but when she really tries, she can make herself weigh about twenty.

Bailey texts to see if I know how to make a stitch video or does she need to walk me through it.

I assure her I can figure it out.

She sends me some talking points to pivot the TikTok conversation from real estate to franchises.

Once I get the gist of what she wants me to say, I turn my camera to selfie mode, welcoming the distraction. The lighting could be better, but I flip through some filters and find one that gives the effect of natural light. Stephanie is perfectly positioned, and I look how I feel. Hard up and in bed. My shirt's already off, so I find an angle that showcases all the finest aspects of the pathetic state I'm in, and I deliver my lines like I'm telling a woman I want to lick her till she comes screaming on my mouth. I send it to Bailey, and she responds with a head explosion emoji.

BAILEY

You just did that right now?!

ME

No, I read your mind and made this one yesterday.

BAILEY

You guys are fucking fire. We're going to win huge.

ME

You're flirting with me now?

BAILEY

Still not my type, golden boy.

Great. So glad the nickname is sticking.

But I can't argue with Bailey's tactics or her approval. Neither can TikTok. By Sunday evening, Ryan and I have made six videos, and our views are up to thirty-three thousand per post.

Whatever we're doing—it's working.

But if I have to see Ryan's sword tattoo one more time, there won't be a distraction in the world big enough to stop me from thinking about what it's pointing to.

CHAPTER NINE

RYAN

It turns out, I don't hate attention as much as I thought I did. As Bud's and my following grows, and I become more confident shirtless on the internet—because the comments I've read are a thousand percent positive—minus the inevitable guy who always wants to argue with me about whatever snippet of advice I dole out, I feel good about this plan. Leveraging social media successfully is a quick ticket to success, and I've always heard the trick is to "just be yourself," but when yourself is a glaring, awkward, cynical dick most of the time, you kinda think it's probably not the place for you.

However—I'm also the guy who works out six days a week, quit smoking pot and started using my brain. I rescued Bud and picked the best tattoo artist in Oregon to decorate my body. Granted, I knew I wasn't hideous, but a certain rejection at a young age has made me err on the shyer side of social interaction. But the compliments I'm getting—on my ink, my muscles, my eyes, my hair—have me enjoying the process a hell of a lot more than I thought I would. Norah never leaves a comment, but she always likes my posts, and I like knowing she's watching.

I texted her Sunday afternoon telling her she could do something similar if she wanted to join the fun, but she sent me a picture of herself with no makeup in a baggy hoodie with the message *no thanks.*

Because this has become my new life now, I've stepped outside my own box and invited an actual person into my home. Calyx is currently sitting on my bathroom counter. I'm standing between his legs with my hands on either side of him while he explains how to make up my eyes so they'll pop on camera without looking like I'm wearing cosmetics.

I hesitated when he hopped up and spread his lean, smooth legs, but he gave me a look that was some combination of come hither and get over yourself, and I walked right in. "You want to bring it just inside your lash line—see?"

"Uh-huh."

"And this mascara is super light because your lashes are so dark, but it'll give them a pretty gloss." He taps my bottom lip. "You're not wearing lip balm."

"I hate it," I tell him.

"Get over it. Or at least use a lip mask at night."

I laugh.

"Your pores aren't terrible, but before I go, we're gonna put in a Sephora order, and when it comes in, you'll invite me back over, and I'll talk you through your new skin care routine. Actually, let's just use Amazon. Sephora takes forever, and I know you're rushing this."

"Sounds good."

"I'm so glad you realized how pretty you are. How many likes did it take?"

I roll my eyes.

He flashes me his rare but brilliant smile. "I'm glad it's working." Using the pads of his middle fingers, he pats something wet beneath my eyes, then lightly smooths it out. "Concealer," he explains.

"What am I concealing?"

"It acts like a highlighter in your case. You don't have bags or anything."

"Good."

"If you're not gonna do lip balm, just like a brush of gloss before you film to make your lips look dewy would work wonders."

I laugh again, my head dipping forward.

"What?" He's obviously laughing, too. "Dewy is youthful and glowing. Dewy is *fabulous*."

"I'll take your word for it."

"You better. Now look at yourself and tell me what you think."

I slide to the side and study my reflection over his shoulder. It's like he put a beauty filter on me. "Nice work."

"Can I film you?"

"Malcolm hasn't posted anything else today," I say.

"He can stitch you, too, you know?"

"Yeah, I guess."

Calyx pats my hip. "Come on. Let me watch you do one. I can help you with your angles and finding your light."

"I thought you said I was doing great."

"You are, *and* there's always room for improvement. I saw a bunch of workout equipment out there. Wanna try using some of that?"

"Bud hates the weights."

"What if you put some tuna or catnip on you?"

"You've got an answer for everything, don't you?"

He simps with a shrug of a shoulder. "I may look like a dumb blond, but I'm a secret smarty pants."

"Speaking of which, you haven't traveled in a few weeks. Is everything okay with your job?"

He sighs, tossing a glance at himself in the mirror. "I just wanted a little break. The traveling was a lot, but fashion weeks will start up again soon, and I'll get back into it."

"Burned out?"

"It's lonely," he says.

"Yeah, I get that."

"I know you do." He slides off the counter and winds his way past me and out of the bathroom to take a look around the apartment. I trail a few steps behind him as he flips lights on and off in different combinations, examining the way it changes the space. We leave my bedroom and head over to Deacon's weight set up.

"Why the fuck do you come to the gym?" Calyx asks.

He's got a point. Deacon has almost everything I use at the gym besides TRX straps. "This is all my roommate's."

"What does he do?"

"Tech stuff. I think he's like a software developer. He's also training for an Iron Man." There. Everything I know about Deacon in a few simple sentences.

"Where is he tonight?"

"I don't know. We don't talk much."

"How long have you lived here?" Calyx asks, dragging his fingertips over the bench press.

"I moved in right before Memorial Day."

He gives me a disappointed look. I shrug it off.

"Grab the cat," he says. "We'll keep it simple with a bicep curl."

He adjusts some lighting while I remove my shirt and retrieve a sleeping Bud from my pillow. The amount of hair he leaves behind is just—ridiculous. I blow some off my mouth while I'm selecting a weight.

"It's gotta be at least twenty-five pounds," Calyx says. "Oh, hold on—I have a thought."

He stages me with a light coating of olive oil everywhere

but my face. He even runs wet fingers through my hair to make it look like I've been sweating. Once I'm where he wants me, I talk about gold, and because he's not done with me yet, and the ideas are popping for him, we film a few more clips in different locations with wardrobe changes and less oil where I discuss everything from stock futures, the bond market, and how to create your own 401K if you're not in a job with benefits.

Calyx directs me all the way through. "Growlier. Give me the bedroom eyes—that's it—you got it. Pet the cat longer."

The process leaves Bud greasy, but I have fun. All Calyx wants in return when I offer to pay him is a mini photo shoot of his own. He does his own makeup and directs himself, but I take the pictures and send him all the shots. The best one is of him wrapped in a bed sheet sitting in the bay window.

In it, he's the perfect, enchanting combination of feminine and masculine—or not masculine, but boyish. It makes me wonder what kind of man he'll wind up with. I picture him with someone older, I think. Someone who'll spoil him stupid and worship at his feet.

He leaves around midnight, and before I go to bed, I send the video of me doing biceps curls via a TikTok message to Bailey and Malcolm, just so they're aware I'm doing something. Once I get a thumbs up from Bailey, I post it.

As I'm about to drop off to sleep after a shower, I get a text.

MALCOLM

Are you wearing makeup?

My mouth twists. This whole night, I've managed not to think about him. Not the way he spoke to me or the way he held me. Not the way I nearly broke down in tears from the pain in my chest and the restraint it took not to press my mouth to his neck. Not the way I'd very nearly told him that nothing had changed for me, and that was the answer to the question as to why he needed to let me go.

I think about it for a while, about whether to respond or not, and finally, I answer the question.

ME

I was

MALCOLM

Where'd you learn how to do that?

ME

My friend Calyx did it.

MALCOLM

Did he film the video too?

ME

Yeah. Why?

MALCOLM

It was good. That's all. Looked more professional.

ME

Not sure how to take that

MALCOLM

It was a compliment.

ME

Oh. Thanks

I want to ask him why he's still up. Why he's got so many questions. Why did he hug me like that.

MALCOLM

Should I wear makeup?

I laugh.

ME

I don't think so, golden boy. You don't need it.

MALCOLM

Neither do you but it looked good.

There. What the fuck is that? How *the fuck* am I supposed to take that? Nothing he said so far was going to keep me up tonight, but that will. That in the context of the hug I didn't ask for but took for every ounce of him it was worth.

ME

Don't do it. You'll look ridiculous if you don't know how to put it on.

MALCOLM

I can watch a tutorial as well as anyone else on the planet.

I curl onto my side. Holding the screen like it's something precious, imagining what it would be like if he were here, curled up just like I am, facing me, saying the words instead of typing them. Would he try to hug me again? Would I stop him?

ME

Unless you have eyeliner, mascara and concealer lying around, you'll have to find a 24 hour store to get all the supplies you need.

MALCOLM

Is that all it was? What did you need with mascara anyway? You've got great lashes.

Well, now I'm just supremely fucked.

ME

Your lashes are fine

Did he ask? No. I just said that. For no reason. As if I want to talk about what Malcolm looks like. I need to go to bed. I'm losing my inhibitions. My mind.

MALCOLM

You think?

I am not fucking answering that.

ME

Go to bed, Mal

MALCOLM

Yeah, okay. Good night.

I flip the phone face down on the mattress and close my eyes, but that's a mistake because my mind transports me straight back into his arms. Into the moment I pressed him to the wall, and he turned the tables on me. When I felt the clench of his hand in my hair and the throb that made my cock rise, I had to force myself to push his hips away.

How is it still possible to want him after all this time and all the shit he threw at me—both the outright disdain, the constant humiliation, and the complete indifference? All incredibly painful. Deserved, maybe? And yet too much. He broke my heart and my brain. He shattered parts of me I can never put back together. Primarily—trust. Specifically, my ability to trust *him*.

But I can't ignore him either. He's in my life again, temporarily at least, and if we somehow salvage a friendship, he could be around for years. I'll get to live through him getting married, having kids. Possibly even with Kaylin, who I don't entirely hate.

I used to think she was an opportunist, but I also knew Mal was better boyfriend material than I was and extremely hard to resist. I honestly can't believe they're still together. I'd have sworn when they first started dating, it was just to stick it to me —Mal's revenge for me fucking up our friendship. But then they just—never broke up.

I don't know what he means by being on a break with her. If that just means she's out of town, and she's allowed to dance with other people, or if it's an official—let's think this through before we get really serious kind of break.

I hate that I care which it is. It doesn't matter. I also hate that I have so many questions I can never ask. I hate that I'm reading into the hug and these texts. His *compliments*. I hate that they mean more to me than the hundreds of similar ones I've gotten from strangers on the internet, or the ones Norah texted me just before I got into bed.

I hate that I'm thinking about what I'm going to wear tomorrow and whether lip balm would make me slightly more attractive to him.

I hate that this is happening to me. That *he* is happening to me.

Again.

CHAPTER TEN

MALCOLM

For the third time this morning, Ryan laughs, and once again, it's got me turning my head. Isla follows my gaze.

"Trouble concentrating?" she asks, annoyed. "I know this finance stuff can get boring, but you did sign up for it."

"It's not the work," I tell her, doing my best to ignore her tone. "I think I had too much caffeine today."

It's got nothing to do with coffee, though, or "this finance stuff." It has to do with Bailey's stupid joke that cracked Ryan up during the morning huddle, and then Miguel showing him something on his phone and making him laugh again. And after that, they'd leaned their heads together and Miguel had talked directly into his ear making Ryan grin like a dope the entire time. And Charlie must really be a joy to work with because he's had Ryan smiling since he sat down with him. Now he's laughing loud enough to turn heads.

Fine. *My* head.

I can acknowledge it's just my head. No one else seems to notice or care that Ryan is in a good mood. That his teeth and tiny dimples have made multiple appearances today, and no one has pointed out that he's breaking character.

This morning in our huddle before Georgie arrived, everyone was talking about our TikTok videos. Piper lowkey accused us of some version of prostitution. Bailey was quick to rebut. "They made it onto your feeds didn't they? Hashtag thirst trap."

That was Bailey's joke and Ryan *laughed*. And blushed. All I could do was grind my teeth and try not to tell them to stop staring at him. To be fair, they were looking at me differently, too, but he's the one taking over my brain. He was in every fitful dream I had last night in varying capacities, and almost all of them were shirtless. One of them featured his cat curled around Stephanie, and she was all peaceful snuggled up against Bud's black and white fur.

Doesn't take a genius to figure out what's going on with me.

The jealousy is new, though, and I wasn't expecting it. I made him cry—they make him laugh. I feel awesome about that. Fucking super.

The spreadsheet I'm fixing is coming along, but at the same time, I'm plotting how to get Ryan alone. Not because I have a plan, but because I don't. It's a test. I want to know what I'll do. It's like when I'm watching a reality show and I'm thinking, what would I do if that were me naked and alone in the jungle? What would I do if I only had five ingredients to work with and one of them was grape jelly? What would I do if I were stuck on an island with six hot girls and six hot guys? And now—what if one of them were Ryan?

My imagination is like the best club in town. Always hopping.

At lunch, he's at the microwaves, staring at the clock on it, humming something that faintly sounds like "The Final Count-down" by Europe. It was one of my dad's favorite songs to play air guitar to. I brought a sandwich, but I've got half a cup of coffee that could be warmer, so I stick it into the microwave next to his and set it to heat for a full minute—a totally unnecessary amount of time. When I glance at Ryan, he's got an eyebrow arched at my timer.

"I like it hot," I say in my TikTok voice. Not on purpose. It's just how it comes out. Overly suggestive. I mean it as a joke. I think.

He meets my eyes. "That should do it," he says, also in his low *fuck me because I know smart shit* voice.

"You're in a good mood today," I blurt.

I get a scowl for that. "Am I?"

"You're smiling a lot."

Did I really just say that? Admit I've been watching him?

He's not smiling now. Those aren't for me, apparently. I *hate* that.

I scramble for a segue. Something to say that will lead to a conversation we can't finish here and need to continue outside of work, because the shit I want to talk to him about is deep. Things he all but ran from Saturday night. None of them are office appropriate, though. I settle for, "What are you thinking in terms of transitioning over to a subscription model?"

He doesn't stop scowling, but he keeps his attention on me as he leans a hip on the counter, crossing his arms. "I said YouTube originally, but I looked into it and now I'm thinking of either a Patreon or a Kickstarter—like say we want to start a podcast, but we need equipment—"

"Which we would if we wanna do a podcast," I say.

"I was talking to Bailey on the way to work about a Patreon. Her idea was to pair it with a Discord so people can ask questions, and we give video responses if you subscribe to a certain tier. She said she could handle lower tiers—like with written answers, but the exclusive videos would come with the highest tier."

I'm following, grateful to be talking about something I actually understand. "If we did a podcast, how would we monetize that?"

"According to ChatGPT, there's like a hundred ways to do that," he says. His timer goes off, and he opens the microwave.

I grab the coffee out of mine and follow him to the booth he slides into. He looks across at me, surprised, but doesn't tell me to get lost. "Ads, paid subscriptions, sponsorships, merch."

"How long do you think until we can start doing that?" I ask. These are all questions I could probably think through and answer for myself, but my brain's not firing on all its cylinders today.

He shrugs as he stirs his plastic tray of pasta. "Depends on if we peter out or keep gaining traction. Bailey thinks we need to start stitching other people talking about finance—like people with bigger followings."

"Do you agree with her?"

He gives me a blank look. "Do you? You're on the team, too."

I don't even remember the question. He's got his sleeves rolled up, which he rarely does at work, and his forearm tattoos are on vivid display. It surprises me how pretty they are. Vines and florals. Ivy and thorns. It's all blackwork, but the shading is so dimensional, I can tell it was done by a true artist.

His father's watch, which used to be too big for him, now fits snugly on his left wrist. Our parents met in a grief support group. His dad died from a sudden heart attack when he was much too young, and my mom died of an accidental overdose. Sort of accidental. I mean—with how much she drank, all the pills she took, and how depressed she was, it was really only a matter of time.

But whereas Ryan barely remembers his dad, I remember my mother: the good, the bad, and the deeply disturbing.

I genuinely thought my father would stay married to Ryan's mom Jill forever—their romance was a whirlwind, and they seemed obsessed with each other for a solid few years, which left me and Ryan alone to become each other's worlds for a while.

I wonder if Ryan knows why they called it quits. My dad only says stuff like "it wasn't working out for us." To my knowledge, he hasn't dated anyone since Jill. He seems fine, though. Always in a good mood whenever I talk to him. He lives in Los Angeles now, so I don't see him as much as I used to.

"Mal?" Ryan prompts.

"Um...we were talking about the podcast?" I ask, trying to replay the conversation that led to my sitting here.

"I was talking about stitching creators with bigger followings. You all right?"

"Yeah, yeah. No, I think that's a good idea. Builds momentum. Did you ask that friend of yours?"

"Calyx?" he asks.

"Such a weird name."

"I can ask him. I'll see him at the gym today."

Do I hate Calyx? I think I might hate Calyx. "What gym do you go to?"

"It's by my apartment."

"Where's that?"

"Lower Haight," he says with a scowl. "Why?"

"Yeah? Cool neighborhood. Is it a good gym?"

"It's fine," he says, but I get the sense I'm veering dangerously close to a firm *none of your business.*

I change course. "Does your cat get along with dogs?"

Ryan arches a brow.

"I was just thinking if we need to meet up again—the three of us, we could maybe do it at your place since you both hate mine, and I don't blame you. But Stephanie gets weird when I leave."

"What does she do when you're at work?" he asks, masterfully sidestepping the apartment topic.

"Day care," I say.

He grins, but it's not the kind of smile he was handing out like candy to other people. This one's more mocking.

"She's Kaylin's dog," I say. "I just follow the routine whenever I watch her."

"Got it. Well, Bud weighs almost twenty pounds so *Stephanie* would be taking her chances."

"She can hold her own," I say.

"Can she?" His look has a challenge in it that I'm not sure is meant entirely for Stephanie.

I answer in kind. "She's more open minded than you might think."

He takes a sip from his water bottle. "Sure, we can use my place next time, if you don't mind my roommate hanging around."

Roommate? "Are they like—always there?"

"No, but I don't know his schedule."

I don't know how to feel about Ryan living with another man. I have questions.

"When should we meet up again—do you think?" I ask, trying not to think about Ryan and his *roommate*.

He sighs like I'm fucking exhausting, and he's not wrong. I'm fucking exhausting myself with this mess of a conversation. "I'm not the team leader, Mal. If you want us to meet up, suggest something. We'll work it out. If you want something else..."

My spine goes rigid. "Like what?"

"I don't know. You're acting weird."

No shit. Because *this* is weird. You'd think he'd get that. Still, I deny it. "I'm not acting like anything. I'm having a normal conversation with you, and you're acting like we barely know each other."

"We don't," he says with that firm edge I was trying to avoid butting up against.

In retreat mode, I fall back into old habits. "Whose fault is that? At least I'm not pretending you don't exist."

"*Today*," he says cuttingly.

I should have said more when I was hugging him and his guard was halfway down. I should have apologized. Now isn't really the time and place, but since I have his attention... "Look, I'm trying. I might suck at it, but this is me, making an effort—"

"Why, though?" he asks.

"Because—" Okay, I can't say the real reason. "Because we have to work together."

"That's it?"

I hesitate, looking directly into his eyes. Very much on purpose. "That's it."

I can see him processing, ruminating on my hesitation, which is a big win in my book. Because *what if*?

What if he grabbed hold of *my* sweater and made *me* stay after Bailey has to go. What if he shoved me into a wall and got in my face again? What if the scent of spice was just a top note, and there's something even more appealing beneath it? *What would I do?*

I'm known among my friends as someone who dabbles. While they've all got hobbies or sports they've dedicated themselves to, I keep trying new things. Pickleball, basketball, frisbee golf, biking—which I do *not* recommend in this town—rock climbing, and once—cliff diving. I don't scare easy except for this one thing. This one thing that I've been running from since I was fourteen.

And I might hate it as much as I hated biking uphill, but I honestly don't think anything could be *that* bad. "I say we try and meet up tonight or tomorrow night and make a concrete plan for the week. Isla's got me pretty busy during the day, but

I've got plenty of free time in the evenings to work on next steps. I don't want to go off on some tangent we're not all in agreement about." There—how's that for a contribution?

His hazel gaze is still suspicious. "All right. I'll check in with Bailey before debrief, then."

"What's your address?" I ask.

His head moves with a subtle shake, and it hits me again how good looking he is. *So* fucking good looking. "I'll text it to you when we have a time set."

I nod and sip my coffee while he finally takes a bite of his lunch. "You're not eating?" he asks after he polishes off half his pasta.

I have zero appetite today. "I had a big breakfast," I lie.

"What'd you have?"

Fuck. Now I have to *really* lie.

"Biscuits and gravy."

"You make that yourself?"

I shake my head. "Delivery."

"You must wake up early."

I couldn't sleep after I stopped texting you. "Yeah. Stephanie, you know? She's got places to be."

He laughs and covers his mouth so food doesn't come flying out.

I smile because finally—*I* did it. *Me.* I feel fucking high off the blush reddening his cheeks and the laughter shaking his broad shoulders.

I wonder what I'd feel like if I made him come?

Whoa. What the fuck?

I clear my throat, my own flush creeping up my neck. *On that note.* "I'll wait to hear from you," I say before my semi gets any firmer. I leave him at the table, the sound of his fading laughter still ringing in my ears.

CHAPTER ELEVEN

RYAN

Deacon isn't home tonight. He left a note saying he'd probably be out until morning, so that's lucky and a good start. Our awkwards don't mix well, and while Bailey and Malcolm aren't people I'm desperately trying to impress or anything, I don't want any side-eyes regarding how little my roommate and I speak to each other. I'd have to do introductions, and Deacon would have to say words, and it's just a whole fracas I didn't want to deal with. I'm glad I won't have to.

Without him here, I can focus all my attention on Mal—his role in the project, I mean. Not his sudden interest in my daily habits.

The thing about my apartment with its living room gym is that the only place to be comfortable is my bedroom. The word I'd use to describe it is cozy, and it's where I spend the vast majority of my time at home. I've got a flat screen mounted to the wall, a desk where I work and eat if I'm not eating in bed, and one of those giant beanbags over by the window where I sometimes read or take a nap. It's big enough to seat two people, but in the same way a love seat does—right next to each other.

But between that, the bed, and the desk chair, no one needs

to be touching. I grab my specially purchased pet hair remover that I use on furniture and start furiously scrubbing cat hair from every surface. Whitesnake is in my head. *Here I Go Again on my own. Down the only road I've ever known...* Luckily, I know all the words to this one. Mal's dad played it a lot in the mornings growing up for some reason. My mom loved it.

Once I'm satisfied with the lack of fur, I clean out the litter box in the bathroom and pray Bud doesn't decide to use it while anyone's here.

Just before seven, I light a stick of incense and gulp a glass of water. I worked up a light sweat, but not enough that I feel like I need to take another shower. I already took one at the gym. I wash my hands, run my wet hands through my hair, and the doorbell rings.

I don't know why I was so prepared for it to be Bailey, but seeing Malcolm on my doorstep makes my breath catch. I clear my throat and steady my breathing. He's wearing a lightweight white sweater which is such a good look on him, and then khaki cargo shorts that aren't. But the sight of his calves, the golden hair on golden skin and his bare ankles—I don't know—it does something to me I'm not at all surprised by anymore.

I've got a thing for legs, and I guarantee I know when it started—tangled up in his.

Those.

"My face is up here."

I glare at said face. "Fuck off." I step out of the way and let him in. I'm about to close the door when I spot Bailey coming up the steps. She smiles and waves, not at all like the evil-eyed woman I sat across from that first day. She's downright bubbly when you take her out of the office. Still a little scary, but more like a good horror movie. She's *Get Out*, if *Get Out* were a person. Entertaining and keeps me on my toes.

"How's my billion dollar black cat?" she asks.

I flex my bicep for her, and she laughs, lifting a tote bag. "I brought a cheeseball."

"Bud will love that."

"I brought him something, too." She sticks her hand in the tote as she approaches the door and pulls out a stick with a tiny stuffed mouse dangling from a string.

"A classic," I tell her.

"It's filled with catnip. You mentioned he's a fan."

"Do I talk about him that much?"

"You do in your comments."

Once she's inside, I turn to find Malcolm right there, looming over my shoulder. *That* almost gets a jump scare out of me. "Did you bring me anything?" he asks Bailey.

"A cheeseball, sweetheart. Like I said."

"Sweetheart? Wow, I'm growing on you."

"Pfft. It's got onions in it."

"Awesome," he says.

He hates onions, but I guarantee he'll suffer through Bailey's cheeseball.

She takes a look around the equipment-filled living area. There's a sofa, but it's behind the bench press. "Um..."

"We can go to my room," I say, gesturing toward the short hallway that separates my bedroom from Deacon's. Malcolm wanders that direction while I help Bailey plate her cheeseball. It's softball-sized and wrapped in cellophane.

"What inspired this?" I ask.

"Gotta keep my cash cows fed and happy," she says.

I laugh and open the box of Wheat Thins she brought before pouring them into a bowl. Bud makes his appearance, leaping onto the kitchen counter and dropping a few hairs before I swoop him back to the floor. "He's untrainable," I apologize.

"He's a cat. I have one, too."

"Any chance he made it into the cheeseball?"

She lets out a peal of laughter. "One way to find out."

"Want anything to drink, Mal?" I call out.

"I'm good," he says *from my bedroom*. I shake my head at the concept—too surreal to contemplate. This evening feels like a mindfulness exercise. Stay in the moment. Focus. Acknowledge the intrusive thoughts and let them glide by.

I make him a glass of water anyway. He'll thank me later. Maybe not out loud, but I'm not picky.

He's on the bed when Bailey and I come in with the food and drinks. That's where I'd mentally placed Bailey, so I have to make a mental adjustment. I hand him his plate of cheese and crackers and the glass of ice water. "Thanks," he says, meeting my eyes.

I nod. Bailey plops onto the beanbag, makes a spot for her food, and immediately pulls out her phone. I sit at my desk and swivel my chair around to face them.

Bailey opens with, "I spent twenty-five bucks. My little brother is all over TikTok, so I paid him to destroy his For You Page to find me all the biggest finance influencers. I found three I want us to stitch. One is a Harvard student, another is a trader on Wall Street, and the last one wrote a book called *Money Sense*. They're all cis men, all white, which is good. We don't want to compete with people who are already marginalized."

She gives us each a look to make sure we understand she's not joking.

Both of us nod agreeably.

"Okay, so the Harvard guy is the absolute worst. He puts the bruh in liberal elite."

I snort a laugh.

"He's all yours to take on, Ryan. You're way smarter than he is."

"Thank you," I say, flattered she thinks so.

She glances at Mal. "You're gonna study up on the author.

He's got some stupid advice, but he's cute, and he's targeting housewives, telling them how to sneak box wine into restaurants to save money. It's so gross. Anyway—we're gonna steal his ladies from him without playing into the mommy juice propaganda."

"Mommy juice?" I ask.

"Have you noticed how alcohol is marketed lately? Directly at women. What am I saying? Of course you wouldn't notice that."

"I'll pay more attention," I mumble.

"What about the trader?" Mal asks, saving my ass.

She scrunches her nose. "I'm gonna send you guys his handle, and you tell me what you think. He's smart, good-looking, funny, and he's got a killer apartment with a view."

"Maybe we leave him alone then," I say, knowing we can't compete with that.

"Maybe we assess the situation first," Mal says. "Put our heads together and see if anything comes up."

I stare at him with my mouth hanging open a little. He's got a half grin and that look he gives the camera when he's giving a smoking hot tip.

"It's up to you guys," Bailey says, oblivious to the sudden shift in the atmosphere, but I certainly fucking feel it.

"Podcast," I blurt.

"Huh?"

I tear my gaze away from Mal and look at our other partner, the one I'm not in danger of getting a boner for. "We need to think about scaling up. We're not earning money on TikTok, and since that's the goal—"

"Right." She stuffs a cracker in her mouth and flips through her phone. She tilts her head toward Malcolm. "Did you tell him about the Patreon idea?"

"Yeah."

"Good. I'm gonna set that up tonight then, and I'll add the link to your TikTok bios. We'll also add subscribe links to your videos. So, we test run that for a week, see if it's getting any interest, and if it does, I'll start building a contact list for potential sponsors."

"We can help with that," Mal says.

She shakes her head. "I appreciate it, but I need you guys making content. For the Patreon, we'll have to give people something they're not getting on TikTok. Diving deeper into money making strategies, yeah, but also behind the scenes stuff. Day in the life maybe?"

"Like what? Pictures of our breakfast?" Mal asks.

"Or your closet—getting dressed in the morning, how you wind down after a day at the office—whatever. You in your glasses for sure, Ryan."

I grimace. "No one needs to see that."

Malcolm raises a brow. "They do, actually."

"He's right," Bailey says.

"People say they like my eyes," I argue.

"This isn't a discussion," she says with finality, so I shut my mouth. "It's a lot, I know. I've been reading a bunch of articles, and I'll put a good resource list together that's exclusive to the Patreon."

"I have a ton of essays from school I can give you," I offer.

"Great!" She looks at Mal.

"I'm not much of a writer. Sorry." He sounds genuinely regretful.

Bailey only shrugs. "Can you devote like an hour a night to interacting on the Discord, then? Answering questions? It doesn't have to be literature or anything. Just bullet points if you want."

"I mean, I'm not illiterate," he snaps. "I can answer the questions."

"Okay. Awesome. What do you think of the cheeseball?"

There's her evil smile. He hasn't touched it, but he does now, scooping a large wedge of congealed cheese and green onions onto a Wheat Thin and shoving it into his mouth.

"Mm..." He smiles and nods as he chews. He chases it with half the glass of water.

"It's good, right?" Bailey asks. "It's my mom's recipe."

"Delicious," he says.

I can't stop my smile from spreading. The way he takes her shit and asks for more is so fucking endearing, I don't even know how to handle being a witness to it.

I finally let myself try the cheeseball as the conversation moves on to the theoretical podcast. In addition to onions and cream cheese, there are also pineapple pieces and pecans. It's weirdly addictive.

There's some argument as to whether our program should be contentious or collaborative. Then we table that and start running numbers on costs. After that, as we're wrapping up, Bailey gives us some quotas to shoot for.

"I'd like to see at least five Patreon subscribers day one. If we get none, we're doing something wrong, and we need to meet up and recalibrate."

"Five is a pretty low number," Mal notes.

I was thinking the same thing.

"I'm a pessimist." Bailey works her way up from the beanbag, which isn't the easiest thing to get out of. Once it has you, it wants to keep you. "Prove me wrong."

Once she's up, I watch Mal, waiting for his move. He's *not* moving.

I stand and take his plate along with my own while I follow Bailey out of my bedroom. A week ago, I would have been ninety-nine percent sure he'd be right behind us. Tonight, I'm at fifty-fifty.

But by the time I'm putting the dishes in the sink and Bailey's ordering a ride home, Mal still isn't out here.

Fuuuucccckkk...

Don't make me be alone with his legs...

Bailey looks up from her phone. "Try one with the glasses tomorrow," she says. "You'll see."

"I got made fun of for wearing glasses until I was seventeen."

Her smile is soft. "Me too. Kids are assholes. Hey, next time, let's meet at my place. I think I slipped a disk in that beanbag."

"It was his idea." I gesture weakly to the bedroom.

"You gonna be okay alone with him?"

The question feels like an attack. "Yeah. What? Why?" Shit, *will I?*

"I don't want you two fighting. Messes with the team dynamic."

"Trust me, the dynamic is already as fucked as it's gonna get."

If she can't tell how badly I'm already suffering, then I'm convinced there's nowhere to go but up.

"See you tomorrow?"

I nod and walk her to the door. On her tiptoes she presses a peck to my cheek, surprising the hell out of me but acting like it's the most normal thing in the world. "Good night!"

"Good night."

Once I don't hear her on the stairs anymore, I walk to the living room window to make sure she gets safely into her ride.

I feel him before I see him. Heat and breath. When I finally glance his way, Malcolm is leaning on the window frame like an expert at leaning. He's facing me with his hands in his pockets and his legs crossed. The kitchen lights are on, but what's mainly lighting his face is the streetlight outside the window. The slats of the blinds make it impossible to read his expression, slashed through with dark shadows.

"What?" I ask softly.

"Nothing," he says.

"It's something."

He shrugs a shoulder. "Maybe, maybe not."

I'd love to bust this up and say I'm not in the mood for games, but I am. I'm very much in the mood for games. Must be the mood lighting. The weird innuendos. His legs. Already my pulse is thrumming, and my blood is warming. I feel every pore on my body, every hair, every molecule alight and alive.

I turn back to look at the street where Bailey is sliding into a car, tote bag on her shoulder. As her ride pulls away from the curb, I step back from the window, into shadow.

"I need the bathroom," I say. "You need anything?"

He shakes his head.

Leaving him there, I go back to my room and close myself in the bathroom where I brush my teeth and gargle mouthwash to get the cheese and green onions off my breath. Don't get me wrong—I don't think after all this time Mal's gonna have some miraculous awakening and want to kiss me, I just don't want to have bad breath if we happen to start talking.

When I come out, I find him sitting on the beanbag like it's a throne, his arms stretched out and his legs spread. Stephanie is curled up beside his right thigh. Bud is sitting like a statue on the window seat behind them, eyeing the tiny dog with suspicion. His tail is in full fluff mode. "I love this," Mal says with a smile, patting the black fabric.

"It was a Christmas present."

"Seems like it can fit two people."

I nod.

"Prove it," he says, and I recognize the look on his face from forever ago. He's daring me.

"No thanks," I tell him. I have limits, okay.

"I thought we could watch the trader guy together."

Manipulative fucker. "Sure. Right. That."

"Yeah," he says with the half smile again.

Walking all the way to the end of my own personal plank, I create some space next to him. He doesn't let his arm drop to drape around my shoulders, but that hardly matters since we're now touching from calf to ribs. My head feels like it's full of fizz. All foam and flavor, but no substance.

"Wanna show it to me?" he asks.

The question sounds filthy. My body reacts, cock stirring in my jeans. "Are you trying to…"

"What?"

"The shit you're saying tonight…"

"Is?"

"You know what it is," I tell him. "You know exactly what you're doing." What *I* don't get is *why*.

His soft laugh sounds slightly nervous. "I don't, actually, but I'm glad it seems like I do."

I dig my phone out of my back pocket, find the message Bailey sent with the TikTok handles in it, switch into the app, and pull up the Wall Street guy. Meanwhile, I'm hyperaware of my breathing and my thigh resting against Malcolm's.

@Inside_traderNY is older than me and Mal—maybe early thirties. In his first video, he's talking about the Nasdaq. He's handsome with slicked back dark hair and a sharp-edged jawline. In a pin-striped suit complete with a navy pocket square and shiny paisley tie, he oozes success and wealth. His apartment is as Bailey described. Outstanding. He's leaning back against a floor to ceiling window with the Manhattan morning as his backdrop, a mug of coffee in hand. Occasionally he tugs a cuff, straightens his tie, smooths an eyebrow, and it's a slick delivery of his expectations for what markets will do today. Or whatever day this was filmed.

"I don't know what we'd do with this," I admit. It's a different vibe meant for a different audience.

Malcolm doesn't say anything. But he does lift the arm he's got behind me and sets his hand on my thigh. I suck in a breath, the contact so sudden and unexpected, my vigilant dick startles. For some reason, I keep my mouth shut. I flip to the next video.

Different suit, rainy morning, same mug of coffee, another rundown of market expectations. I click on the comments to see if this is working as a thirst trap, or if the people following this creator are a bunch of dudes who want to know where to move their money.

Before I can read the first comment, Mal's hand is between my legs, *on my cock*. I jerk so powerfully, my phone goes flying. "What the fuck are you—"

"Shh..."

"No, I won't shh—" I reach for his wrist to get his hand off me, but he locks his elbow and gets his fingers around my length, which is already throbbing and growing and apparently desperate to humiliate me. "Mal, what the fuck are you doing?"

"Let's not talk about it. Would you just relax?"

"We *have to* talk about it."

His tone is faintly pleading when he says, "Ryan...shut up. Please?"

I close my eyes and throw my head back, trying with everything in me not to get any harder than I already am. He's not moving his hand, and there's two layers of material between his palm and my dick, but he's gripping in exactly the right place. What the hell is he thinking? *Is* he thinking?

"Breathe," he tells me.

I do. It's sharp, fast, jagged and embarrassing as fuck. It doesn't help. "You can't just—"

"No talking."

"Fuck that," I grit out. "You can't just touch someone like this without their permission."

"I couldn't figure out a way to ask. Forgive me?"

I think I hate the word forgive. The whole concept of forgiveness in general. "Fuck you," I say with no heat whatsoever.

"Am I hurting you?"

"No." *Yes, goddamnit*, everything he does hurts me. His existence is a festering wound on my soul. I have to admit, when I was thinking about games, I was thinking it'd be verbal—not physical. This is going way beyond my field of expectations.

"Then may I?"

Shame on me, shame on my stupid ass. "Yes. Fucking *asshole*," I add under my breath.

He relaxes his grip and lets his hand rest there, like it was originally. "Thank you,'" he says. "And I'm sorry."

"It's fine." I don't know why I say that. Nothing about this is fine. What was only a mild remembering of wanting him is now a raging inferno of need—specifically for a hand job.

We sit like that for a while. A few dozen seconds. A minute where I deep breathe and try to focus on the pulse in my neck and not the one throbbing in my groin. Despite any mindfulness techniques he suggested or I attempt, I have a significant erection, but his hand is more in the region of my shaft and balls. The sensitive tip has moved out of the way, and I hope he stays the fuck away from it because it'll start leaking any second, and the last thing I want to be is *wet for him.*

Right now, there's just a hand on my cock. I'd probably get hard if it were my hand, too, just like anyone would. Leaking only happens when I'm genuinely aroused, but I don't know what he'll read into it.

Enough. He'll know enough.

I start to wonder if he's ever going to move. As much as I

want him to stop, there's a big part of me, no pun intended, that wants him to do more.

"Talk to me, Mal."

"What do you want me to say?" he asks quietly.

"I want you to tell me what the fuck you're doing."

"I'm feeling your dick."

"Why?"

"I wanted to know what it felt like."

"Again…why?"

"It's something I've been thinking about. A lot."

"Say more," I demand, and it comes out like a growl. It's taking effort not to move. And I'm not talking about moving away. I'm talking about lifting my hips and rubbing my cock up and down his hand.

"So, you're straight?" he asks.

"More or less," I say, aware that now's not exactly the time I can assert my "straightness" to its full effect.

"How's that work?" he asks.

"I've never been with a guy. Just girls."

"Never?"

"Nope." I bite my lips and suppress a groan. The restraint I'm exerting is monumental. Epic. I'm legendary.

"Is this making you uncomfortable?"

I don't know how to answer that. "Um…yes and no…"

"Same," he says softly.

"Then stop."

"But I'm more okay than not. Here." With his right hand, he takes my right hand and puts it on his lap, right between his legs, directly on top of his rigid boner.

My eyes are still closed, but they're *wide* shut now. He's *hard* hard.

"There," he breathes. "Not so bad. Right?"

I swallow and will my hand to stay still. I'm excessively salivating. "It's...fine."

"You okay if I move my hand a little?" he asks.

I want to say it's fine, do whatever, act casual like I do this all the time, but what ends up coming out is a whispered, "Please."

He lets out a soft huff of surprise and very slowly moves his palm up my shaft, caresses the tip of my cock and then slides it back down my length. My hips lift slightly, pressing into his hand. "Sorry," I say, trying to get back under control.

"No worries. I get it. I don't mind."

"Since when?" I manage to ask because that's what I really want to know.

"You want a date?"

"Just a general idea."

"That's a tough one. Let's call it a week."

"Is that the truth?"

"It's *a* truth." He sighs. "It's complicated."

No shit. "You about done?" I'm still not looking, but I feel his breath on my cheek when he speaks next, meaning he's facing me.

"I mean, we made it this far...do you want to stop?"

"I..." Something wet touches my knuckles and I jerk my hand off him. He whips his back, too. It takes me a second to realize Stephanie just licked me. "Sorry—your dog—"

"Oh," he says, looking and sounding a little dazed as he turns toward the Yorkie and the huge tent in his shorts. "Forgot she was there."

"No, it's fine." I start to get up, but he pulls the same shit he did on Saturday night and grabs hold of my shirt.

"Wait."

I'm sorry. I can't. Sanity has to prevail here. "This is nuts, Mal," I tell him. "You don't want this."

Somehow, showing a hell of a lot more maneuverability on

this chair than I've ever been able to, he moves onto his side and plants a hand on my chest. Then he does the only thing that could possibly submit me. He puts his leg over mine, trapping me with it, his knee an inch from my balls.

"I want *something*," he says. "But maybe you're right. Maybe I don't need to feel your cock. Maybe I just need to be close."

I squirm beneath him, without a clue what to make of this. "Are you high? What the fuck is going on?"

"Will you stop asking that?" His hand slides across my chest and then his arm wraps around my shoulders. He tucks his head into the crook of my neck. "Just be here with me. I'm sorry I was an asshole to you, and I fucking miss you, all right? Is that what you want to hear?"

Jesus *Christ*, my *heart*. My body that was resisting this with all its might acts without any thought behind it, tilting his direction, layering my other leg on top of his, and hugging him to me. Because yes. It *is* what I want to hear. If I'm being honest, I've been waiting years to hear it.

Holding him feels...

So fucking good.

He sighs. Hot breath on my neck that smells like cinnamon. He did something about the cheese and onions, too, I realize, and that shouldn't make me harder, but it does.

"You don't have to touch my dick to tell me you miss me," I say once I wrap my mind around the fact that this is happening. We're making up.

"That was different. I just wanted to be sure I wouldn't freak out on you again."

"I hate to tell you this, but I think you are freaking out. You might even be losing it. This isn't you, Mal."

"You don't *actually* know everything, Ryan. Not about me."

My fingertips flex into his back at the ideas those words put in my chest. "Maybe I don't."

"Don't you hate that?" he asks. "I hate that."

"Yeah," I admit. I don't know what's making me speak so freely, other than the fact that I can't see his face. It could be that his grip on me is so strong. Like he doesn't want me going anywhere.

"Yeah," he agrees and melts softly in my arms, like every muscle in him relaxes at once.

I try to do the same, but I have to go one limb at a time. First, I let the full weight of my leg settle onto his. Then I relax my back, my shoulder dropping, which causes him to nuzzle in more. Finally, I loosen my neck, and my head rests heavily against his. My erection is pressed to his hip, and I think I feel his on my thigh, but there's a lot going on—a ton of contact I'm only barely processing. "You all right?" I ask him after another few minutes of quiet.

He doesn't answer right away, and I think he might be sleeping. But then he says, "Honestly...I could be better."

CHAPTER TWELVE

MALCOLM

Ryan feels so fucking good, I barely remember why we ever stopped doing this. Unfortunately, I *do* remember, and I can't believe I would give *this* up because he basically told me he liked it too. That he loved it. That he loved *me*.

Just the fact that he's allowing this—that he never once turned me away no matter how messy or random I can be. This is him—accepting me any way I come at him.

Like what the hell could be better than that?

My cock seems to think it knows one thing that would.

I'm so hard, I'm *aching* in my shorts. It's the one part of me that keeps getting more worked up while the rest of me is finally settling the fuck down.

"Better how?" he asks.

I'm so nervous, my mouth is dry despite the cinnamon gum I'm holding in my cheek. But I don't want to think too hard about anything. I just want to feel. I want my body to tell me what it wants, and right now it wants one thing in particular. "Can I kiss your neck?"

He groans. Not like a lustful, fuck yeah kind of groan, but more like a put upon, I can't believe he's asking me this kind of groan. I expect another why or what the fuck, but he says, "Sure. I guess."

I was serious about not wanting to freak out on him. I'm ninety-nine percent positive I want this, but the other one percent is still there with big doubts. Yeah, I get that it was weird and a little uncool to put my hand on his dick, but I needed to know I could handle it, so to speak.

It was fine. More than fine.

I already know I like holding him. I was reminded of that very powerfully Saturday. Kissing a man on the mouth, though, feels like a line—like if I do it *and* I like it as much as I think I will, it'll mean something about me that I've spent a lot of years adamantly denying. But his neck is smooth, and it smells good, and it's warm, and I very much want to taste it.

So, I do. My slightly parted lips meet his fever hot flesh, and I sigh heavily as I close my mouth around the spot I found beneath his ear. His breath shudders in and out.

After everything I've done and said to him, by all rights, his feelings for me should be long gone, and if he's really decided he's straight, then he's being very fucking nice to me right now in a way I know I don't deserve, but appreciate so, so much. So fucking much, I kiss him again, and again with only my lips, but all over the side of his neck I have access to.

When I feel his hand in my hair, gripping the roots, I brace to be forcibly removed, but Ryan just breathes and adjusts his grip, lightly pulling and releasing the strands, letting me explore. I run my hand down his well-defined arm, surprised by how smooth it is—that the tattoos, which look so three dimensional, have no texture. I kiss him as I squeeze his biceps, his shoulder. I kiss the side of his throat as I trace the hairline behind his ear and finally, I run my fingertips along the side of his jaw until I'm cradling it in the palm of my hand.

And I keep kissing him, getting used to the texture and scent of his skin. His taste—earthy and somehow like home. Like I've been here before. I only stop when all I can taste anymore is myself. When I've covered him in me. "Okay?" I ask, letting my thumb rub back and forth over the hollow of his cheek.

"Yeah."

"I'm so fucking hard," I admit.

He nods, his fingers tightening their grip in my hair for a longer second this time.

"Can you feel it?" I ask.

"I'll take your word for it."

"It's you," I feel the need to assure him. "You're what's making me hard."

He snorts softly. "Okay."

"Did you ever get a boner when we did this before?" I ask.

"You never did *that* before."

"You know what I mean," I say.

"Did you?" he asks.

"Yeah," I admit. "But my dick was pretty small back then."

He laughs again with barely any sound, but I feel the shaking of his chest.

"So did you?" I ask again.

"Maybe once or twice."

"That's it? Because it happened to me like—quite a few times. I asked my dad about it—not like—in terms of hugging you, but just whether it was normal to pop so many boners in general, and he told me it was, so I just figured it happened to everyone."

"It *is* normal," Ryan says. "Puberty and friction."

"How do you explain it now?" I ask.

"I have no fucking clue what's going through your head right now," he says.

"Want me to tell you?"

He lets go of my hair and runs his hand down my back, stopping just above the waistband of my shorts. "Are you finally ready to?"

I might not be ready to confess everything, but I want to tell him something. "I like how you feel."

"Deep," he says, in his most cynical voice, calling me out, like he still knows me just as well as he did back then.

"You want it to be deep?" I ask.

"I want you to be honest with me. And yourself."

"Then it's like I said. I like how you feel, and I miss being with you."

"That's beautiful, man."

"Fuck you, asshole," I murmur against his almost too-warm skin.

"Mind if I try something on *you*?" He makes it sound like a dare. His heart might not be in it, but if his body is, I'll go along for the ride.

"Go for it," I say. "As long as you don't try to leave this beanbag."

He slides his hand down further, to my ass, then he lets it rest where my thigh meets the cheek. He cups it and gives it a squeeze. I grin.

"That was it?" I ask when nothing else happens.

"That was it."

"You don't wanna try anything else?"

"I think I should stop here."

"Why's that?" I ask, because if there's anything I don't want it's for him to stop. I feel like we've made it across a desert and we're just now seeing water. It'd be a shame not to take a long, indulgent drink of it. Right?

"I'm pretty fucking hard, too," he says.

"That's why I asked if you're sure you wanna stop."

More curiously, he asks, "What else can I do?"

My heart picks up its pace. My brain spins through fantasy

after fantasy. All relatively tame for someone who's been sexually active since fourteen, but this is new territory. "Wanna kiss *my* neck?"

"Do you want me to?"

"If you want to."

"Um..." He hesitates. "I'll try it."

Elated, I move my head, and with the hand I've still got on his face, I bring him in. The second his wet lips meet my skin, I groan. "Whoa."

He jerks away, but I grip him by the nape of the neck and pull him back. An "umph" sound escapes when he makes contact again, but then his mouth is opening and sucking skin, which is way more than I did, but now I have more regrets to stack on the pile.

"Fuck," I whisper. "Damn. That feels really good." I've got something new to say with each kiss, it turns out. It's probably annoying, but I can't stop. "Ryan. Yeah. Shit. Mm..."

He moves a hand up my back, over my shoulder and presses it into my right pec. I press back, liking that, too. He gives it a squeeze, and I make another stupid sound. My dick is buried underneath him, somewhere in the beanbag chair, but I'm thrusting and grinding, regardless. "It'd be so embarrassing if I came like this."

"Mmhm," he agrees, squeezing my ass again and sucking at another spot on my neck.

"Are you anywhere close?" I ask, hips pumping away at the chair.

"It's your turn to shut up, Mal."

"I'm trying," I say, meaning it.

"I'm gonna move now."

"No," I groan, trying to hold him in place, but he's lifting his leg and letting go of me. I grab for him, but he keeps moving. I roll onto my back to find him and get a better hold on him, drag him back, but he's a step ahead of me, already between my opening legs and kneeling on the floor.

"Yeah?" I ask, nearly exploding in my pants at the sight of him like that—for *me*.

He nods, and I open my pants faster than I've ever done anything in my life. Either he doesn't trust me to go through with it, or he wants this as much or more than I do, but he's got his hand inside my underwear as soon as the waistband is exposed, pulling out my cock and leaning in.

To my utter mortification, but not surprise, I come the second his lips are around me and his tongue hits flesh. "Fuck, oh, fuck...oh my *god*..."

I don't recognize my voice, but the whine that comes out of me as he goes ahead and sucks me into his mouth anyway, swallowing my gushing cum and sucking and licking *everywhere—goddamn making out with my dick*—isn't human. I yell his name, and I think I might growl, too, but the aftershocks buzzing through me go from excruciating to insanely good over the space of about fifteen bobs of his head, and I swear to God, I'm gonna die right here in this beanbag chair with Stephanie watching.

When I open my eyes, I see my hand in his hair, his eyes on me, and his lips red and swollen as they slide up and down my slick cock.

"What's it like?" I pant.

He winks at me and keeps sucking.

"It's not gross?"

He shakes his head and doesn't stop. Whatever he's doing is keeping me from getting soft. I feel a major reset coming on.

"Not even swallowing the cum?"

He pops off and glares at me. Fisting my dick with one hand, he grabs my wrist with the other. He's very strong, and he's got my complete attention. "Do you want me to stop?"

I shake my head. "Not unless you want to."

"Did it seem like I wanted to?"

I shake my head again.

"Well, you already came, so I guess I'm done." He lets go of me and tucks my dick back into my boxer briefs.

He's not getting away that easy. Not after he gave me a crazy good orgasm. I need him to stay close. I grab him by the shirt and return him to the chair at my side. He doesn't resist, but he does reach down to adjust himself, wincing. "You made that so fucking weird," he says.

I get that. "I wasn't thinking. It was really hot, though. I liked it."

"Yeah, well..." he sounds all defeated. A little frustrated. Embarrassed. I can feel it in the new stiffness of his body, too.

That reset feeling? It's also the feeling of a moment passing, and I want to hit rewind and start over. I fucked this up. I made it weird and unsexy, and now he's barely touching me. Probably second-guessing everything when he did everything right and then some.

He stretches out on his side, facing me and rests his head on his arm. I stare back at him, afraid to say anything else.

He looks good, though. Really good. Warm and big, and I want him back. Back in my arms. Back in my *life*. "Are you pissed at me?" I ask.

"No," he says on a heavy sigh.

"Can I kiss you?"

His eyes widen slightly. "Kiss me where?"

I focus in on and touch his bottom lip.

"Don't do me any favors, Mal. I don't need a pity peck."

"What about like...a gratitude grope."

His lips twitch out of their sour pout for a split second. "Don't grope me. I don't want to come in these pants."

"What's so great about these pants?" I ask, then register what he's saying. "Wait, are you close?"

"I *was...*"

In whatever way I can, I scoot closer. It involves rolling onto my side and slinging my leg over his hip, but I make it. "Pity peck it is," I say, planting my lips on his and making a loud smooching sound before I draw back a few inches.

"You can show yourself and your dog out now," he says.

"I want a good night hug."

He rolls his eyes. "I knew you were gonna say that. You know, I don't think you grew up much at all."

I grin, sensing he's going to give me what I asked for...again. I like this side of him. This indulgent side. It's grudging, but still. The way he acts like he hates it makes it sexier. I put my hand on his waist, and he drops one of his to hold the back of my arm. "Seriously," I say. "How're you doing?"

He breaks eye contact. "I'm fine."

"Can I come back again sometime?"

He shrugs.

I think I understand what's happening. I kissed his neck, but he *sucked my cock.* It's the whole *I was hugging him and he said he loved me* all over again. He thinks he got ahead of himself—that he showed his hand. He's embarrassed. I can't have that. Not again. This *isn't* like last time.

"Hey. Look at me." I give him a shake, my hand moving from his waist to his hip. With the way he's stretched out, my thumb grazes a slip of exposed skin, and I feel a ridge of oblique muscle that makes my heart thump harder. Jesus, he gets hotter by the second. I knew sexuality was a spectrum, but I didn't expect it to be a *journey.* This feels like being on a fast-moving train headed straight for the guy with the sword tattoo. "Are you good? Because I'm great. I promise."

He hugs me, and it comes on quick. One second, I'm staring

at him not staring at me, and the next, we're in full frontal contact again. He holds me tight. I feel all his muscles clenching. I feel his rock hard cock jamming my abs, his hair covering my face. And then, there are his eyes again, a gentle touch lighting up my cheekbone, and his mouth on mine.

It's barely a kiss, but I'm absolutely counting it. My lower lip is slotted in the crease between his, and he lingers there, like he's letting me get used to it. I nip at him, a little like I did at his neck earlier, but with less lip. Less mess. His mouth caresses mine, closed and soft. We kiss like that repeatedly, and it should get old, but really doesn't. I love it. I love it so much, I never want to stop.

But then it gets a little wetter. He's barely opening his mouth, but it makes a huge difference, and I love this way fucking more. I let my lips part and actually kiss his mouth like I was kissing his neck. "Mal," he whispers with an urgency I'm not feeling, but makes my dick react.

"Don't stop, please."

"Fuck. *Mal*..." He opens my mouth with his and sweeps his tongue across the surface of mine.

I grip the waistband of his jeans and hang on because my body responds to this kiss like someone just turned on my ignition. I roar to life, taking every inch of space between us and my own taste of his tongue.

I get what the urgency was about now. He was warning me. He was trying to let me know he was about to take me the fuck apart. Maybe he thought I wouldn't let him? But if there's a line I was thinking about crossing earlier, I am fucking leaping over it now. I give him whatever he wants, opening for him, tousling with him, leaning in when he sucks me closer. His teeth get involved, tugging at my lower lip and making me hurt for him. Our bodies rub and rock together as the kiss goes from dirty to fucking filthy.

There are strands of saliva, tongues in mid-air, pornographic grunts and a full takedown of the mask I've always worn while I clutch at him, begging without words for more and *everything*.

He breaks back on a harsh breath, his cock hard against my own, and his body shakes—almost like it did when he was laughing earlier, but the sound he makes isn't anything like a laugh.

He's coming. He's fucking *coming*, and I am elated. High off the fact that my gratitude grope was a huge success, but still sorry about the pants he didn't want to mess up.

He doesn't seem to care, though. He's already kissing me again, and I'm right back in it. I am *not* going to make *this* weird. *This* has to happen again. Soon. Honestly, I don't see any reason for it to stop.

He's slowing down, though. His grip on me is loosening. I get it, I do. I got my hug and then some, but he's gotta be second-guessing everything. I flipped our life script on him tonight, and while it might make perfect sense to me, I haven't exactly given him a thorough explanation.

When he pulls away, I lean in and give him one final kiss. "That was like...the best thing that's ever happened to me," I tell him.

He groans, putting his hand over his eyes. "Shut up, Mal."

"Seriously," I say.

He shakes his head, refusing to accept the praise or the compliment or whatever this is bursting from my chest that needs to be acknowledged. He needs space.

"I'm going," I tell him. "I promise."

"It doesn't feel like it."

"No, I'll show myself out and let you change your pants in peace."

He nearly smiles.

"And I'll see you tomorrow," I say. "At work."

He nods without taking his hand off his face.

"I might record some content after I take a shower," I tell him.

"Make sure Stephanie looks wet, too."

I laugh because that's a funny idea. She looks ridiculously tiny when she's had a bath.

"You should do one, too...after I post mine."

"I'm going to bed."

"It's nine o'clock."

He finally takes his hand off his face and looks at his watch. "Feels later."

"No makeup, okay? You look good like this."

"Like what?"

"Like you just kissed someone till you came."

He shoves me in the chest. "Go."

I zip up my shorts and struggle my way off the beanbag chair. I hate my life slightly more the second I'm not touching him, knowing what I'm going home to, which isn't much.

"Come on, lady." I scoop Stephanie off the floor and kiss the top of her head. She's been very patient with me tonight. Suffering silently while I let someone else get up in my space.

I look down at Ryan, sprawled out and disheveled. Thirst trap? Fact check: true.

It's not until I'm halfway home that I remember he used to be my stepbrother, and I'm *not supposed to be gay*, and that *shouldn't have happened*.

What in the actual fuck is happening to me?

CHAPTER THIRTEEN

RYAN

I've been down this road before. I know all the twists and turns, the hills and the valleys—all the overgrown brush that can scratch the shit out of me if I don't watch my head. And I don't mean Malcolm's curious experimentation last night. I mean his total indifference today.

He barely looks at me during the morning huddle.

Despite his supposed plans for when he got home, he didn't make any content last night, and Bailey is annoyed. I watch them whisper argue across from me at the conference room table while I chew on my nauseating feelings—a mix of resentment and desire. Regret and wanting—longing. It's a bone-deep, fucked up love that feels like a curse someone put on me a long time ago.

There's a mark on his neck. It's not big—and if I hadn't known what he was up to last night, I might have mistaken it for a shadow, but it's right beneath his left ear, and I remember that spot. How sweet it was. How I couldn't help myself from taking just a little more. Tasting it just a little longer. I wanted it to be his mouth. I was imagining what it would be like to have his lips moving with mine.

But I took too much. I overstepped. I acted when I should have stayed still. He asked for a hug, and I gave him a fucking *blow job*. He gave me a peck, and I shoved my tongue down his throat. Well done, Ryan. Way to fucking go. Why not tell him you're still fucking in love with him while you're at it? I might as well have.

An argument could be made that he started it by palming my crotch, but Malcolm is nothing if not impulsive. He was always in trouble in grade school and at home for playing with something until it broke, like the toaster or the DVD player. Once, he broke the gas grill on our deck because he couldn't figure out how to light the burners, which looking back, was probably a good thing.

He's always gotten bored easily—always wanted to try the next thing, play a different game, watch a new movie. He never finished anything, which is why the fact that he got two degrees from Stanford is stunning. I wonder if he's on ADD meds. Maybe he forgot to take them yesterday, and that's what all that experimentation was about—him totally going off the rails.

At lunch, I'm sitting by myself, eating my sandwich and scrolling my phone, trying not to relive my entire adolescence in a single hour when Bailey appears with Malcolm's arm in her hand and an accusatory look on her face.

"Did you two fight after I left?"

"Yes," I say.

"No," he says at the same time.

I glare at him, and he responds with a slightly less harsh one.

"Was it about the challenge or some stupid stepbrother shit?" she asks.

He and I continue to stare stonily at each other. If all of a sudden *now* is when he's gonna finally shut up, I'll have to drive this narrative. "As usual, he can't make up his mind."

"About?" Bailey asks.

"Anything. But if you're asking about last night—"

That's when Malcolm speaks up. "Last night, Ryan wasn't being very supportive. I just felt like my contributions to the project were under appreciated."

I lean back in my seat. "Oh, is that right?"

He waves a hand at me as if to say, *see*—zero appreciation.

"Look, you two," Bailey says, sitting across from me and dragging Mal into the booth with her. "We *have* to work together. It's too big a project to have anyone dropping out now. We all agree on that, right?"

I give a stiff nod, and Mal says, "Right."

"I support you, Malcolm," she tells him with more earnestness than I would have thought her capable. "Does that help? I think you're doing an amazing job. Your set ups have been really creative, and your chest muscles are super good."

His expression softens as he looks down at her, "Thanks."

"Give him a compliment," she tells me, her tone stern.

I jerk. *Actually?* I have deep barrels inside me full of compliments and complaints about Malcolm Walsh, but it's not the compliment barrel I'm digging through today. My contribution is, admittedly, a copout. "I agree about the chest muscles."

He levels a glare at me. Do I deserve that? What the fuck did I do this time? *Besides wrapping my mouth around his dick when he was only planting soft kisses on my neck.*

"I'm a little concerned about how much reassurance is required here," I say. "If you feel like you're in over your head, speak up."

"I'm fine," he grinds out.

"Well, I think your communication needs improvement. That's what the group text is for. If you don't feel comfortable saying something to our faces, maybe put it in a text."

From the look on his face, it's clear he gets my meaning, but he only glares at me.

"Mal?" Bailey looks at him expectantly.

"We are all grown ass adults," I add.

She shoots me a look that says shut the fuck up.

Mal finally mumbles something. "Maybe it's just like—performance anxiety."

I snort.

"Stage fright," he says louder, ignoring me. "This idea of having a big following—it takes some getting used to."

"I get that," Bailey says. "The bad news is, it's probably gonna involve some growing pains. The good news is, it's working, and people love it."

"Do they?" he asks.

I feel like this is all aimed at me, and I'm no better. Every word out of our mouths seems to have a double meaning. For someone who claims not to be a good writer, he sure as fuck has a way with words. Or maybe I'm reading too much into it.

Bottom line is, he let me suck his dick, he freaked out once he left, and now I have no clue where his head is at, but I can certainly guess based on past experience. At least he's not banging an associate in the supply closet, because that's pretty much exactly what he did when we were in high school, and he somehow always managed to get caught. Imagine that.

His sexploits were everyone's favorite topic in school. It didn't do Kaylin any favors, but Mal's reputation as a straight guy who had a lot of sex was golden. I'm surprised there's not a statue of him in the trophy cabinet—most lays in a high school career. Lifetime achievement award.

"Of course!" Bailey's saying. "You have forty-eight thousand followers and counting. We just need you and Stephanie to start selling those subscriptions."

"Right," he says. "Sorry. To be fair, he didn't make any content either."

"I did *actually*," I say, annoyed as fuck. "I just haven't posted it yet."

His eyes flash to me. They're bluer today than usual. Maybe something to do with the dark circles under them making them really pop. "You did?"

I cock my head. "I did. I thought I looked good last night, so I went ahead and made a few."

His jaw works as he stares me down. "Sorry for fucking up the flow," he finally says.

"No problem," I say easily. Maybe a little blithe.

Abruptly, he stands and leaves the table. Bailey gapes after him and then turns to me. "What the hell?"

I shrug.

"What happened? Seriously?"

"Seriously? He and his girlfriend are on a break, and I don't think he knows how to be alone."

That's FACTS.

"Oh. Yikes. I know how that feels."

"Maybe you should go to his place tonight and keep him company," I say.

She makes a horrified and slightly pissed off face.

"I didn't mean like that. *Jesus.* I meant as moral support. Encouragement. You could hold the camera while he makes some content. Tell him he looks smart or something." *Give him a nice long hug. He loves those.*

"I can't tonight. We're having dinner for my mom's birthday, but good idea. You do that, and hopefully by tomorrow we'll have some subscribers, and he'll be in a better mood."

"I can't tonight either," I say quickly, the epic backfire blasting my face and turning it red hot.

"Why?"

"The gym and I've got...I've got..."

"Nothing to do. Go help Mal. We need this to work, Ryan. I'm not losing to Piper for fuck's sake. If you make me lose to that bitch, I will never forgive you."

"What happened with Piper?"

"Have you not seen the comments she's leaving on the videos?"

I haven't. I've had to stop reading the comments. There are too many to keep up. I shake my head.

"Well, she's leaving them, and she's stitching some of the videos, too. She's doing this get ready with me bullshit while she basically contradicts everything you guys are saying."

"She's what?" That's *sabotage*. "Why would she do that?"

"Because we have a winning plan, and they probably don't. Or she's just a bitch."

"I will tear her apart," I say under my breath, my anger with Mal easily redirecting itself.

"Good. You should. If I had the looks, believe me, I'd be doing it myself, but—"

"Hold up—Piper's a Barbie doll. You're far more interesting to look at, and if you wanna play her stupid get ready with me game, you should, because fuck her."

Bailey's silence surprises me, but her stunned look has me rethinking what I just said and wondering if I owe her an apology. "My makeup routine consists of putting on moisturizer and combing my eyebrows," she says.

"And you look great," I tell her.

She frowns.

"What?" I ask, not understanding.

"I mean..." she touches the corner of her eye. "I guess I could learn to do more..."

This reminds me of Calyx, and it gives me an idea. "You could always have my friend Calyx over and let him teach you about skin care. That way you can talk about how to have a natural glow instead of all that shit she puts on her face." I'm not sure where that came from—especially the "natural glow" part, but Bailey's current expression is now the definition of it.

"Yeah..." she muses. "Like...stripped down. No bullshit. No Botox, no contouring. No overly complicated advice."

"Exactly," I say cautiously.

"Maybe," she says, just as warily.

I tear my sandwich in half. "I can't believe she's doing that. What's her handle?"

"Forget her. We need to deal with Malcolm."

So much for throwing her off that topic. "He won't want me at his place. I'll probably make it worse."

I will definitely make it worse.

Catastrophic, even.

Bailey—for the first time ever, cracks. "Look, I can't manage *all* of this, all right? Especially if I have to show my face on the internet. From now on, you're in charge of content, Mal's in charge of public relations, and I'll deal with the website and costs. That means *you're* on duty tonight to make sure he posts something good. We need those subscribers, and we need them soon. Fair?"

It is fair. More than fair.

It's simple really. All I have to do is show up at Mal's shitty apartment and tell him to forget last night ever happened. Don't worry about it. Didn't mean anything. All the same bullshit I've been telling myself for years.

We can move on. And if he needs me to say I can keep this strictly professional, I'll agree. And if he doesn't—then I'll say it myself. This was a one-time thing, and Malcolm Walsh is not my future. He never was.

$$$

I show up at Mal's place without calling or texting first. I figure I have a better chance of being allowed in if I catch him off guard. Best case scenario—we'll end up friends again, but I'm not holding my breath.

He continued his petty ignoring me bullshit all day today, and I had no reason to believe he'd answer a call or return a text, so here I am with pre-written content and a shit ton of determination to put last night behind us.

Only thing is, he's shirtless. He's got the dog in one hand, his phone in the other, and he's wearing charcoal gray sweats. His hair is wet and slicked back from his face. He looks like a goddamn athletic wear model.

His nipples up close and in person are striking. On the videos, they've caught my eye, but in the flesh, they're a rosy brown, and they don't lie flat on his chest like some men's do. No, of course not. His form tiny, perfect, bite-sized mounds directly in the middle of his lightly hairy pecs. I immediately want to cover them with pasties.

Fortunately, he's too confused by my showing up to notice the lingering look of what I'm guessing is pure longing I give those nipples.

"Did Bailey send you? Or did you come on your own?"

"Bailey," I tell him.

"Awesome," he says in a tone completely lacking awe. "I don't need a babysitter."

"She thinks you do, and she put me in charge of content."

"Yeah, I heard. It was in the *group text*."

Ignoring the tone, I ask, "Can I come in?"

He sighs. "Do you want to?"

"Look," I say. "My patience is limited, and we need to start making money, so yes. I'm here, I'd like to come in."

He makes a noise that usually prefaces something like, "unbelievable," but he does let me inside and closes the door.

"I'm filming in the bedroom." He walks past me in that direction.

Since we're alone, I don't see any reason to not speak bluntly. "What the hell is wrong with you? And I don't just mean today."

He waves off the question and disappears around a corner. I follow him.

"Don't blow me off, asshole. You were acting fine when you left last night. What happened? Gay panic?"

He barks a laugh.

"Laugh it up, but it's fucking rude as shit to act how you acted last night with me and then treat me like I don't exist today."

He whirls to face me. "Is it? Is it kinda like trusting someone to be there for you a certain way and then finding out they had something else in mind all along?"

My head rears back. "No. Actually, it's not. It's more like being used and tossed aside because you got bored or changed your mind again. It's like feeling disposable."

His jaw sets, and a muscle in his cheek twitches. "Sorry," he somehow manages to force from his mouth.

I don't like this feeling. The constant uncertainty. The desperate wish for this to be a simple case of boy loves boy who loves him back, but that was never us, and it won't ever be. It hurts, and I fucking hate it. Why I keep coming back for more is a mystery, except maybe it's like getting tattooed. You get addicted to the burn. The permanent marks that prove who you are to yourself and the world.

Is it a badge of honor? A sign of strength? Or a cry for help?

"Don't worry about it," I mumble. "Let's just forget about it and move on, minus the hostile ten years in between. Can we do that?" I honestly don't know if I can, but if he's willing to try, I am, too.

He frowns, an odd stillness coming over him. "Can I tell you what happened when I left last night? Before you move on?"

"I was there. I already know what happened."

"No, I mean after I left."

I narrow my eyes. "Okay."

He sits down on the edge of his bed, putting Stephanie on the mattress next to him. She snuggles into this side, pressing against his hip and promptly falling asleep. He glances at me, sees I'm not moving from the spot I've staked out in the doorway, and looks down. "I was actually pretty happy when I left. I mean, I wasn't ready to leave, but I could tell you needed your space."

I didn't need space. I was afraid to ask him to stay. Afraid of the way he'd look at me when the sun came up. Or whether he'd still want to look at me at all. Big difference.

"I wanted to talk about it more, you know? Tell somebody you and I were... Anyway, the first person I thought about telling was my dad. And then I remembered you and I were brothers for what? Twelve years?"

"Thirteen," I whisper.

"Yeah, right. Thirteen. And I used to ask him all these crazy questions about sex—like no filter, you know?"

I don't say anything, but it's true that he lacks a filter—or at least, he used to.

"And I didn't want him thinking you and I were like—inappropriate way too young, and I figured he might think that, because I think we kinda were. You know?"

"No we weren't," I say, surprised he thinks so.

He wipes at his nose and sniffs before bracing both hands on the mattress and tilting forward slightly. "I think I was. Not on the outside, but like—in my head."

Malcolm looks and sounds totally unlike himself—incredibly small and uncertain. Troubled, even. I tread lightly. He was in therapy a lot as a kid, dealing with his mom's death. I wouldn't be surprised if he still sees someone. I know losing her was hard for him, and he was no fan of talking about it. I know his dad took good care of him, and my mom loved him a lot, but he had a lot of nightmares and was prone to losing his temper over small things. The way he turned on me was an extreme example, but neither of our parents would call him an easy kid.

"Can I just say something happened a few times before my mom died that made me a little more aware of sex than I probably should have been?" he says softly.

I swallow hard. "Yeah."

"Okay. I'll leave it there, then."

"Okay," I say, barely above a whisper.

"Thanks. Anyway, it wasn't gay panic or whatever—it was holy shit, he's my stepbrother, and I decided a long time ago it was wrong. Like really, really wrong to look at you like that. But you don't look the same, and you're basically a stranger now." He laughs softly. "Which is weak, but that's all I've got. Momentary lapse of judgement or whatever."

"So last night was wrong," I say, just to clarify.

He meets my eyes and asks, "Don't you think?"

"Sure," I say weakly, the bullied kid in me raising his hand to agree with Mal's assessment that I'm both a freak and a pervert. It's only sort of okay because I think he's saying something similar about himself.

We're quiet awhile before he looks over at me and asks, "Did I freak you out?"

"Last night?"

He shakes his head. "Just now."

If I'm being honest... I nod.

"I'm not as fucked up as it might sound. I don't want you to think I'm some kind of psycho. Or like...*damaged*."

"I don't," I say.

"What *do* you think?"

I've got no clue what to say. I don't even know where to be right now. Like, does he *want* me here? Am I too close? Too far away?

What I think, however, is that I might not be the one who broke him, but he sure as fuck broke me. And everyone's damaged. "Maybe I should go."

He frowns. "Don't do that. Please. I'm sorry I was weird today."

"You gonna be weird tomorrow too?"

"No promises," he says.

I take a deep breath and think through my next move. "You want help with filming?"

"I was about to do the shower thing we talked about."

I gesture at the dog. "You think she'd let me bathe her while you're in there?"

He laughs, and the sound surprises me. "Why? You don't think you can contain a four pound, pissed off Yorkie?"

I raise my brows.

"I'm kidding," he says. "She loves baths." Malcolm scoops up Stephanie and hands her to me. For all her hair, she's surprisingly bony, and she looks at me with wide, searching eyes, licking the air between our faces.

"Look at you all naked," I say because she's not wearing the bow or a collar.

Her head lurches forward like she wants to smell me closer.

Malcolm goes into the bathroom, then comes back out with a bottle for me. "Her shampoo. It doesn't take much. You can use the kitchen sink. Make sure the water's not too hot, okay?"

Stephanie looks between the two of us, and Mal gives her ear a scratch. "I'll see you in a minute," he says, looking from her to me. I can't tell who he's talking to.

He returns to the bathroom, closing the door behind him. I go into the kitchen to do my first dog bath. I can say a lot about how great cats are, but one of the best things about them is they're more or less self-cleaning. The only time I ever had to wash Bud was right after I took him in.

But it turns out Mal was right. Stephanie likes baths, and she's easy to clean. Of all the shitty things this apartment has, the spray nozzle on the sink isn't one of them. It's the perfect strength to wash out the suds and not knock her on her skinny ass. I let her shake it out once I'm done, and she looks pitiful.

Her hair makes her look three times the size she actually is, and even she seems distressed by her raggedy appearance.

"You done?" Mal calls out.

"Yeah."

He laughs when he comes into the kitchen and sees her. It's the purest smile I've seen on his face since sometime yesterday. He takes her from me and turns to wrap her in a fluffy white towel matching the one around his waist. He's still wet, especially on his back with droplets dripping from his hair, between his shoulder blades and down to the divot above his ass.

I have an urge to put my hands on his shoulders, hold him still, and suck up every drop, but I refrain.

"Stay in here, will you?" he says. "I'll get nervous if you're watching me."

"Yeah, all right."

He looks at me. "But like—don't go."

"I'm not."

"I wanna get this over with, but when I was in the shower, I realized there was something else I wanted to talk with you about."

I nod. How many ways do I need to say I'm not leaving? "I'll wait out here."

"Okay."

He glances from my eyes to my mouth, then he inhales and leaves the kitchen. That familiar tug of attraction has me watching him until the last possible second. The smooth tanned back, the well-endowed ass that looks insanely good in a towel, his bare calves that I have very strong feelings about in general.

My physical attraction to him is stronger than it's ever been, especially since last night. The whole "I'm in love with you thing" still feels like a core truth. He's right, though—we don't know each other. There are things to like about him, and there are also things I barely tolerate.

What we have in common—a shared past and a similar career path—aren't small things, but he's still the golden boy with his long term girlfriend and his charming grin. He's still good at pretty much everything, and I'm hyper-focused on the small handful of things I know I excel at with no interest in expanding my skill set except as it pertains to finance or making money. I wonder, randomly, if Bailey has a favorite between the two of us, or if Georgie does.

Malcolm's back in the living room after ten minutes, still in the towel, but without the dog. "I made two." He flings his phone onto my lap and plops down next to me on the couch. "I don't know how to add the links."

"Oh."

Fuck, he smells good. Shower fresh—sweet and soapy. He puts a bare foot on the coffee table, exposing his entire left thigh and leaving his crotch barely covered. I lick my lips, swallow some excessive drool, and open his video. He's giving a house-hold budgeting tip that helps people allocate funds toward luxu-ries like spa appointments or haircuts. I guess he was paying attention to Bailey last night when she said what market he was meant to go after. He even remembered to ask for subscriptions at the end of both videos.

Also, he looks hot, pretending like he's perfecting his hair while occasionally looking into the camera. He's also found the perfect setting for his ring light because he glows. No makeup, filter, or concealer needed.

I add a subscribe button that links to the Patreon and jot out a quick caption with our usual hashtags. Then I hit post. "Oh," I say as it's loading. "Guess I should've shown you how to do that."

"I was watching." He takes the phone back. "I'll post the other one before I go to bed."

"I'll stitch it when I get home," I say. "So, what's up?"

I halfway expect him to tell me we'll talk after he gets dressed, but of course he doesn't. I try to stop imagining what it would feel like to run my hand up his leg. I also try to stop remembering what it felt like to have his spasming cock in my mouth, but that particular sense memory seared deep. He tasted so fucking good. I'm close to pulling his same trick from last night and casually resting my hand where I think his dick is. It was a guerrilla tactic, but it obviously worked for me.

I've never been as attracted to anyone as I am to Malcolm. It's like comparing the light from a star to the light from the sun. I'm exponentially more attracted. There's literally no part of him I don't want to consume. I'm interested in all of it.

"This is a little embarrassing, but I think if you'd have texted last night, I would have been more okay today," he says.

"You...*huh*?"

"I mean you kinda kicked me out, and you could tell how into it I was, right?"

I can't help it. I'm frowning at him.

"Like—was it okay for you?" he asks.

"I mean...which part? In general?"

Stress lines appear on his forehead. "Was *any* of it good for you?"

"Yeah, of course. I mean, you were there. I ruined my pants."

He rolls his eyes. "They're not ruined."

"Until I do my laundry, they are."

He blurts out, "I wanted to tell you I've been lying to you."

Jesus Christ, the tangents. How am I supposed to keep up? "Are you on meds?" I ask.

"I'm not high, Ryan—"

"No, I'm asking. Do you take anything for your brain?"

He scowls. "Yeah. Why?"

"And you're not skipping days?"

"No," he says. "This is me. You don't have to like it, but I'm trying to be up front with you. It probably seems like I've been all over the place since the internship started, but there's a through line here that I want to point out to you since you seem to be missing it."

"Okay, fine." I sigh, giving him my attention, eyes on his face, not his bare naked leg or chest or erect nipples. Mostly.

"I'm not straight," he says.

I swallow again, fighting to keep looking him in the eyes and keep my expression blank. "Since when?"

"Like ever. Like from before we met. Like I was born this way."

"And you realized this..."

"Realize is a complicated word," he says. "If you're asking when I was sure—it was last night. If you're asking when I started having questions it was before we met."

"What about high school?"

"You mean me and Kaylin? Or me and you?"

I shrug. Whichever. Any clarity is welcome.

He rubs his mouth and sighs. "Two things can be true at once, right?"

Okay, I'll bite. "Sure."

"So," he says, "I can want to have a traditional life with a woman and kids and not have anyone looking at me funny, *and* I can want a man to fuck me into a mattress until I'm sobbing, too."

That wakes my dick up. It was stirring with the sight of his bare leg and all, but the imagery he just put in my brain—I don't bother to hide the fact that I need to adjust myself, and he doesn't hide that he's watching.

"Look," he continues, "Do you think I would have done what I did last night if I wasn't pretty sure I wanted it?"

I think about that for a minute. Because what other motive is there, really? To palm another man's crotch and kiss his neck and hug him like you want to merge with him? "I guess not."

"Admittedly," he adds, "I wasn't sure I wouldn't freak out. Like all the wrong I tried to tell myself it was back then would come surging back, and I'd puke or something, but obviously I didn't. I mean, I almost did when I got back here, but like I said—panic. Not *gay* panic—brother panic."

"You're bisexual," I say.

"No, I don't think that's it," he responds vaguely.

"But you wanna marry Kaylin, put babies in her *and* fuck men."

He laughs. "Is that what I said? I don't think that's what I said. It doesn't sound like me."

"Would you know what sounded like you if you heard it on a loudspeaker?" I ask.

He narrows his eyes. "I fucking hate you. Still. Sometimes."

"Same," I tell him.

"But also..." he leans in slightly and doesn't finish the sentence.

My mind somersaults at his sudden proximity. I find I don't care so much how he identifies as I do that his lips are extremely close. "Yeah?" I whisper, staring intently at his mouth. I shouldn't do this. I should *not* do this. He basically just described himself as a person who doesn't know what the fuck he wants except that he wants everything—except his former stepbrother. Today. But not necessarily yesterday and maybe not tomorrow, but probably, we'll see.

The problem with me is, I think I *am* still in love with him. I think, in fact, that I am so fucking in love with him, I can't see straight. He's a fucking mess, and I love it. I'm *crazy* about it.

It was one thing knowing he didn't want me and learning to live with that. But this idea of maybe not having to live like that? God, it's like he's offering me a million dollars to put myself completely at his mercy. An offer too tempting to resist.

But I *should* resist it, right? I don't have to give him my heart again. I don't have to make any promises. I can just take what he's offering—if he offers anything. Enjoy it while it lasts. Find out if it's been worth the misery and the inability to fully offer myself to anyone else. The thing is, I still have these recurring dreams featuring the hazy image of the two of us fifty years from now, still holding each other and whispering quietly, just like when we were kids.

But that's not what's on offer here. My dick is obviously on board with getting physical, but I'm not sure my heart is willing to take the chance.

I don't have to love him to fuck him, though.

I don't ever have to say those words to him again.

What he doesn't know won't hurt him.

Unless I want it to.

CHAPTER FOURTEEN

MALCOLM

I'm throbbing *everywhere*. What I've said to Ryan since he walked in the door is a hot mess, I realize that. It's just that I can't articulate this particular conundrum: I want him because I've always wanted him, but I never wanted to want him like this.

I didn't want the feelings I had for him to mean that my feelings were like *this*. That doesn't make sense—none of it makes sense. When did it get so goddamn complicated? How do I explain to him that yes, I'm just now figuring this out, but these are old feelings. Deeply familiar and just as uncomfortable as they've ever been, but not half as uncomfortable as my untouched cock threatening to knock the towel off my lap.

"Would you wanna go lie down?" I ask. "Watch something on TV maybe?"

Ryan nods, and I exhale with relief.

I stand up, and the loose towel falls. He reaches to grab it, but I put a hand on his shoulder and say, "Leave it."

He looks at my erection, and I let him. It's so hard, the tip is a scary purple.

"Your legs," he says so softly I almost miss it.

"Yeah?"

He lifts a hand and runs it up my right thigh, barely touching me, but it's electrifying. I want more. Badly.

"This okay?" he asks, glancing up at my face as the pads of his fingertips tickle my leg hair.

"Anything," I tell him. All the reasons why seducing my former stepbrother is a bad idea leap out the window. It doesn't *feel* wrong. What it feels like is long overdue.

"Anything," he echoes in a whisper, gaze roaming down my chest, my abs, settling on my cock. "Do you give a fuck if I'm bad at this?"

If he's saying what I think he's saying... "You won't be," I whisper.

"I want you," he whispers, and it's like a song I've been dying to hear, though I don't think he meant for me to hear it.

I inch closer, leaning into his light touch, wanting him to want me. Wanting him unable to resist me.

"*Mm...*" His hand wraps firmly around my thigh, and I find myself pitching forward. He's still sitting on the couch, and then my knee is on the cushion, too. His other arm is banded around my ass, but the main thing—the single most important thing— is the way he's running his lips down the side of my cock and rubbing his face in my pubes.

"Fuck," I grunt, as he nuzzles and licks at my base. His chin grinds against my balls as he scents and tastes me. I put one hand on his shoulder and one hand lightly on the back of his head so I don't collapse at the raw hunger he's allowing me to see.

Was this there when he walked in the door? Is he that good at hiding it? I would have thought he'd stoically accept my advances if I got really slutty about it, but this feral, primitive shit is *doing it for me*.

I'm leaking precum onto his cheek by the time he wraps his lips around my right nut. "Jesus Christ," I gasp, my fingers digging into his deltoid. "You're so fucking hot, Ry. So hot." Because Ry is *my* name for him. It's *always* been mine. Fuck Miguel for even *trying* to take that from me.

"You smell so fucking good, Mal. I wanna suffocate in you."

My mouth drops open, and my eyes flutter shut as my body rolls toward him. *Did he really just say that?*

"*Mm...fuck,*" he groans, kissing his way up my shaft. He laps at the precum and shudders. He's holding me so tight, I shake, too. And then my cock is in his mouth. I cry out sharply like no one's ever sucked my dick before. But it's more like no one's ever tried to *consume* my dick before.

It's somewhat terrifying if I'm being honest, but it's also the best, the hottest, the wettest—his mouth is the *ultimate* hole. He sucks voraciously, groaning and squeezing my body closer to him.

Like he can't leave them alone, he takes breaks from my cock to mouth and suck my balls. One at a time, both at once, but never letting me move more than the space it takes for him to catch his breath.

Jesus, is this how much he wants me? It feels like a lot. If I'd known it was this much...

I can barely breathe it's so much.

Not that I'm complaining. I want it. All of it. I just hope what I have to offer is enough to satisfy him. Because I want that, too.

His hand slaps my abs, and his forehead digs into my pubic bone. He breathes, hot breath on my wet cock. "Sorry..." he says, inhaling again, and letting his breath out shakily. His hand gripping me goes from firm and forceful to gentle and soothing, barely touching again. "Sorry. I'm sorry."

I run my fingers through his hair and take his face between my palms.

He shakes his head, refusing to let me look at him. "We can lie down," he says, then again, "I'm sorry."

Using the strength I have left, that he didn't just inhale or suck out of me, I put my other knee on the cushion, straddling his lap. I force his face up, making room for myself to slide onto his thighs. I wrap my arms around him, pressing my mouth to his neck. "Sorry for what?"

"I'm not like that," he says. "I just...you were naked, and..."

"You wanted me."

He nods, his chin digging into my shoulder.

"I want you too," I tell him.

"Let me chill out a minute."

"Like this?" I ask.

"Yeah," he breathes. "Like this is fine."

Good, because that wasn't really a question. He would have to throw me off him. I ignore my painful erection and rub his back, taking my chance to breathe him in, soak up his warmth, and settle into the secure circle of his arms. It's the polar opposite of the way I felt when I got home last night. That was wild and erratic, nearly a frenzy.

This is calm and centered and stable. This is the way only Ryan has ever made me feel. This version of me belongs only to him. And it's the truest version of me I can think of. Naked, slightly trembly, a lot uncertain, and needing something stronger to hold onto.

This is what I meant when I said I was born this way. I wonder sometimes if I had a twin who died in the womb and got reabsorbed. I've read about it—disappearing twin syndrome. And I wonder if I was already attached when I lost him. I've never felt like a whole person, complete all by myself. There's always been something missing.

But if it wasn't a twin, then I think it might be Ryan, because being close to him like this almost makes those feelings go away.

Almost.

"Are you gonna put some clothes on?" he asks once his breathing settles.

"I wasn't planning on it. You can take yours off too, if you want."

He pulls back and looks at me. His eyes narrow. "You just wanna lie down and watch a show, huh?"

"I'll do whatever you want." Anything to get him to stay. "Even put on pants."

"I don't know how to take it when you're nice to me," he says.

I grin. "Am I more likely to get what I want if I'm an asshole?"

"Probably not."

I shrug like well—there you have it. Nice it is.

"Put on some pants," he says. "Please."

I make a face. "Are you sure?"

He nods.

"Can I ask why?"

"I just need to slow down."

"And if I say I don't need you to?"

"It's got nothing to do with you," he says.

"Okay." I let go of him and grab the towel from the couch. When I stand, I wrap it around my waist, covering my hard on and my ass.

I swear he sighs with relief. Throwing myself at him is obviously not the move. I tell myself to back off and give him some space, but I'm not sure I can do it. I'm not sure I remember how to. Not when we're alone. What seemed like a terrible, impossible idea when he first got here feels like the only option now. I want him close. Closer. *I need it.*

Ryan follows me into the bedroom, and I like the sight of him lying down on my bed after he kicks off his shoes. I go into the bathroom and pick up the pants I was wearing before I took the second shower where I was mainly making sure my asshole was clean, because I took a shower right before he got here, too.

I turn the TV on before I get into bed with him, putting on "Battlestar Galactica"—the most recent version. We used to watch it when we were kids, and I've watched it many, many times since. I notice his scowl when he sees what it is, and I crawl into bed, making myself comfortable on my side, propping up on my pillow so I can see him and the TV. For the moment, I keep my legs to myself.

"I don't need space," he says after a minute, reading my mind like I think he's always been able to, even when we weren't friends.

I don't question him, I just move over, slotting my leg between his and putting an arm around his waist. I rest my head on his chest, hoping he'll run his fingers through my hair, and he does.

From this angle, I study the waistband of his jeans. They're a good fit, not loose like my sweatpants. It wouldn't be a smooth move if I tried to get my hand inside them. I'd have to unbutton, unzip, dig around...it'd be an event. Whereas, if he wants, he can just slide his hand down the back of my pants and play with my very clean ass. I sigh.

"You okay?" he asks.

"Yeah."

"I'm better now, too," he says. "Sorry about that."

For slurping up my dick? "Still nothing to apologize for."

"You might think differently later," he says.

I think I get what he means, but I'm pretty sure he's wrong. If he wants to be feral, I'm confident I can match his energy. My balls are so blue they might bruise.

"Are you really on a break with Kaylin, or is she just out of town?" he asks out of nowhere.

I wish he wouldn't bring her up while I'm literally all over him, but I guess it's a fair question. "It's a real break. She and I are on the same page about it."

"Why did you need a break?" he asks.

"It's just not going anywhere. We're great friends, and the sex is okay, but it's not like I'm ready to have kids. I don't even have a real job yet."

"Is that what the break is for? Once you get the job you'll re-evaluate?"

I reposition so I'm looking at his face. I'm propped up on one elbow with my other hand on his chest. "The situation's a little different now."

His scowl deepens. "Say more."

"Okay...I don't know if she's what I want. *Sexually.*"

"Is she experimenting too?"

"Fuck if I know. And please don't use the word experimenting again. That's not what this is."

"Exploring, whatever—"

"Maybe don't try to define it unless you're a hundred percent sure. Then you can tell me all about myself."

Half his mouth tilts up in a smile. "Yeah, all right. I'll let you know when I figure it out."

I stare at him a long moment, hoping for *something.*

He threads his fingers through the hair on the back of my head and draws closer, pressing his mouth gently to mine in the briefest, softest kiss. My eyelids flutter shut, but just when I think he might do it again, he's resting back on the pillow. "You don't have to stop," I say.

"Let's pace ourselves."

Yeah, no. Fuck that. "I can pace you," I say. "I can make you go super slow."

His eyes sparkle, the light from my lamp catching his irises just right. God, he's fucking gorgeous. The most beautiful man I've ever seen.

I descend on his silent mouth, giving him a kiss that's slow and tender and deliberate. I keep my eyes open and watch his fail to close. I smile against his mouth. "Trust me," I tell him.

"It's not you."

I don't believe that. "Sure it's not..." I kiss him again, longer and taking slightly more lip between mine. His eyes finally close, and I shut mine, too, focusing on the velvety feel of his mouth and desperately wanting in. With my hand still on his chest, I feel his breath catch, and that makes mine do the same thing.

We sink deeper into the kiss, his fingers mapping my face, feeling my cheekbone and jawline, the corner of my eye, my brow. Our legs, still interlocked, move, and our hips align. I wish we could lose the pants. I want to feel him everywhere. I've never craved the feel of someone's skin as much as I crave Ryan's tonight. Pacing myself is fucking hard. But I'm not pacing myself —I'm pacing him.

I lick lightly into his mouth before sucking his lower lip. He lets out a soft moan. I grind my erection into his hip and carefully nudge his with my knee, reminding him that I'm here to grind against, should he decide he needs it, too. He grips my side and then lets go to rest his hand there. I want to press it down again, make him touch me harder, but he's treating me like I'm glass.

I know what I need to do, but last night when I thought about it, I hesitated. I talked myself out of it, and then I had my freakout. But today, after telling him as much as I told him, which, I admit wasn't much, but it's more than I've ever told anyone, I must have broken through whatever was holding me back, because it would take a bulldozer to stop me now.

I put my hands over the placket of his jeans and thumb the button. "Please?" I ask as I kiss his chin.

His hand covers mine.

"Please, Ry."

He lifts his hand, and I unbutton his jeans, then unzip them.

He lets out a shaky breath as I kiss my way down his throat and use my leg to make room for my body to rest between his thighs.

He's got his hand in my hair, not letting go. He's not forcing anything—just hanging onto me. "Take it out?" I ask.

"Mal..."

"Please."

"You don't have to," he says.

The fuck I don't. There's so much strain in his voice, it's like he's trying to lift up a car. Besides, we're not just gonna kiss and hug for the rest of the night. I took two showers, and he looks like a goddamn wet dream. "I really want to," I tell him in case he needs me to spell it out.

"Are you sure?"

I must look sure enough because he reaches into his maroon underwear and pulls out his cock. This is my first time seeing it. The jeans last night hid a lot from my hand. A *lot*.

TikTok isn't the right place for him. He *belongs* on Only Fans. He'd make thousands of dollars showing this beautiful thing off. It's seriously an exquisite dick. I'm immediately jealous. Mine's fine—it's whatever. It's not embarrassing or anything, and requires the occasional position adjustment during sex, but his? Fuck. I've seen dildos less perfect. As I'm staring at it, a drop of precum forms at the tip. *That's mine.* He made that for *me*.

I take it with the flat of my tongue and taste, and oh Jesus, *oh fuck yeah*, I like that, too. I like all of this. This is good. It's *right*. I mouth the crown of his cock, kissing it and getting it wet.

"Oh, God," he groans, sounding only halfway okay with the fact that this is happening. His free hand floats nearby my head, like he might steal his dick back any second. I take more into my mouth before he can change his mind, letting him slide down the length of my tongue and settle just before I have to open my throat. He lets go of my hair, and I glance up at him.

He's staring at me with his lips parted and his chest rising and falling quickly. His eyes look darker. Hooded. He's fisting the comforter near his thigh. I hold his gaze as I take him deeper, gagging slightly on my first attempt, but so fucking determined not to the second time, that I get *way* farther. He grunts and curses while I choke him down.

His dick throbs in my mouth, and I draw back to take a gasping breath, eyes watering so hard, tears are pooling on my cheekbones.

"I'm close," he whispers, looking concerned. He's warning me. "Don't make me come in your mouth."

That's just stupid. I shake my head and go down on him again, sucking harder and glaring at him like this is his punishment for underestimating me.

"Mal...*Mal*..."

As his copious precum coats my tongue, I force my way to his base, taking a deep breath through my nose before burying my face in his pubic hair. I figure this proves I'm not straight. Deep throating first time out of the gate? Looks like I've finally found something I'm passionate about.

I gulp around him until he comes with a shout, and I keep swallowing until I'm lightheaded and breathless and I've memorized the clean, salty taste of him. I pull back, but I don't stop sucking or licking, I keep kissing his cock until I'm sure I've got every drop of what he made for me. When I'm satisfied I'm done, and he's a jerky, quivering mess, I push myself up and press a kiss to his lower abs, right between the cum gutters. He tastes good here, too.

He grabs my arm and pulls me up. "Come in my mouth," he tells me.

I don't question him or hesitate because *finally*. Fuck. I've been focused on taking him—proving something, but I'm edged so bad, this could be messy. Still, I need it like I need him in my bed right now. I shove my hand into my sweatpants, bring out my cock, and straddle his chest.

He grabs my ass, working the pants down in the back to grasp my bare skin, which feels so fucking perfect, I'm that much closer.

He parts his lips, and I slide my dick between them. The sight of that is phenomenal, but the feel of his tongue on my sensitive flesh sends a jolt up my spine and puts a clench in my legs. Once again, I come nearly the instant I'm inside him. He shuts his eyes and drinks me down, his hands kneading my ass cheeks as I catch my overloaded body on the headboard and gasp my way through the mind-blowing release.

"Oh fuck, oh shit..." I pant as powerful bursts shoot into his perfect mouth.

He looks drugged, rapturous, and lewd with his lips stretched around my less than perfect but still decently fat dick. I pull out before I overload and put myself at risk for a seizure or something. I'm literally that fried. He licks his lips and swallows before he opens his eyes to look up at me.

There—I paced us both. No need to freak out. We're on the same page. I sit back on his thighs and pull up my sweatpants so he doesn't have to watch my dick slowly deflate. It's much better looking when it's hard. His probably looks good all the time. I'll take a peek in a minute to prove my theory, but right now, I'm more interested in his sexy as fuck face. "Okay?" I ask evenly.

He nods, swallowing again. He's got his hands on top of my thighs, and I like them there, too.

"Need anything?" I ask. "Water?"

"I'm good. You?"

"I'm good. Wanna watch the show?"

Bewildered, he blinks a few times. "Sure."

"Want some sweatpants?"

"No, I'm all right."

"They're more comfortable. You're not planning to go, are you?" Yeah, I get it's a leading and slightly manipulative question, but it's safe to say I've lost all sense of shame when it comes to him.

"I can stay a little longer, and these pants are fine."

"You're making this harder than it has to be." I lie down and snuggle up to him again. I get a glimpse of his cock before he tucks it back into his underwear, and yep. It's a motherfucking work of art.

That better not be the last time I ever get to see it. I'll be so pissed. He only thought I was an asshole in high school. Wait until he sees what I'm like when I actually know what I want and can't have it.

At least this time, when I tangle our legs, he turns in bed to face me, which I take as permission to kiss him again.

He's way more chill about it this time, leisurely kissing me back as I explore the taste of myself mixed with him. What a fucking turn on. How did I ever manage to delude myself for any length of time—much less *years*—that this wasn't for me. "This is so good," I accidentally say out loud.

I get a peck on the cheek and the loss of his tongue in my mouth for that.

He's looking at me like I'm a puzzle he can't figure out. I let him, content enough to be in his arms, close to him. Not alone.

"Anyway," I say, "I'm glad you're here."

"I can't stay the night. We have work tomorrow."

"Yeah, I get it."

"If you ever wanna get out of here, though...you can spend the night at my place. It's closer to work."

My stomach does something wild when he says that. Flutters of something—excitement, pleasure, promise? It's the most generous thing he's said to me since...well...*before*. I want more of it. Unfortunately, he looks like he's about to take it back.

"I just mean—"

I interrupt him, just in case. "That'd be great. I can sleep on that beanbag."

He laughs, and that, beyond everything, makes my night. "You really need a better place."

"I know. It was slim pickings when I moved here. Every place I liked and could afford was taken by the time I said I wanted to fill out an application."

"Well, it sucks."

"I know. Thanks for coming anyway."

"You're welcome. We still have a lot of money to make."

"Yeah. Right."

An explosion on screen catches both of our attention, and it's a great episode. We maneuver ourselves so we can both watch, and after that one ends, he stays for one more. But then I'm walking him out. At the door, he doesn't give me another hug, which I totally understand. Really. We've been holding each other for three hours.

But he does give my forearm a squeeze and says, "I'll text you when I get home. In case you're freaking out again."

"I won't."

"We still used to be stepbrothers, Mal."

"But we aren't anymore. I got over that like two hours ago."

He gives his head a disbelieving shake. "All right. Well, if you do freak out after I go, just don't be a dick tomorrow."

"You know what would put me in a good mood?" I ask.

"What?"

"If you asked me back to your place after work. To film content or whatever."

"I go to the gym after work," he says. "But yeah. Maybe after that."

"Maybe doesn't guarantee a good mood."

He smirks. "I'll take my chances."

CHAPTER FIFTEEN

RYAN

What the fuck *was* that?

I mean—I know *my* answer—it was me totally losing my mind on him like a lost, starved animal and reeling myself way the fuck back in, but *him*? Who even was he? *That's Malcolm Walsh?*

Look, I wasn't kidding when I asked about his meds. I almost had to physically restrain myself from going into the bathroom and raiding his cabinets and drawers for either prescription meds that might be making him delusional or illicit substances that are changing his entire personality. The thing is, I kinda like him like this?

It's just nothing like how I expected him to be in whatever fantasy or nightmare I dreamed up. He's always been the douchey jock—reluctant participant—or the dude who punches me in the face for trying to go down on him. Never, ever slutty "leave the towel" guy. Never once *straddle my lap* guy.

Half the time I was in his bed, my brain was too busy rewiring itself to take in what was happening—how long have we been kissing? Was that his noise or mine? I halfway convinced myself that mine wasn't the first cock he's ever sucked

—he was so fucking good at it. Meanwhile, I'm over here gobbling him up like I'm a pig in a trough, not even thinking about what might actually feel good to *him*.

Thank fuck I was able to rein it in. If I freaked him out after last night, I'd have had him in an institution if I kept up like that.

The more distance I get from his apartment, from his bed, the more I think about what he told me tonight balanced against what he used to be like before my horrible confession lost me everything I cared about.

For example, I remember very distinctly the first time he ever rolled over and put his arms around me while we were watching TV. The Simpsons were on. We were ten, I think. I thought he was saying good night because we'd hugged before. Not all the time, not every night, but when it was convenient and made sense, we'd give each other a hug before going off to our separate rooms for bed.

But that night wasn't a hug. It was the first time he snuggled up to me, put his leg between mine and sighed like he'd finally gotten comfortable for the first time in years.

It surprised me, but I'd liked it. He was warm and managed to fit himself perfectly into all my hollow spaces. It was before bed, so we were both clean and showered, and it was just so... *cozy*.

"You're comfy," he'd said.

I think I said something like *thanks*.

So, after that night, he'd say things like "let's watch a show and get comfy." And I knew what he meant.

Sometimes I'd wake up in the middle of the night, usually close to daybreak, and he'd be snuggling up to me again. I'd pretend to be asleep, and he'd usually get up before I did and slip out of the room, but sometimes I'd let him know I was awake and make room for him. Sometimes we'd wake up together and laugh about it.

Why the hell was that inappropriate? I didn't start crushing on him for years after that. So what was he talking about? I'm gonna get obsessed with having more answers. It's only a matter of time before I won't be able to go on with my life before I *need* to know what the hell goes on in his confusing head. I respect that he doesn't want to talk about it, but what a weird thing to say. Especially when it preceded him all but throwing his naked body at me and speaking the words aloud: *I'm not straight.*

His timeline was confusing as fuck for that, too, but I can't deny he was acting exactly like someone who was way more confident about being with a man than I am.

Did he mess around with guys at Stanford?

If he did, I'll be pissed. He was at his homophobic worst when we saw each other for holidays in college. I didn't even spend the summers at home because I knew he'd be there. I stayed in Portland and worked, only venturing to the Bay Area for Thanksgiving and Christmas—the occasional birthday. I'd stay two days max because watching him feel up or fuck Kaylin in every room on every conceivable surface was crippling.

I was physically ill after the first time I caught him having sex with her. We were sixteen, and they were in the laundry room. He had her on top of the washer—during the spin cycle obviously—and she was coming unglued as he was thrusting steadily into her. I'd literally thrown up in my bathroom afterward. But after that time, I guess I got used to it.

To hear him say tonight that their sex life is "okay" is in direct contradiction to the way it looked to me on that and several other occasions following that. He'd seen me, too—that day in the laundry room. He winked at me with a shit-eating grin on his face. He wanted to get caught. I knew that. He was showing me who he was. Proving it. Over and over and over again. He liked pussy. *Loved* it. And he wanted to make damn sure I knew it.

I perfected the art of giving him no reaction. I'd watch a few seconds, make sure he knew I knew what I was seeing, take his stupid fucking wink and walk away with fury burning my insides and hurt devastating the landscape of my feelings for him.

I hated Kaylin, too. Not that she ever noticed me walking in on him banging her brains out, but I hated her for being the object of his desire.

She'd let him do her in just about any position, in any room, no matter how likely they were to get caught. Bathroom with the door half open? No problem. Kitchen—sure, why not, mom's out for a walk and dad's out back mowing the lawn. Should be fine. Bent over the living room sofa when mom and dad were upstairs wrapping presents? A perfect time to fit in a quick, indiscreet fuck.

So sue me for not trusting his reckless ass.

His plump, round, *perfect* ass that turns hard as a rock when it clenches during one of those infamous thrusts.

While I'm showering, I remember what he said about getting pounded into a mattress.

Another mind fuck.

I'm a few months older, but he's a few inches taller than I am. He's slimmer, too. Lean but not lanky. Still, he's got a different build than me. I'm not huge, but I'm dense, packed with muscle. I'd guess we weigh about the same, it's just distributed differently. He's height and ass. I'm shoulders, chest and thighs. Mostly thighs. It's impossible to find jeans, which is why I didn't want to come in them—I only have two pairs that fit right.

So, can I picture it? Pounding him into a mattress? Fuck yeah, I can, especially after tonight with him pouring himself all over me the way he did. But the mind fuck is that those are moves of his I've never seen—never could have imagined his body doing. The casual drape—the loaded upward glances—the slow seductive body roll. He was hot before, but he's *sexy* now.

I text him when I get out of the shower, unable to stop worrying about what tomorrow's gonna be like. I'm not sure if I can handle him flipping out on me again. I'm messed up enough already. "Once Bitten, Twice Shy" by Great White is stuck in my head. Only the chorus, of course. No mystery how that one got in there.

ME

You still up?

MAL

Barely. My mattress wants to swallow me.

ME

You good then?

MAL

💯 You?

ME

I'm fine. See you tomorrow.

MAL

Tomorrow night too?

ME

I told you, we'll see.

MAL

Did you have a good night?

I blow out a breath, thinking about how to answer that. In all honestly, I feel wrung-out. Emotionally hung over. Uncertain. Other than a few minutes while he was sucking me off, I was overthinking *everything*. I was trying to separate my feelings from what we were doing, trying not to conflate the two. But something about the way he kisses me is—I don't know what the word for it is—*fond?* What a stupid word. Is it even a word? It's definitely not a sexy word. And the hugging. Goddamn, the hugs. They're like marathons.

It feels good to be turned on—it felt incredible to come down his throat—best orgasm of my life, no contest, but I also feel ashamed of it. Like I was taking something that isn't mine to have.

But in the interest of not putting him into a dark, belligerent mood, I respond casually.

ME

Yeah, it was a good night. Sleep well.

MAL

You too.

Long story short—I don't sleep well, but Bud sleeps like a champ.

The following morning with the same song stubbornly stuck in my head, I'm dragging ass getting ready. I see I missed a call from Norah. I debate about whether to return it, and I ultimately do, but I only last a few minutes on the phone, barely able to speak in complete sentences. She assumes I'm struggling to wake up, which is at least half true, and I promise to catch up with her after work.

Deacon, who sees me spill nearly a whole box of cereal, which I have to clean up while wanting to cry, brings me a double shot of espresso while I'm shaving my face.

I nearly come out of my skin when I see the gentle giant behind me in the mirror, but he holds up a hand like he means no harm and offers the drink with his other. "It's got ginseng in it."

"Thanks, man."

He gives me a weak, shy smile and disappears.

The shot helps. By the time I'm on the elevator at Marks & Baker, I'm sharper, and as a bonus, my hands aren't shaking like they normally would be with so much caffeine in my system. Piper and Nathan are on the ride up with me, and I notice Nathan's looking a little smug. "Any subscribers yet?" he asks.

I scowl at him. "Why? You like my tips?"

Piper grins. "*I* like your tats. And your cat." And then she snickers.

"Thanks for all the comments," I tell her.

Nathan shifts, looking away, but Piper gives me a sly, half grin. "No rules, right?"

I cannot express coherently enough how much I *hate* people. I got used to being the butt of a joke in high school, but Portland was a welcome reprieve. PSU was a great school full of normal people from normal families without any of this San Francisco classist shit. Even the jocks were only mediocre. But I'm back in the Bay Area now where things like who your family is can matter—how much money you have and what kind of car you drive definitely matters to people like Nathan and Piper. She screams former cheerleader—prom queen.

I get why Bailey can't stand her. She's too good looking, and she knows it. She's also looking at me like she thinks I'm not so hard on the eyes either.

I've never cared for cheerleaders, though. I like a sexy nerd. Band girls like Norah who used to play the clarinet. I never had sex in high school, though. Malcolm made sure I was treated like I had multiple contagious diseases. It was great. Didn't fuck with my self-esteem at all.

So when a woman like Piper looks at me like she appreciates

what she sees? It pisses me off. *Once bitten...* "What's the saying?" I muse. "Imitation is the highest form of flattery?"

She scoffs. "I'd hardly call it imitation."

"No," I agree. "You'd have to give good advice to call it that." I've watched all six of her stitches—all on Malcolm's videos. She uses huge words with no context, acronyms no one outside the finance world would understand, and it's obvious she's reading from a script unless she's talking about her concealer, which, I've noticed, isn't the right color for her skin. Under the elevator lights, it's almost comically wrong. "Do you not believe in makeup blenders or something?"

Calyx gave me that line yesterday when I showed him what she was up to, and I'm looking forward to telling him about the bitch-slapped look on her face.

"It's just a little—" I gesture to my own face. "Obvious."

She huffs. Rolls her eyes. It's a dismissal. But there's also a twitch to her lips that has me picturing her in the office bathroom mirror blending and smudging with her fingertips the moment we get off the elevator.

Calyx had no shortage of ideas for how Bailey could neutralize her, some nastier than others. I did have to remind him I have to work with the woman. However, face to face with her, I see her for who she is. She needs attention. The more, the better, and she doesn't care who she has to step on to get it. She's the girl in a high school movie who tells her popular boyfriend that someone like me tried to flirt with her and all of a sudden has the entire football team slamming the guy who dared into lockers.

In real life, for me, it looked more like embarrassing pictures of me circulating on Instagram with rumors that I touched people inappropriately or something equally disgusting. In real life, my mom and I got people suspended from school, and in one case expelled. While what Piper's doing on TikTok doesn't rise to that level, we all grow up and get smarter. It's still sabotage, and I might want to watch my mouth before she gets her entire team on it.

Nathan takes over while Piper stresses about her contouring. "How's working with Bailey going?"

"Oh, you know Bailey," I say, turning my gaze to the floor readout.

He chuckles like Bailey is someone we should all be laughing about, and it scrapes like a metal hook on a chalkboard. I need to get Bailey and Calyx in a room together as soon as possible. We've gotta win this—and in a spectacularly humiliating way. It's true that competition brings out the best in some and the worst in others. I've known these people for a little over a month now, and it's possible some of them could be my colleagues for years. I'm not prepared to make a final decision about anyone yet—other than Bailey. She's already in my keeper column.

It's a very small list of names. My mom is on it, and Norah. Calyx, too. Malcolm is there as well, but in invisible ink, only so that I don't have to acknowledge how weak I am when it comes to him.

Mal and Bailey are sitting in their usual seats in the conference room. This morning, instead of sitting across from them between Nathan and Miguel, I sit next to Mal. He squeezes my knee under the table the second I sit down, and my ass nearly comes off the seat. I shoot him a warning look, but he's already let go.

It wasn't sexual—more the equivalent of a football player slapping another's ass in congratulations. He smiles and says good morning while my dick thickens in my pants, overreacting to him as usual.

"A hundred and eighteen," Bailey leans forward and tells me in a stage whisper.

"What?" I ask.

"Subscribers. A fucking hundred and eighteen! By eight a.m.!"

"That's good, right?"

"Better than five," Mal says.

"Have you had any time to make content for the Patreon yet?" I ask her.

"Oh, totally," she says. "I've got links up, pictures of Bud and Stephanie, and a podcast poll."

"What's the poll about?" Mal asks, which is what I was about to say.

"It's super simple. I put five topics for you guys to talk about in an exclusive video, and the subscribers vote on which topic they want first."

I take a deep breath, the pressure to perform hitting harder than ever. Talking into a camera is easy enough, I remind myself. And there are plenty of things I can rattle on about for fifteen minutes if I just say what I'm thinking and don't worry about who's listening.

"When does the poll close?"

"Five," Bailey says. "You'll need to film tonight."

"Topless?" Malcolm asks.

"I'm still debating that," she says.

"Can I say I don't think it should be shirtless?" I offer. "It's one thing on TikTok, but if we're offering real content that dives a little deeper, maybe it's better for them to see what we're actually like? I mean—not what *I'm* actually like, but at least how I dress."

"What's wrong with what you're like?" Malcolm asks.

Bailey looks like she's wondering the same thing.

"Nothing," I say defensively, not wanting to get into it. "Forget I said anything."

Bailey's not done with me yet. "Do you mean off-putting and cynical? The step the fuck away vibe?"

Mal interjects, "He's not—"

"Look who's talking," I say, not letting him finish. I don't need Malcolm defending me. It's too fucking disconcerting.

Bailey shrugs. "I'm self-aware. My therapist says that's a good thing."

"You see a therapist?" Malcolm asks, turning toward her.

"Yeah. So?"

"So, nothing. I do too."

She nods at him. "Respect. Okay, Ryan, we'll try it your way, but if we lose subscribers, shirts off. And don't look like a slob, okay?"

Ouch. When have I ever looked like a slob in front of her? "You want us in suits or what?"

"No, I just mean, no piles of laundry in the background. No tacky t-shirts. But you can look real. I'm fine with that. For now."

"I might have better luck keeping my shirt off," Malcolm mumbles.

"You look good in clothes, too," I say and immediately want to find a stapler to shut my mouth.

"Ryan!" Bailey exclaims. "You complimented your step-brother!"

"Shh!" No one else here needs to know *that* about us. "He's not my stepbrother anymore," I add quietly.

"Not for more than two years now," Mal adds quickly.

"Whatever. You grew up together. You're brothers."

"We're not," he insists, and he sounds a little tense.

She lifts her hands in surrender like Deacon had in the bathroom earlier. "Fine. Whatever you say."

"I'm saying we're not fucking related," he mumbles, slumping back in his seat.

There goes his mood. Georgie walks in before I can say anything to him, so I send him a quick text.

ME

Don't fucking go there

He reads the text and looks at me. His mouth is tight, and there are a million things going on behind his eyes I couldn't follow if I tried.

"*Don't.*" I mouth.

His nostrils flare with a deep breath.

One last text because he doesn't need to feel bad about something I could have stopped if I had any willpower whatsoever.

ME

Come over tonight and we'll record our responses for the poll.

He reads it and then turns his phone over on the desk, but his lips part. He lets out a breath and visibly relaxes as Georgie says good morning. Underneath the table, he slides his right foot around my left foot, effectively wrapping our calves together. He's not wearing socks.

I am utterly fucked.

DEACON IS MAKING a stir-fry when Malcolm arrives. My roommate is wearing a muscle shirt and thin gray joggers shoved halfway up his shins. I tell him I've got the door as he turns to abandon his sizzling pan. "You expecting somebody?" he asks.

"Yeah," I say. "Friend from work."

"I can make more," he offers.

"Thanks. We're good." I had a smoothie on the way home from the gym, and surely Malcolm's not expecting me to feed him.

When I open the door, though, the first things he says is, "Smells amazing."

To which, Deacon immediately responds, "I'll make more."

Mal's wearing a simple button down in mint green that brings out all the teal notes in his eyes and makes his tan look incredible. His *neck*—Jesus.

Stephanie is dressed up, too, with a white ruffle collar.

"Deac, it's fine. Mal, this is my roommate Deacon."

Deacon smiles and waves. He's like me—he looks totally different when he smiles. He's got deep dimples which are apparent despite the dark scruff on his face. Mine are barely there, which is just as well because I don't smile much either anyway.

"Deacon this is Malcolm. We work together."

Mal's eyes narrow slightly as he looks between my roommate and me. Then he gives Deacon a nod and a hey.

It's an odd moment because Deacon is also sort of—I don't know—sizing Malcolm up?

"You ate already right?" I ask Mal.

"Yeah."

"We're good," I tell my roommate. "We're working on a project, but enjoy your dinner."

"Okay," Deacon says. "Good to meet you." His smile is less impressive this time, not crinkling his eyes or popping the dimples. I nod Malcolm toward my room, stopping short of physically dragging him there.

"Good looking guy," Mal says once we're behind my closed door.

"Deacon?" I ask.

He nods, looking suspiciously at me.

"He's not—I'm not—do I really have to explain the concept of roommates to you?"

"No. I've had a gay roommate before, too."

"You—? Never mind." I don't press because he'll probably say something I either won't like or will confuse me about him even more. He's had me in a tailspin since the second I sat beside him in the huddle this morning.

How to describe what he wore to work without sounding problematic...

The black shirt he had on underneath his camel colored suit had a slight sheen to it. His pants were slimmer cut, tapered at the ankle and, like I noticed under the table, no socks with his brown Amberjack loafers. It wasn't *flamboyant*. Not exactly. Not in the showier way Miguel is. But I got the feeling Mal had never worn those items of clothing in that precise combination before because it made him look...less than straight. And Malcolm, in my experience has never looked anything less than perfectly *ramrod* straight down to his golf shirts and khaki shorts.

Tonight, the mint shirt—very flattering on him with his body type and skin tone—isn't paired with cargo shorts. He's wearing faded denim jeans that fit him like a goddamn dream. In addition to carrying Stephanie, he's got a full on garment bag with him, slung over his shoulder.

"Wardrobe change?" I ask, following my rambling train of thoughts.

"It's a suit," he says.

"Like—a work suit?"

He nods. "Can I hang it up?"

"Uh...sure." I gesture toward my closet. He sets Stephanie on the floor, unfolds the garment bag, makes a space for it on the rod, and hangs it up.

"Did you bring a toothbrush too?"

He looks over his shoulder at me. "Don't act like we didn't talk about this."

I'll take that as a yes about the toothbrush.

"You're welcome to change your mind," he says. "I won't unpack yet."

I can't think about him spending the night or how fast all this is moving. We've got actual shit we need to accomplish tonight. "Can we just do the work? Please?"

"You're ready?"

"To talk about early retirement for fifteen minutes? Yes." That was the topic that won the poll.

"Where do you wanna do it?"

"My desk, I think."

"Want me to film?"

"It's better than me doing it with you staring at me from the side the whole time. Yeah, you can film it."

He arches a brow. Admittedly, I sound prickly. But then he smiles like it's all par for the course and goes over to sit in the beanbag. It's a good place to film from. We'll get the sunset light and a view of my room that I've haven't used before. I close the bathroom door and make sure nothing "slob"-like winds up in the shot.

Malcolm is making himself comfortable again because I really do think he loves that chair, and says, "I wanna do mine right here."

He'll be talking about turning side-hustles into full-time money makers.

I have a seat at my desk, run a hand through my hair, and ask how I look.

"Really fucking good," he says, his voice low with a hint of a rumble.

I put my hands on my cheeks to make sure they're not getting too hot. "Behave."

"I'm just sitting here."

Yeah, sitting there looking like he'd whip out his cock and start jerking it for me if I asked him to. Has he always been this slutty?

Yes, I remind myself. He has been. It's just never been directed at me, and that's why it looks different. I'm normally not a fan of a strong come on, but maybe he's the exception. If his advances were any weaker than full throttle, I don't think I would have come within a foot of him after that one time I backed him up against the wall. I lost my cool that time. That won't happen again. He's a walking red flag.

"Okay," I tell him. "I'm ready."

He positions the phone and starts recording. I start talking. I talk and I talk, and then I think of something else I want to say, and I talk some more. It's honestly helpful having him here. It feels less like I'm performing, more like I'm sharing something with him I'm passionate about—the way I used to talk about how much I wanted to live in a mansion with two kitchens.

He smiles from time to time and nods like he's in agreement with where I'm coming from. Eventually he gives me a signal like wrap it up, and I do, adding in a request for people to hop on the Discord and leave their thoughts and questions. He gives me a thumbs up. I stop talking, and he lowers the phone. "Come here."

I shake my head. "Nope. Your turn."

"Ryan..." He runs his hand over his crotch, leaving a nice outline of his erection.

"Tough for you, bro. Toss me the phone."

"I can't talk right now. I need to..." he swivels his hips and lifts them slightly. "Come on. Help me clear my head."

I'm staying strong on this. My cock is another story, hardening fast at that slutty hip thrust. "Forget it. We've gotta do this *and* make videos for TikTok. You need to tell your inner slut to take a seat for an hour."

"*Mmph.*" His hips move again. "Fuck. Call me a slut again."

Fuck me, he's hot like this. Scalding.

"Mal, I need you..."

"Yeah?"

"To talk about scaling up a side hustle."

"Fine," he groans. "Shit. Okay, go."

I get the video going, and he starts talking, his voice all growly and sexy, though his expression manages to stay tame. I react less to his content than he did to mine, but only because I've trained myself not to react to him for so long, it's a habit. He tends to talk with his hands when he's not holding Stephanie. She's currently curled up on the corner of the bed with Bud spooning her. She's a needy little thing—Stephanie. She likes a big warm body to rest against, and Bud couldn't care less.

When Mal wraps up, I take a few pictures of the dog and cat together before I have to start thinking about what to record for TikTok.

"Hey," Mal says. "Since your shirt's gotta come off anyway, why don't you let me help you with that."

I bite my cheek, trying hard not to smile. "Because I want to finish this."

"Why? So you can give me your undivided attention?"

"Sure, Mal. Whatever you want to tell yourself."

"It's a coffee break. We just did so much work. We're so fucking productive. Come here, and I'll make sure you've got that just been fucked look all your followers go crazy for."

I widen my eyes at how goddamn brazen he is. "You sure you're all right? Taking your meds as prescribed? You don't need to go in for an adjustment?"

"I thought I made it pretty obvious back in the day, but sex is kind of a thing I like to do. A lot."

"Explain to me again what's not working out with Kaylin then?"

He sighs and runs a frustrated hand through his hair. "I *would* tell you. If you'd stop being such a sarcastic dick."

"I don't see that happening anytime soon."

"The other day in this chair you were pretty cool with me. There was like—almost half an hour before you said something shitty."

"We didn't have stuff we were supposed to be doing."

"I'm trying to be patient with you," he says. "But you're not making it easy."

"*Me*?" He's the one with his legs spread.

"Yeah. You."

"We've already hooked up twice," I argue.

"I'm a sex on the first date guy."

"How would you know? You've dated one person," I say, testing him.

"That's how I know," he says.

I frown, annoyed that he didn't take the bait.

"I don't need you to get it, Ry. I just need you to come here."

CHAPTER SIXTEEN

MALCOLM

Ryan's starting to give me a complex. I have enough esteem issues and self-doubt to power a rocket to Mars, but obviously I'm going about this wrong. The problem is—I don't know how else to say it. If we do it his way—film the content and post it, who's to say he won't think up some other excuse. If he doesn't want this, I need to know so I can stop embarrassing the fuck out of myself.

He walks over to the beanbag, looming over me. "*I* need to get it. Otherwise, you gotta go."

My mouth immediately dries up, and my guts twist. I try to pivot off the topic I know he's getting at. "You think I'm cheating on Kaylin. You want me to call her? You want to talk to her yourself?"

Ryan shakes his head. His eyes are boring into mine. "Do you love her?"

"Sure," I say.

"Are you *in* love with her?"

I shrug.

His eyes narrow to dark slits. "Have you been with anyone besides Kaylin?"

"You," I say.

"Anyone else?"

"No."

"Never?"

I shake my head. I'm not sure he believes me, but Kaylin is my entire sexual history. Now, if he wants to know about the intimate and very well-maintained relationship I have with my collection of flesh lights, that might give him a different perspective, but it's nothing I feel compelled to share. Since Kaylin went to UCLA and not Stanford with me, I got used to taking care of myself. No one at school ever sparked my interest more than she did, so it wasn't that difficult to stay faithful. Keeping up with my schoolwork was challenging enough.

But now that we're on a break, I feel the need to make up for lost time. Since my recent gestalt, I've been wondering what I would have done with the break if Ryan weren't around. Would I have started cruising the Castro looking for guys to try new things with? I think...maybe.

In all honesty, I'm not sure anyone but Ryan could have unlocked the door where I've kept this secret all these years, even from myself. But if he ditches me... I'm almost certain I won't go straight back to dating women.

My need to get off is one thing—it's gotta be at least twice a day. My sex drive however—in terms of wanting to have sex with another person, had all but disappeared before Saturday night. I thought it was my meds, which my doctor and I have changed and titrated over time, but clearly, those aren't the issue.

I just don't want Kaylin anymore. Not like that. Not like *this*.

Ryan is standing just out of reach, and I'm sure that's on purpose.

"And you say wanting to be with guys is nothing new for you," Ryan says, studying me.

"That's not exactly what I said."

"You didn't say much," he doesn't hesitate to remind me.

I tilt my head. "What do you need to hear?"

"I don't know."

"You don't know, or you don't wanna say?" I ask.

He looks at the floor, kicking the toe of his shoe into the rug. Ooo...I got him. He doesn't wanna say. Interesting.

"You know, I don't really feel like talking either," I tell him.

"You just want what? Me to take my shirt off?"

I grin. "To start."

"What else?"

"Would you consider fucking me?"

His eyes meet mine sharply. His shock is obvious. "*Tonight?*"

I nod.

"I think that's a terrible idea."

"Can I ask why?"

"Because I don't know what this is, Mal. It makes me nervous."

"Oh." He doesn't seem nervous, so the words get my attention and help me understand that coming on so strong is likely what's making him balk. But then I remember the way he apologized for his intensity yesterday like he didn't want to scare *me* off.

Communication it is.

"Okay, let's talk," I say.

"And then we can make the content?"

"No, you're right," I acquiesce. "Let's get that out of the way. Then we'll talk. Deal?"

He looks relieved. "Deal."

We spend some time clipping the videos we just made. He works from his bed, and I stay on the beanbag.

I post a clip to TikTok and add all the stickers and links to the full video that I upload to our Patreon. After I'm done with that piece, I take off my shirt, grab Stephanie, and pull her onto the beanbag with me where we make a one minute and ten second video about starting small when you're diving into entrepreneurship. By the time I'm finished, Ryan's getting comfortable, lying on his side on the bed with Bud stretched out in front of him, belly up. He runs his fingers through the lazy cat's fur while he stitches my video and talks about how risk is part of the reward of being your own boss.

He's inspired *me* to want to risk something by the time he turns his phone face down on the bed. I mean—with him looking like that, it doesn't take much.

He glances over at me. A long moment passes before he asks, "Do you want me to come over there, or do you want to come over here?"

I want to tell him I just want to come period, but I hold that in. "You look comfortable." I go to the bed and lie down facing him. I prop my elbow on the pillow and rest my temple on my fist. He cradles his cheek in the crook of his arm and looks up at me.

"Can I use a metaphor?" I ask. "Is that gonna annoy you?"

"Depends. You can try," he says.

"Okay, then I'm going for it."

He nods.

I'm pretty sure this will make sense—if we were as close as we used to be, I know it would, but so much has happened. Still, lying here like this makes it feel like we know each other better than we actually do. "So let's say there's this room in my head. It's been there since I was little. I used to hang out there a lot. I liked it there. It was interesting and exciting, and maybe a little scary, but in the good way."

He squints, trying to follow me.

"And then the light went out inside it, and I didn't understand anything that went on in it anymore. I couldn't see the toys or whatever. I couldn't play the games. I was just fumbling around outside it because I wanted to be in there—I knew I liked it there, but it was hard to remember why. You with me?"

"More or less. Maybe."

"And then—when you were sick that time, the door slammed shut. Lights out, locked out—caution tape everywhere."

"Okay."

"So, it was basically a crime scene. Like I didn't belong in there, and I never had, and the room kicked me the fuck out, and I was basically supposed to forget it ever existed and pretend I never went there."

Ryan's squinting. "If this gets any more complicated, I'm gonna need you to move off the metaphor."

I hold up a hand because I think I'm about to make it clear enough. "When you pushed me into the wall, and I thought you were gonna kiss me Saturday night, the door flew back open. Monday night, the light came on. Tuesday night, I was back in the room, and it wasn't scary anymore because I knew what everything was. I remembered what brought me there in the first place."

"Which was?"

"You ask too many questions," I say, looking down at the bedspread.

"Prepare yourself because I have another one," he says. "How do you know it's not gonna kick you out again?"

"Because I'm not a child anymore? Because repression only works until the memories resurface? Because I'm in control of my brain now? How do those reasons sound?"

"Plausible."

I can sense he wants to ask me something, so I wait.

Then he comes out with it. "Were you hurt, Mal?"

"No," I whisper. "Not like that. No. But if it's okay, can we not go there? It's got a lot to do with my mom, and I don't want to..."

I trail off, ignoring the flashbulbs going off in my head, illuminating the memories. The things I saw. The things I felt. The betrayal. The jealousy. The yearning.

Ryan's hand on my arm makes it all stop. I'm back with him, in his bed, staring into his gorgeous eyes—the one part of him that hasn't changed at all. "It's okay," he says.

"What about you?" I ask. "What are you not telling me?"

"I just don't want you to turn on me again, and..." he hesitates. "That's basically it."

"You sure?"

He nods then says, "I don't think I'm ready for sex."

"Okay," I say, hoping my disappointment doesn't show.

"But if you insist on spending the night, who the fuck knows, right?"

A smile breaks on my face, so big it hurts my cheeks.

"Just remember I have a roommate," he says as he moves to hover over me. I roll onto my back, listening to him talk and wishing he would just shut the fuck up and make out with me already. "And he's shy and weird, so you have to control your noises."

I don't trust myself to make that promise, not when I'm about to *need* to undo my pants. I don't know how he stands it in those jeans with that huge dick. Does he enjoy suffering? "Maybe put some music on?" I suggest.

His chest meets mine just before his mouth does. I immediately wrap my legs around him and bring him crashing down on me. I kiss him hard. My tongue too eager, my lips too aggressive, but I can't help it. He's been edging me since I walked in the door, and now, shirtless—with our nipples touching, I can't be expected to control myself, can I?

"Jesus, fuck, I want you," I say as his teeth graze my jaw.

"I see that."

"I want out of my pants."

"Of course you do." He kisses me again and keeps me busy doing that for a few heated minutes, but I'm just gonna keep bringing it up. He's gotta breathe eventually. Christ, but I like this part, too. He's an unbelievable kisser. I hope I'm halfway decent at it, only ever having kissed the one person, but he's not complaining or trying to force anything different out of me. Although, I don't kiss him the way I kiss Kaylin for a lot of reasons.

One, I haven't wanted Kaylin this much since we first started dating. Second, Ryan is more of a force to reckon with. Third, he's got a bigger mouth in general, so I have to work harder to fill it.

His thumbs brush my nipples, and I gasp, shocked by how good that feels. His hands move down my sides, and we turn slightly so he's not crushing me. I still have my legs locked around him, but now he's able to grab my ass and let me know he likes me where he's got me. Good.

Except it sucks because *I need out of these fucking jeans.*

I slide my hand down the back of his pants, making them tighter, *hoping* to make this insufferable for him, too. It's the first time I've touched his bare ass, and it's hard as a rock. He's a brick house and all that. Fucking *fantastic.* He groans, maybe because I just tugged his lip with my teeth—maybe because I'm putting more pressure on his big dick.

"Ryan," I whisper. "Come on. Please."

The next noise he makes is more like a whimper of defeat. He sucks in his abs enough to get his hand between us and works open both our jeans. Immediately, my hand slips further down his ass, and I dig my fingers into the muscle, pulling at it, wanting to take a piece of him with me.

"Whoa, damn," he says, his forehead landing on mine while he lets me grope him a few more times. With every squeeze, he grinds his hips against mine, and I'm dying to tell him to just fuck me already. He might not be *"ready"* for it, but we both want it, and I don't need a better reason.

I take another risk, loosening my legs from around his back and letting go of his ass. I start taking off my jeans. "Do it," I tell him. "Get naked with me."

For some reason, he does. He sits back on his heels and opens his pants the rest of the way. As I'm pushing mine past my hips, he's doing the same thing.

Closer, I think. *We're getting closer.*

His cock appears in all its perfection and glory. My ass clenches, wanting it so fucking bad. I've never much considered my asshole as a space, but lately I'm hyperaware of how empty it is. How hungry it is to be filled.

Do I have a virgin hole? Yes. Do I care? Fuck no. I want that dick to split me in half. I want it *yesterday*. I want to get the first time over with so I can make Ryan fuck me all the time. The unisex bathroom at work comes to mind. It's a single stall with a door that locks. Not that I give a fuck about a locked door, but he probably would.

I've also counted at least a dozen surfaces in this very room I want him to bend me over. Especially the beanbag. I think I could make it really good for both of us on the beanbag.

He's got his pants halfway down his thighs, but I'm naked already, watching him and waiting. He's staring down at me, his gaze roaming from my chest to my erection, and he freezes. Like he stops. Stuck.

"Ry?"

"Uh-huh?" He doesn't move. Doesn't take his eyes off my cock.

"I wanna see you."

His next breath is shaky, but slowly he keeps undressing. Once his jeans are off, and I see he's got a hip and thigh tattoo along with everything else, I get that high feeling again. Euphoria. Like I'm not responding to gravity anymore.

I reach for the tattoo—his hip. "That is the hottest fucking thing I've ever seen."

He glances down at his leg like he forgot what his own tattoo looks like. It's the only one with color. A rosy orange that looks gorgeous on his skin makes up what looks like poppies surrounding a Celtic cross. There's something sort of familiar about it but fuck if I can remember what it is right now. The poppies are what spread up to his hip while the stone cross takes up most of his outer thigh. It's beautiful. He is *so* fucking beautiful.

I was too young and stupid to appreciate him before, and maybe he needed what I put him through (not that I'm excusing myself for it) to become this magnificent man. Like how diamonds are formed from pressure and heat. This hot as fuck version of Ryan was forged with my denial and hate.

Maybe.

I reach for his ass, but he grabs my wrist. "Turn over."

"Actually?" I ask, like he just offered me a job I'm in no way qualified for but want really bad anyway.

He nods and guides my hips as I roll to my stomach. "Just like that," he whispers, moving my legs apart and dragging his fingers up the backs of my thighs. I moan, thrilling at the sensation. I'm sensitive back there. I didn't know.

He squeezes both my ass cheeks at the same time, and I feel them spread, my hole stretching open. My immediate instinct is to get my knees under me—arch my back, offer myself up, but when I start to move, he presses my hips to the mattress, massaging my ass like he took a college course in butt massage.

It feels incredible. The majority of my body melts into the bed. My cock, however—it might as well be back in my jeans for how trapped it is.

"Mal…" He says my name in that shaky, warning way he has when he doesn't trust what's about to happen. It's also how he says it when he's about to come. *Please don't come yet, Ryan…*

"I can take it," I tell him. "Please."

"I'm sorry," he says. "I'm so fucking sorry."

"Ry—"

I shut up when I hear him spit and warm liquid pools in my asshole. Barely a second later, his mouth is on me. My shocked gasp is loud enough to send his cat leaping off the bed. I gather the pillow beneath me and stuff my face into it as he spits again and sucks. *"God, oh fucking god, fuck that's so fucking good yes fuck yes."*

Whatever he started doing to my crotch yesterday that he apologized profusely for? He's doing that *times ten* to my hole. His face has to be buried between my ass cheeks. His tongue enters and licks me. He's practically snarling, and I am so goddamn glad I prepped again and way more thoroughly than last night. I'm talking—I stopped by the store on the way home and picked up some things. My only concern is whether I'm sweating, but judging by the way he's trying to eat my ass for dinner, he must really, really like it.

In my wildest dreams, I never could have imagined how good this would feel. My face is on fire. My balls are aching. Excitement swirls deep in my core.

Oh shit, I think I'm gonna come. He's holding me firmly in place, the only movement I'm getting is when he nudges his face into me really hard, but there's so much heat, so much mess, so much pressure on my taint I don't think I'd even *need* a dick to come from this.

Fuck, he's gonna hate that. If he didn't want jizz in his jeans, he's really gonna hate it on his comforter. *"Ryan…"*

He thrusts his tongue deep inside me. I cry out his name again, and he growls around my hole.

"Ry, fuck, I'm about to come."

With his hand, he lifts me by the ass cheek and his fist wraps itself around my cock.

My thighs tense as the orgasm pulses my tight balls. He pulls my dick between my legs, the stretch excruciating and impossible. And then it's in his mouth, once again, just in time. Apologies to the roommate, but I come so hard and so loud, no amount of pillows or music would have helped muffle it. It's so extreme, I drool and convulse. It's the most shocking thing that's ever happened to my body. Electric and dangerous and absolutely fucking *miraculous*.

For long moments, I don't feel anything but pure ecstasy. It overloads me, causing the opposite of numbness. I feel *everything,* and it's all *good*. Static fills my head. I'm deaf and blind. I'm locked in the perfect expression of what my body is capable of achieving in its most heightened state.

And when the weight of gravity pulls at me again, when I can hear my breath against the pillow, I still feel his mouth on my cock, sucking gently, licking lightly, tasting and warming me.

It's intense. A lot. Almost too much. But I fist the pillows and squeeze my eyes shut, wanting this part too. Once I give it a minute, it's all good again. "I like that," I say quietly, not expecting him to hear me.

His mouth engulfs me, and it's as big of a relief and turn on as sinking into a flesh light. I groan when his nose hits my balls.

"Fuck me, Ryan. Please."

He doesn't say a word. Neither agrees nor disagrees. But he slides his mouth off my cock and wraps his hands around my hip bones. My eyes fly open, and I hurry to get my knees underneath me. He reaches for the nightstand, and I *thank God*.

CHAPTER SEVENTEEN

RYAN

This needs to be over. All of it. I'm out of control, and I can't fucking take it. He'll hate this. He'll freak the fuck out, and we can be done. Or I'll hate it. I don't know. I just know I need to do it. My mind needs it. My body certainly fucking needs it. And my stupid fucking tormented soul does, too.

I don't have to love him to fuck him.

I don't have to love fucking him.

I don't have to fucking care at all.

Even with a condom on, my hand feels good on my dick as I coat it with lube and stare at his tiny hole, still wet and glistening from what I did to it. It's the same exact color of his nipples—or it was before I attacked it with my mouth. Now it's even redder and smaller. Scanning up from there, my gaze follows the long line of his spine and the broadening, inverted triangle that forms from his lean torso. His arms are stretched out, his head turned toward the closet, his chin tilted down so he can see me.

He looks wrecked. Sweaty hair stuck to his forehead, eyes glazed and bright, lips bitten to a garish pink. Fuck. Hot.

He's never, ever looked better.

I never pictured us like this. Not once. With the way he used to rail away at Kaylin, I always imagined if there ever was a time for us—or when I would happen to dream about it, I was the one bent over, ass up, taking his punishing thrusts.

But I see all that differently now. His naked ankles, his draping legs, his breathless, gasping mouth and the needy whimpering noises he makes between all the swear words. He's a slut, and I love a slut. Sluts know how to break through my walls. They know how to wind me up and get me inside them when I can't always see my way there.

They make sex fun and uncomplicated.

Nothing about this has to be complicated.

I slide my slick cock up and down his crack, transferring some of the excess lube.

"Fuck yes, *please...*"

His begging is hot, too.

"Put it in me."

I almost laugh. "You're a fucking psycho."

"Put *something* in me."

I probe him with my fingertip, and his hole opens, swallowing it. I groan as I spread the lube over his hot walls, the sinking feeling a preview of what my cock is all too eager to experience.

His hole works me like an expert cunt. Clenching and releasing as I stroke back and forth. "More. Fuck," he groans. "That feels so good."

My middle finger joins the first and he gasps. "Yes..." he moans. "Oh fuck... God, fucking help me, I want more. I want you to *hurt* me."

"Hurt you?" I repeat quietly.

"Give me what I deserve. Please. *Fuck...*"

I don't want to hurt him. I want to get off, yes—and I want to stuff my cock into his pretty hole—*this slick needy cunt*—but hurt him? For what? For hurting me? Upending my life? For breaking my heart?

Aren't we supposed to be forgiving each other?

I remember what he said, though, the other night, about wanting to be fucked into a mattress until he was sobbing. Going based off proportions, my cock should accomplish that.

"You sure?" I ask, because I can't imagine how this *wouldn't* hurt.

He groans, fucking back onto my fingers when I'm not moving fast enough. Greedy. Slutty.

I'm keyed up, edged, needing to come. Does wanting to hurt him just a little make me an asshole?

I never said I wasn't, and I'm looking at the man who turned me into one.

"I'm sure," he says. "Do it. Fuck me, Ryan."

A sudden case of nerves along with all the heightened arousal has me shuddering.

I rest the tip of my cock against his hole, apply the slightest bit of pressure, and wait with my hands on his waist. "You want it so bad, come and get it."

"You know I fucking I want it," he says. Moving his hands to the headboard, he presses back. It's like meeting a wall. He takes a deep breath, blows it out and tries again.

"*Ungh...fuck...*" he groans as my crown pops through a tight band. He's determined—I'll give him that. I guess it's flattering? His body trembles, and he breathes heavily while we both adjust. The sight of my cock penetrating his ass is jarring and filthy. The way he feels? So. Fucking. Tight. Like he could snap my dick off if he moved a certain way.

But I need him to move, too. This is excruciating. *Nearly.* There's an anticipation building inside me that's actually very, very good. Another deep breath, another stretch of his arms, and another inch of me disappears inside him, compressed in the tightest space my cock has ever squeezed through.

In a low, low voice that sounds nothing like him, he says, "I need you to move, Ryan."

"No," I grit out, stubbornly suffering because I guess that's what I'm used to.

"Move," he breathes harshly. "*Goddamnit*," and that's a sob.

For a faltering moment, I don't know what to do. I'm tempted to pull out, call it a nice try and then... Then *what*? What if I never wind up here again? Do I really want to let this moment pass?

My decision made, I get a grip on his waist, and I pull him onto me—compromise, right? The feel of my cock sheathed fully inside him makes me cry out in shock and mind-blowing pleasure.

It's a little like falling. All that resistance—the compression—gives way as I sink inside him, and my balls slap his. *That*—that is a crazy good feeling, and one I wasn't anticipating. He makes a noise like I'm ripping off his arm and goes limp on the pillows.

My cock twitches inside him as the rest of me freezes solid. God, I need to fucking come.

"*Move goddamnit*," he shouts, and I can tell he's crying or very close to it. The words are thick and wet. I can't help *but* move. Not like the way he used to fuck Kaylin, all power thrusts and speed. No. I fuck him the way *I* like to fuck. Slow and deliberate so I can feel every inch of his insides dragging against my cock. After a few strokes, he's panting, and I've never been this deep.

I get used to the tight squeeze—the sinking feeling—and close my eyes. I find my rhythm and the smoothest glide of my life. I run my hands up his back and it changes the angle, pulling my dick down, and he jolts, gasping again and again as I move my entire length from the shallow end to the deep end.

Pressure builds in my balls as they tap his. One of his hands leaves the headboard and disappears beneath his body. I can only assume he's touching himself.

I don't object. Whatever he needs to get through it.

I'm almost there. So fucking close because goddamn it just keeps getting better. Hotter. And then I realize that's because he's not being still. He's fucking me the same way he took my fingers. He's clenching his ass and tightening his hole. He's rocking in opposition with me, and that's why our balls are now *slapping*.

"*God...*" he groans, the word guttural. "Jesus fucking God. Oh...*God.*"

"That's it, Mal," I say, encouraging this. I wrap my hands over his shoulders, managing to bend down and lick the back of his neck. He lifts his head, arching for me, and I get a better hold on his nape, sucking the skin between my teeth and latching hard enough to leave a mark.

"I'm gonna come," he gasps. "I'm gonna fucking come again."

I usually last a lot longer during sex, but this is different in every single way than anything I've ever experienced. His words shove me past the breaking point. My balls pulse in rapid blasts, and my cock throbs hard. Cum fills the condom in burst after burst, and he chokes out a gasping sob, once again going limp beneath me. All but the breathing. His back expands and contracts, and he pulls his hand slowly out from under him, his fist clenched.

Did he...?

The primitive part of me rears its twisted head again. I pull my dick from his hole and grab for his wrist.

"Ryan—I—"

Moving quickly, I drop onto the bed next to him, bringing his hand to my mouth and prying his fingers open. When the first taste of his collected cum hits my tongue, I start licking, finishing this thing we just did in the most depraved way I never could have thought up in my sickest dreams of us.

After that it's kind of a hazy mess for a few seconds while my humanity tries to seep back into my bones. There's blood on us both. Not a lot, but enough that I feel compelled to get a cold, wet towel and press it to his ripped hole. Not gonna lie—blood during sex isn't new for me. This wasn't my first inexperienced hole.

"Am I okay?" he asks.

"Yeah," I say. I checked before I put the towel on him. It's not bleeding anymore. A small anal tear. He'll be fine in a day or two. "It already stopped."

"Bleeding?" he asks.

"Yeah, Mal. Bleeding."

"Oh. Good. That was crazy."

I guess he's fine, then. He's had his eyes closed this whole time, but he opens them now while I'm staring at him.

"Your dick," he says.

"Yeah?"

"It's big."

"You knew that. You had it in your throat last night."

"Yeah. I did. Now it's been everywhere."

"Not your hand."

"No?" he asks. He sounds drunk.

I shake my head.

"I just used my mouth?"

"Yep."

"Wow."

I smile because I can't seem to help it. "You're wrecked."

"Did you like it? It was your first time in a guy's ass, right?" he asks.

"First ass, period."

"So?" he presses.

"Of course I liked it. Big dick, tight hole."

He laughs softly. "Fuck you."

"Still wanna spend the night?" I ask.

"*Yes*. Jesus. Why do you keep acting like I'm gonna change my mind?"

I lift my eyebrows.

"Don't answer that," he says. With a groan, he winces as he moves closer to slide his leg between mine. We're both still naked, so the effect of this particular comfy snuggle is exponentially different. I can feel a nipple, his cock, the hairs on his leg. And I can see his entire face. I sweep some of the stuck hair off his forehead. The love I didn't allow myself to feel while I was fucking him hits me squarely in the chest. *Shit.*

It's more potent than the orgasm, and it totally fucks me up. "Are you okay?" I ask.

He smiles faintly. "Yeah. I'm perfect. Fuck me anytime."

That coaxes a smile from me, which only broadens his. It's so stupid. Both of us. Here. Now. Smiling like idiots at each other when neither of us has a clue what the fuck we're doing.

Just because I fucked him, doesn't mean I have to say it, but it's right there, wanting out worse than it's ever wanted out. But I'm not on drugs, and I am *not* an idiot. Not for him. Not anymore.

But while I've got him, I go ahead and kiss him.

$$\$\$\$$$

FOR THE SECOND night in a row, I don't sleep. Whereas the night before last, I got a few stretches of forty-five minutes or so—last night, with Mal wrapped around me, I got nothing. I can account for every minute.

Every breath he took that landed on my neck—every shift of

his body against mine. Every erection that lived and died from either his presence or a memory of what we did.

Over his long stretch of uninterrupted sleep, he's sacrificed exactly zero inches between us. For every body part that moved away from me, another one got closer. Now, as dawn is breaking outside the window, he's practically smothering me. His surprisingly flexible leg is hitched around my waist, while the straight one is lined up flush with mine. His chest is resting on my chest, and his head is right next to mine. His breaths blow through my ear—loud like a thunderstorm.

I'm hot, and I've been sweating since he fell asleep. We're still on top of the covers—still naked. The arm of mine he's more or less trapping is wrapped around his waist, allowing him to stay on top of me, slightly lifted from the bed. My free arm and hand can't decide what to do. There's been a lot of rubbing my eyes and face. But I've done some touching too. Him for the most part, and occasionally, when I have access to it, my cock.

I haven't jerked off, but I've humored my erections to an extent. Drawing them out, enjoying the warm, tingling sensation of arousal without getting myself to the point of needing release. Mostly, though, I've been stroking him. Long, light strokes not meant to rouse him but to remember him.

He's either a deeper sleeper than he used to be, or sex knocks him out.

When my alarm goes off, he clenches around me. The hug he gives me is suffocating. I reach out to silence my phone on the nightstand and wrap my free arm around him, too.

He moves on top, and fuck me, but I help him get there. He starts kissing my neck without so much as a good morning. I slide my hands down his sides, settling on his hips. This time, my legs are spread to accommodate him. My latest erection rubs against his, and he makes the most of that position by rocking his body back and forth.

It's...*amazing*. I don't want him to stop. The only thing that would be better would be if I were inside him again. I want to feel *that* again. The way his body seemed to draw me in and reward me for how deep I could get by keeping that outer constriction—like fucking through a glory hole. A hole that was a bit too small to fit comfortably inside but the tight hold it had on me was fucking everything, and his heat engulfing me—*fuck*.

I've been up all night like I'm trying to prepare a diary entry for it, but the truth of the whole thing is, it was the best sex I've ever had—in a physical sense.

The rest—the implications and the emotional turmoil—I was only able to push away for the length of time I was inside him. The rest of the night has been a wrestling match between the deepening of my sense of entitlement when it comes to my former stepbrother and the lived experience of losing his affection—and worse.

I've slept with the enemy—my tormentor in every possible way. The line between love and hate is practically invisible. In any given moment—all night—I've found myself on both sides infinite times.

But never once did I want to push him away. And I'm not about to now, either. I'm much more likely to take both our cocks in hand and give us both something to fuck. Together.

"Want you," he whispers.

"Shower," I say.

"Mm...no. Now. Here."

"You're injured."

"I'm tough."

"Shower," I say again.

"Bath."

"We don't have time to run a whole bath."

"Let's take a sick day."

"Absolutely not." I get out from under him in a quick move

that has him face planting with a grunt. Then there's the groan as he gets up and follows me into the bathroom, walking carefully with small steps.

I turn on the shower. If all I had going on was morning wood, I'd take a leak, but while I do try, I can't manage it. I'm too turned on. The water can't get hot fast enough. While Malcolm is trying to look at his asshole in the mirror, I'm checking the water. It's barely warm enough, but I drag him behind the curtain with me. "Worried about your hole?"

"No," he says with a note of defiance.

"Let me take a look."

"Ryan—oh shit," he grunts when I drop to my knees and turn him around. The warming water is angled down his back, so when I put my mouth on his puffy, red hole, I get a full drink of it. I put a hand up to block the stream from drowning me as I lick softly at his angry rim. The light tang of chafed flesh threatens to send me into cannibal territory again, but I tighten my other hand on his thigh, channeling my baser instincts into a show of strength.

He muffles a cry. It sounds like he's got his mouth wrapped around his arm or something. At first, he raises to the balls of his feet like what I'm doing hurts, and he needs to get away, so I press open mouthed kisses to the entrance that took all of me last night, and he settles back down, pressing his ass out for more after a minute or two.

I lick just inside the swelling, careful not to stretch the abused tissue. I handle his balls with gentle pressure and his cock with long, twisting strokes. He's whimpering and speaking in incoherent bursts. His legs tremble, knees wobbling, but I've got a good grip on him. He's not going anywhere.

Ultimately, because he's him, and he brings out the worst in me as often as he calls on my better angels, I restrain my mouth to tender kisses and use my hand to get him off. His load sprays the gray tile, and something twisted in me wants to lick the wall. It's one of the hottest things I've ever seen. Fuck, I *really* need to come. I stand, tugging at my own dick. He hasn't moved much, still heaving breaths while he holds himself up on the wall, and I'm too close to wait for him to help me out.

The orgasm rockets through my core, sending a few impressive jets of cum directly onto his ass. The water quickly washes it away, and I groan as another contraction makes me shoot more. He looks over his shoulder at me—at what's happening, and then our eyes meet. His mouth moves in a silent "*fuck.*"

"You like that?" I ask, almost laughing.

He nods.

"Wash up," I tell him, letting go of my cock.

He fumbles the shampoo, and it falls to the floor. I pick it up for him and squirt some into his hand before I take some for myself. As he lathers his hair with his back to me, I watch his hands working through the strands I stroked half the night. I last about five seconds before I'm covering his back and taking over. He reaches around to grab my ass, holding me tight to his body.

A little too tight now that I've come. "Careful," I say. "Full bladder."

"You don't piss in the shower?" he asks, sounding all blissed out as I massage soap into his scalp.

"No."

"Easy clean-up," he says.

"You're..." I go quiet because I don't know what he is other than a huge fucking turn-on ninety-nine percent of the time.

"Say it."

"What?" I ask.

"Call me a slut. It's what you're thinking."

"You don't know what I'm thinking," I assure him.

"Say it."

"Fine," I choke out as he leans back against me, pushing my

bodily control to its outermost limits. I give him what he asked for. "You're a fucking slut. Is that what you're going for?"

"Just need someone to call me on it. I pick you."

I grunt with discomfort when he bumps backward again.

"Just go, Ryan."

"I'm not pissing on your leg."

"That hurts my feelings."

"Do you have feelings?"

He laughs darkly. "I do. You'd rather mark a toilet than me? Ouch."

"A *sick* slut," I mumble as I try to get away from him to rinse out my hair so I can relieve myself in the appropriate place.

"Oh, I like that. Call me that." He squeezes again, not allowing me an inch of space. "Make me *that*."

"How do you live with yourself?" I ask as my need to go gets urgently necessary.

"I don't," he says. "But you're bringing me back to life."

Jesus. He can't say shit like that. I slide my hand around his neck; covering his throat with my palm and apply pressure. "Are you trying to make me hate myself?"

His voice strains to get through his windpipe. "I just want inside your head."

"You're there, asshole. You've always been there."

"Prove it. Do this with me."

I make myself stop thinking. I'm fucking exhausted, and I just came, and he's wet and squirmy and hot, and what fucking difference does it make? We're in the shower.

I bury my face in his neck and let the stream loose. "Ryan, *ohmyfuckinggod*, I *feel* you. Oh *fuck*. What the fuck are you doing to me?"

Me? I want to ask. Scream. He's got me marking his leg like a fucking animal and it's somehow *my* fault?

"I'm going, too," he says because he can't let a single thing happen in silence. Nothing goes unnoticed or unremarked upon with him. I have this awful realization then, that if he asked, I would have let him piss on me, too. It would feel like—*closure*.

What I'm doing to him feels wrong, though. Like the same reason I shouldn't have left a mark on the back of his neck last night is the exact same reason I shouldn't be marking him like my own personal fire hydrant. But the flood gates are open, and I let it flow until I'm done. My body feels better but my mind feels sick and dirty.

He, however, is now washing himself with reverence, seeming to relish every stroke of his leg and his ass, his chest. He's showing off, and it's better than porn. *Good luck thinking about anything else today, Ryan.* Maybe I do need to take the day. Just—not with him. I need the fuck away from him for a few hours—if not a day or two. He's got me ready to commit myself for physical and emotional exhaustion.

As I'm rinsing off and he's running his hands all the fuck over my body, I start mentally shutting down.

I can't handle this. If he were anyone else—maybe. Maybe I could deal with this like a mature adult, but he's rapidly regaining traction in both my mind and heart. This can't be real.

I'm part of some fever dream he's in, and I can't allow myself to get swept up in it like it means something for him. Or us. *Especially* for us.

In a couple weeks, Kaylin will be back, and he'll snap back into his reality where he wears boring suits and tech vests and goes to brunch or sports bars with his straight friends or whatever the fuck they do together. I'll finish the internship and get my dream job in Seattle where Norah is lowkey waiting for me to hold her hand in the park.

Malcolm will remember—like he did when we were fourteen—that he doesn't want me "that way." That whatever room is suddenly open in his head is a place that leads to a life he doesn't want, no matter how much fun he has playing in it from time to time. It's as much of a threat to his future now as it ever was, and he's just being reckless.

I can't allow him to be reckless with me.

He gets dressed in the bedroom while I'm in the bathroom. I closed myself in as soon as he went to grab his suit. The steamy air does nothing to wake me up or clear my senses, but the empty space around me is welcome. Work will be hell today on no sleep, but I've got to power through. Focus.

I've got to shut him out and not allow my mind to wander.

This all proves absolutely fucking impossible. At work, my brain is as substantial as unset Jell-O. Constantly melted with flashes of him out of the corner of my eye—the sound of his voice across the worktable, the memories of things he said, things I did. The feelings I'm utterly defenseless against as they beat at my chest and deeper...like they're part of my DNA.

After lunch, I go narcoleptic. Charlie tells me to go splash some cold water on my face and get an energy drink.

I don't notice Mal's following me until I'm in the unisex bathroom. I chose this one because I thought I might start crying from pure exhaustion on top of everything else, and I'd like to keep that shit private.

But he's inside the small room with me before I have the sense or the reaction time required to stop him. I'm beyond defenseless as he walks me into the wall, his hands underneath my jacket and his lips sucking needily at mine.

My liquefied brain does nothing. My body responds to his with equal fervor. "You look terrible," he tells me. "Hot as fuck but terrible. Did you not sleep?"

"Mm..." is all I manage before he's rubbing his tongue against mine again.

I'm not sure how it happens, when or why or who does it—I guess him—but he's got both our cocks clenched in one fist.

"We can't," I say weakly while we both look down at our leaking dicks. Our foreheads are pressed together, and he's not wasting any time. I want to come. I need to come. I'm close. This is my favorite. I love him.

"Good, right?"

Fuck, did I say that out loud?

"So fucking close Ryan. I've been thinking about this all day. Come with me."

Okay, maybe it wasn't out loud. I don't even know. There's a rustle near my head, and it's him grabbing a wad of paper towels from the dispenser, holding them near our cocks, ready to catch what comes out.

Distantly, somewhere in my addled brain, I think how much better this would be with lube and maybe we do this again later —in the shower maybe—after the gym—and I realize no way can I go to the gym today, which also makes me want to cry because I've been on such a good streak.

"Mal..." I breathe, and it comes out like the most pathetic sigh. It doesn't even sound like me. "Coming...shit...don't let me make a mess. Please...*Mal...unfph...fuck...*"

"I've got you. Shit, me too...hang with me, baby, fuck...yeah... oh God so fucking close."

I'm spilling cum, and it's probably getting everywhere, but I also feel half asleep. I register the low sustained groan he makes as he jerks us—me with my far too overstimulated dick—and drops his head to my shoulder. My hands are on him. Somewhere. They're in fists, and I unclench them as the intensity of the orgasm and aftershocks pass, leaving me even stupider and more drained.

His kiss is sloppy and sexy and long while he holds the soaked paper towels over our still joined cocks. When he pulls away and makes sure we're free of cum stains, he tucks me back in and does up my pants before taking care of himself. "Let me take you home."

"I'm..." Okay isn't the word. Not even close. But no—I need to get the fuck away from him. That was too much. *This* is too much. "I need to sleep."

"We'll sleep," he says. "I'll let you sleep all night. Promise."

I put a hand on his chest and hold him back because he's about to kiss me again. "No. Stop. Mal, I'm so sorry, but we have to stop."

CHAPTER EIGHTEEN

MALCOLM

Andrea, my long-time therapist hands me a fresh box of tissues because I used up what was left of her other one.

To be clear, I'm not weeping or anything, but the tears are flowing nonstop. They have been since I left work. Since Ryan stopped me from kissing him and told me to back off. He did it again today. For the second day in a row. Not in words so much, but he might as well have said it. Yesterday was bad after he ducked out of work early to get some sleep, but it was understandable. He hadn't looked as rough or tired today, though, which I assumed meant he caught up on his rest.

But then he went off and had lunch with Miguel. Somewhere not in the building. When we were in the office, he never once left his desk to go to the bathroom, and he didn't return any of the texts I sent him where I made it abundantly clear I wanted to see him tonight.

I feel like I'm finally getting my long overdue punishment. Like what we did—sucking and kissing and fucking—was a trick to get me to fall for him, and now he's pulling the rug out— same as I did to him way back when.

I'm crying because I know I deserve it. Because I know he's right to use me and leave me lost and broken.

"Can we go back to this room metaphor?" Andrea asks gently, but also like we're definitely circling back, whether I want to or not.

I heave a sigh and wipe my leaky eyes again. "What about it?"

"It had to do with your mother's affair?"

I've been seeing Andrea since my mom died. She's the same age mother would have been had she lived, which means there's been a lot of transference she and I have both had to work through over the years. I've been needy, petulant, rebellious, regretful, unfair, ungrateful, and angry with her in each new phase of my life.

She's a grief therapist, so that's how this all started, but now she's the person I vent all my issues at for fifty minutes a week. When I'm done, she gives me a thing to do to deal with something I've been nervous about or avoiding. Whether it's having a conversation, paying a bill, or replying to an email—just something so I don't let my anxieties fester or sabotage myself.

"Sort of," I say, not wanting to talk about this with her either.

It's one thing to tell someone my mother had an affair. It's another to disclose who she had an affair with and what any of that had to do with me.

It's all so fucked up. "Do you think I'm normal?" I ask.

"I've never liked the word normal," she says.

"Do you think I'm fucked up?"

"I think you're human. Perfectly imperfect."

"What if I told you I'm in love with my stepbrother?"

"I'd remind you that you no longer have a stepbrother."

"Is that really a label that goes away, though? Former stepbrother, ex stepbrother, are you catching the brother part?"

"I remember Ryan, yes. You haven't talked about him in a while."

"I thought he was gone," I say. "But he's in my internship."

"Why haven't you mentioned that?"

"I was processing it." And we've mostly been talking about the break with Kaylin. Ryan hasn't come up, and I guess that was on purpose. But now that the "room" is lit up like a fucking carnival, it's harder to avoid.

"Love feels like quite the leap," she says.

"It's not," I say, sighing again. "It's more like a laying down of arms."

"Hm. I know sex isn't your favorite topic—"

"It's fine," I say, in full surrender mode. I feel like shit, and if this makes it worse, who cares? On the off chance it might help, I'll talk about Ryan *and* sex. "It's just complicated, and I don't expect anybody to understand it, except I thought maybe he would, but he's not talking to me right now, which is fair since I made his life hell."

"I don't recall you being particularly happy at that time either."

More tears fall remembering how miserable I was in high school. The soul shriveling loneliness. How being with Ryan was unthinkable, but being without him was just—fucking *devastating*. I abused alcohol and Adderall. I had sex with Kaylin literally any chance I got just to be held and stop thinking. I tried out for the goddamn football team for the body contact for fuck's sake while also hoping to find a friend I could be close to the way I'd been with Ryan, but maybe not mix so much love in with it.

Back then, I refused to admit I missed him even to myself. And I didn't just miss him as my friend and someone I could say anything to, I missed *everything*. The physical closeness. The safety and containment. The unconditional acceptance no matter how rotten I was.

Something about losing a parent when you're that young makes most people weird around you, especially kids. Everyone I told, with the notable exception of Ryan peeled themselves away from me like it was *their* fucking mom who died. I felt like an infection.

Andrea helped me reconcile that piece. I understand grief better now. She was okay with my decision to stop telling people my mom died. She was also okay when I started lying and claiming she was still alive, living out of state.

Andrea said as long as I was honest with her and my father, I was allowed to cope however I needed to. But part of my teenage rebellion involved not telling her about what happened with Ryan. At the time, it was because it embarrassed me. Now I'm mostly embarrassed that I was embarrassed. The thought of trying to explain it all so long after the fact is exhausting when all I can think about is whether he's going to start turning everyone against me the way I did to him.

But in answer to her question—about how fucking miserable I was in high school, I say, "I didn't understand what I was feeling. I didn't get what I liked about him or what I wanted."

"But you do now?"

"Yes."

"In retrospect as well?"

"Yeah."

"Which I'm assuming was a more physical relationship?"

"That's what I'm assuming, too," I say, so frustrated with my brain's inability to wrap its arms around the totality of who I am. "I'm still really confused about a lot of it."

"Well, why do you think that is?"

The real answer for that is what I don't want to talk about because it nauseates me that it's still something I think about. It shouldn't be. Ryan is separate of all that, but my question is *can he really be*? If I'm still affected by it, can I really say it's not spilling into my feelings toward Ryan, too?

Fuck, I want to talk to him so bad. There's no one else I trust with this, but I don't know if I can trust him anymore, either. I wish I'd told the Ryan who showed up at my apartment after work Friday night. Friday night Ryan was listening, and I hadn't crossed any major lines with him.

Now I've had sex with him, and the need to have sex with him again is impossible to ignore—for me at least. Conversations like this one I should have with him feel secondary. I want to connect with him both ways, but my physical desire is out of control.

I need more time with him. Time without TikToks or Patreons or *fucking Miguel* coming between us. Time to hold him and whisper all my secrets to him and let him tell me my past doesn't make me fucked up beyond repair or wanting.

Goddamn, I'm needy. Selfish, too. Is that what's pushing him away? I'm making it all about me?

"Because he's not talking to me," I say. More tears. Goddamnit. I grab two tissues and shove them both against my eyes while I lean over, elbows propped on my knees. I'm such a fucking mess. Christ. This obsession I have with him isn't cute or endearing. It's psycho, and I'm sure it shows. I've seen him look scared at least a few times already, but I took no for an answer... didn't I?

Fuck.

"When we were fourteen, he told me he was in love with me. It wasn't something I could hear at the time. The way people talked about LGBTQ kids at school—like they were freaks—and here I've got my fucking *stepbrother* telling me he's one of them and maybe he thinks I am too—I just flipped out on him."

"But you were close before that," she says.

"Yes."

"Best friends?"

The very best. "Yeah."

"If he'd only told you he was gay would you have reacted the same way?" she asks. "Or was it more to do with the fact that his feelings were directed at you?"

"I don't think he *is* gay," I say, which just puts my thoughts into more of a snare.

"But back then."

"Back then—if he told me he was gay—I mean..." I think about it. About the way we held each other. About the way we'd whisper talk about random things—TV shows, teachers, dinner, giving the most mundane conversations the veil of intimacy and importance. "I think...I think..." I take a deep breath. "I think I would have told him I was, too."

"Oh."

The room goes completely silent for a long moment.

"But that's not how it happened," I say in a rush.

Fuck, now I really wish that had been how it happened.

"What bothered you about knowing he loved you?"

"Not loved—*in love*. I don't know. It was about twenty steps beyond where I was at? It was like having all this pressure on me all of a sudden, but it also changed the context of our whole past —or the previous year or two at a minimum. Like he'd been luring me or grooming me or something."

"Grooming?" she asks, sounding even more surprised.

"I just mean I thought maybe he had ulterior motives."

"Do you still think that?"

"Obviously not."

"I don't know why the hell you think that's obvious," she says.

"I felt the same way," I tell her urgently, needing her to

understand what I'm just now beginning to grasp. "I was just too stupid to realize it at the time. And I thought it was wrong."

"Which was it?"

"Both," I insist.

"To clarify," she says, "You pushed him away out of a misguided sense of wrongness, not your feelings for him."

I nod. I like the way that sounds. Not because it gets me off the hook, but because it sounds way better than saying I was the asshole.

"And that did damage to you both," she concludes.

I exhale. "Yeah."

"You need to back off," she says. "Don't you think?"

I grind my teeth, and another tear falls, but I nod again.

"Yeah," she says quietly. "Let him know you're available if he wants to reach out, and back off."

"Why is this so hard?"

"Well, I'll have to think about that. You've dropped a lot in my lap today. Granted, I feel pretty strongly that you should officially break up with Kaylin because neither of you are doing each other any favors by staying together, but I didn't realize you were contending with a sexuality issue. I'll have to re-contextualize my thinking on our prior sessions."

"All of them?"

"Don't worry about me, Malcolm. I have a good memory."

I roll my eyes, wipe my face again, and lean back on the couch.

"I have one more question before we wrap up, though."

"Fine," I say.

"When did you start questioning your sexuality?"

The last two days without Ryan have given me plenty of time to pinpoint that. "It was the first day of eighth grade. There was a gay kid named Ivan who'd just transferred into our school. He was out and obvious about it. He was wearing rainbow Converse and had painted nails. By the end of the day, he also had a bloody nose and a black eye. Courtesy of the defensive line of the football team. He never came back to our school after that."

"You...liked Ivan?"

"No. You asked when I started questioning myself. I already knew I liked boys. That's when I started questioning whether I should or not."

"You were thirteen?"

"Yes."

"And you'd known you were gay since...?"

"Since I was seven."

"Mal," she whispers.

"What?"

"Why didn't you tell me?"

"Because...it wasn't a big deal until I knew to be ashamed of it, and then once I was ashamed of it, why the fuck would I tell you?"

She makes a pitying noise, and I don't mind it. I'm glad someone feels at least partly as sorry for me as I do for myself. "I guess the genie's out of the bottle now," she says.

"Yeah. Well... solves the Kaylin problem."

She laughs. "I can cross that off the list. Same time next week?"

I nod, wipe my hands on my pants, and stand.

"Text me if you need anything?"

She always says that, and I sometimes take her up on it, but she doesn't usually respond until the next day. She has better boundaries with her phone than I do.

As I'm leaving her office, however, I do send Ryan a text.

ME

> Officially backing off. When you're ready to talk, I'll be available.

When he leaves me on read again, I go home, and after I stop leaking tears, I make a TikTok about estate planning with my shirt on.

It's the first time I get any negative feedback from women.

I show up at Bailey's apartment Saturday afternoon unshowered, unshaven, and ungroomed in general. I put on deodorant before I came over, but that's about as far as I went in terms of sprucing up. Long story short, I'm not feeling very slutty today. It's been a warm day for San Francisco and sunny, which means everyone looks happy. Couples are out en masse celebrating the beauty of love and the world and tank tops.

I, too, am wearing a tank top because it was clean, and I haven't done laundry. It's a black undershirt paired with red gym shorts that I also dug out of the back of a drawer. Tying shoes felt like too much work, so I've got on a pair of black knock-off Crocs, and my feet are sweating.

Bailey's porch is packed with ferns and flowers in full bloom, which is not what I expected. I was imagining something more along the lines of a thorny wreath and a sarcastic doormat. The whole apartment complex is fucking cute. Peak San Francisco modern hippie vibe. Macrame, wooden wind chimes, bougainvillea, and everything.

"Whoa," she says when she sees me.

Her tank top says RESIST in pastel Pride colors. Her curly

hair is up, and her penguin pajama bottoms signal to me she hasn't been out enjoying the sun today.

"Hello," I say.

She looks me up and down. "What happened to you?"

"Nothing," I say giving her an up and down perusal that's just as obnoxious, I hope. "Nothing at all. Nice pants."

"Thanks. Watermelon marg?"

I think I might love Bailey, too. "Fuck yeah."

She smiles. "I was hoping for a taker. Ryan—"

"Doesn't like watermelon," we say at the same time.

"I know," I add. "Crazy, right?"

"Seriously."

She steps out of the way, and I enter her incredibly cute apartment. It's the kind of place I thought only existed on TV. The kitchen is quaint and hasn't been updated, but it's clean and bright with lemon and lime colored accents. The living room, where Ryan is by the way, has a green couch, two bright yellow chairs—Ryan is sitting in one—and a shit ton more plants crowded around two narrow bay windows where an orange tabby cat is sprawled in a ray of sunshine. The rug is multi-colored with a watercolor effect.

The thing that reminds me most of a movie apartment is the set of French doors leading to another room, maybe an office, maybe a bedroom where more light pours in.

"Hey," Ryan says.

"Hey." I don't make eye contact and stick with Bailey, holding a glass while she pours a margarita for me. I take a sip and nod my approval. I needed this. I honestly don't know how much help I'm gonna be today. When I left work Friday afternoon, my finance brain shut off and my poor-me-I'm-so-lonely brain started running full steam. I had a couple of extra videos I made when we were just starting out that I posted, and I envied that guy who looked like he had his shit together. That guy had potential and things to look forward to.

Friday night Malcolm was dreading fake Croc Malcolm having to be within six feet of the man who gave me an anal tear and I let piss on me because it seemed really hot at the time. And it was. It was really, *really* hot. I think about it way too much.

Bailey's work project stuff is taking up the entire couch—a laptop, a notebook, a bag full of pens and highlighters—so I sit on the other yellow chair and avoid looking at Ryan in favor of trying not to guzzle my margarita.

It's a perfect summer drink and in direct contradiction to my mood, which is dark and sour. It tastes sweet and optimistic. Fucking delicious.

Bailey plops down amidst all her things and gives us the updated subscription numbers. We're at nearly two-thousand, which is mind-boggling. Starting next week, she wants Ryan posting a video every Tuesday, Thursday and Saturday, while I'll pick up Monday, Wednesday, Friday. Sunday is going to be Bailey's poll day.

One of the worst parts of this week from a social media standpoint is that the secret of Ryan and I knowing each other is out. In the first video we posted on the Patreon of Ryan, the corner of his bed where Bud and Stephanie were sleeping together was in the frame. I hadn't noticed because I was too busy ogling him, but I'm sick of answering questions about it on the Discord.

I let the subscribers know we're working at the same investment company, and now they want content with the two of us.

It's the one thing I need to bring up in case Bailey somehow missed it, and given the piles of other stuff she's been doing, I'm assuming she hasn't been able to keep up with the chat. *I* can barely keep up with the chat, but it's the one thing keeping me sane. Talking with online strangers has been the only thing to look forward to because they'll respond when I talk to them. They're even excited to hear from me.

Granted, I stopped trying to talk to Ryan after he never responded to the message I sent after leaving Andrea's office, but he's still ghosting me in plain sight. If this is meant to be a taste of my own medicine, I guess I have ten more years of it to look forward to—that would make us even. At least I'm not in high school. I would not have survived what I did to him. One more way he's always been the strong one.

"So, we have about ten grand on hand," Bailey's saying. "What would you guys think about paying a PR consultant seven hundred bucks or so to give us some ideas for branding and merch?"

"Fine by me," Ryan says.

I grunt and nod.

"I talked to my mentor about using the offices for a podcast, and she showed me a smaller conference room on the ninth floor with a nice set up for video calls. There's a mounted ring light and a mic. She said we could use it on weekends. It's not ideal, but it's a starting point."

"What's not ideal about it?" Ryan asks.

"I mean—it's a boring conference room. I want the aesthetic to be a little friendlier, I guess."

"I assumed it'd be audio," I say.

"Well...no—I mean, the podcast would be, but it'd be recorded from the YouTube Video."

"Oh." How'd I forget about the YouTube part?

Easy—because all you've been thinking about is having Ryan's giant cock in your ass.

"Can I get another one of these?" I ask.

"Help yourself. They're not very strong."

In that case, I'll take a double. I get up and shuffle into the kitchen, scratching at the itchy scruff on my face. While I'm pouring, I accidentally glance at Ryan and catch him looking at me. Pain zaps me directly in the chest. I look away first.

If it's gonna be like this the rest of the summer, I need to start looking for a different job.

Bailey has a lot to talk about, and I finally start taking notes because there's no way I'm gonna remember any of this. It helps me concentrate to write it down, even if it's just in my notes app with a ton of autocorrections that won't make any sense later.

She's still talking after my second margarita, and while she was right—they're not all that strong—I'm ready for a nap.

"Look," I interrupt her mid-sentence. "I gotta go. Stephanie needs to eat and I...whatever. Oh, also, the Discord group wants content of me and Ryan together since they know we know each other now."

"What?" Bailey looks at Ryan who looks as confused as she does.

"Yeah, so, figure out how you wanna do that and let me know. I haven't changed my number or anything, so anyway... thanks for the drinks."

"Seriously, are you all right?" she asks, standing when I do.

"I'm awesome. Your ideas are all good. We're definitely gonna win."

"Okay, Captain Monotone. Do I need to call you a ride?"

"No thanks. This one's on me."

Surprising the shit out of me, she gives me a tight hug. "I know it's a lot," she says, "But you're doing great."

"Thank you," I say out of a genuine sense of gratitude. She smells like watermelon and mint. A hint of vanilla from her curly hair. It makes me feel disgusting for not showering today. "Sorry if I smell."

She laughs. "You don't."

I glance at Ryan, and he's standing, too, looking at me.

My heart starts beating like I just sprinted across a football field. Is he going to hug me, too? I might cry if he does—I might kiss him in front of Bailey and everything.

Before that can happen, I let go of her and back away. I need to go, or I'll make a scene. I'm feeling too much all of a sudden, and it's really better if I'm not around him when it all decides to come spilling out.

CHAPTER NINETEEN

RYAN

So, I might have made a slight miscalculation when it comes to Malcolm, but in my defense, he seemed fine at work yesterday. Better than right now anyway. Right now, he's breaking my fucking heart.

I've never liked seeing him sad. It's just that I haven't seen him like this in a very, very long time. I assume it's because of me, but it's possible something else happened. I knew I was going to see him today—we've had this meeting planned since Monday, and I also knew ignoring his calls and texts was kind of a dick move, but every time I thought about responding or reaching out to him, my phone was basically a hot pan I didn't want to touch with my bare hand. So I figured—wait until Saturday, but it looks like that was too long.

In my defense, I haven't talked to anyone this week. Calyx has been out of town, and I haven't spoken with Norah either. Sometimes I just need some alone time. I don't mind it. It's helped clarify some things for me.

Namely that I have an apology to make. I squeeze Bailey's shoulder as I follow Malcolm out.

"Wanna grab some food?" I ask from behind him as he's walking down the stairs.

"Not really."

I should probably know better than to ask this, but, "You want a drink?"

"Nope."

Good. He's hard enough to deal with when he's sober.

"Wanna come home with me?"

He stops at the foot of the stairs and turns around. "Seriously?"

"Yes."

He puts his hands on his hips. "You don't talk to me for four days, and now you're asking me to come home with you? What do I look like? A Tinder hook up?"

"I need to talk to you Mal—"

"Could have fucking fooled me."

"Okay, listen—"

"Is this payback?" he asks. "For high school?"

I have to take a deep breath because *yes*, there's a part of avoiding him that was, maybe a small percent, spiteful. Do I want to admit that? No. But do I want to move past this? I do. "Not completely."

"But some," he says.

"Maybe."

"Nice."

"Sorry," I say because I actually am sorry. It was immature and stupid, and I wanted to know how much he'd care. I wasn't trying to hurt him, but I didn't mind if it hurt, if that makes sense. Seeing it up close is different. "I needed space, but...I should have just said that."

Malcolm drops his head and rubs his face with his hands. "You did. I just...Ryan, it might not seem like it, but this means something to me."

"What?" I ask.

"What?" he says, his face blank.

"What does it mean to you?"

"Oh. Well, I feel like you think I just want to get off with you, and I mean—that's not a small part of it, but I want it to make us closer, not push you away."

"Okay." I guess I can accept that. For the moment. "But it's kinda overwhelming." Not to mention out of character. Out of the blue. Driving me out of my mind.

"I get that," he says. "And it's the same for me, but you shutting me out fucking sucks. And I know I did it to you—worse—I know there's a lot of really bad, shitty history between us, but this isn't some random idea I had—this is *who I am*. Whatever you thought you knew about me in high school, I can guarantee you got it wrong."

"Like what?" I ask.

"Like—" He lowers his voice. "Like if you thought I was happy. I wasn't. I was miserable."

Fuck. Of all the things he's told me, *that* resonates. It makes a lot of what he did back then make more sense. If he'd been happy, he might have been kind and understanding. Instead, he was the opposite—angry and cruel. His confession gives me the soft urge to hug him, but I don't. "That sucks."

He rolls his eyes and lets out a huge sigh. "I'm not trying to say I had it worse—"

"I get what you're saying," I tell him. "It's not a competition."

"I'm really fucking sorry, Ry."

"I know." I take another step down, another step closer. One stair remains between us. "It's hard for me, though. Trusting you is hard for me." I want to be clear. I need him to know that whatever it is he wants from me—friendship—a hook-up—any kind of relationship really—needs to start from scratch. I have to accept what happened to me after he threw me to the wolves, but I've also *got* to understand why he felt like he needed to hurt me. Even if it was pure malice, I deserve to know that. I need to know who the fuck I'm dealing with. It's the only way we can wipe the slate clean and move on.

He looks up and meets my eyes. His are so blue with the sky reflecting in them. "I want to work on that," he says. "Trust. You mean so fucking much to me, but I want you, too. I want you like crazy. I don't know what to do with how much I want you."

In terms of things that turn me on—this whole moment ranks pretty high.

"I'm gonna ask you this one more time," I say, taking the next step, literally and figuratively as I slide my hand into his. "Can I buy you dinner?"

He shuts his eyes like the question itself hurts, but then he nods. "Yeah."

WE'RE one of many same sex couples in the quiet seafood restaurant I picked for dinner. Bailey lives in the Castro District, which is widely known as the gay part of town. It's actually awkward for me to be here, having identified as straight with the one exception for so long. Malcolm doesn't seem to notice, but then again, he's rarely awkward—at least from what I can tell on the outside.

He orders a beer, and I order water.

"Do you not drink?" he asks.

I force myself to be honest. It's what I want from him, so I'll lead by example. "I don't want to say anything out loud I didn't mean to say. I'm just being overly cautious. When we decided to team up, I decided I wouldn't drink. It's not a huge sacrifice for me. I always liked weed better anyway."

"When did you stop doing that?" he asks.

"When I had to pass a drug test." I smile.

"How's that going?"

"I'm less hungry."

"You don't have to be careful what you say around me," Mal says just when I started to think we'd be moving smoothly past that part.

"I'm also kind of an asshole when I drink," I add.

He snorts a laugh. "Would anyone be able to tell?"

"Funny," I say flatly.

Malcolm leans back in his chair and looks around the restaurant. It's a low lit, narrow space with shiplap walls and atmospheric fairy lights. There's a fake candle flickering between us on the table. "This feels like a date, and I look like shit."

He doesn't look like shit. Not at all. He doesn't look like himself with his disheveled hair, facial scruff, and the tank top, but in terms of how sexy I find him in comparison to anyone else in the room, he's number one. But I'm beyond biased. He's sexier to me than anyone on the planet. If I thought I had it bad for him before I had sex with him, I'm a fucking goner now.

"You're fine," I say. "So how did people on the Discord figure out we know each other?"

"Bud and Stephanie."

"On my bed?"

"Yeah," he says.

"Shit. They don't know we're in San Francisco, do they?"

"Yeah. Someone guessed, and I confirmed."

"Why?" I ask.

He shrugs. "Why not? It's a big city. We're not criminals."

"Do they know this is like—a scheme though?"

"No. They're just genuinely curious. Don't worry, they like you."

"I wasn't..." Okay maybe I was going to ask what they thought about me. "Good. I'm always kind of insecure about how I come off."

He looks closely at me for a long moment. "Intimidating," he says.

I scowl. "How's that?"

"You know—the surreal good looks, the nearly creepy but very sexy eyes, the little frown line..." He draws a line down the space between his eyes. "That makes you seem annoyed, but really you're just concentrating. The constantly perfect hair."

"It's not," I assure him.

"No?"

"No," I say running a hand through it. "I work hard on this. It's very well trained. Like Stephanie."

"Don't make me name your hair."

"Yeah, don't."

"I might," he says.

"What would you call it?"

"Alex."

I laugh—hard. If I had water in my mouth, it'd be everywhere.

His smile is huge, and that's its own reward. Without putting too much thought into it, I lock my calf with his beneath the table. His shoulders drop, and he lets out a breath, his smile going soft. His relief becomes my relief. Touching him comes with a set of complications I'm not sure I'm prepared to deal with, but it also comes with a peace I can't find anywhere else. If peace can be scary, though, this particular brand of it *is*. Still, what he said earlier, about how much I mean to him? That was the lifeline I didn't know I needed.

To change the subject, I hope, I look down at my menu, waiting for the words on it to make sense. In terms of dates I've been on, if we're going to call this a date, it's definitely less awkward, and the butterflies or whatever in my stomach aren't something I usually have to contend with. Has Malcolm always been a flirt? Is he this quick and easy with Kaylin? Am I going to keep thinking about her every time I'm with him, because I wish I wouldn't.

I also wish I could take his word for it when he says he's ready to move on from her, but this whole "we're on a break" thing implies that at some point the break will end. Does that happen when she comes back from her trip? Will he be done with me by then?

These are all questions I want to ask, but now doesn't feel like the time. He's smiling, and I'm fucking smiling, and his leg is warm against mine, and I like us like this. Not because it reminds me of old times, but because it feels new and fresh and like something I want to try.

Try being the operative word. Not *invest*. He's way too risky. He's like a shiny new stock on the market that everyone's talking about, and I have this chance to get in on it early when I know the smarter thing to do is sit back, wait, and watch to see if it's really going to perform—live up to the hype.

But it's also based on a product I have a built-in affection for. I want it to do well, and I want the long term gains, with or without sex.

He must settle on his order because he puts aside his menu and looks at me without the smile. "I assume you brought me here and put a table between us so we could talk."

I glance around again at the couples engaged in low conversations that all appear to be amusing based on everyone's grins. It's been such a pretty day for this town, and everyone *should* be in a good mood on a day like this. Mal's right, though. There's a reason I wasn't leaping at the chance to go straight back to my place. Instead of wanting to dive deep into my issues or his, though, there's an opportunity here to *not* do that.

There are other things I want to know, too. What was it like going to Stanford, why Marks & Baker? When did he decide on finance, because the last I heard, he wanted to be a Marine for whatever reason. I always assumed he wanted to blow shit up or do something more mechanical. He was always taking things apart, wanting to put them together "better." I would have picked him as a doctor over financial advisor if someone had given me a multiple choice question on what Malcolm Walsh would be when he grew up.

So I start there. With Stanford, with why he decided on his major. He, in turn, asks me similar things about when I decided I wanted to be rich, what it was like to live in Portland, and did I have a lot of friends still in the area, to which I just laughed.

The conversation moves easily to the internship and the other interns. I tell him about Piper's TikToks and our encounter in the elevator. He asks where I went to lunch with Miguel. I don't tell him much about that because I'd found Miguel crying in the men's room, and I doubt he'd appreciate my talking about it with Malcolm, so I circle back to Calyx's ideas for Bailey's TikTok's to counter Piper's.

The other thing I avoid mentioning is the fact that I want to ask Miguel to join our team. I'll save that for when Mal and I are back on steadier footing. He's never been the best about adapting to change.

He talks to me about what it's like working with Isla, most of which I'd gathered from watching them together those first couple of weeks, and he asks why Charlie is in a wheelchair. It's multiple sclerosis, and I tell him both what Charlie's told me about his experience with it and what I've looked up.

My plate is clean, and I'm now talking about how Deacon and I ended up being roommates. He's surprised how little I know about the guy I live with, and I tell him I'm terrible with people.

"Why would you say that?" he asks before draining the dregs of his second beer.

"Personal experience?"

"Like what?"

"I don't know. Maybe it's like you said. Maybe I'm intimidating."

"But you don't think so," he says.

I shake my head. "No. I think I'm shy. But I also think I'm smarter than most people." I say this second part with a laugh.

"I think you're shy, too. We were living together for a month before you could say a whole sentence to me with eye contact."

"I mean... I was eight."

"Did you feel different at school because you didn't have a dad like the other kids did?"

I shrug, wincing slightly at how personal the question is. I don't mind him asking, but it's something I would have preferred to hear in a whisper. Up close. Or maybe I've now been properly seduced and want to get him home. Alone.

"I guess I did," I answer him.

"I only asked because when my mom died, I felt like a freak. Like I'd grown a second nose and everyone noticed, but no one wanted to say anything about it—or look at me. I was glad to change schools. To have someone my age like you with something in common like that."

I swallow on a lump of emotion. "Me too."

He leans in, putting his face nearly over the candle. "I have more I want to talk to you about, but here doesn't feel like the place to do it."

"Are you ready to go?"

"To your place?" he asks.

"Yeah."

His gaze slips to my mouth, and then he blinks, backing up.

Another turn-on my dick definitely notices. "I'll try to behave myself," he says.

"Don't try too hard," I hear myself say.

"He's gonna mess with me now," Mal mumbles. "Awesome."

"Not messing with you," I assure him. Tonight was everything I needed. For the first time in a long time, I know where I stand with him. I feel like more than an experiment. I feel *important.*

The waiter stops by, and I hand him my debit card. "This was a good date."

"You think?" Mal asks.

"Yes. Thank you for humoring me."

"This isn't me humoring you, Ryan. This is me fucking missing you after not talking to you for four days."

That's fair. I hope I've made up for it over the last hour and a half because this dinner, as mundane as it was, covered a lot of ground and made a big difference for me. It's a much less confusing fresh start than jumping straight into a blow job. It's also got me incredibly horny. "That won't happen again, okay? No matter how this turns out."

"Meaning you'll return all my texts from now on even if you're pissed off at me?"

"Yeah, sure, even if it's just to tell you to fuck off."

He grins. "Good."

We're quiet, engaged in a heated staring game until the waiter drops off the check. I calculate the tip, sign the bill and stand up, offering him my hand.

He takes it, and as soon as he's on my side of the table, I slide my arm around his waist. His drops around my shoulders. A few steps down the street, I turn to him, back him up against a brick building, and kiss him. He grips my waist, pulls me close, and kisses me back.

He gets hard fast. His cock springs rapidly from his thigh to his hip, and while that's what I'd really like to suck, I decide to leave a mark on his neck instead. "You like to be watched, don't you?" I ask.

"How'd you ever guess?" he says in a breathy, dazed voice.

"Do you like to show off for me?"

"Everyone likes showing off for their big brother."

I freeze, my hands still gripping his side.

"Sorry," he says quickly. "Don't let me make this weird. I'm sorry."

I'm hard as a fucking rock, so maybe his weird works for me. My mouth comes back to his, landing hard and hot. I grind against him on the street for anyone passing to see. He groans into my throat, and I have to make myself care that there are public decency laws, even in San Francisco. "Let's get home. I'll let you be as weird as you want."

"Yeah?" he asks with the starry eyed hope of a child who's never had anything nice.

"Yeah, let's go be freaks together."

It's a stumbling, heated, forty-five minute walk home that should have taken twenty. It's Saturday night, so Deacon should be out, and I'm thrilled to see his note on the counter saying he is and to let him know if I need anything.

Not tonight, Deac. Everything I need is right here.

Malcolm's feeling me up from behind as I read the note, as if I need to get more turned on. "How's your ass?" I ask as I turn to back him into my bedroom.

"Ready for your big dick." He's already panting and flushed. "But I need a shower."

"I'll get you clean for me," I tell him.

"In the shower," he says, while I lick a line up his neck. "I'm serious."

I like the way he tastes, though. Salty with a faint trace of alcohol. His natural scent reminds me of spring. Petrichor. I honestly don't want to cover it up, but I get it. His ass was meticulously clean the night I ate it out, so I gather he cares about that kind of thing. He's *serious*.

"Okay, dirty boy. Let's get you all washed up."

He relaxes as soon as the hot water hits his naked body, signaling to me that he was wound up tight about not being clean enough. I lather up his chest before moving my hands around his thighs, washing his groin, his balls, and his cock thoroughly while he braces an arm on the wall and responds sensually to every touch with thrusts of his hips and low groans.

"Turn around."

"I can—"

"Turn around."

He stops arguing and turns, his hands on the tile and his head directly beneath the spray of water. It cascades down his back and his ass. I use conditioner instead of soap, wanting the extra softness, the extra slide.

"Oh, God," he sighs when I slip two fingers into his hole. I kiss his shoulder as I massage in and out, letting the water wash away the suds and whatever else he's afraid is in there. The way it feels to touch him like this has me dying to be inside him again. I stroke my cock as I slowly clean him up. He passes me the spray nozzle and I almost laugh. "You're clean, I promise."

"Humor me."

"Do it yourself," I say, moving to accommodate his makeshift bidet. I jerk his cock the same way I'm jerking my own while he shudders and moans loudly.

"How's it looking back there?" he asks.

"Like I could eat off it, now come to bed and feed me."

"Fuck," he says as I pull him into my arms again and kiss him hungrily as the water sprays us both, washing away what's left of the soap.

"I just wanna be pretty for you," he says.

"You're fucking perfect for me." Jesus. Was *that* necessary?

He doesn't shy away from the praise, though. He kisses me again. I shut off the water, give his ass a squeeze and then a light slap to get him moving. I follow him out of the shower, making a half-hearted effort to dry off while he's more meticulous about it. Once he's done rubbing the excess water from his hair, he drops the towel, and I nod for him to meet me on the bed.

He takes my hand and pulls me into the bedroom with him.

CHAPTER TWENTY

MALCOLM

Tonight has felt like a series of small miracles. Ryan's desire is more potent than it's ever been, and mine is close to suffocating me.

"I need you to fuck me," I say when the backs of my knees hit the mattress.

"Good, because I need to be inside you." Ryan positions our cocks between us, both erect—mine leaking like crazy. Once they're side by side, he pulls me close, pressing them between our lower abs. With one hand on my ass, he uses his other hand to grip my jaw and pull me in for a long, muscle weakening kiss. His tongue drags along the surface of mine, his plush lips covering my mouth.

I've never cared much for kissing. It's necessary foreplay, a means to an end, but never something I've derived much meaning from, or placed any importance on. Kaylin's kisses are small and sweet, more lips than tongue. In high school, she was more audacious, but as we grew up and got used to each other, the heat dissipated. It's not like either of us were going to come from kissing, so we usually just fast forwarded to the orgasm making.

But now, in the wake of Ryan's kiss, I have another word for kissing Kaylin. Dispassionate. His assault on my mouth is erotic torture. It's got me wanting things I didn't know to want. It's got me dying to put my mouth on every inch of him, taste his sweat and blood. It has me near desperate to pull the words from his chest—the ones he told me years ago—with my fucking teeth. He's taking me the fuck apart. *Again.*

I want to break away to say please, Jesus, make it stop, fill me up, shut off my heart, my brain, but I can't stop letting his tongue into my mouth.

I'm on the bed somehow, and he's on top of me, grinding our cocks together and kissing the fuck out of me. My legs are locked around him, and I'm rocking with him, my balls tight and hot, my hole wide open, stretching enough that there's a slight burn I crave more of.

His head drops to my chest, and I throw my head back to gasp for air. His mouth closes around one of my nipples, and I jerk with the electric shock that lights up my spine. My balls pulse viciously, and it's like a bonfire flares in my pelvis. I come so unbelievably hard my back comes off the bed, and the cat yowls at the noise I make.

Did that just happen? What the hell? When did I get so easy?

"Fuck," he groans. "Turn the fuck over."

I don't think *I* do it, I think *he* does. A few seconds later, anyway, I'm on my stomach and cold lube is stuffing my ass on his thrusting, curling fingers. "Shit, oh shit..." I whimper, trying to get on my knees. He lifts my hips and holds them in place with an arm beneath me, buying me time to make my body work again.

"You want it like last time?" he asks.

"Yes. Fuck yes."

Or no... No, I want him to punch into me. Make me feel it

everywhere. Shock me and push me to my limit. Make me feel every ounce of pain I deserve, and the pleasure I can't help but take. But all I can say is his name. *"Please, Ryan..."*

I hear the rip of a condom packet, and I manage a no, too.

"No?" he asks.

"No condom," I tell him. "Just you."

"I always..."

"Please...just you."

He kisses my back, his hair grazing my shoulder blades. His hand moves up and down my thigh. I can sense his hesitation, but more than that—his silky, hot cock rubbing against my hole, telegraphing his need.

"I love you. Please..."

His hand on my thigh stills and grips. His lips close around a kiss on my shoulder. I lose the hand on my leg, but I gain the direct nudge of his crown on my hole. Holding my breath, I let him in. The stretch is exquisite. A burn so bright and intense, all my air comes out in a deep *"Uuummph."*

His forward progress is careful, and he hisses like he's the one on fire. I reach down, touching my belly, wanting to feel him as he stuffs his thick cock into my ass. I'm not sure what I'm feeling until my balls snap forward to graze my fingertips as his hips drive his dick in as deep as it goes. Flesh smacks flesh with a bold, thudding noise. His teeth dig into the strained tendon that connects my neck to my shoulder, and then his hand is in my hair, holding my head against the mattress.

It's so *much.* So all-consuming—extreme—I think I'll never fully get used to it, and I love that. I love that this one part of him will always torture me just a little. Beyond enough.

When he moves, it's not more than an inch or so, but it undoes me. Curses fly from my mouth, along with praise and pleas for *more* and *worse* and *deeper.* Keeping his hand on my head to hold me down, he fucks me. He fucks me until I'm sputtering and drooling, unable to shut my mouth to properly swallow.

His long, thick cock hollows me out and fills me up. He tunnels in deep and withdraws until the burn nearly has me screaming, and then he pounds home again.

I hear myself say "harder," and I feel him comply.

His hips hit my ass so hard, my butt cheeks heat like they're being spanked. Then, in feral Ryan fashion, he hooks one of his legs over mine, changing the angle to drive downward, nailing my prostate with each ramming thrust. He's got speed, power, and so much fucking finesse, I can't imagine anyone being better in bed, and I don't think I'm being biased.

My semi-erect cock bobs back and forth, slapping my abs and my balls as he jams into me over and over again.

"So fucking tight," he grunts. "So fucking good. I'm gonna come so fucking hard in your ass, Mal. You'll leak all the way into next week."

Shit...Is he saying that to *me*? Why is his dirty mouth so goddamn hot?

"Give it to me," I grunt. "Give me all your fucking cum."

His makes a fist in my hair and pulls, adding something new and delicious to what's already epic overload. "That's what you want?"

"I need it."

He lets go of my hair and braces his hand on my shoulder, using his grip to hold me still so he can rail my ass as hard and fast as he needs to get off.

I hear him break before I feel it, a ragged gasp and a low, short groan. "*Mal...*" His cock throbs his release inside me. Hypersensitive and raw, I feel every spasming contraction of his dick and every hot gush of his long release. The vibrations aren't much in the grand scheme of things, but my prostate thinks they're the best thing that've ever happened to it. My barely erect dick squirts out a thin stream of cum that does no justice to the orgasm taking over my entire body. It's got me roaring, toes curling, abs quivering, ass clenching, and my tight, reactive clench has Ryan crying out in shock. Or aftershock.

Like I said—it's all a little extra. A bit too fucking much. We're like two chemicals that shouldn't combine without major precautions being taken first inside a sealed room. Explosive only begins to cover it. He slides his cock out of me slowly before carefully lowering me back to the bed. His weight then disappears from the mattress, and I lie there limply, legs half-splayed, trying to catch my breath as my own aftershocks snake through me, making me quiver and breaking chills out on my skin.

My eyes close, but I feel his weight return and the warm, wet towel against my hole. "No blood," he says.

"Good." I had myself half-convinced the bleeding was what put him off me for four days, so I'm proud of my hole for not letting me down this time. "Does that mean we can go again later?"

His laugh is warm and soft. "Depends how fucking crazy you make me. We'll see."

"Gonna make you so fucking crazy, Ry."

"You sound high."

"I am...high off your dick."

"You need to shut up."

"I'm shutting up. Sort of. Wanna talk to you. Wanna hold you. I wanna tell you all my shit."

The gentle wiping up he's doing stops. "You don't have to."

My eyes squeeze tight. Hot tears threaten behind them. Maybe he wouldn't call that a rejection, but it hurts. Or maybe I'm just too fucking emotional after getting fucked like *that*.

I pinch my eyes with my fingers and get myself under control. What comes out is a weak attempt at a joke. "One minute you want it, the next minute you don't... What the fuck am I supposed to do with you?"

He huffs. "Give me a second."

He goes into the bathroom again, and when he comes back, he pulls back the covers and gets into bed. "Come here," he urges.

I shift around, finally managing to wiggle under the covers with him. He's got an open arm I lie on, and he pulls me against his side. I rest my hand on his stomach, lightly tracing the line of dark hair on his lower abs. It's even better and sexier than it was in my daydreams.

He reaches out and turns off the light. I don't think it's all that late, but the sun has set. The streetlight outside his living room puts plenty of light into his bedroom, though. In the outline of the bay window, Bud is sitting up, looking out.

"Shit," I whisper. "Stephanie's all by herself."

"Fuck. You want me to go grab her?"

"Like take a Lyft to my place, pick up the dog, and get a ride back?" I ask in disbelief.

"I mean..."

"No, I'll just...I'll go home in a little bit."

He holds me tighter. "Wish you didn't have to."

"At least you'll be able to sleep," I say. Also, the fact that I have an excuse to go definitely limits my options for launching into the dreary subject of my homosexual origin story. It's not the kind of thing I can just drop and run. I'd lose my mind without talking it out. It's one of those things that requires multiple levels of explanation and probably provokes more questions than it answers.

"Can you come back in the morning?" he asks. "Bring her with you so you don't have to worry about it?"

"Um. Sure," I say, surprised by the request.

"Okay, good." Ryan turns to face me, his leg wrapping

around mine this time before he kisses me like we didn't just have the most intense sex of my life. I touch his face, feeling his jaw move and his lashes flutter. I run my thumb against the grain of the short stubble on his cheek. He pulls away slowly, his hand smoothing circles on my ass. "You feel okay?"

I nod. "You?"

"Yeah. Does it hurt?"

"Now or during?"

"Either?"

"It's intense," I tell him. "You're huge."

"Sorry." He ducks his head, pressing his forehead to mine. Our noses bump and I can't help my small, stupid smile.

"Don't be," I tell him. "I love it."

"You're throwing that word around a lot tonight."

"I said it twice."

"You said it way more than twice."

Maybe. Who knows what the fuck I was saying when he was tunneling through my insides. "Told you it was intense."

His mouth grazes mine in an almost kiss. I follow it up with a real one, only stopping when my cock threatens to thicken again. I guess he follows the *it doesn't count if you say it when you're fucking* rule.

I wonder if it counts when you're doped up on cough syrup.

"Can we start tomorrow like this?" I ask.

"If you want."

I hate that answer. "What do *you* want?"

"For you to let me go get the damn dog so you don't have to sleep by yourself tonight."

This time, I think he might mean it, but that doesn't stop me from double-checking. "Are you being serious?"

"Yeah."

"Okay," I tell him after a long second. "My keys are in my shorts."

"Rest up then, gorgeous. I expect a tip when I get home."

RYAN VALE IS A FUCKING DREAM. My goddamn hero. I love him so much, I can't stand it. I give him such a thorough blow job when he gets home with the dog, it makes us both come. If I could have said anything with his gorgeous cock filling my mouth and throat, it would have been *MINE*, on repeat. He's so blatantly fucking amazing, so hot, it's hard to believe I get to be the one in his bed. After everything I've put him through, *I* get to hear his groans and feel his fingerprints on my scalp. *I* get to drink his cum and listen to all his filthy praise.

I never want to forget today. From the lowest of lows to the highest of highs on one of the prettiest days this city has ever seen, I've got Ryan's smile.

I refuse to let myself fall asleep until he does. Mainly because I want to make sure he does. He spends a lot of time looking at me and running his hands through my hair. I ask him why he didn't sleep the first time I spent the night. He says, "I thought it might be the last time."

I shake my head and kiss the tip of his nose. "No. And this won't be either."

"I feel like I should get a say in that."

I sigh, determined to keep my eyes open as long as he does. "Obviously. But as a point of fact, you were the one who wouldn't let me leave."

"You didn't want to go," he says simply.

"You're fucking exhausting."

Ryan brushes his thumb along one of my eyebrows. "You want me to admit something?"

"Yeah," I say.

"What do you want me to admit?"

"I'm gonna start pulling out your armpit hairs one by one..."

He laughs. "I really, really wanted you to stay."

"Because you wanna fuck me again?" I ask.

"Or I just want eyes on you. Which one is more pathetic?"

"You're not pathetic," I tell him. "I wore Crocs today."

"They made your calves look good," he says.

I kiss him because I can't tell him I love him again. I'm already the king of overkill when it comes to Ryan, and I wasn't kidding about him being intimidating. He still scares the shit out of me in so many ways. Unless he's holding me, in which case everything is pretty much okay.

When I separate my mouth from his, I say, "Go to sleep."

"I will."

"Anything I can do to help?"

"Stop being so beautiful," he says almost too softly to hear.

Almost. "I refuse," I whisper.

"Maybe sleeping is a stupid idea," he says, his tone different, frustrated. "Maybe we should make a snack and watch a movie."

Okay, I'm not sure what's going on here, but for whatever reason, he can't relax with me. He's not restless, he's not uncomfortable, he doesn't want me gone, but there's obviously an issue, and since he spent the last four days avoiding me, I have to assume it's me. I know there's a conversation that needs to be had, but I'm hesitant to ruin this day or even risk it. But the idea of risking tomorrow is worse.

"I don't want to watch a movie," I tell him. "Instead, why don't you put some clothes on and give me something to wear. I wanna talk to you."

"About what?"

"About what I said earlier."

"Which—"

"Just put some fucking pants on." I let go of him and sit up.

He stares at me for a long moment before slowly rolling over and getting out of bed. I follow him to his dresser. He hands me a pair of white briefs. Despite our different builds, we're both medium-sized through the middle.

I pull mine on, not used to wearing anything other than boxer briefs—not since I was a child anyway—so I take a second to check myself out in his full length mirror. "My ass looks amazing."

He glances over as he's pulling his pants up. Even in the dim light, I notice his gaze heat. "Pants too." I hold out my hand.

He tosses me some gray flannel pajama pants with a navy plaid print. They look like part of a set. Like something Jill would get him for Christmas. He's got on a much sexier pair of sweats, but the important part is I won't be quite as tempted to grab onto his cock and stuff it back in my mouth.

"Am I not allowed to touch you either?" he asks.

I'm flattered. "Don't be crazy. Come beanbag with me."

After a long stare he ends by shaking his head in defeat, Ryan crosses the room to the beanbag chair. He sits first, and I straddle his lap, wanting to look at him.

"What's this about?" he asks, settling his hands on my upper thighs.

"Why can't you sleep?" Okay, that's a copout, but I've got to warm up to this. It would really help if he came out and asked me why I'm all of a sudden so eager to take a cock up my ass.

"I guess it'd be stupid to say I keep wondering what your angle is."

Thank God. That's damn near close enough. I shake my head. "No. I changed overnight, and I know why, and you don't."

"You said it wasn't overnight."

"It wasn't, but I get how it looks like that, and why it might be keeping you up."

His eyes warm as he tilts his head and looks up at me. The

expression is so affectionate, it makes me want to keep doing whatever I'm doing right.

Talk. Keep talking, Malcolm.

"So...this is partly about my mom."

His hands move to wrap around my hips, getting a better hold on me, which I can't describe how much I appreciate. "Okay."

I'm so fucking nervous. I've never said any of this out loud. I don't know if I've ever put these particular thoughts into words. It's images mainly and feelings that only started to make sense when Ryan pushed me against the wall, and I realized I *wanted* him to kiss me. I take a shaky breath. "And my mom's cousin."

CHAPTER TWENTY-ONE

MALCOLM

The near murderous look on Ryan's face has me rushing my next words. "I told you no one hurt me. I wasn't hurt. There was no touching or molesting or anything like that. I promise this isn't anything like that."

"Okay," he breathes out evenly, a hint of veiled rage still underpinning his tone.

"I promise. I've been in therapy since I was eight. Same therapist. I mean, she doesn't know about *this*, but she'd know if I was abused or whatever, and I wasn't. Not like that. Not like anything really. Honestly, this is so fucking embarrassing."

"Who was the cousin?"

"William. His name was William."

"Was?"

I shrug. "I haven't seen him since her funeral."

And I still remember the hug he gave me that day as he left the graveside to go to his car and disappear. *"Hang in there, sweet boy. Remember she loved you so much,"* he'd said.

"And he never touched you?" Ryan asks.

"No...I like... It was more that I had a crush on him. He was nice to me."

"How nice?"

"Just nice," I tell Ryan. "He'd hug me and bring me Pokémon cards. He'd pick me up from school sometimes, and we'd throw a football or play catch or whatever. He was just like—my mom's cousin who I liked, and I wanted him to like me, too."

"How old was he?"

"Maybe our age. Twenty-five-ish. I don't remember what he did for a living, but something in healthcare. He always had scrub pants on when he'd pick me up from school. He was one of those guys that was good at everything. He taught me to play chess and cards and all the rules of all the sports. He was at our house a lot."

"But he didn't live there?" Ryan asks.

"Honestly, I'm not really sure. He might have for a while. There was definitely a room I thought of as Will's room."

"A room, huh?"

I look Ryan in the eyes for the first time since I started talking. "Not the metaphor room. That literally was just a metaphor."

"Then what does he have to do with anything?"

"I just said. I had a crush on him. Like a crush."

"You were how old?"

"Young. I was little."

"How was it a crush?" Ryan asks. "Sounds like hero worship."

I rub my face. I might be sick. Inhaling deeply, I try to translate all the uncomfortable images in my head into words. A question comes out instead. "How'd you learn about sex?"

He scowls in that way he does when he's baffled or annoyed or focused. "Um...my mom had the talk with me when I was ten, I think. Around the time they were teaching it in school."

"You hadn't run across any porn at that point? No sex scenes in regular movies?"

"No, and my mom wouldn't let me anywhere near the internet. You remember how she was."

"What about from kids at school?"

He scowls at me. "What kids? I didn't have as many friends as you did. No one who would show me porn for sure. Did you?"

I shake my head. "Not in grade school, no. But I knew about sex."

"Since when?"

That's when I come out with it. "I walked in on my mom and Will doing it when I was seven."

Ryan's eyes widen. "She was fucking her *cousin*?"

I nod.

"Like they were actually related?"

"Yeah. He was her aunt's son."

"Oh. Damn."

Yeah, talking about this is weird. Go figure. I've never been more grateful for the fact that Ryan never met my mother. "I didn't understand what was happening the first time I saw it. They were wearing clothes, mostly, so all I could see looked like a hug. Like a really good, full-body hug. Anyway, when I saw them like that, I asked if I could have a hug, too." I swallow hard, remembering the way they reacted. Like I'd opened fire on them. I remember Will coming at me, putting his pants together, and guiding me by the shoulder out of the room.

I remember my mom wailing.

I remember Will's flushed face as he knelt down to talk to me. "Will told me that sometimes adults hug differently, and he was sorry I saw that."

One might assume that since they'd been caught, they'd stop, or at least be more discreet, but that's not what happened.

"I watched them a lot," I tell Ryan.

"It happened more than once?" he asks, shocked.

I nod. "A few times a week."

"Why did you watch?"

"I was just trying to understand. You know—what was so different about grown up hugs."

"It didn't upset you?" he asks.

"It upset me a lot," I admit.

"Your dad didn't know?"

"I don't know. I never said anything."

"How could you keep that to yourself, though?"

"I mean, I didn't. I talked to my mom about it."

Ryan looks even more freaked out. I feel compelled to remind him, "I was seven. Granted, she didn't know I was sneaking around to watch them every chance I got, she just thought I caught them the one time and they were dressed that time, so..."

"What did she have to say for herself?" he asks.

"She said something along the lines of the way Will loved her was special. I can't remember exactly how she put it, but I remember how I felt about it."

"How *did* you feel about it?"

"Jealous," I admit, finally. "I was really fucking jealous."

Ryan's jaw looks painfully tight, and I want to rub the muscles in it to get it to relax. He says, "I'm really trying hard not to assume or jump to conclusions, so...spell it out if you can."

"I asked her why Will wouldn't hug me like that."

"Jesus."

"What?" I ask. "What are you thinking?"

"Did you realize what they were doing by the time you asked her that?"

I nod. I realized it the second time when they were naked. When I saw *everything*. Will's naked body, his cock, his ass. When I heard the way he moaned when he was inside her. The way he held her and rocked himself against her. When I wished I *were* her because she sounded happy. He could make her laugh and gasp in surprise. He made her purr with contentment and say things like *you feel so good*.

And I thought if the kind of hug *I* got from him felt good—the kind she was getting must be even better. I was so fucking jealous of her.

And I was mad at her because she wouldn't share.

"I mean, I didn't know they were engaging in an act of adultery or that it could result in pregnancy, but I saw they were close, and it looked like it felt really good for both of them, and it gave me a funny feeling in my stomach."

"And now?"

I sigh. "Well, now I think I had to have been a pretty fucked up kid to be looking forward to watching someone fuck my mom."

"Jesus, Mal."

"I've always cared more about what guys think of me than girls," I say, moving off the ugly topic that created my reality and had no small part in shoring up my sexual identity.

Ryan narrows his gaze. "I guess that tracks."

"Does it track with anything else you can think of?"

"You mean me and you?"

I nod.

"Is this what you meant about being inappropriately physical? Because you weren't."

"Wasn't I?" I ask. "Do all preteen boys snuggle together to watch TV? Or wonder what it would feel like naked?"

He gives me a suspicious look. "Is that what you were thinking about? Because you never said anything. Not about sex or porn. Nothing, Mal."

"Will you hate me if I say I thought about it a lot?"

His eyes widen. "You...? Okay..."

"Is it?" I ask, not knowing what to make of the incredulous expression on his face.

"I just want to understand," he says.

"That answer makes me sick to my stomach," I admit.

"Is Will the reason you say you're not straight?"

"Partly," I say. "Will and everything after."

"Including me?" Ryan asks.

"Yes."

"But—"

"Listen," I interrupt him. "You weren't Will. You were a kid, and he was an adult. It didn't start out like that for me with you."

"Was it ever?" He sounds dubious, and I get it.

"It's *always* like that for me. By the time I realized what sex actually entailed, it wasn't long until I heard about how guys could do it with each other, which meant Will lied, and that's another whole mess of fucked up, but a bunch of the kids I hung out with in junior high all had older siblings with access to porn, and it was kind of all I thought about."

Ryan goes from looking troubled, then confused, then annoyed. "So, what the fuck happened?"

"Well, around the time I was regularly getting boners every time you touched me, was about the time my friends started calling guys fags and making being gay sound like it was disgusting and wrong."

He sighs heavily. "What the fuck am I supposed to do with this?"

I think it's a rhetorical question, so I don't answer. I start to move off his lap, but he holds me in place. "Wait," he mutters, but doesn't tell me what I'm waiting for.

I pretend he's piecing together the room metaphor, hoping he remembers it well enough for any of this to start making sense. For *me* to make sense.

"What about Kaylin?" he finally asks.

"What about her?"

"Does she know any of this?"

"No. I've never told anyone this."

"Other than your therapist," he says, like he's speaking for me.

"No. Not her either."

"Why not?" he asks.

"Because it's fucked up?"

"Isn't that what therapists are for?" he asks.

"It might not seem like it at the moment, but I do have some dignity I'd like to keep intact. Telling my therapist I wanted my mom's cousin to satisfy me sexually isn't exactly the kind of thing that would reassure her I'm adjusting well."

"You couldn't possibly have understood that at the time."

"No," I agree. "But I understood enough. And I definitely understood it with you."

He blushes. Full on, red cheeks, blushes. I don't take it as necessarily positive.

"So what was the problem?" he asks. "What stopped you?"

"I thought I was vile, Ryan. I thought I'd lose you if you knew."

"But..." he trails off, and I have a feeling he's thinking about what he told me that day. When he had the flu.

"Fantasy and reality were two different things. I was old enough to understand that, too. I could want something—but if what I wanted was unacceptable, then it couldn't become a reality."

He presses his lips together and looks down. I can't see his eyes anymore. His hair falls to obscure his face.

"I don't want to fight this anymore," I say quietly. "I don't want to fight anymore, period."

"So, you're gay."

There's not much room to argue it. "Yeah. I'm gay."

His hair flips back, and I get the annoyed look again. "Then what the fuck was the deal with Kaylin?"

"I can't possibly be the first gay teenager who tried like hell not to be."

"And then what?" he asks. "I showed up with a decent haircut, and it all clicked?"

"Yeah," I say simply. And I wish it really were that simple.

He scoffs at that. Understandably.

"I might need some time with this," he says.

It's the last thing I want to hear, but it doesn't come as a surprise. "You want me to go?"

"No...not really."

I climb off his lap, and he allows it this time. I sit beside him so he doesn't have to look at me if he doesn't want to.

He turns my way anyway, lying sideways in the chair and sighing heavily. "Listen. I wanna be honest with you. I'm not planning to stay in San Francisco," he says. "This is a sublet. The plan is to leave at the end of summer. The end of the internship."

I take this in without reacting immediately. I let each word settle as they pelt me. My eyes start blinking beyond my control. My stomach takes a very unpleasant turn. He's speaking in present tense. "Why?" I ask, but it comes out as a whisper.

"There's someone I've been interested in. She lives in Seattle. I thought I'd take a chance. See what happens."

"You said you didn't have a girlfriend."

"I don't. It's not like that yet."

The "yet" is excruciating. I rub my face, covering my mouth for a few seconds to make sure nothing's going to come up. "Okay," I finally say.

"Is it?" he asks.

"If that's what you want." Props to internal screams. They're super quiet.

"You broke the fuck out of me," he says quietly.

I clench my jaw and nod, taking it.

He goes on to say, "I've never wanted anyone the way I want you."

"If you want me to cry, you're getting pretty close to making that happen."

"No, Mal, that's not what I want. But when I said we needed to talk, I meant both of us."

Swallowing hard, I say, "You've been acting like you wanted to win the challenge. Like you want a job at the firm."

"At the Seattle branch," he says.

"Oh." I forgot there were other branches.

"But as a reminder," he says, "You *do* have a girlfriend."

I shut my eyes. "It's over," I say weakly.

"Does she know that?"

"What difference does it make?" I ask, feeling truly hopeless.

"I mean, nothing's written in stone," he says.

"But you don't trust me," I say.

"I want to."

My head shakes. "Not the same thing."

"No," he says. "I know it's not."

"So, what do you want me to do?" I ask.

"I like the honesty."

"Really? Because it feels like it totally backfired for me."

"It's only July, Mal."

"Are you saying—what are you saying?"

"I don't want to fight anymore either," he says.

I don't want to hear what he doesn't want, but maybe his inability to tell me what he actually wants is a relic of the way I broke him. "You're not kicking me out, right?"

"No."

"Then let's go to bed," I say. I don't know if I can talk anymore.

"Are you sure?" he asks.

"Why wouldn't I be?" I'm on the verge of pouting. I get up and take the two steps to the bed, throwing back the covers and getting in. It takes Ryan a minute, but he joins me. Pants on and everything. I hate it, and I'm more than ready to escape to sleep now that the perfect day is so obviously fucking over.

CHAPTER TWENTY-TWO

RYAN

It's too soon to reconsider everything I planned for my life, and much too early to tell him I still love him. I always knew my feelings for Malcolm ran deep. Bone deep. He's in my marrow, and over the years he's made me, and he's broken me. Love, hate, it's all passion. When he hurts, he hurts like being eaten alive. But when he feels good—Jesus. Pure euphoria.

Worse, the capacity for me to hold these feelings is limitless. I know because I love him even more for everything we just experienced together—everything we just said. What it feels like he and I found tonight is beyond any closeness or connection I've ever experienced. Because of that, touching him feels spiritual. The next time we have sex might be fucking transcendent. And this is all so dangerous. Delusional maybe.

I don't want to become my own cautionary tale but just fucking look at him. Sleepy, hooded eyes, the mess of his hair that somehow looks perfect. The light stubble on his cheeks and jaw. The anxious chewing on his lip and the small crease in his brow. This must be how Bud feels about catnip. I want to lie down in a field of him.

I wrap a hand around the back of his neck and maneuver

him onto his side, facing me. "Don't overthink it, okay? Nothing good happens when you overthink something."

Malcolm grimaces. "It's kind of my brand, though."

"I'm not sure I knew that about you."

"You should by now," he says.

"The picture's clearing up."

"Do you hate it?" he asks.

Hate it? Vulnerable, beautiful, pouty, fawning, *gay* Malcolm?

"No." I press my lips to his. "But it definitely looks different up close."

"Sounds like you hate it."

I shake my head slowly, staring at his face.

"Would you rather I was straight?" he asks.

"No," I say, surprised by the question. "I just hate that you thought you had to hide this from me. From everyone."

"I would do a lot of things differently if I got a do-over."

"Like what?"

"Like not treated you like shit," he mumbles.

"If you can forgive me, I can forgive you," I tell him, meaning it. Or at least, willing to attempt it.

He sighs. "You shouldn't."

"I think I might try anyway," I tell him. "If that's okay with you."

His hand wraps around my arm in a soft caress. It gives me chills. He says, "I wanna ask if trust comes with forgiveness."

"Trust is..." I stare into his amazing eyes. Do I know what trust looks like when it comes to him? It's not something that comes naturally to me in any circumstance. I've been made a fool of too many times. "Complicated for me."

"I trust *you*," he says, not like it's a competition, more like an assurance. "Thanks for being honest with me about the summer."

"Thanks for saying...everything."

His gaze drops away from mine. "I know it was weird."

"Not for me," I tell him. "It's just hard to imagine what it was like for you."

"You shouldn't overthink *that*."

"I'm relieved no one hurt you."

"No. I only ever hurt myself," he says.

His words give me a sense of unease, like the first rumble of an earthquake. "Is that what you're doing now?"

He sighs, his eyes blinking a few times before meeting mine again. "I don't know, Ryan. Is it?"

I frown. "What do you mean?"

"Are you planning to keep hooking up with me?" he asks.

"Obviously I'd like to."

"It's not obvious," he states. "Nothing about you is obvious. So, what does it look like in your head? A summer fling or whatever?"

The idea of Malcolm Walsh thinking I can reduce him to something as fleeting as a fling makes me think I haven't shown him how important his willingness to spend *any* amount of time with me outside work is. However—I'm not ready to call this a relationship. Not even close. Right now, I want my best friend back, and I see him in front of me again for the first time in too many years. And if sex is part of our new dynamic—the evolution of the innocent snuggling we used to do? Fucking bonus.

I get how friends with benefits is portrayed in general. That someone's always more invested than the other. But I'm a cautious investor. Risk isn't something I like to dabble in. The idea of putting my love out in the open again is a risk I'm not willing to take—not while he's in flux.

I'm not without misgivings either. I'm certainly in love with him, but there's a part of me that wonders—and this is the part of me that's only ever been with women—whether being with a man will be enough for me. While I've never had a long-term, romantic relationship with a woman, this thing I have going on with Norah has managed to heal a lot of old wounds. Wounds inflicted by boys and men and high school mean girls.

The opportunity to develop a relationship with a mature woman who's probably never been any meaner than an occasional private gossip session, fells like a real chance to move on from this old, doomed crush. I haven't been *pining*, per se. I'm a fucking realist. But when he's right here—looking at me like this —my goddamn soul wants to intertwine with his. There's a sense of never being able to be close enough.

But is that really what I *need*?

I can want him. I can even love him. But in order to change my plans, my future, I shouldn't be able to picture my life without him in it, but something in my mind won't let me go there. I keep coming back to Kaylin. Their decade long relationship as evidenced by the dog who's now sleeping on the beanbag chair because Mal left her there staring after him longingly.

At any rate, I can't think past tomorrow, much less the rest of the summer. I'll see how we get along if he agrees to hang out for the day, and then maybe I'll have a better sense of what's possible.

But in terms of the other question he keeps asking me— what do I want? I want to be sure of him. Even if it's just as a friend, I want to be sure I can count on him to be there.

"Can we play it by ear?" I ask.

"Are you always like this?" is his follow up question.

"Like what?"

"Like afraid to commit to anything? I only ask because—well —it sounds like it, and I'm the same way."

"I wouldn't say I fear commitments, no."

"Just me, then."

"I'm not afraid of you either," I say, before realizing it's not true. He's got a piece of me. A chunk, really, but when we're lying here like this, it doesn't feel like it's missing. If we were to lose touch again, or worse—turn on each other again—I'm not sure I'd ever feel this complete. "Okay—maybe a little. What do you want me to commit to?"

"Just be honest with me," he says with a defeated sigh. "And if you ever find yourself doing something because you're feeling sorry for me—like buying me dinner for instance—don't."

"Hey," I say. "Is that fair? That's not what that was about."

"So, if I'd shown up at Bailey's wearing normal shoes and acting like nothing was wrong, you still would have wanted to have dinner?"

I hate that I don't know the answer to that. The bottom line is, dinner was great, and it was something *I* really needed. I let his neck go and roll onto my back. He doesn't make a move to get closer. Fine. Whatever. We can see what this looks like in the morning—*if* he stays. I'm not gonna fucking force him. God forbid he thinks I feel sorry for him—that I have an ounce of compassion.

"I had a good time at dinner," I say to the ceiling. "If you didn't, just say no next time."

"There's gonna be a next time?"

"Oh, fuck off, Mal." I flip over again, giving him my back.

"I did have a good time," he says.

"Then why are you acting like I was bending over backwards to do some favor for you?"

"Were you?"

"Why are you asking?"

"Because," he says, sounding as frustrated as I am. "You've been really hard to read, and I don't want you thinking you need to throw me a bone because I had a rough few days."

"No? So you'd rather I didn't go pick up the dog?"

"No. I love that you picked up the dog. I'm pretty sure I let you know how much."

If he's referring to having him on his knees sucking my dick while I sat on the edge of the bed thrusting into his throat, then yes. He showed more than enough gratitude. I wish he hadn't brought that up. It's gonna make me hard again, and I'm determined to prove I can sleep with him in the same bed. "Then what is this about?"

"I guess what I'm saying is you scare the shit out of me. Meaning you make me really fucking nervous, so don't be surprised if I keep fucking up."

"You haven't fucked up at all," I argue.

"That's not what it feels like."

I groan. I'm done talking. This is going nowhere. "Look, I turned over because I don't know if I can sleep with you all up in my face."

"Does spooning count?" he asks.

Spooning requires a cock against an ass. Pants or not, where there's friction, there's fire. But if it shuts him up…

Without a word, I turn toward him again, give him a look, and he turns away from me. I stuff one arm underneath his pillow, wrap the other around his waist, and tuck my bent legs against his.

He slides his hand up and down my forearm and lets out a long breath. There's a shakiness to it that makes me believe him when he says I make him nervous. I don't mind because it levels the playing field. I wouldn't call the way I get when he's around anxious, exactly, but out of sorts, maybe? Fucked up? Confused.

And now, as I very much suspected I would be once I got this close to him, aroused.

It doesn't take much. My dick against his ass. One slight squirm of him getting situated in my arms, and I'm ready to dry hump him.

He turns his head to look at me, and I stare back with narrowed eyes. "What?"

"Nothing," he says. "Good night."

"You good?" I ask.

"Yeah. You?"

"Sure."

"If you get uncomfortable, let me know. We can adjust," he says.

"Thanks," I say.

He settles his head on the pillow, shifting his ass slightly against my cock again. I bite my lip so I don't hiss.

I close my eyes and try to ignore the fact that his hole is *right there*. I have plenty of things to think about. A podcast script for example. I could think about that. Topics we should cover. What dynamic we want to aim for. Guests we could have. All things I can talk with him about tomorrow. Surely it won't be this difficult to concentrate once I've had some coffee and we have an agenda to tick through.

But what if he sits on my lap again? Why do I like when he does that so much? What's so hot about him straddling my thighs? What is it about that one move that flips a switch in my head from thinking of him as my childhood nightmare to my filthiest fantasy?

What would it be like to fuck him like that? Pounding up into him while he looks down at me and I can see every expression on his face.

"Need something?" he asks, likely in response to my actively twitching erection.

"It's fine."

"If you say so." Then he just comes out and asks. "Did you wanna go another round?"

"I'm pretty comfortable, but I won't push you away."

He laughs softly. "I don't know why you're making this so difficult."

I deep breathe. Then I do it again. Then one more time. "I wasn't exactly easy on you earlier."

"Did I complain?"

"If I can't control myself..."

"What?" he asks.

"You said I scare you," I remind him.

"I didn't say your dick scared me."

I bury my nose in his hair. "I don't think it's a good idea to do it twice in one night."

"If you're not gonna do it, then at least tell me how much you want to."

Despite the tumult in my head and my throbbing dick, I grin. I like this. It's permission to speak freely, but I remind myself the topic is sex, not our relationship. "You want me to talk dirty to you?"

"Mmhm."

"You want me to tell you how much my cock is dying to get back inside that hot, tight hole. How bad I want to stroke that spot inside you that makes you leak?"

He groans softly, ass pressing into my crotch harder. "Yeah, you can talk about that more if you want."

I rest a hand on his pec, noticing his erect nipple beneath my palm. "How it feels like you're strangling me and swallowing me at the same time?"

"Is that what it feels like?"

"Yeah." I give his chest a squeeze. "Feels so fucking good." My hips move, my cock sliding up and down his crack. What would that feel like between his bare cheeks with some lube? Fuck, that'd be good, too...Not to mention how hot it would look.

"Opening me wide and stretching me out?" he asks.

"Fuck yeah. Your pretty ass looks so goddamn good taking my cock."

"Your huge cock."

"My big, fat cock."

"Ryan..." He pushes at my forearm, then makes sure my hand finds how hard he's straining against the flannel pants. "I'm not a shoe. You don't need to break me in."

"You've gotta be sore, though."

"Not as sore as the first time."

"Mm..." I groan as I grind myself harder against him. "You're asking to get fucked again."

"No," he breathes harshly, rubbing his cock against my hand. "I'm *begging* you to fuck me again."

"You gonna take me raw like last time?"

"Always."

Nothing in me is able to resist the words or the feel of him. "Then show me that pretty hole. Let's make sure it's ready for this big, hard dick."

"Oh, God," he moans, tugging at his waistband.

I reach back for the lube.

Once his naked ass is exposed, I take hold of his bare hip.

"Jerk yourself while I open you up," I tell him as I slide down his body to soften and stretch him with my mouth.

His groan is unholy. It's a sound I crave deep, deep in my bones.

"Why is that so good?" he whispers.

"Because you're a filthy slut." I spit on his hole and run my tongue along his rim. My dick jerks hard in my pants. I reach down and set it free, stroking it as I continue to suck and tongue him. I move to get his balls into my mouth, trying to decide unsuccessfully what my favorite part of him is.

"Fuck...*Ryan*..." he whines. "I love that. I love you. I need you so bad."

The way he runs his mouth will never not fuck me up just a little bit. But I do love the way he responds to literally everything I do with rampant enthusiasm. So perfectly fucking *needy*.

"You're gonna make me come. You always make me come so fucking fast. *Shit*," he pants, like he's desperately trying to hang on to the edge.

I go ahead and put some lube on my fingers, testing his opening in case it's swollen again.

It is, but the sound he makes when I slide two fingers in instantly tells me he wants more. "Fuck yes. Christ that feels so fucking good. Right there, oh my god." His thigh slides forward to open himself wider. Letting go of his cock, he grabs his ass cheek and spreads himself.

The sight, even in the dim room sends a shock of lust through me. I add a third finger.

"More," he says. "More. Please. *You*."

After biting his lower ass cheek hard, I hold him open wide as I readjust my body. Finger fucking him and lubing my cock at the same time isn't the easiest thing I've ever accomplished, but I manage. I'm so goddamn hard, it's killing me not to be inside him.

"I'm ready," he pleads. "Fuck me with that perfect dick."

"You want this fat cock in your tight, slutty pussy?" God, help me. He's turning me into an animal.

He moans, gripping his ass harder to show off his hole where my fingers are still moving in and out. "Yes. Fuck. So wet for you. Please. Jesus."

Okay, that's fucking irresistible. Later, I might wonder how many of Mal's soft kinks are related to his bizarre sexual awakening, but speaking as a man who's only ever been with women before him, this particular kink aligns nicely with mine. Not that I'm pretending he's a woman. I fully appreciate the fact that his cock is as hard as mine is and dripping precum all over my sheets.

But as someone who's more or less bisexual, he's offering me a small taste of both worlds in a way only he can. Because he's the only man I want. The only *person* I've ever truly wanted with my body and soul.

Lining up my slippery cock with his hole, I take hold of his writhing hip and hold him still just long enough to stuff myself inside him.

His growl is deep as he buries his face in the pillow beneath him. All his muscles clench, like taking me is a battle he has to brace for. My hand slides to his abs as I do my best to hold still and let him adjust. I stroke his belly in smooth circles, kissing his shoulder in a way that totally belies my need to pound roughly into him.

"Okay?" I ask.

"Feels so goddamn good," he gasps.

I'm not sure I believe him, but I'm not really in a position to argue. Holding my cock still in his snug, hot asshole is fucking *agonizing*. I give him a slight thrust, and he grunts again, this time with a punched-out "fuck yeah."

Testing a theory, I give his ass a light slap as I shove in deeper.

He quivers, practically mewling as he starts jerking his cock again.

I knock his hand away and take over, my hand still damp with lube. With that, he drops his head back, giving me access to his neck, and surrenders to my takeover of his body.

His skin is hot when my lips make contact. I thrust slowly and jerk him in time. "You like that it hurts, don't you?"

"It doesn't—*yes*," he says, like he can't bother with bullshit anymore. "It's a good hurt, though. So fucking good. Fuck."

"Want me to stop going easy on you, beautiful?" I ask.

"Please, yes. I want you to use me to get yourself off. I wanna be everything you need."

When he puts it that way...

It doesn't take much with Mal. Getting myself inside him is all it takes for me to hit the edge. If he told me to come right this second, I absolutely could. It's lucky I already came twice tonight though, because my stepbrother wants to be *used*.

Closing my eyes and keeping my mouth on his neck, I lose myself in the sensation of sliding back and forth in his perfectly clenching hole while he moves with me. I cover his pec to palm one of his pornographic nipples while I seek the edge of my orgasm without going over. I fuck him slowly, rocking my hips and squeezing his cock from base to tip.

I wish I could say I last longer. I wish I could say I'm immune to the sounds he makes, the words and pants and curses erupting in a steady stream from his perfect mouth, but the truth is he turns me on like a fucking power plant and then some. Too soon, my balls are so full, and my body is so lit up, that when he comes with a cry, and I feel the first gush of his load coating my hand, I detonate.

Fucking without a condom is crazy intense. The sensation of sliding through my own cum has me needing to spill every last drop inside him.

His slutty ass is all too willing to take it.

It makes him the sexiest person to have ever graced my bed, and fuck me because I never want to let him go.

We're both still shaking when I pull out, and I feel the window for sleep open wide.

He peeks over his shoulder when he hears me yawn.

I use his discarded pants to gently wipe him up, then flip his boneless body over to face me. Wrapping my arms and legs around him, I feel his heavy, contented sigh against my chest.

"It gets better every time," he says.

"Shut up," I say before giving him a long, deep kiss where I feel him laugh faintly before kissing me back.

"You don't think so?" he asks, when I pull away with my eyes still closed.

"I do think so. I thought you wanted me to sleep."

His hand moves through my hair and he plants a soft kiss to my forehead. "Good night, Ry."

"Night, Mal," I say and happily surrender to sleep.

MY BRAIN WAITS until the sun comes up to start second-guessing. Why I can't just let myself enjoy this, I have no idea, but here I am, determined to find something wrong. The only time those thoughts go quiet is when we're messing around. When I've got him fastened to some part of me.

Out of a sense of self-preservation, I get out of bed before he wakes. I shower alone. I know I'm running the risk of pissing him off or *hurting his feelings,* but once again, I feel the need to scale this back. *This* meaning whatever's going on between us. I need time to process and think, and whether he realizes it or not, he needs it at least as much as I do.

I've never been the impulsive one of the two of us, and I can't shake the sense he's headed for some kind of crisis over his sexuality. What he told me last night makes sense—the dots connect—but sometimes what we physically enjoy isn't what we need to live a happy life.

Sometimes, it's the exact opposite.

He does look annoyed when he wakes up to find me fully dressed and working at my desk, but he takes himself to the shower without complaint and emerges walking only a little funny. "Has Stephanie been out?"

"Yeah," I tell him. "And I got you a smoothie."

"You did?"

"It's in the fridge."

He frowns but leaves the bedroom. When he returns, he's slurping the hell out of the peanut butter banana smoothie I knew he'd like. "This is amazing."

"You're welcome."

"What are you working on?"

"Ideas for the YouTube. Do you know how hard it is to make 401Ks entertaining?"

"That's what you want to talk about?" he asks, taking a seat on the beanbag chair. I notice he's leaning on his left hip, like his hole hurts. I scowl at that but return my gaze to the computer screen. *Why does he want it if it hurts?*

Why do I care if he has a sore ass? I certainly didn't give a fuck last night. But I was careful, wasn't I?

Maybe I have some things to learn about anal sex. It's not like I've ever done it before. Already dreading *that* Reddit search.

I answer his question. "I mean, I know people are looking to get rich quick, but we're trying to give *good* advice, right?"

"Could we do like a good cop bad cop thing?"

"Meaning what?" I ask.

"Like you hand out conservative money-making strategies, and I counter with 'but if you wanna make a few bucks fast...' That kind of thing."

"You want people to watch us arguing?"

"You asked how to make it entertaining."

"I guess," I mumble, making a note on my ever-growing spreadsheet. "I should send this to Bailey." I also need to mention the conversation I had with Miguel, but since I haven't heard from him this weekend, maybe things have smoothed out between him and his team.

"How soon do you think she'll want us to get started?" Mal asks.

"Soon," is my guess. If we're going to build off the TikTok

momentum—especially now that Piper's getting her hands into it—we need to diversify our audience before someone else comes along and starts doing what we're doing better. Not that I'm worried that person will be Piper, but the more attention we get, the more people will hop on the trend. "We have to establish dominance," I say.

"You shouldn't have any problem with that," he says, making it sound loaded.

"Yeah, well...we both know you can take me."

Mal laughs, and I slide a glance his direction. He looks incredible. The smile. The wet hair. My t-shirt hugging his chest and a pair of sweats I don't remember having. He must have really been digging through the drawers. His exposed ankles and bare feet catch my attention. I think I might have a fetish or something. I drool for the sight of his skin.

While I consider whether I want to tackle him and pin him to the bed, both our phones ping with a message from our group text with Bailey.

I open mine first and see the TikTok link. This time, Piper stitched one of *my* videos. Mal and I watch as she pointedly uses a makeup blender and picks apart my explanation of the commodities market in laymen's terms. She dismisses it as simplistic and once again tries to make herself sound smarter by using fifty-cent words and speaking way over the heads of a TikTok audience.

"What the fuck is this?" Malcolm asks. "Are they doing the same thing?"

I forgot he didn't know about this. "I think it's just Piper. I'm trying to talk Bailey into picking her off."

"You told Bailey you wanted her to put makeup on?"

I laugh. "No." I explain my idea about skin care and involving Calyx.

"When do *I* get to meet Calyx?" Mal asks.

"You want to?"

"You talk about him all the time," he says with a pout in his voice.

"I don't actually think I do."

"Do you think he's hot?" he asks.

I try to hide my smile. "I think he's confusing."

"Because he looks like a girl?"

"He doesn't, though. That's why it's confusing. Do you think he's hot?"

Mal makes a dismissive sound. "No. Not my type."

"You have a type now?"

He cocks his head and stares at me.

"Is it the tattoos or the shoulders?" I ask, making the decision to enjoy this.

"Neither."

"Then what?"

"I'm not telling you why you're attractive," he says. "Dream on."

"You wanna know why you are? Would that help?"

He laughs. "No."

"It's your nipples," I say.

He grabs the nearest pillow and tosses it at me. I catch it easily and stand, tossing it back before I tackle him to the bed. He struggles, sort of—as much as a person can when his natural instinct seems to be to wrap his legs around my waist.

I kiss him hard, driving his head into the mattress as I grind my cock against his. We're both half-hard already, and as we kiss, it only takes a few seconds to form full erections.

"I should message Bailey," I say when I break away to take a breath.

"You're thinking about Bailey right now?"

"Just wanna stay on track. Money's not gonna make itself."

He grabs my ass and makes me thrust against him, gnawing at my chin with his teeth. "I didn't throw *myself* onto the bed."

"But you were asking for it."

"I wasn't."

I shove up his shirt, exposing his chest. "You were making me think about your nipples."

He laughs and then yelps when I bite down on one. Soothing the sting with my tongue, I rub my cock against his relentlessly. Our phones ping with the group text again, but we ignore them in favor of moving further up the bed and shedding our clothes.

CHAPTER TWENTY-THREE

MALCOLM

I can't stop thinking about fucking. Ryan was stingy yesterday, and I got laid a grand total of twice. Once in the morning and one more time when we took a shower before bed. I did get to sleep over again, but I left early this morning to go back to my apartment and get ready for work. It's for the best anyway since he walks to work with Jia, and it's not like I'm not going the exact same place.

I wind up in the elevator with Miguel and a few other people I don't know. He's dressed in one of his usual statement suits, this one in a stunning garnet. He's sneaking looks at me like he wants to say something and keeps chickening out.

I have no relationship with him whatsoever, so I don't help him out. I pretend not to notice. Now that I'm in the building, I'm remembering Piper's shitty attempt at undermining our project, and since he's on her team, I've got nothing to say to him.

That all changes when I follow him into the conference room, he makes a beeline for Ryan, and they immediately leave together. Suddenly, I have plenty to say. To both of them.

Bailey doesn't seem to notice, only gives me a once over

when I sit next to her. "You look better," she says. "You and Ryan make up?"

"We're fine," I tell her. "What's he talking about with Miguel?"

She shrugs, her gaze shifting to the door where Nathan and Piper are coming in. I don't miss the look Piper shoots in Bailey's direction. It's smug. Derisive.

"What's her problem with you?" I ask.

"No clue. Maybe she's one of those girls who thinks everybody wants to have sex with her. Like in this case, my best guess is she and Nathan are probably fucking, and she thinks because I'm a lesbian that would make me jealous because obviously I'd want to fuck her, too."

She got a lot from one look.

"Maybe she's just a bitch," I say.

Bailey snorts. "That, too."

"Are you gonna stitch her videos? I liked Ryan's idea."

"I need to be focused on the project—not her petty bullshit."

"You could do it just for fun," I suggest.

"My idea of fun does not include putting my face on the internet."

"I mean literally nothing by this, but do you ever wear makeup?"

She glares at me. "No. Why? You think it'd make me easier to look at?"

"*Noooo*." Did she miss my whole I mean nothing by this thing? "I'm saying something more like you don't have to be yourself when you're on the internet. For all anybody watching knows, you slay in makeup. You could straighten your hair or something—look even less like yourself."

"Look, I know I'm not finance Barbie, but it is so fucking rude to comment on another person's looks."

"You do it to me all the time."

"Oh, like you care what I think about what you look like."

"I'm actually very sensitive," I tell her, sounding like I'm joking, but I'm actually not.

"Golden boy really is the perfect nickname for you," she says.

"Yeah, *you* don't get to call me that."

She arches her brows. "Who does?"

"Mind your own fucking business, Bailey," I say without any heat, and she snickers.

Georgie enters the room, followed by Ryan and Miguel. Miguel has his hand on Ryan's shoulder and is leaning in close to speak into his ear. Either he's a close talker in general or he likes to put his hand on *my guy*. Either way, I hate it.

Ryan is nodding at whatever he's saying as he glances around the table, looking first to the other group, then to Bailey, and finally me. As he takes his usual seat between Nathan and Miguel, he gives me half a grin, but I don't return it. I don't even try. Because I'm a complete psycho, I text him even though we're not supposed to have our phones out during the huddle.

ME

What's going on with you two?

Either he has his notifications off or he's got a perfect poker face because he doesn't blink. I shift in my seat, restless, then wince as I put too much pressure on my hole. Funny how having Ryan's cock in it is no problem, but sitting on it makes me feel like it's being stabbed with a hot poker.

What Georgie's talking about isn't interesting to me with Ryan six feet away, so my mind wanders to butt plugs. Vibrators. Vibrating butt plugs. By the time we wrap up and I have to face Isla, I've got a semi and a hole desperate to be filled.

Ryan and Miguel remain glued together until Charlie waves Ryan over to the couches. Logically, there's nothing wrong with

Ryan talking to other people, and I'd probably be more fucked up if he were talking to whoever that Seattle woman is, but yesterday was special—at least to me.

It was making out in the beanbag chair and a buffet of takeout Chinese food. It was practicing good cop bad cop for the podcast while I kept messing with his hair to annoy him—or get him to touch me. Tackle me. Do whatever he wanted to me.

What's stressful is that he runs so hot and cold. One minute all he wants to do is talk about the project—the next, he's all over me, and I can't tell what I did to get him there. If I had it my way, I'd glue him to me. Our conversations however, since Saturday night, haven't been deep. Not that I'm knocking them, we've laughed a lot, but I don't feel any closer to knowing what makes him tick—or more importantly—what it would take to get him to choose me over Seattle. Which means I have to assume what he told me that night still holds true.

This is just for the summer, and he doesn't know how to trust me. And how the fuck do I overcome that? He doesn't seem to have believed me when I told him I love him. Or he blew it off as a heat of the moment thing. He hasn't said anything close. And I don't count how many times he said he wanted me. I mean—I did count—it was four times—a mere fraction of the times I said it to him—but it's not the same as the feeling of not being able to breathe for the fear of losing him all over again.

Isla is being very short with me today, so I don't ask too many questions. She's been harder on me since I turned into a vapor trail that night at happy hour. I get it. I led her on, and didn't put out. It was a shameful lapse of judgement, both because of Kaylin and because I think I embarrassed Isla, which she didn't deserve.

If she were interested in actually getting to know me, maybe she'd understand, but I get the feeling my mentor is just as big of a mess about what she wants as I am.

I get a return text from Ryan around 9:30 which says he wants to have lunch with me and Bailey and asks if I mind if Miguel joins.

I respond with a totally chill, *What the fuck is going on?*

He responds with, *Meet us at Big Bites.*

Us? *Us?* He and Miguel are an *us?*

There goes what was left of my focus.

At eleven, I get up to grab a coffee. When I pass the unisex bathroom on my way back to the workroom, I hear grunting on the other side of the door. A man's grunt. A *sex* grunt.

I nearly have a heart attack until I find Ryan seated on the couch with Charlie, right where I left him. Isla's missing, though.

I sit down, sip my coffee, and scan the room to see who else isn't here.

No Piper and no Lisette, but their mentors aren't out here either. Nathan is missing, but his mentor is at the communal worktable on a call. There are a few other men unaccounted for, both senior analysts. If someone's fucking in the unisex bathroom, fuck if I can figure out who it is. But damn, it makes me horny knowing it's happening.

I text Ryan that I have a better plan for how to spend our lunch hour.

I can practically feel his smirk when I get his message.

RYAN

Miss me, golden boy?

ME

Do you have a problem with that?

RYAN

I have a problem with the way you keep flashing your ankles

I light the fuck up. He's thinking about me.

ME

Why's that?

RYAN

It makes you look like a slut.

I cross my legs, trying to disguise the hard on rapidly tenting my pants, and also exposing my ankles even more.

ME

I get so hard when you talk like that

RYAN

Then maybe stop texting me at work?

ME

Someone's fucking in the unisex. Should be us.

RYAN

Jesus. Stop.

ME

Can't. My ass needs to be stuffed. Need to touch my dick.

RYAN

Who's in the unisex?

Goddamnit, Ryan. It makes me crazy how impervious he is to me unless I'm literally sitting on top of him. He started this. He was talking about my ankles. How was I supposed to take that besides flirting? I try again.

ME

No clue. Are you hard?

RYAN

I'm trying to work.

ME

Am I distracting you?

RYAN

Obviously.

ME

So are you hard or not?

RYAN

I'll see you at lunch.

If I could find one sliver of myself that still hated him, I would put it to use for that text. But these days, I'm a bonfire of burning love—the operative word being *burning*. This erection —this one-sided erection—is solid and insistent. It's taking all my will power not to touch it in the middle of the workroom. The financial report on my laptop might as well be a faded Sanskrit scroll for all I can decipher it. My brain is parked in neutral, and my dick wants to plow full steam ahead.

Isla returns to the table with a flush on her cheeks and a faint sheen of sweat on her neck.

I glance around the room to see who else is back, but I'm too worked up to remember who was missing in the first place. I stop short of asking her if she was the one being screwed, because it's pretty obvious she was. I'm jealous. Not of whoever had her, but of the fact that she just had a cock inside her from the looks of it.

"We'll need to send a report to Stevenson by three. Where are you at with that?" she asks, and I swear to God, she hasn't even caught her breath yet.

"Struggling," I admit, pathetically.

She sighs. "Risk assessments are part of the job. Even if you don't like analysis, you still need to develop a base level of competence. What are you not understanding?"

Oh, *now* she wants to teach me something? Great. Perfect timing, Isla. I wonder if anyone else's mentor is as chronically checked out of mentoring as mine is.

"It's fine," I mumble. "I think I might need to work someplace quieter. Is there an office or a conference room I can use?" My ADHD and the constant activity in the communal workspace don't go well together. Add in Ryan and covert bathroom sex, and I'm screwed in the worst way when it comes to learning anything.

She looks utterly exasperated with me. "Whatever." She slams her laptop closed and stands. "Well, come on."

Damn. Did she not come or something? There's a pretense of politeness and deference I try to use when I speak with her, but I'm frustrated with how this internship is going for me in general. "I can work alone," I say, just shy of snapping at her, though she didn't give me the same courtesy.

"Can you, though? No offense, Malcolm, but—"

I stand, easily a foot taller than she is, and look down her. "Let me stop you right there. I don't know who just ruined your day in the unisex, but it wasn't me, so why don't you stay here, I'll find a quiet place to work, and I'll message you any questions that might come up."

She gapes, her pale cheeks flushing scarlet. "I don't know what you're talking about."

I shrug. "Me neither. But it's obvious you've got other things on your mind. I'll touch base with you later."

I leave her at the common table in search of an empty office. When I don't find one, I wind up in the lounge. I take a seat in a booth, pull out my phone to ask Google any questions I have, and lock in.

About twenty minutes later, Bailey slides in across from me with a coffee and her laptop. She and I work quietly until I ask her a question about the report I'm trying to write.

She answers it with no judgement. Quick, clear, and concise. A few concepts snap cleanly into place, and I fly through the rest of the report. Is it perfect? I doubt it. Is it good enough?

Bailey gives it a nod after a quick skim. "You got it," she says.

"Thanks."

"What do you think Ryan and Miguel are up to?" she asks.

"Guess we're about to find out," I say after a glance at the time on my phone.

She and I walk together to Big Bites, which is two buildings down from Marks & Baker. Ryan and Miguel are already seated at a table, side by side, waiting for us to join them. On the way, I told Bailey what I overheard in the unisex and my suspicion it was my mentor on the receiving end.

"She's too sexy for her own good," Bailey said to me.

In return, I asked, "Do you think she's got some kind of issue?"

"Liking sex isn't an issue, but when it interferes with your work, it might be time to find a therapist."

Since I already have a therapist, I recognize the need to bring up the situation I have with Ryan to Andrea. I'm not exactly focused in the workplace either. And holy fuck, I hate seeing him sitting next to another man in a booth with their heads ducked together, speaking in low voices.

Bailey scoots into the corner, and I wind up across from Ryan. He sits back and puts a hand on Miguel's back. The hairs on my neck stand up as Miguel gives us a timid smile.

I narrow my eyes, physically unable to return it.

"What's up?" Bailey asks Miguel directly.

"I'm wondering if there's room for me on your team."

Oh for fuck's sake. I slouch in the booth and glare at Ryan, who spares me a quick glance and continues to explain. "He majored in communications before he got his MBA."

"I've also got a YouTube channel," Miguel adds.

"Oh yeah? About what?" Bailey asks while I remain silent.

"I used to do movie and TV show reviews. Like breakdowns and analysis. I quit when I got into grad school, but I have a lot of equipment and a dedicated office space at my apartment."

"And experience with editing—all the stuff we don't know much about," Ryan adds.

I finally speak up. "Why do you want to leave your team?"

Miguel and Ryan share a look I hate from the core of my being. It's a knowing look. A look that implies that they understand each other on some level. Like they're deciding whether to reveal something intimate. I feel both violent and violently ill.

"There's been a lot of personal drama," Miguel says.

"Like what?" I ask.

"You don't have to say," Ryan says, all protective of him.

"No," Miguel says, glancing at me. "I get it. It's mostly Piper and Nathan. Piper's a bitch, you all know that."

Bailey leans in, elbows on the table in a very *tell me more* pose. "And Nathan?"

"She likes him. Like she wants him."

"Has she had him?"

Miguel nods. "But Nathan's not exactly picky about who he's with, you know?"

Bailey grins and shakes her head, eating this shit up. "No. What do you mean?"

"I mean he likes to get laid. A lot. And Piper likes to play games, so…"

"He just goes around talking about it?" I ask.

"Look," Ryan cuts in. "We don't need all the details. The point is, things aren't working out for Miguel with their team, he's still got forty-five dollars and a setup we can use to move our team to the next level."

"No offense, Miguel," Bailey says, sitting back, "But Piper's already got a sabotage agenda she's not being shy about. That makes this a little hard to trust."

"We can trust him," Ryan says without equivocation.

"How do *you* know?" I ask.

He gives me a harsh glare. "I just do. This is low risk, high reward. What's the worst case scenario? He finds out what we're doing and reports back? They already know what we're doing. Piper's made that extremely clear. It doesn't mean they can compete. We've already built the foundation we need to be successful, and if Miguel can help, which he's offering to, then we can get started on the podcast this weekend."

"I hate this." I don't mean to say it out loud, and when Miguel looks genuinely stricken, I almost apologize, but I clamp my mouth shut.

It's not like he seems untrustworthy in terms of the challenge. What I don't trust him with is Ryan. Ryan who's mine, but only temporarily. Ryan who I deeply betrayed and hurt and who is generally an asshole to people but not Miguel. Ryan who says he doesn't trust me but *does* trust *him*.

Is he attracted to him, too?

"Can I have a word with you outside?" Ryan says to me. It's not really a question.

"Want me to order for you?" Bailey asks.

"We already ordered," Ryan says, and I wince.

"I'm not hungry," I say.

Ryan shakes his head, grabs me by the arm, and drags me out of the deli. "What the hell is your problem?" he asks as soon as as we're out the door.

"What's going on with you two?" I ask.

He blinks in surprise. "What do you think is going on?"

"Don't fucking play with me. I'm barely hanging on here, just tell me."

"Barely hanging on?" He looks baffled.

"Fine," I say. "You want me to ask, I'll ask. Is there something going on with you and Miguel?"

"Jesus Christ, Mal."

"That doesn't answer my question. Stop being an asshole and tell me."

He leads me out of the flow of sidewalk traffic to the other side of a mailbox. He doesn't touch me, but he stands close. "Last week, I found him crying in the men's room. He and Nathan have been hooking up, and I guess Piper found out and started talking a lot of shit."

Whoa. "Him and *Nathan*?" I know Nathan. Kind of. Never in a million years—

"I get the impression it was just fucking around, nothing serious, but Piper took it personally."

"He was crying, though? Sounds like *he* took it personally."

"Look," Ryan says, his voice lower. Softer. "When you're being bullied, it's not unheard of to have a breakdown in a men's room."

My jaw tightens. "Are you speaking from experience?"

He won't look at me. "This isn't about me and you."

Why doesn't he get that everything *is about me and him?* "I made you cry?"

He shrugs it off. "I was a kid."

My heart feels like it's crumbling. "I don't know what to say."

"We can deal with that later," Ryan says. "You're okay with this, right?" He gestures toward the deli, meaning Miguel being on our team.

Whether he meant to or not, he cut me down to size, so I can't say no. Ryan's right. It's worth the risk in terms of the challenge, but this whole business of Ryan making friends—ones that aren't me? Do they hug, too?

"Sure," I say quietly.

"Good. We'll meet up tonight?"

"Your place?"

"No—I mean all of us. At Miguel's place to check out the set up."

"Oh. Yeah, all right."

"We'll play it by ear after that," he says, which I guess is all I'm gonna get.

I follow him back into Big Bites with my heart in my stomach and my hope hanging on by a thread.

CHAPTER TWENTY-FOUR

RYAN

Miguel has a very nice place in the Castro. Evidently his stint as a YouTuber set him up nicely for a while, and he was able to buy the upper floor of a townhome. His office is exactly the cozy kind of space Bailey wanted, but at the moment, it's a blank canvas with good lighting and a ton of recording equipment. The walls are a warm, dark green.

The four of us work together to set it up. We bring in two chairs from Miguel's living room and an end table to put between them. Bailey's heart is set on calling the show "Finance Bros," and as much as I hate it, and I think Mal does, too, there's no talking her out of it, especially when Miguel agrees. If we hadn't spent a good chunk of our life actually being brothers, I don't think it would bother me so much, but it's not an aspect of our relationship I want to advertise. It's awkward enough that Bailey knows.

A white neon sign with the name of the show costs a hundred and eighty bucks and will be delivered next week. We leave a spot on the wall for it, then decorate a bookshelf, pull in a rug, and do some test shots.

With Miguel's experience and equipment, we'll be able to film from three angles: one camera on me, one on Mal, and the other on the two of us.

A few beers and two pizzas later, we've got a filming schedule and a list of topics for the first two shows. Mal seems to be settling into the new arrangement, but he's short on jokes and smiles. He's annoyed, too, that Miguel won't tell him what the other group is working on, but that's on me. I told him it'd be better if we didn't know, even when he said he had no problem telling me. All I know is we're doing better, and that's all I need to hear, which is probably why Piper's been lashing out.

Something about Malcolm pouting hits all my buttons, and by the time ten o'clock rolls around, I'm near dying to be alone with him. I managed to forget about our sexy text exchange earlier because I have to be able to compartmentalize while I'm at work, but watching him move furniture and sneak glances at me while our plan is coming together is a big turn on. Even the way he and Bailey bicker gives me a warm, connected feeling inside. I don't know how much longer I can go without smashing my mouth to his—among other body parts.

He brought Stephanie with him to Miguel's but no overnight bag. When I see him yawn, I say, "We should get out of your hair," to Miguel.

"Thank you guys again. I'm so glad there's something I can do that's useful."

"Oh, don't worry," Bailey says. "We'll make sure you're useful."

"You," I say to her, "Need to get with Calyx."

She grimaces. This, I'm beginning to understand, is a tell of hers. She wants to take Piper on. She just needs a push.

"Why don't I bring him by your place tomorrow night when we're done at the gym."

"Fine," she sighs. "Whatever. Have him send me a list of things I need to get from the store."

"Seriously?" Mal asks. "You're gonna do it? Even if it involves makeup?"

She backhands him in the chest.

"I can help, too," Miguel says. "I know my way around a contouring palette. Drag was a hobby of mine in high school."

"If you try to make me look like a drag queen—"

"Chill, mama. I'm just saying, I know how to make you look like AI Barbie."

Bailey startles. "Oh my God, that just gave me the best idea."

"Care to share with the class?" Mal asks.

"Not with you, no."

He huffs and tightens his hold on Stephanie as he rises from the couch. "One of these days I'm gonna surprise you, and you're gonna be so sorry you underestimated me."

"Yeah, okay," she says with a laugh.

I look at her with raised eyebrows, and she frowns. "Is he right?"

I shrug and stand, too.

"I'll believe it when I see it."

I'm tempted to kiss Malcolm right then and there. Make him melt against a wall and show Bailey what he's *really* like. But our relationship is confusing enough without dragging other people and their opinions into it.

We say goodnight to Miguel before Mal and I walk Bailey home. Her cute apartment complex is only a few blocks away. She loves Miguel being part of our group. "Seriously, boys, I'm getting dream team vibes," she says.

"Yeah, he's so dreamy," Mal says flatly.

"What crawled up your butt by the way?" she asks him. "Do you not like the direction of the project?"

"I love the project," he says, then adds in a lower mumble, "I just hate the job."

That's the first I'm hearing about that, and I look over at him. He's got his eyes on the pavement with Stephanie under one arm and his other hand shoved in his shorts pocket. It's a cool night. He and I both have on hoodies over t-shirts. I'm wearing pants, though. He's got his sexy legs on full display. "The job?" I ask. "Or Isla?"

"Both."

"You still wanna win, though, right?" Bailey asks.

"Yeah. Sure."

Jesus—was he always this moody?

Yes. Of course he was. It's just that I haven't been allowed to see the way he cycles through his moods for so long, I forgot what it's like—the turbulence of him. I forgot how much I love it, too. Back when we were close, he turned to me like I was the eye of his storm, and I remember the way it felt to have his heart slow its pace against my chest.

Being his safe place—the one he always turned to—was what I built my identity around. Losing that when he turned to Kaylin—it *killed*.

As soon as Bailey enters her apartment, I dig his hand out of his pocket and wrap mine around it.

"I have to go home tonight," he says.

"You don't." I tell him.

"I had a shitty day."

"Is this because I wouldn't fuck you in the unisex?"

He takes his hand back. "Not funny."

"I'm asking."

Apparently, he's reached the end of his tether, because he more or less snaps, "I've got actual feelings for you, you know?"

The words give me a jolt, and I find myself struggling to swallow.

"I wish you'd take it seriously," he adds, softer.

My mind flips through all the things I've done over the last few weeks, the ways I've acted, words I've said. He thinks I'm not serious? "I...do, I just..."

"What?"

"It's sudden." I don't know why I say that. I've had feelings for him the majority of my life. In retrospect, the evolution of our relationship makes sense to me. It scares me, too.

"What do I have to do to let you know I mean it?" he asks.

That's not the right question. I already know he's serious about us. He's locked in. *For now.* That's the way he is. He does things with his whole chest until he stops. I don't know what he'll do once Kaylin comes back from her trip next week. I don't know how much of what's going on with us is due to his poor impulse control or an actual desire to build something new with me—or repair what we broke. Worse, I'm not sure what the fuck I want from him either.

I mean, I definitely want more. And I want him around. I don't want him to spend tonight alone. I don't want to *be* alone, either, not if being with him is an option. This is *Mal* for fuck's sake—making me and breaking me all over again.

"I think what I need to hear is what *I* need to do for *you*," I say because the way he's making it sound, I'm not meeting some need of his. "Besides sneaking off with you at work. What's got you all twisted up?"

"You're different," he says.

"Than when I was fourteen? I fucking hope so."

"No, I mean in the last couple of weeks. You're friendlier. You're making friends. You seem chill and kinda happy."

I scowl, but he's not wrong. Work is great. I think we're killing it with the challenge. I *am* making friends—finding people I actually enjoy being around. Most importantly, Mal's not actively trying to make me miserable even though we see each other every day. Is there some uncertainty? Sure. But it's the good kind of uncertainty. The kind that leads to excitement rather than dread.

"Why are you not?" I ask.

"*Are* you thinking of this as a fling?"

I wish I were. If I could put Mal into casual territory, it would make my life so much easier, but that's never been the way my stupid heart deals with him. What he actually is—is a complication. A wrench in my well-laid plans. He's a person I don't know if I'll ever be sure of, no matter how much I'd love some sign from the universe that says *he's yours. Take him.* "No, I don't think of it like a fling," I tell him.

"Why not?"

Now he's fishing.

I sigh. "Because you're important to me."

He stops walking. So do I, and we face each other. "Why?" he asks again.

"Why do you think?" I ask, and immediately feel bad about it. He needs more. I need to give him more. I just don't know how when I feel this distance parting us again. When his hand isn't in mine.

"Because we have history?" he asks.

"Guess again," I say.

His gaze is a plea, and I know what he wants me to say. He wants me to tell him nothing's changed for me. That I'm still "like completely in love" with him. And how can I not be? I am. But that's no longer *all* I am. I have a life and plans that have nothing to do with him. Building a new identity without him was what I had to do to survive. Whether I wanted it that way or not—*I didn't*—it's happened.

"I feel like you want me to slow down, but I feel like if I do, you'll be gone before I've even got a chance," he says.

"A chance to what?" I ask, my heart threatening to throw itself on the tracks.

"To be with you."

"I'm right here," I tell him, knowing how far that is from his point. He's being so careful, though, and I love him for that, too.

He takes a deep breath, shuts his eyes a moment, and nods. "Yeah. You are."

"So come home with me."

"I can't fucking say no to you, Ryan," he complains.

I grin. "Good."

"You're not cute. I tell you I'm barely hanging on, and you laugh. I say I'm serious about you, and you change the subject. I ask if you want me to slow down, you tell me to come home with you."

"Then that should answer that question," I say, reaching up to pet Stephanie, sidling closer to Malcolm in the process.

"So, you *don't* want me to slow down?"

"I don't mind you at full throttle. But I might move slower."

"Why?" he asks.

"I don't know why," I tell him honestly. "It's just how I'm built." Fuck, I've never had to explain this to anyone before. I don't know how to put it into words.

"Is it because I'm a guy?" he asks softly.

"No," I whisper. "No, that's never been it. It's more about how close I feel—like when you let me in—when we share a look or finish each other's sentences or something—make each other laugh. That's when I want you most. Like tonight. Like now. This connection, when it feels like we're on the same page."

"Are we?" he asks.

"If you're serious about coming home with me. Yeah."

He frowns slightly, studying me. This probably makes as much sense to him as his room metaphor did for me, but I kinda got it. Maybe he'll kinda get this, too.

This is where never having been in a relationship before is a problem. I'm used to taking things a day at a time. One encounter, one conversation, one night. This has felt different from the beginning because it's *him*, but I'm still me. Still gun shy. Still, also, obsessed.

He slips his hand back into mine and squeezes. "Let's go."

We make it back to my place without much more conversation. He heads straight for the shower, telling me he'll be a few minutes, which I take to mean he wants to be alone.

I get us both some water in the kitchen and nod hello to Deacon when he peeks out of his bedroom. He sees the two glasses of water and retreats behind his door. A moment later, music comes on. I close my door and lock it. The shower's still running, so I take off my shirt, grab Bud and do a few recordings I came up with throughout the day.

Ideas come easier now that I know what kind of content gets the most engagement. Also, my hair looks good, so there's no time like the present. I'm on the beanbag adding tags and links to the post that needed the least editing when Mal comes out of the shower. Maybe Miguel can take over all the editing. It's way easier to film the content than it is to prep and upload it.

"You're in my seat," Malcolm says from the bathroom doorway with one of my gray towels around his waist.

Unable to help myself, I say, "You look fucking great like that."

"I smell good, too."

I guess he's in a better mood. "Prove it."

With Stephanie circling his feet, he walks over to me and drops his knees onto the beanbag outside my thighs. The towel doesn't come loose, but with his legs spread, it might as well.

He's exposed—cock and balls, his goddamn nipples in my face. I wish he'd grabbed the lube on his way over. My own cock is thick and heavy, wanting out of my pants. I want to fuck him like this. Facing him. Kissing him. Looking into his eyes. Thinking about that, I wrap a hand around his neck and pull him down for a kiss.

He humors me a moment, licking a hot wet trail through my mouth before shaking his head slightly and pulling away. "I love you," he says, gaze locked on mine like he's daring me.

I nod.

"What do you have to say about it?" he asks.

"I believe you?"

"Yeah?" he asks.

"Yeah, you've said it like twenty times. I believe you love me."

"So the tables have turned, I guess."

I frown. "Meaning?"

"Meaning only one of us knows how the other person really feels again," he says.

Does he think I've changed *that* much? That I would let him anywhere near me if I didn't love him fundamentally? The trick here though is that he doesn't just love me. He thinks he's *in love* with me. It's hard to believe this is actually happening. Having sex with him is easier to wrap my mind around than us being in love with each other.

I always sort of thought—if he ever forgave me for what I said, and he accepted my love—that we wouldn't have to have a physical relationship. Not any more than holding each other and maybe sharing a bed at night.

I imagined it monogamous and intimate, but not necessarily sexual, not if that was a bridge too far for him. I could have lived without it. After all, when you fall in love with someone at thirteen, believe it or not, sex is not the primary motivator. Just affection. Being close. I wanted to be his partner. The only one he ever touched the way he used to touch me. I wanted him all to myself.

It sounds stupid now with my dick straining to get to him—

wanting him so much it stretches credulity. "I love you, too," I tell him, which isn't a lie.

His mouth twists at my tone. Granted, my delivery was a little flat. "You do, huh?"

"You want me to think about it?" I ask.

He sighs, wilting. "Not really. You'll just start remembering all the reasons you have to hate me."

I reject that. "No. I know you're sorry. Dumb kids do dumb shit, right?"

"It'd be very generous of you to let me off the hook on that logic," he says.

I counter with, "I mean, it's obvious I don't disgust you anymore."

"Never," he says. "You fucked with me, but you never disgusted me."

"You had a lot of people convinced I did," I remind him.

"I almost had myself convinced, too," he says as he runs a hand through the hair above my ear. "Almost."

"And then I showed up with an eight pack?"

He puts his other hand there, on my abs. "I'm not sure I'm *that* shallow."

"But you missed me?" I ask.

"Yeah," he says quietly.

"And you forgive me."

"Fuck, *yes*. Of course I forgive you. I was the one who shit all over what we had. You didn't do anything wrong, Ryan. You were the best thing that ever happened to me. You still are. So, am *I* forgiven?"

Wow. "A hundred percent," I tell him, meaning it.

"But you don't trust me."

If he keeps talking to me like this, I won't have a choice. "I'm working on it, Mal."

"Are you?" he asks.

I hold his gaze and nod.

"Loving you *hurts*, Ryan."

Fucking *same*. I sigh. "I know exactly what you mean."

He leans in, and I think he's going to kiss me, which he does, but his lips touch my forehead. "I'm so sorry," he whispers.

"I'm sorry, too."

With his hand on my jaw, he tilts up my face and presses his mouth to mine. I want him so much at this point, it's hard to keep the kiss from turning into a feeding frenzy. Nevertheless, the feel of his tongue lashing through my mouth works me up. It's got me urging his hips closer, putting his ass over my erection to give myself some friction.

"*Mmmph...fuck...*" he sighs.

It's such a turn on to know that if someone walked in and saw us right now, they'd see him covered in a towel, while I've got a view of *everything*. His dick is hard and ruddy, the tip shiny with arousal. The skin of his inner thighs is soft and lightly dusted with hair that's softer than the hair on his calves. I run my thumbs over and over it, kneading the muscle and grazing his warm, tight sac.

"Grab the lube, would you?" I ask between kisses.

"In a minute," he whispers as he keeps kissing me. I'm practically melting into the chair. I don't want to let him go either, but it'll be worth it. It'd be easy enough to get my cock out and jerk us together—I'm genuinely desperate to get off, but I'd much rather be inside him.

He caresses my face and pulls back an inch, his lips hovering near mine. "Is this why sexting you doesn't work? You prefer seduction to propositions?"

"Sort of."

"Conversation, then?" he asks.

"I think you're getting warmer."

He smiles. "I love you," he tells me again.

"Get the lube, Mal."

Biting his lip, he climbs off me, the towel falling to the floor. I watch him walk naked to the other side of my bed and retrieve the bottle from the nightstand.

By the time he's handing it over to me, I've shucked my pants and underwear, my own cock so hard it's hitting my abs. I catch Mal staring at it. "Turn around," I tell him.

He rips his gaze from my dick to my face, a mournful look in his eyes before he does what I say.

I squeeze the lube onto my fingers and rub them over his hole, pushing some inside, first using one finger, then adding a second. "Shit," he gasps, bending over to brace his hands on his thighs, his legs already quivering. Once he finds his balance, I torture his prostate gland for a few, slow, firm strokes, each one causing him to pant heavily.

"Ready?" I ask.

"Yes. Fuck yes." He starts to sit back, but I catch him by the hips, turning him to face me again. I let him watch while I cover my cock in more lube. I go slow, not trying to come before I even get inside him, but it feels so fucking good with him looking at me like that.

"Wanna sit on my lap?"

His breath comes out in a sigh. "Yeah..."

I spread my legs slightly, causing him to have to part his thighs wider to straddle me. Holding my cock, I watch it disappear as he lowers himself onto it, his hands braced on my shoulders. His nails dig in at that first hissing penetration. Then, as he adjusts and sinks deeper, a low groan I feel down to my nuts erupts from his throat. "*God...*"

I watch as his eyelids flutter. His irises nearly disappear as they roll back in his head. His lips are parted, and that's all I see before he drops his head and fully seats himself.

I sink back into the ever-accommodating chair and bear the

sensation of being fully sheathed inside him—something I never managed with a woman. The heat is something I'll never get over. Grabbing his ass, I roll my hips up. His hands move closer to my neck, and I remember why I wanted him like this in the first place beyond the blatantly fucking obvious.

I seek out his mouth, and once we make the connection, he wraps his arms around me, and we fall into the beanbag together.

Massaging his ass cheeks, I work them around my shallowly thrusting cock as his tongue delves deep into my mouth. He delivers his moans directly to my throat, my chest. Our movements are limited, but that only makes the closeness more intimate.

Slight clenches of his hole put us in sync, and we maintain a lazy rhythm, as languid as the kiss. Fucking him like this is intensely erotic. I've never been so turned on—so locked in—so *connected* during sex. I wish I could think of a better word for it, but the only one coming to mind is special. This is so fucking *special.*

Letting go of his ass, I run my hands up his back and make sure he's pressed as tightly as he can be to me. When I feel his leaking cock on my abs, I work my stomach muscles over him until he turns his head to gasp and whimper. "Jesus, Ryan...it's so good. You feel so fucking good."

I kiss his neck while he's catching his breath, but soon enough our lips are sealed together again. Our tongues move in that frenzy I was trying so hard to put off before, but I'm starving for him now, rapidly approaching the end of my control because this is Mal. This is *Mal* making love to me and giving me shadows of feelings past, but also new ones—huge ones.

What the fuck am I so afraid of? Why do I think this unending feeling can be pushed aside like it's nothing? Why did I *ever* think it could? What difference does Kaylin make when I know how completely I've fallen for him? The fantasy of loving him was one thing, but the reality of it is unlike anything I could have imagined. It's worse in some ways—admittedly. He's needy and messy and moody as fuck, but in the ways it's better—it's exponential.

He's *into* me. He might even be lowkey obsessed with me. He's possessive and passionate and beyond affectionate. He also takes me so fucking well—and for me, who's never felt like I've belonged anywhere—I fit perfectly here.

A quickening in my groin locks and loads my balls. Biting his lip, I break away. "Close," I whisper.

"Touch me," he begs, his breath shaky and stretched thin.

I do, sliding my hand between our abs and fisting his cock. He gives me just enough room to move, but mostly he thrusts through it as I shove into him, chasing our release. I want him to come with me.

Our mouths find our way back to each other. The kiss is wet and sloppy and delicious. Too good. "Mal..." My voice breaks. "I can't. You feel so fucking good."

"Yeah," he groans. "God, Ry, fuck, yeah. Come inside me. Fill me up, baby."

Oh *God...* I bury my cock deep in his ass and let the bone-shattering orgasm take me. Shuddering and grunting, I do my best to keep holding him, keep kissing him as blood drains from my head and leaves me dizzy and stupid. A rutting animal.

Mal gasps once—twice—and his warm cum slicks my hand and abs as his cock throbs in my tight fist.

My orgasm is still wrecking me, my dick still pulsing out erratic spurts spurred on by everything I notice about him. His catching breath. His wet lips. His sweat-slicked chest and his quivering body. I run a hand up his spine and grip his neck while we quake against each other, riding it out.

When every drop has left us, I let his dick go, and he

smashes his body to mine, burying his face in my hair and holding me tight.

I return the embrace as his spasming hole sends intense aftershocks zapping across my hips and down my legs. "It's so fucking good with you."

He kisses my neck, and that's how I know I'm the one who said it. His response is quiet and non-intrusive. "Maybe you'll wanna keep me around, then."

CHAPTER TWENTY-FIVE

MALCOLM

Ryan swallows my load and looks up at me. "Why do you keep apologizing?"

"I don't know," I pant, collapsing onto my back.

"I liked it better when you just said I love you on a loop."

"I think I just..." Fuck knows what I'm thinking. He just sucked out my brain cells. "I'm sorry."

He chuckles. "Stop."

He crawls onto the sex chair—aka the beanbag—with me and presses his erection against my hip. While I catch my breath, he messes with my nipples. Stroking and squeezing them, watching them blanch and then redden up again, all the while getting more and more swollen. I'm a shivering mess—I think I might still be coming.

"Seriously," he says, finally laying off my nipples and resting his chin on my shoulder. "What are you sorry about?"

"I figure—I don't know...you don't wish I could go more than once a day?"

"Go?"

"Take your dick?"

"You have," he reminds me.

"Twice," I remind *him*.

He wipes some sweat from my brow and runs his hand over my hair. "I got the impression that position from earlier wasn't exactly good for you."

"It wasn't *bad*," I argue.

"Harder then."

It was actually harder. Taking his huge cock while I was leaning over the sink in the unisex was a new kind of uncomfortable.

"You can always tell me to stop or change it up," he says.

"I didn't want you to stop. I came, didn't I?"

"Yeah. You did."

Thinking of it now—watching Ryan watch me in the mirror, his hand over my mouth to muffle my noises while I was red-faced and in perfect agony put me over the edge. It was only my second time coming completely untouched—nothing but air on my dick—and the first time had been a second orgasm. This one was ridiculous. Annihilating. I'd come everywhere, and Ryan had to clean it up because I was a useless wreck afterward.

"I ordered a butt plug," I say.

He laughs again. "What the fuck?"

"I want you to be able to fuck me anywhere, anytime without worrying about it."

"And you think that'll help?"

"I do," I say.

"I don't need to fuck constantly. That's you."

"I'm sorry," I say, aware I'm still apologizing. "I know. But it'd be like our secret. Something only you and I know. And I like knowing you're thinking about me."

"Mal...there hasn't been a single day since I met you that I haven't thought about you multiple times."

"What does that mean?" I ask. "Is that a bad thing or a good thing."

"It's just a thing. About me. I think about you a lot."

"I think about you constantly," I confess. "I'm useless for how much I think about you."

"Yeah?" he asks.

"You think I don't?"

"I mean...I wonder."

"I wish you wouldn't," I say. "The only reason I'm not texting you constantly is because I'm trying to show some restraint. There hasn't been a single day I haven't wanted to talk to you. And I'm not just talking about this summer."

"I needed to hear that," he whispers.

"It's true. It's worse now, though," I admit. "I want you. I worry. I feel like such a mess."

Ryan sighs and digs his forehead into my shoulder, his fingertips returning to circle my right nipple. "I've always liked your mess, so don't worry about that."

I try to smile. "Okay."

"I know work's sucked for you this week, but are you excited about the podcast?"

We're filming our first episode tomorrow at Miguel's. Our plan is solid, mostly introductory. Bailey and Miguel scripted the talking points, the intros and outros. We get to keep our shirts on.

With Kaylin coming home Wednesday, I'm going to need to start phasing Stephanie out. I've been thinking about getting another dog, but I'm also sort of preemptively mourning the loss of my bond with Stephanie. She's grown on me these last few weeks. I understand her better now that I have an obsession of my own I'm constantly tracking and missing when he's not in my sight.

I've been good about not bringing up Ryan's plans for after

the internship. We have about a month left, and maybe that seems far off for him, but to me, it feels like tomorrow. For my part, because I've had a less than stellar experience working at Marks & Baker, I don't think I'm likely to be offered a job no matter how the challenge turns out, and if I were, I'm not likely to take it, which leaves me at yet another loss as to what comes next for me.

I'm all out of ideas. Although, if Ryan's gone, what difference will it make whether I hate my job or not? What difference would anything make?

When I said that to Andrea yesterday, she pounced all over it, wanting to know if I was taking my meds or having any thoughts of harming myself.

I gave her two truths and a lie. Yes, I'm taking my meds. No, I'm not thinking of harming myself. *I'm fine.*

Still, I am looking forward to the podcast, so I tell him yes. "It should be fun."

"It will be," he says. "Now be a good friend." He takes my hand off my own leg and puts it on the bulge in his sweats.

I feel like I should apologize again for neglecting his needs, but he doesn't give me a chance. As soon as I've got my hand in his pants, he's kissing me and fucking my fist, precum the only lube, and it's not all that good for jerking someone off. He doesn't seem to care. He keeps molesting my nipples and licking into my mouth like all is right in his world, and then he comes with a jolt and a soft series of groans against my lips.

It's all so stupidly hot, I've got another semi thickening in my lap. Fuck, I can't get enough of him. I need to figure this shit out or he and his Seattle lady friend are going to wind up with an unwanted roommate with a severe clinging problem. Hope she's cool with sharing.

Ugh. I twist away from him and struggle my way out of the beanbag chair, bracing myself for a cold shower.

I should just ask him. I have three questions I need answers to, and I just need to ask them and get it over with. 1. Are you in love with me? 2. Are you leaving me? 3. Can we still be together no matter what?

The problem is the wrong answer to any one of those questions would nuke me.

I'm not expecting him to join me in the shower, so I don't bother to lock the door, but he's a minute behind me. "What?" I ask when he pulls the curtain shut.

"I just came in my pants."

"Right." I turn my back on him and let the cool water soak my face.

"It's cold. Shit." He wraps his arms around me from behind and I look down at all those tattoos crossed over my midsection. He's so goddamn gorgeous. So fucking sexy. Strong and contained and smart. I never used to think of us as opposites until we were in high school when I did everything I could to differentiate myself from him.

And I guess it worked.

"I love you, Mal," he says against my ear. His mouth there sends another wave of chills over me.

"I know," I sigh.

"No," he says, like he's reading my mind. "I mean, I'm like—completely in love with you."

My hands fly up, locking onto his wrists. "Is that...did you?"

"Sound familiar?"

"Are you fucking with me? *Now*?"

"I'm not fucking with you. And I'm not doped up either."

"I mean, you just came..."

"How long after I come do I need to wait to talk to you then?" he asks.

"You don't. I'm sorry. I wasn't expecting you to say that. Those particular words."

"Hope it's not a trigger or anything."

"No," I say quickly. "Definitely not. I didn't know if I'd ever get to hear you say it again." *And I've needed to hear it more than I could possibly convey.*

He presses a soft kiss to the base of my neck. "There you go."

"I'll handle it much better this time. I swear to God."

"I know."

He knows? Does that mean he trusts me?

"What does it mean?" I ask.

"It's literal," he says with a distinct smile in his voice. "It defines itself."

I wish that were true for anything with me, but maybe I won't press my luck right this second. I have one of my answers at least. It's not the heaviest, but a weight lifts nonetheless. I let his wrists go and turn in the circle of his arms. He looks into my eyes, the soft smile still on his face. I return it, pushing his half wet hair away from his beautiful eyes.

The look in them is all-encompassing—like there's no part of me he can't see. I'm still over here searching his, but the love is there—written plainly and perfectly.

A line forms between his brows after a moment. "Jesus, you're hard."

"Ignore it," I say, slamming my mouth to his. He backs up a step, but in the next second, he's got me pinned against the wall, his thigh between my legs and his mouth hot on mine.

I HAVE MIXED feelings about the butt plug. Girth-wise, it's about half the size of Ryan, which was what I was going for, so I'm happy with that. I already had a near constant awareness of my asshole, so it's not like having it half stuffed makes me all that much more preoccupied by it.

Anyway, I've got the plug in while Ryan and I are running our separate Saturday errands before we're scheduled to meet at Miguel's. I wasn't counting on it arousing me.

I guess I was thinking of it like a shoe tree. Something I could stick in there to keep me propped open so when Ryan wanted in—or I beg Ryan in, my hole would be more resilient. The plug isn't big enough to stimulate my prostate—at least not while I'm upright. When I'm sitting however—like I have to while I'm getting my hair cut—all I can think about is how badly I need to get off. I calculate how long the walk to my apartment is as I get harder and more desperate.

I don't make it any farther than the barbershop bathroom. The good news is I come fast. The bad news is I can't look anyone in the eyes on the way out because I do think I made a loud enough noise when I came that I embarrassed myself.

Such a good orgasm, though. Best solo work I've ever done.

Thinking of solo work, my array of flesh lights come to mind. While my laundry is running and after I take a shower, I pack for the rest of the weekend, including one item from my nightstand I think Ryan might like.

I meet him at his place with Stephanie on a leash, but we only have time for me to drop off my things and collect his before we need to head to Miguel's. It's another gorgeous day, perfect for a walk and for him to hold my hand apparently. With our fingers locked and palms pressed together, we make our way up and down the hills of San Francisco and finally Castro Street with its porn cookie shops and sex toy stores, its amazing restaurants and array of rainbow flags.

"You feel like you belong here?" I ask.

"Here as in…?"

"This neighborhood." It was all I started out meaning, but

now with the door to ask him about staying in the Bay Area wide open, I consider pressing the issue.

"Why? Because we're fucking?" he asks.

Because you're in love with me? I swallow roughly and say instead, "I feel like *I* do. Like I have an all-access pass."

"I used to work at that bar," he says, pointing across the street, "For about a month before the internship."

"Seriously?"

"I thought I'd still be able to pick up shifts, but with the challenge it's been—"

"But you said you'd never—"

"I hadn't."

"Been with guys," I go ahead and finish in case he can't actually read my mind.

"Women go to bars, too."

"So—back to my original question," I say, exasperated, "You feel like you belong here?"

"Belonging isn't something I feel very often," he says. It's an honest, unguarded answer, and it makes me realize how measured his responses to my questions usually are—or they used to be. Maybe that's changing.

"I guess I have something to do with that."

He squeezes my hand but doesn't say anything. Obviously what I want to say is do you feel like you belong with *me*? And I might, later, but I'm really trying not to actively obsess over him when we have our first episode to film.

We pass couples of all varieties as we walk. Stephanie gets a lot of attention, and she eats it up. She's been spreading her love around more lately, coming out of her shell. When I spend the night with Ryan, she prefers to sleep snuggled up with Bud more often than not. I'm not *jealous*. I just happened to notice, is all.

Miguel welcomes us with a broad smile and offers us beer.

We're not holding hands anymore and straight guys drink beer, I guess. I accept the offer, but Ryan wants water.

Bailey's already in the office, surveying and perfecting the setup. She scoops up Stephanie as the tiny dog runs toward her. Bailey gives me a sheepish look. "You'd think I was gonna be the one on camera with how nervous I am."

"You think we're gonna fuck it up?" I ask.

"No!" she says, sounding unexpectedly supportive. "I think it's gonna be amazing. I'm literally all tingly. I have a really good feeling about this."

"Yeah?"

She nods with enthusiasm. "You look fantastic, by the way."

I don't know how to deal with her like this. I'm wearing gray slacks, a white button down with the collar open, and an Old Navy tech vest I bought last year. When Bailey asked if I had one, I told her I did, and she snorted. Ryan didn't get the same question.

The group text has been popping all week about how to brand "Finance Bros." Like *how bro do we want to go?*

The consensus opinion was to maintain the opposites vibe Ryan and I have and go half bro. Accessible Bro, hence the open collar. Ryan, in contrast, is wearing that black sweater of his that short circuits my brain, his father's old Rolex, and black slacks. His hair is in its natural state, dark waves perfectly framing his face. When he shows up in the office with Miguel, his sleeves are pushed up to reveal his tattoos.

"Are we ready?" he asks.

Miguel rests his hand on one of the mounted cameras. "We could warm up by filming the intro and outro. You guys look perfect. I want to take some photos, too. What would you say to a little make-up?"

Ryan loves this, patting his under-eye. "Yes. Can you take care of these bags?"

"Of course, honey. Come with me."

Because I'm not letting Miguel be alone with Ryan for more than a minute, I follow them. Miguel's bedroom is more of a boudoir, and it answers a lot of questions I probably would have eventually had about him.

The walls are painted a dark gray with a high platform bed as the centerpiece. There's also *a mirror on the ceiling*, which makes me wonder if movie reviews were the only thing he used to record with all that equipment. Off to the right, he's got a vanity fit for a Broadway star.

The rug is huge, white, and extremely plush. I'm terrified of Stephanie soiling it somehow, so I take her from Bailey to make sure her paws don't touch the floor. Miguel gestures to the stool at the vanity, and Ryan has a seat.

I lean back on the sill of the bay window to watch.

It's quick, a dab of concealer beneath Ryan's eyes, a pressing of anti-shine powder on his face, and a few plucks of eyebrow hairs, which Ryan bears like someone who's covered in tattoos.

It's good work. I can't even tell he has makeup on. Miguel looks to me, and I want to say no—the prehistoric part of me screaming *gay! Gay! Too gay!* but no way am I listening to that voice anymore. Pride makes a hell of a lot more sense to me now. It used to bug the shit out of me. Like why do people have to be so loud about it—so in your face?

But the truth of it is that it's a necessary, adaptive reaction to shame—both the external hate and the internalized second-guessing that every confused kid has to deal with when they realize something about them is different than the majority of their peers.

I recall to my horror the time I told my college roommate that Pride was one of the seven deadly sins, and he looked at me like I was the biggest asshole to ever walk the earth.

In retrospect, I think I was only trying to understand, but it is

—as he said—the shittiest thing he'd ever heard someone say about the queer community. I'm not even religious, so I had to have been really reaching.

Still, it's not like I can claim "pride" since I'm technically in the closet. I glance at Ryan as Miguel spruces up my face. He's staring back at me with a faint smile. It's the kind of smile that makes me want to kiss him. Hold him close. Whisper things to him both sweet and filthy. It's the kind of look that makes me want to say *I adore you, too.*

He seems to sense my thoughts and draws a dollar sign in the air—I guess to remind me to get my head on straight. Miguel dabs lip balm on my lips and declares me ready to go.

In the mirror, I see a version of myself that's refined and refreshed. "Nice," I say.

Miguel beams.

It takes several tries for Ryan and me to warm up to the new, more formal set up, and Miguel is a perfectionist. We film at least a dozen versions on an intro, then switch to taking promotional still shots. Stephanie gets a quick photo shoot, too.

I'm glad I had a beer because it makes me less stiff. It takes Ryan a little longer to warm up, and I want to pour a shot of whiskey down his throat. But eventually, we're laughing and giving each other the usual shit, and it's time to film the actual content.

It's interview style, where we ask each other questions about how we got into finance, where we went to school, what we feel like is different between school and the "real world," and what we want to achieve with this webcast.

It goes smoothly. Neither Miguel nor Bailey interrupt. We take a quick break before we move into the finance portion—the winning poll topic from the Patreon: building wealth. It's a broad topic on purpose, meant to open the door for more nuanced conversations down the line.

For another uninterrupted fifteen minutes, Ryan and I toss the conversation back and forth. He argues for a patient, measured approach, and I argue for calculated risks. We wrap up with an invitation to subscribe to the Patreon for the rest of the conversation. After another break, he and I really get into it, leaning in and gesturing. His passion for finance is showing, and I love it on him.

It's easily the most substantive conversation I've had with Ryan about anything other than our weird relationship, and it's *fun*. He's incredibly smart, but I know more than I thought I did, too, and we each manage to score a few unarguable points.

Bailey is practically vibrating with excitement as we interrupt each other and start showing off a hint of our actual relationship, which is naturally argumentative and teasing. Granted, it took us a while to get here—trying to forget the cameras and focus on each other—but once we do, the chemistry between us is undeniable, and I get why Bailey's happy because so am I.

I don't have any idea how much money we'll make from this, or if it'll take off in time to win the challenge, but I'm confident it's something Ryan and I can do—and well.

Finally, he wraps it up, saying, "Okay, okay, enough. Don't make me come over there and wrestle you. You and I both know who'll win."

Thank God for makeup because I'm definitely blushing when I tell the camera we'll be back Wednesday with another episode and invite them to discuss and ask questions in the Discord.

Miguel calls it a wrap, and Bailey throws herself on top of Ryan, giving him a hug.

He laughs and rolls her over to sit on his lap. She ruffles his hair and fucking *giggles*. "That was amazing! Miguel, what did you think?"

"I think Piper's head might explode, and I'll sell tickets to anyone who wants to see it."

Ryan glances my way and grins. "Nice job."

Smitten as fuck, I bite my lip and smile back at him. "You too." It's a crime that I can't remove Bailey from his lap and take my place there. I *need* to kiss his face and tell him how fucking proud I am of us. The first day I saw him sitting at the conference table, I thought I was in for the worst summer of my life.

Not like it's been easy, but this moment right here makes it all worth it. I do stand, and Miguel offers me another drink. I nod and start following him to the kitchen.

Everything goes to shit in a heartbeat. It starts with Stephanie. I notice she's at my feet, in danger of being stepped on. To avoid the inevitable squish, I shift my weight and wind up off balance. Over-correcting in the opposite direction, I lose my footing entirely. Vaguely, I register falling.

The next thing I notice is a white hot pain in my left wrist and Ryan's hands on my face.

"Baby, did you hit your head?"

Bailey's laughing. Apologizing for laughing, but laughing. Heartily.

"What?" I ask.

Ryan is crouched beside me as I clutch my arm to my chest. Someone shoves a pillow under my head, and Ryan snaps— "Should you be moving him?"

"I don't think his *neck* is broken." That's Miguel.

Bailey asks through her laughter, "Is your hand okay? You're holding it."

I understand what's happening here, and there's definitely an injury, but the pillow is a nice touch, so I look at Ryan and tell him I'm okay.

His hand explores my head, feeling for lumps or cuts. I close my eyes as his fingers run through my hair—a welcome sensation to counter the pain in my wrist.

"I'm sorry," Bailey's saying. "I laugh when people fall. I can't help it. I don't actually think this is funny." She snorts and giggles again, so it's hard to take her word for it.

"Can you sit up?" Ryan asks.

"Yeah," I say, like this is a totally ridiculous question.

With one hand under my neck and the other beneath my shoulder blade, he helps me sit. "It's my wrist," I tell him like we're having a private conversation.

"Let me see."

When I lean my head on his shoulder, he takes my left hand gently in his. I hiss and Bailey gasps.

"Is it that bad?" I ask.

"Um..."

I register that I'm slumped fully against Ryan, dependent on his body to hold me up. He's warm everywhere. Against my chest, my neck—*am I going into shock?*

"Are you two...? Oh my God, no wonder."

"Bailey—not now," Ryan says.

"Sorry. I know. I'm sorry. You want me to call an ambulance?"

"He's not having a heart attack," Miguel says rationally. "Nothing's bleeding."

"That's good news," I murmur into Ryan's neck.

"Dude," he says in a low voice I think only I'm meant to hear.

Does he seriously care whether Bailey and Miguel think we might be fucking? Does he think chemistry like what just happened is random? Does he think I can resist him after all that and *this*—him fussing over me. Worried about me? In *that* sweater?

"Can you move your fingers?" he asks.

Doubt it. Don't even want to try. The pain is just this side of bearable. If I try moving my hand, my odds of passing out become a sure thing. "I don't think so."

"You should take him to a hospital," Miguel says.

I groan. "What about Stephanie?"

"Miguel's right," Bailey says. "I can watch her."

"I fucked everything up." Everyone was happy, and now they're all serious. Why does that always happen around me? *How do I always manage to ruin everything?*

"Nothing's ruined," Ryan says. "Is your wrist the only thing that hurts? Not your head."

"My head's fine."

"You're sure?" he asks.

"Positive," I tell him.

"Good." He sounds relieved.

"Here," Bailey says.

A bag of frozen corn appears, and Ryan takes it, placing it on my wrist as carefully as he can, but it causes another jolt of pain to shoot up my arm.

I hold the bag in place myself, and Ryan puts his arms around me. "I'm really sorry," I say to everyone. Especially him.

"No worries," Bailey says. "Miguel and I can do all the editing. Just go get checked out and text us when you know what's up."

"Thanks, guys," Ryan says as we work on standing.

"Seriously, you guys were fire. We'll barely have to do any work," Miguel assures us.

"It's true," I say. "We are fire. That's facts."

"Shut the fuck up, Mal."

"I think the cat's out of the bag," Bailey says.

"What gave it away?" I mumble.

"It was the hand in the hair for me," she admits.

Miguel adds, "It was the chest rub and the kiss on the neck for me."

Did I kiss him? Shit.

"Missed that," Bailey says. "But you're right. Definitely seals it."

"Okay, okay," Ryan says. "Sue me for wanting to make him feel better."

He kissed *my* neck?

I can walk fine, but Ryan keeps an arm around my waist all the way to the car he ordered to take us to the ER.

"You think Stephanie's gonna be okay?" I ask.

Ryan shakes his head and laughs.

CHAPTER TWENTY-SIX

RYAN

Mal shakes the bottle of narcotic pain pills in my face. "You want one?"

"No," I say firmly because this isn't the first time he's asked. I don't know what he thinks I'll say to him that I haven't already said. It's Sunday afternoon, and we both woke up late after six hours in the emergency room. His left wrist is broken, but doesn't require surgery, so he's in a cast that covers half his hand and his entire forearm.

Bailey dropped off Stephanie around ten, and she peeked in on Mal asleep in my bed. "How long?" she'd asked.

"About three weeks," I told her.

"Doesn't he have a girlfriend?"

I sighed. "They're on a break or something."

"Is it rude that I like him about ten thousand times more now?"

I huffed a laugh. "Me, too."

"I didn't know you..."

"It's him," I admitted. "It's kinda always been him."

She'd looked up at me like she might cry. "That's so sweet."

"Is it?" I asked. "Because most days it feels colossally stupid."

She left us alone after reassuring me that she approved.

Now, I shove his hand and the pills away. "You get forty-eight hours with those, then you're weaning."

"I broke a bone," he argues.

"You're suffocating when you're high."

"Oh, and you hate that," he says, rolling on top of me to prove my point, and maybe his, because my dick immediately perks up.

What I do hate is having no self-control around him. I was all over him after he fell. I'm surprised I didn't start undressing him to check for wounds in front of Miguel and Bailey. Kissing him on the neck once I got him off his back was a moment of pure helplessness. Relief.

"You should eat," I tell him with his mouth an inch from mine.

"Good idea." He dives in to kiss my neck and starts working his way down my chest.

I grab him by the hair to stop him. "Deacon made soup."

"Soup? I'm not sick."

"You are if you think I'm gonna let you suck me off eight hours after we left an emergency room."

"You're not making sense," he says, his lips wet and red. Tempting. "That's not a rule."

"You need to eat."

"I'll make you a deal. If I eat, you do whatever I want after."

"I can't agree to that," I tell him.

"If I told you what I want doesn't require me to use either of my hands, would you agree to it?"

"Maybe..." I say, picturing things. Sucking him...eating him... fucking him.

"I need more than a maybe," Mal says, those teal-blue eyes arresting mine and holding them hostage.

"Fine."

"You can do better," he taunts.

"I'll let *you* do whatever you want. Satisfied?"

He smirks. "I will be."

I ease out from under him and get out of bed.

I'm surprised to find Deacon didn't just make soup—he made clam chowder. I'm more surprised when it's one of the best I've ever had. "Deac?" I call out.

I don't get an answer. I guess he left. I'll have to save my gratitude and compliments for later. He was really great when we got home in the middle of the night, making sure we had everything we needed and letting me know I could text him if I needed him to run out and grab something else.

But Mal's fine. His wrist hurts, but there's nothing more to be done about it. This chowder, however... I can barely work a stove, and Deacon made *this*.

Norah made a clam chowder once, and I thought it was good, but Deacon's is the perfect amount of creamy and peppery. Hers was thinner and not super memorable, so why the fuck am I thinking about that now? Maybe because I talked to her for an hour yesterday while I was rushing from store to store, picking up groceries and vitamins and lube.

It wasn't an overly intimate conversation. It was about work and how things are going with the challenge. She had a rough week with her assistant, so she vented about that for a while. It was less flirtatious than some conversations we've had, but it did remind me how well we get along. How what I might have had with her would have been good. And yes, I'm already thinking of it in the past tense. It's not like I can tell Malcolm I'm in love with him and actively picture a future with someone else.

I feel guilty for not talking to him about it, though, which does make me more willing to let him have his way with me once he's had something to eat.

I bring two large mugs of chowder into the bedroom and

hand him his along with a spoon. He's propped up with some pillows against the headboard. Stephanie and Bud are soaking up the sun in Bud's bed on the window seat. I sit facing Malcolm to make sure he eats.

"I think I left my work badge at my apartment yesterday," he says.

"You shouldn't go in tomorrow. Not if you're still taking the pills."

"Twist my arm," he says around his spoon. "Just not the broken one."

"You really hate the job?" I ask.

Malcolm avoids the question and says, "This is really fucking good. I think your roommate has a thing for you."

I laugh, despite the abrupt subject change. "Why do you say that?"

"Comfort food like this? Soup? It's a love language."

"What the fuck are you talking about?"

"Like how Mom always made us soup when we were sick," he says.

"That's cause she thinks it's a cure for everything."

"She's a nurse. She knows what cures things."

I grimace. "Don't make me have to think about Deacon like *that*."

Mal laughs but doesn't take it back. I don't let my thoughts go there. "He made this for you, too."

"Maybe he wants in on the action."

I nearly spit out my mouthful. "Stop. Jesus, Mal."

"Doesn't appeal?" he asks.

"No!"

"That was adamant. You used to be pretty good about sharing."

"*With* you, not...*you*."

His blue-green eyes gleam with satisfaction. "Careful.

Sounds like you might want to commit to something."

"That's not anywhere close to what I'm saying," I say, but in terms of holding my ground in this conversation, he's got me on my heels. I perform an ungraceful turning of the tables. "Besides, your girlfriend is back in two days. You won't be my problem anymore."

His mouth drops open, and I swear his skin loses a shade of color. "What?"

"Isn't she coming home Wednesday?"

"I'm your *problem*?"

He's always been my problem, but in this case I was joking— about that part, at least. "Look, I just needed you to shut up about Deacon—"

"You think you're getting rid of me Wednesday?"

"Am I not?" I ask.

"*No.* Are you fucking kidding?"

The chowder isn't settling well. I reach over and put the mug on my nightstand. "It's hard to imagine you not being with her."

"It's impossible to imagine not being with *you*," he says.

My stomach does a one-eighty flip.

"But if that's some kind of *problem* for you..."

I take his soup and put it aside, too. Call it a moment of weakness or whatever, but those words, more than anything he's ever said to me, dissolve my resistance. I put my arms around him and swing my leg over his hips. I pull him close, pressing a kiss to one cheek while I cradle the other.

He takes advantage of my obvious vulnerability and kisses me firmly. My heart can barely tolerate it. I'm broken open. Exposed. I'm the same stupid kid with a crazy crush he had no business having. All that talk about the risks he loves so much slips into the space he opened up, and I'm ready to take one. "I want this," I tell him.

"Good. Now, tell me how much."

I put him on his back. "You know how much."

"You're not even hard."

"It's not always about that, asshole." I grab his face and kiss him again. "Sometimes it's not a feeling in my pants, it's a feeling in my chest."

"Can you go ahead and take that warm, fuzzy feeling and get hard?"

My dick is already working on it, but I hold his head in place and kiss him again and again.

"Wait—hang on—wait."

"What?" I groan, pressing my forehead to his in frustration. I don't want to talk anymore. He fumbles around under the covers next to him. I turn to look at what he's doing, and my eyes widen at the huge flesh light. "What the fuck?"

"Do you have any of these?" he asks.

"No," I say, frowning at it.

"But you know what it is, right?"

"Yes, Mal. I've been in a sex shop before."

"This one should fit us both."

"*What?*"

"Shit, Ry, it's not that weird. You said anything I want."

He's right on both counts. I did say that, and on the spectrum of Mal's kinks, this is a relatively mild one. "It doesn't look big enough."

"It'll be tight," he says, his voice low and sexy.

"What does that one do?" I ask. Though I don't own one, I'm aware that there are different kinds.

"It's pretty basic," he says. "It's got a little suction if you want."

Ready to be naked with him in any capacity, I reach for the lube and push off my underwear—the only thing I'm wearing. I help him out of his before he holds out the toy for me to squirt lube into.

"Put some on our dicks, too," he tells me.

I do, getting him ready first while I watch his face. His eyes hood as I stroke him. "It's gonna be like fucking you," he says.

"You want that?" I ask.

"I want this."

"You're welcome to fuck me," I tell him.

He shakes his head. "I like how things are with us. Unless you don't."

I guess "how things are with us" is still pretty new in the grand scheme of things. Since we've been fucking, I haven't thought about bottoming for him. But before—back when I was forced to watch him fuck his girlfriend any chance he could make it happen, I always pictured being on the receiving end of him. But that wasn't really him, it turns out. It was a show he was putting on for me—maybe for himself, too. "No," I say. "I do. I fucking love being inside you."

"You wanna do this with me?" he asks, sounding less than confident for the first time. "This probably wasn't what you had in mind a second ago. You were being really sweet."

I kiss him softly, and he leans into me, taking more. "I do want to," I assure him. I'm so turned on, so desperate to be as close as possible, I can't wait to stuff my dick into a flesh light with him.

He bites my lower lip as he draws away. "Then get yourself wet."

He's only got the one hand, and he's holding the flesh light with it, so I lube my cock and arrange myself to face him. He pushes a discreet button on the toy, and it makes a soft swishing sound. Then he hands it to me. "You do it."

We've got to get extremely close for this. I grab his thigh and pull it over mine, then line our erections up between us. Wrapping a fist around them, I stroke them both, and he groans. "Fuck, your dick feels so good."

So does his. Hot and rigid and slick. It takes a few tries to get us into the soft, slippery hole together. There's some cursing on my part and some breathy laughs on his, but once I get the aim right, and we sink into it together, we both gasp sharply.

"Jesus Christ," I groan.

"That's so fucking tight. Ryan...oh my God."

The toy is filled with silicone, I think. It's a squishy, wet, mess, but with his rigid length smashed against mine, I don't know how I can last more than a few seconds.

Holding the toy still, I find his mouth with mine and kiss him.

He grunts in response to my tongue entering his mouth, and his good hand grips the back of my neck. "Is this too weird? he asks breathily.

"No," I manage. "It's incredible. I love it."

With my free hand, I grab his ass and we start to move into the toy. Angles being what angles are, we each only get about halfway in, but with the mild, vibrating suction and the hard heat of his dick on mine, it's more than enough.

"Shit," I grunt.

"Mmm... God... Yes. Fuck my cock, Ryan. I love fucking you like this."

"I love you," I tell him.

"Fuck. Me, too, baby."

Our kiss is messy and wet, interrupted with his whimpers and my grunts of restraint. I could come on command, but I'm doing everything I can to hold it in. He's in a zone, languidly stroking with tight rolls of his hips and long licks of his tongue. It's another dimension of sexy, and when I match his rhythm, it's so good—so fucking good, I have to confess I'm screwed. "Gonna...unh...fuck...*come*." The word is barely out before I'm nutting into the toy and all over his cock.

The pressure inside gets extreme as my dick thickens and throbs.

"Holy fuck," he breathes, hand on my shoulder suddenly as his hips buck, and everything inside the flesh light gets hotter and filthier. We look at each other and our mouths slam together. I shove the toy onto our erupting dicks, and we pound into it together, crying out against each other's mouths as we empty ourselves thrust after relentless thrust. The pleasure is mind-blowing. All the atoms in my body are in their most excitable state. Bliss is sweating through my pores.

Empty and overstimulated, I remove the fleshlight, trying to be careful with the mess we left inside, but there's no good way to do it. I resolve to keep a stack of towels by the bed from now on.

"Well?" he asks, once I've laid it carefully on the floor and made my way back into his arms.

"So fucking hot," I murmur into his neck. "You're so *fucking* hot."

"You sure you didn't take any of the pills?" he asks with a laugh in his words.

"Shut the fuck up. I did exactly what you wanted."

"Yeah. You did." He runs his fingers through my hair and looks into my eyes. "And I fucking love you for it."

I might never understand it, but I take his word for it. "*Ugh.* Mal. I love you so much."

Then. Now. And I'm guessing always.

BAILEY GRABS my arm as I'm stepping into the conference room Monday morning and rushes me across the hall into the lounge. "Did you see the numbers this morning?"

I study her face, the feverish gleam in her eyes. "Which numbers?" Given where we work, she could mean anything, but I'm guessing this is more specific to us. Subscribers, likes, follows, shares, views.

"We're in the *hundreds* of thousands."

"*Dollars?*"

I can tell she's getting frustrated by the thin, pressed line of her mouth, but she at least pretends to have patience with me as she shakes her head. "Views. YouTube subscribers. But if you want to know about dollars, those are rolling in, too. We've had more than *six thousand* Patreon subscribers since Saturday. The Discord is blowing the fuck up!"

"Are you serious?"

"People *love* you and Mal."

I'm literally stunned. "I—I can't believe it."

"I know. Me neither, but you got *something* that's working."

The veiled dig amuses me, and I smile with her. "That's incredible."

"This morning, I got an email from an online trading company who wants to sponsor the next episode."

"No shit?"

"No shit. I know we need to get to the meeting, and I want to know how Mal's doing, but I'm so excited!"

I can tell. And it looks good on her. "Mal's fine. He'll be back tomorrow."

"I'll send a group text in a little bit with all the stats. You think we'll be okay to film tomorrow night? Will Mal be up for it?"

"Yeah," I say with confidence. "Just let me know what you want us to talk about. I'm assuming you've got thoughts."

She gives me one of her jump-scare hugs. I lift her off the floor and spin her around once, in a perfect mood. She screams a little before dissolving into laughter.

When I set her down, we join the morning meeting, sitting next to each other with Miguel. I notice the dirty looks he's getting from everyone but Nathan. The look he's getting from him is…different. It's angry, but there's something else in it, too. Frustration, maybe? Regret?

Curiosity killing me, I lean in to ask Miguel quietly, "You okay?" He's buckled under their mean vibes before, and the room is full of them today.

He cups a hand to hide his mouth and whispers in my ear, "Nathan came to my apartment last night. He wanted me back on their team."

"Did something happen?" I ask, barely moving my mouth.

"Have lunch with me," he says.

I nod and refocus on Georgie who's explaining different ways of writing a risk analysis to Jia, who I've gathered from previous meetings isn't having the best time with her mentor either. For someone who used to be so outgoing and quick to smile, she's seemed down lately, and we've stopped walking to work together. I wonder if she feels the same way about this internship as Mal does—that maybe it isn't a good fit for her.

I count myself lucky again to have been paired with Charlie who's teaching me something new every day. For the first time in a long time, I've got nothing to be pissed off about. It's hard to know what to do with myself. Is this how normal people feel?

My good mood persists while I have another productive morning with Charlie before meeting Miguel for lunch at Big Bites. Face to face with him, I notice the signs of sleep deprivation on his face. His large, dark eyes are weary, and there's a little frizz in his hair that's usually much better tamed—like he forgot to put product in it.

He doesn't look bad, he never does, but he doesn't look as put together as usual. "First off, congratulations," he says. "I can't believe those numbers."

I can't help my smile. It's crazy that our shouting into the void plan that began with bare chests and cute pets is actually working. "Honestly, I can't either, but I'll take the win."

"Oh, it'll definitely be a win. The other team's falling apart."

"Okay, yeah, what's up?"

"This goes nowhere," he says, palms flat on the table, tone serious and low.

"You've got my word."

"So, Nathan came to my apartment last night. Just showed up around nine. I thought he was gonna give me shit for leaving the team or make sure I wasn't telling you guys what they were doing—not that it matters because there's no way they can beat you guys—"

"Us," I remind him. "You're part of it, too. Right?"

"Oh—yeah—no question. No, this isn't me saying I'm bailing —trust me—as long as Piper is drawing breath, I'm going nowhere near that shit again."

"Okay," I say, reassured.

"No, he was actually upset. Like asking what he did wrong— why I left."

"Too much drama, right?" I clarify.

"*So* much fucking drama, which is exactly what I told him. And he was like—" Miguel puts his hand on his chest like he's mimicking Nathan. "From me?"

I raise my eyebrows. I know gossiping is shitty, but at the same time, it's hard to resist. And technically this isn't gossip since Miguel is just relaying a story of something that actually happened to him.

"So I said, sort of—yeah. Him, Piper, Lisette."

"What about Jia?"

"Poor Jia. She's doing most of the work while everybody else snipes at each other *and* her."

"That sucks."

"I mean, I'd tell her to bail, but she's too deep in it now, and if they do end up making a decent amount of money, she could easily make the case it was primarily her doing, so I'm just keeping my fingers crossed for her."

I nod, sort of wishing we had room for one more on our team, but I'm not sure how much thinner we can stretch ourselves and still allocate proper credit.

"But that's not what I want to talk about," Miguel says.

"Okay, I'm listening."

"He *kissed* me."

"*Oh.*"

"Yeah—like—no preamble, no permission—just grabbed me and laid one on, which was hot as fuck, but obviously not okay."

"Right," I say carefully because he's looking at me like he needs me to agree.

"*Exactly.* And also—I know I said we hooked up, but there wasn't any kissing involved. It was a BJ in the bar bathroom. Technically two—two separate occasions."

"Is he *okay*?" I ask. I don't know why I'm concerned with everyone's mental health all of a sudden, but maybe it's because I've never seen so many people crack under pressure all at once.

Miguel shrugs, looking baffled. "Once I got him off me, I asked the same thing. He started *crying.*"

This is almost impossible to picture. Six-five, wall of muscle, cocksure Nathan breaking down because Miguel wouldn't let him kiss him? I need more information.

"He said he can't stop thinking about me, that he wants me. It's a trap, right?"

"A trap?" I ask.

"To get me back on the team."

"Why would he want you back on the team that bad?"

Miguel looks confused, and I swear more of his hair frizzes at the question. "I don't know. He doesn't like to lose?"

"Nobody likes to lose."

Miguel's eyes widen. "What are you saying?"

"Nothing, just...he was *crying*?"

"I mean haven't we all cried at least once about this job this summer?"

"I haven't."

"Well, I have plenty. It's a lot."

"It is a lot," I agree, but I think Miguel might be missing something here. "Do you like him?"

"Who? Nathan? I mean, he's hot. He has an incredible dick."

I try not to laugh.

"But he's basically a **sex addict**."

"You think?"

"*Obviously*. I don't think he can make it through a day— honestly," Miguel says. "And he's not choosy."

"Maybe he just needs a friend," I offer as an unlikely alternative.

Miguel grimaces. "Maybe. He's got a weird way of going about it."

"If you like him..." I trail off, not sure what I want to say.

"I think I just needed to tell someone about it."

"Feel better?" I ask.

"Yeah. Kind of. Anyway, if you see or hear anything..."

"Yeah, sure," I say, understanding Miguel is more interested in Nathan than he wants to admit.

"So...speaking of which, you and Malcolm, huh?"

I smile, unable to help myself again. "Yeah. Me and Mal."

"Is it a big deal, or...?"

Interesting question. And incredibly personal when I think about my answer. Confusing, too. "Yeah," I say, trying to sound dismissive or vaguely indifferent about it. "But it's not something I need everybody knowing about. At work, you know?"

"Oh, of course not. But Bailey?"

Bailey knows a little too much in my opinion. I hope she didn't tell Miguel that Mal and I used to be stepbrothers after I took him to the ER Saturday night. Why I care is a question for another day, but being the subject of office gossip—any kind of gossip—isn't something I'm interested in.

I shrug in response. "I trust her." *Who am I?* A dude who gives trust out like candy, apparently. Love really does make people stupid, and it turns out, I'm not immune.

We talk some more—about Mal, mostly. I share with Miguel that it's our first time in a same sex relationship, and he seems surprised by that. Not the fact that Mal is gay—according to Miguel it was *obvious?* But that I'm bi, which, not gonna lie, is something I can't wait to tell Malcolm later.

After we wrap up lunch, I spend the rest of the afternoon tackling Charlie's to-do list—returning phone calls and emails mainly. Mal texts me around three, asking if I mind going to his place to get his work ID. I tell him no problem.

MALCOLM

And if you find anything else fun you want to bring over, my nightstand drawers are deep and full of surprises.

That gives me an eyebrow raise and throb in the groin region. I've never been one for toys, but I have to admit—the flesh light experience was one of the hottest things I've ever done. I have to force myself not to think about it to get through the rest of the day.

The debrief has a tense vibe. Bailey and I are fine, but no one else seems to be. Piper and Lisette look seconds away from pulling each other's hair out, Jia appears to have had a recent cry, and Nathan is staring down Miguel who is trying like hell to pretend he doesn't notice.

"Looks like he wants to eat you alive," I murmur to Miguel, getting close enough to him to make Nathan's fist clench on the table. Admittedly, I'm testing a theory, and Nathan's tell proved it correct. I can't speak for every man, but once a dude has sucked your dick, it's hard to imagine letting a woman do it. No shade to all the lovely women who've wrapped their mouths around mine, and maybe all guys aren't as good at it as Malcolm is, but I'd bet good money Miguel is.

Bottom line, it's a relief to get the fuck out of the Marks & Baker building, even though I have to go to Mal's depressing apartment before I head home to him.

His place is worse in the daylight. All the finishings look cheap and slapped on. The kitchen cabinets are hung slightly crooked, and cold white light from the cutout windows doesn't do the anemic paint job any favors. I'm half tempted to pack all his shit and bring it back to my place, but again, I need to pace myself.

His work ID is on the small kitchen island. I assume wrangling Stephanie and his garment bag must have distracted him from grabbing it on his way out Saturday. I put the lanyard around my neck, and decide to check out his nightstand.

Sitting on his bed, I open the top drawer. There's a bottle of lube and one, smaller flesh light, but he led me to believe there was a more extensive selection.

The bottom drawer is where it's at. There's nothing crazy. A set of handcuffs, three more flesh lights, which makes me laugh because he's obviously a fan, a wand vibrator he's probably used on Kaylin, or it *is* hers, and I'm therefore not touching it, and an elaborate silicone cock ring. I do grab that.

When I reach for the lube in the top drawer because it's a better brand than the one I got from the store the other day, a bunch of other shit tumbles out of place. Not that the drawer was incredibly organized to begin with, but I do my best to make less of a mess of it. I move a few batteries and a remote control, and then my fingers land on a small velvety box.

Picking it up, one look at it makes my stomach drop. I inhale once, deeply, and flip the lid.

The large diamond engagement ring catches a ray of sunlight, and sparkles scatter everywhere.

CHAPTER TWENTY-SEVEN

MALCOLM

Ryan wakes me up from my afternoon nap with his hand running up my back and his body stretched out in front of me. "Hey," I murmur, before he softly plants a kiss on my cheek.

"Hey."

"How was work?" I ask.

He sighs like he's letting the whole day out. Cracking my eyes open, I see he's still dressed, just with a loose tie and no jacket. He skipped the gym? Do I care? I wrap my hand around his tie to keep him close.

"Kinda crazy," he says. "How was your day? How's your wrist?"

"Fine, fine. Define crazy."

He throws a leg over mine and runs his fingers through my hair, snuggling as close as he can get. "Girl drama, boy drama."

"Any fucking in the bathroom?"

"Not that I noticed."

"Shame."

Ryan laughs softly and kisses my face again. "Do I need to take Stephanie out?"

"In a minute. You feel good."

"Yeah?"

"Yeah," I hum, closing my eyes and soaking him up. Despite his long day, he smells good. Like hair gel and his sexy cologne. Even the warmth of his skin has a scent to it. I could pick him out of a line-up now using only my nose.

He surprises me with a full kiss on the mouth. I keep mine closed at first, conscious of the fact that I just woke up, but he's insistent, and it's like the words "hold on" or "wait" or "no" have left my vocabulary. As soon as I part my lips, his tongue takes me over, and I groan as my dick swells.

His hand grabs my ass and squeezes, forcing our cocks to rub together. He's half-hard, and he uses my body to get himself rigidly erect. Me, too, obviously. I want to ask to what do I owe the pleasure, but he's not giving me a chance to say much more than "*Mmmhhh.*"

Since I've been mostly in bed all day, being lazy as fuck, I'm only wearing underwear, which makes me ridiculously easy to access. I love the feel of this. Not just what he's doing to me, but being in his bed mostly naked like I've been waiting for him. Thinking of him and wanting him. Not entirely false, but I slept a lot, too, and I also texted with Kaylin for a few minutes.

We're meeting Thursday for the Stephanie hand off and the official break up. I didn't mention that second thing to her because that would be too much like breaking up over text, and I know better than that.

But back to Ryan's hand in my underwear and his fingertip probing my hole. Gotta admit, he usually takes longer to warm up, and this is a slight red flag that maybe his day wasn't as bland as he claims, but fuck if I can care when desire is burning like a brushfire through my body, incinerating every cell.

I feel like a whore. *His* whore in the best possible way— yielding to him and writhing against him, ready to open for him.

I'm wearing a pair of his white briefs because I liked the way he looked at me when I was wearing them last time. That was another thing I did that was productive today—ordered a six pack of tighty whiteys from Amazon.

"Let me fuck you, baby," he says.

Fuck, I love it when he calls me that. If he keeps up with it, I'll let him do more than fuck me. I'll let him marry me. Gladly, I roll over and offer him my ass.

Ryan doesn't waste time. As soon as he's peeled off the briefs, he's pushing lube into me. As rushed as it feels, I'm still rocked by the suddenness with which he's wedging his cock inside. The feel of his pants and his shirt are distinct on my skin, and I almost ask if he's okay, but I'm too preoccupied with taking him to speak. It's a mess of adjustments and deep breaths and bearing down to let him tunnel in deep.

Once he's where he wants to be, he bands an arm around my chest, presses his mouth to the nape of my neck, and pounds his cock into my ass. I touch myself thoughtlessly, my body beginning to understand that the more I involve my own dick, the easier it is to get fucked by his. Granted, I'll take it any way he wants to give it to me, but I like that it's getting better every time.

He gives up on my neck, resorting to panting in my ear as his pace picks up. He pinches my nipple hard, and I gasp as the pain makes me fist my cock tighter. Whatever the fuck magic that was, I hope he does it again. A few more times, and I'll come so fucking hard...

He doesn't though, and I lose myself in his rough, quick strokes, the sound of his hips slapping my ass, his heavy breathing, and the wet squelch of lube. God, he feels so good. I'm torn between wanting to keep jerking my dick and wanting to grab onto him somewhere and let him take me on this wild ride.

"Yes, *please*," I praise him. "Just like that."

He tries, but soon enough his breaths quicken, and his hips

lose their rhythm. Shoving in deep, he holds himself there and throbs out his release, gasping as it takes him. When he starts milking his cock in my ass, I go over the edge—the slide too slick, too hot for me to ignore. "Fuck," I grit out, my hand flying over my erupting dick. "Jesus—mother*fuck*."

He's back to kissing my neck and running his thumb over my nipple, his length still buried in my ass. "I love you," he says.

"Baby," I reply.

"Yeah?"

"You meant to say, I love you, baby."

"Did I?"

He removes his cock from my hole. Warm cum trickles down my crack and thigh crease and I stare at the mess I made on his sheets. I never fully appreciated how messy sex is before, but I almost wish it could be messier. I love it.

However—"Why are you still dressed?"

"Couldn't wait," he says. "And I have to take the dog out."

I find myself frowning and smiling at the same time. "How crazy *was* today?"

"Am I not allowed a quickie?"

That didn't answer the question. "Is that what that was?" I ask.

"I went as fast as I could."

"Are you all right?"

A hesitation and then he says, "Yeah. All good."

Oh man... This guy's got so many walls up—walls I absolutely blame myself for—I need to start working on a map of them so I know which ones to start tearing down next.

$$\$\$\$$$

Aᴛᴇʀ ᴡᴇ ᴡʀᴀᴘ up filming our second episode, Bailey stands in front of me with her hands in her overalls' pockets, giving me a look I don't think I like.

"Sooo…about that wrist of yours."

I scowl up at her. "What about it?"

"Well, I mean, you didn't talk about it in the episode."

"That's because gold has nothing to do with casts. One of the reasons."

She swivels back and forth, all innocent looking. It's a trap. Avoiding my eyes, she says, "I'm just saying, people will have questions. We're at the point when we need to think about the fans…"

"You want me to make a TikTok about it?"

"No…that won't be necessary, if…"

"If what?" I ask. "Could you just spit it out?"

"Well, the thing is, we have the whole fall on video—from three different angles."

"Oh—you mean while you were laughing hysterically at the fact that I broke my wrist?"

"That one, yes."

"That's not going on TikTok."

"Oh, I completely agree. I mean mostly. It'd be like an outtake on the Patreon."

I'm glaring now. It's obvious she's trying not to laugh, and I'm pretty sure it's because she's remembering how funny she found the incident before she realized I'd broken a damn bone.

"Fine," I say.

"And just like a tiny snippet on TikTok. Like a teaser."

"Do you seriously think people are gonna sign up to pay twelve ninety-nine a month to watch me trip over a dog?"

She keeps swiveling. "I mean…*I* would."

I look around for Ryan to back me up here, but he's left the room, and Miguel is too busy managing the equipment to help save my dignity—what's left of it.

"Are you forgetting what happened after I fell?" I ask. Me and Ryan—neck kissing.

"No, but I'll cut most of that."

"Most of it?" I ask, appalled. "The other interns watch our videos."

She waves her hands dismissively. "I can't worry about them anymore. They've got their own mess to deal with. I've got a ship in the making, and a fall that was fucking hilarious. Sorry, but it's a thing. I'm not the only person in the world who loses it when I see someone fall. It's *gold*, Mal. There—there's your crossover."

"Yeah," I say. "I see what you did there. Do I actually get a choice, or is this more an illusion of a choice?"

"I guess think of it more as a heads up."

Ryan is back in the office with a glass of water. He frowns at me and the *help please* look on my face. "What?" he asks.

"Bailey wants to put a video of me falling on the Patreon."

Ryan shakes his head. "No. Absolutely not."

"Okay, but hear me out," she says.

"He said no," I say.

"All due respect to both of your nopes, but I'm on this team, too, and what the hell have I been wrong about so far?"

Ryan and I share a look.

He says, "What about the part where I—"

Bailey faces him. "I won't show the part where you tried to make out with him, okay? God. But I do want to show you running to his rescue."

"Why?" Ryan asks.

I'm still stuck on the tried to make out with me part. "What'd you do?"

"I just—kissed you for a second. Not on the mouth."

"You kissed *me*?" I ask, beyond happy to hear this confirmed.

"It was like—a reflex or whatever."

Bailey snorts a laugh, and I smile. "That's the move, huh?"

"Shut the fuck up," he says, and then to Bailey, "You're not posting that."

"The kiss—right. Cutting room floor. Swear to God."

"No, *I* swear to God," he says. "If that kiss makes it anywhere near the internet, I don't care how much you've done for this project—I'll fire you."

Her eyes widen. "Mal, you might need to take your cat home. His claws are out again."

I stand, ready to follow her instructions, but Ryan is still looking at her. "Can I have a minute please?"

"Sure," she says, then, "Oh! You mean with me?"

"Yes," he growls in that slightly feral way that makes my balls get tight.

He and Bailey leave the office together, and I ask Miguel if he needs any help.

He eyes my cast. "Not sure how much help you'll be, but I appreciate the offer."

"Do you think it's funny when people fall?" I ask.

"Depends on the person. Depends on the fall. Since you fell in my house, I didn't find it particularly funny, no."

"It was the dog's fault," I assure him. That's why we left her at Ryan's tonight.

Miguel nods over his shoulder in the direction Ryan and Bailey went. "He's protective of you."

"Yeah?" I ask, unable to help the small smile, and helpless against the blush.

"I hope you don't mind, or you can forgive her, but Bailey told me you used to be stepbrothers. He didn't mention that."

I could fucking heat a room with my face. "We were more like best friends," I say.

"I have stepbrothers," Miguel says. "Three. I hate *all* of them."

"Younger? Older?"

"Older. Assholes. And not a one of them is remotely attractive, which probably explains why they're such dicks."

I huff. "Maybe."

"Anyway, they're very much in a different category than my actual brother, who I don't care for much, either, but there's a difference."

"So, you don't think it's like—sick or wrong or whatever?"

"*No,*" he says emphatically. "It's actually really romantic."

"I wish our history was romantic."

"Was it not?"

"We had a rough patch." Or as I like to think of it now: a decade long mistake, although *mistake* doesn't really do it justice.

"All better?" Miguel asks.

"I hope so. I think so."

"Anyway," he says, "My point is, whether it's weird for your families or whatever, it doesn't matter what you start out as— just where you end up. Because that's what was meant to be, you know? You can't help how you met."

I take a deep breath and consider the whole of it. I get where he's coming from—what he's trying to say. It's different than meeting the love of your life on a bus in fourth grade, but how Ryan and I know each other seems a lot less important than what we *mean* to each other. And obviously, it hasn't stopped me. Or him.

Do I want to advertise it? No. But I can't change it either. Nor would I want to. "Yeah," I say. "I can own it."

"Good."

"Is this where you tell me love is love?"

He scoffs. "No. It absolutely is not. But it is where I tell you love is fabulous when it's not the worst fucking thing ever."

I laugh. "Yeah, no I get that."

Ryan and Bailey reappear. Bailey doesn't say anything, but Ryan locks eyes with me and asks, "You ready?"

"Yeah."

"Let's go."

Yes, sir.

Once we've been silent for half a block, I ask, "What did you need to say to Bailey that you couldn't say in front of me? I realize what I'm asking."

He exhales a harsh breath. "I just reminded her that you have a girlfriend."

My thoughts about protectiveness and us being meant to be screech to a halt. I stop walking. "Seriously?"

He faces me. "What?"

This is so fucking frustrating. Why is he like this? Why can't he just be with me without trying to find some major impediment to it? "I mean, I appreciate you thinking about that and everything, but I'm just surprised, I guess. You haven't said a word about her in a while."

"She's coming home tomorrow."

"Yeah, and I'm gonna talk to her on Thursday when she comes to get Stephanie."

"Talk to her?"

"Break up," I specify because obviously I need to state it for the damn record.

"Yeah, okay."

"Are you worried I'm gonna see her and all of a sudden forget that I'm in love with you?"

He looks down at the sidewalk, his hair falling to cover whatever view I might have had of his face. "I don't know what's gonna happen, Mal. I'm doing my best, okay?"

"Doing your best?"

"To trust you."

"Have I given you a reason not to?" I ask. I've barely let him out of my sight.

"No," he whispers, sounding choked. "But I don't want..."

I wait, not the world's best at being patient, but trying.

"I don't want you to feel like you've got something to prove or you're—whatever—trying to make up for something."

"You think I'm doing you some kind of favor?" I could almost laugh if he didn't seem so twisted up.

"You have history with her. A whole relationship."

"Yeah..." Where the fuck is he going with this? If he tries to break up with me—

"I just want you to do what's right for you," he says. "Don't worry about me, okay?"

"Ry, are you kidding?" I step toward him, and he looks up, into my eyes.

He bites his lip, and there's a slight tremble in it. "Having you in my life is enough," he says. "You not hating me is enough."

"No," I whisper, putting my fully functioning hand on his face. "It's not. Not for me, it's not."

"But when you see her again—"

"Ryan. Come on—do you see my face? I *love* you. And it's not fucking new."

"I love you, too, but—"

"But?" I ask, verging on losing it. "But *what*?"

"I get that you might...*want*...something else."

"More than I want you? You're crazy."

"I'm just saying it doesn't have to be like...the way it's been."

I narrow my gaze. Is he saying we can go back to just being friends? He's gotta know I'm too far gone for that. Right?

I don't know what he's saying or not saying, but this is about as open as Ryan gets, and I think for once I know what he needs.

"On the off chance I wouldn't change a thing..." I'm joking because there's zero chance of me wanting anything less than everything, and I hope he gets it. He *should* get it, if we're as in love as *I* think we are.

His half smile says he does. "I'll keep your side of the bed empty."

"My side, huh?" He and I could sleep on a twin bed and still have room for another person. A small person, but still.

"Fine, my side. Whatever."

"You make me crazy," I tell him, but then I kiss him, wishing I didn't have to wait for Thursday to get him to start trusting that the only person I want anything from is *him*.

CHAPTER TWENTY-EIGHT

RYAN

It's Friday morning and I haven't heard from Mal since he left work to meet up with Kaylin Thursday, but that's how I wanted it. I asked him not to reach out—told him I'd see him today. I turned my phone off so he couldn't text or call me. Why? Because I'm psycho, and I can't get the image of that engagement ring out of my head.

I figured if I knew I wasn't going to hear from him, then I wouldn't drive myself nuts waiting and wondering.

It's not because I think he was going to propose to her last night—but because at some point *he was planning to propose*. It's safe to say my trust, such as it is, has been stretched to its outermost limits, but it's hanging in there.

Would it be so fucking difficult for him to at least be on time this morning, though? Of all mornings? Jesus.

"Where's your boyfriend?" Piper asks, unexpectedly taking a seat next to me at the conference room table.

I can't say I wasn't expecting this. Bailey cut out the neck kiss and me calling him baby, but there was enough in the video of Malcolm's fall to prove one thing at least—I have more than a passing interest in his well-being. In my defense, I've seen too many movies and TV shows where a fall to the ground cracked a skull, and in the moment I ran over to him, the first thing I was looking for was blood pooling around his head, signaling the end.

Piper however, whether she realizes it or not, gave something away with the question. "Do you use your own money to subscribe to our Patreon or the group cash? Either way, we appreciate the support."

She sidesteps my dig. "I just wonder what Jonathan would think about fraternization…"

"Do you? So, you and Nathan never…" I make a lewd gesture with my hands.

Her mouth twists into an unpretty shape. "Who told you that? They're full of shit."

Apparently not.

"What are we talking about?" Bailey asks, taking her seat on my other side, her eyes on my hands.

"Fraternization," I tell her.

"Fun," she says.

Piper rises without a sound and moves to sit in her usual spot next to Lisette. Just then, Malcolm walks through the door. He's not wearing one of his sluttier suits, and that's the first thing I notice, but then I remember he spent last night at his place—theoretically—and maybe all his newer looks are still in my closet. The second thing I see are the dark circles under his eyes, betraying a lack of sleep, and as he gets closer, I notice the puffiness of his eyelids. Like he's recently spent a hell of a lot of time crying.

Before I have time to ask him anything, Georgie breezes in and starts talking before they're even sitting.

"Sorry folks, this'll be brief. We have company today, and I have another conference to get to. There's a shareholders' meeting this afternoon, so the senior investors and analysts are all here to make presentations. If your mentors are okay with it, you're welcome to sit in, and please make your own introductions. Any questions?"

We all, to some degree, look at each other. I barely understand a word Georgie just said, but I blame that on Malcolm and my urgent need to talk to him. But before I can, Isla appears in the doorway of the conference room and gestures for him to get up and come with her.

He and I share a look. "Later," he mouths, and he looks fucking miserable.

It's not the first time one of the mentors dragged us out of the huddle early, but it's the first time Isla's taken Malcolm. I can only assume she's got one of the earlier presentations.

He gets up and goes with her. Bailey says, "Would have been nice if they gave us a heads up about this say—any other time than this morning."

"Yeah." I pick up my bag and push my chair back from the table. I'm already cursing my own stupidity for icing Malcolm out last night. In retrospect, there was no good reason for it. What if he needed to talk? Or needed to see me? Why couldn't I have just assumed he was going to do what he said he was planning to do rather than have some last minute change of heart?

Charlie's at the common room worktable, looking chill. Malcolm and Isla aren't there. "You don't have one of these presentations?" I ask, taking my spot next to him.

He chuckles. "No. But I'm helping Jess with hers later. You're welcome to sit in."

"Thanks," I tell him before picking up some work I was doing yesterday and trying my best to concentrate while the room is buzzing with tension and more conversation than usual. With at least twenty tabs opened on my browser, I'm zoned in on a market analysis for a small business client when I feel a light tap on my shoulder.

I turn and look up, then I nearly come out of my skin with shock.

"Hi," Norah says softly.

I'm standing before I can make any words come out, the instinct to hug her overriding any sense of where we are or what's appropriate. She laughs as I put my arms around her, and she hugs me back.

The smell of her transports me immediately back to Portland nights. Sitting next to her in a cafe, across from her in her office, watching a movie with her on her couch after a study group broke up for the night.

Remembering where we are, I pull away and take a look at her. Her dark hair is thick and straight but styled with a soft wave at her shoulders. It's glossy, and I remember the one time I kissed her, the way the strands slid through my fingers like silk.

Her big brown eyes are large and round, lined with long lashes. She has perfect pale, rosy skin and glossy burgundy lips. She's in a pencil skirt and a white silk blouse with tiny black polka-dots that I remember. It makes me realize it really hasn't been that long since I've seen her. A few months.

"Why didn't you tell me you were coming?" I ask.

"I didn't know until two days ago, and then I thought it might be a fun surprise."

"I'm surprised," I say, still taking her in. This is—

Not good, actually.

I mean—it doesn't have to be bad, but it's definitely less than ideal. I haven't been exactly straightforward with her about how I've been spending my time outside of work and the challenge. And I haven't been exactly honest with Malcolm about how often she and I talk.

I know she's seen the TikToks, and she might have thrown us a bone by subscribing to the Patreon, but I haven't told her about Mal. Or me and Mal. While the tone of our conversations has been a lot less future focused, especially over the last two weeks —more friendly—the last thing I told Mal about her was that she was where I saw my future.

And with her here...

"Hey, Norah. How's it going?" Charlie asks from behind me.

I step out of the way so they can talk.

"Great! Did you know Ryan was a student of mine during my year at PSU?"

"I wondered if the two of you crossed paths." To me he says, "Norah was in my internship."

"Oh yeah? That's cool." I say like she didn't tell me that day one of this job.

"Would you mind a lot if I borrow Ryan for the day?" she asks him.

I stiffen at that. I'm not sure why the idea of spending the day working with her is such a threat, but it feels existential. There's a reason I've been slow to commit to anything ongoing with Malcolm, and while Kaylin was a big part of it, Norah is arguably the bigger one.

Choosing between two people is one thing, but choosing between two entirely different lives is another. Up until very recently, my plans for the end of the summer hadn't been in question. I was convinced what Mal and I were doing together would run its course. He'd freak out, get bored, or otherwise back away, and I relied on this back up plan to keep myself from feeling anything too deeply. It's really only been in the last week or so that I've found myself leaning into him. Allowing myself to imagine a future with him at the center of it.

But that engagement ring—the reality of Norah. How safe she feels even now—when I know I'm not in love with her.

The truth is I've only ever been in love with the idea of her. The idea of starting over and leaving the past behind.

Mal is a risk. He's like the living embodiment of risk. He

changes his mind, he moves onto the next thing, he goes hard and gives up so fast it can make heads spin. I'm not even sure I'd call him stable. Not that I think he needs to be committed or anything, but if I only look at the last month—how he went from insulting me to attaching himself to me on the turn of a dime...

Don't second guess him, I tell myself firmly. But the other voice in my head that's staring at Norah is saying, *don't be an idiot.*

"Sure—take him. Teach him something useful. As you know, you're in good hands, Ryan."

"Yeah," I tell Charlie. "Thanks."

Norah smiles up at me, her eyes shining. "Shall we?"

I swallow nervously and nod. As she walks, and I follow, I glance around the room, only to find Malcolm's heavy-lidded aquamarine eyes trailing me. The look on his face puts me through a wringer of guilt. He's got no idea who this is, but the next time I see him, he'll have probably found out. And then what?

Meanwhile, Norah is speaking. "They gave me a tiny little office to set up in. I'm presenting at two. I don't know if you'll actually learn anything, but you can listen to me stress."

I have to look away from Mal as I turn down a hallway with her. As soon as no one is around, she slips an arm around my waist and walks close. I reflexively do the same. "Good to see you," she says.

"Sorry," I say. "I'm just really surprised."

"Good surprised, I hope."

"Yeah, I mean...you look great."

She laughs. "So do you. I've been watching your videos of course, but in person, it just takes it all up a notch."

"Ha. Thanks."

"Are you guys raking in the cash or what?"

"Kind of."

"You think you'll win?"

"I'm pretty sure."

She lets out a subdued but excited squeal. "Isn't that the best feeling? Not being a thirst trap—I know how you are—but winning?"

The *best* feeling? I mean—it's good. Who doesn't love to win? But the best part of the challenge by far has been sharing it with Malcolm and Bailey, now Miguel. I'm honest with Norah. "It's something I can see us doing long term. Helping one person at a time is great, and giving specialized attention, but building a community..."

"That's what I loved about teaching," Norah says. She lets go of me to open a door and gestures me into a tiny office with a sliver of a window. There's a bookcase full of what looks like old ledgers covered in dust, a desk, and three chairs. Her laptop is on the desk along with her pink Stanley and a half-eaten protein bar. The déjà vu is strong.

"So," she says, pulling a seat up next to hers and sitting. "Is Isla still terrorizing all the men? Tell me everything."

$$\$\$\$$$

I COUNT myself lucky that Norah is the way she is. I think it would take an act of God, or at least many shots of tequila for her to actually make a move. She's flirtier long distance than she is in person, and so she really does want the office gossip and to vent about her presentation. Her smiles and lingering looks are the only hint that there's ever been a spark of heat between us, but the morning I spend with her is almost completely platonic.

It's over lunch that the conversation veers into more personal territory.

We're at Big Bites. We cut out of the office around eleven-thirty, earlier than most people leave for lunch. She said the protein bar wasn't cutting it, and I suggested the deli.

She eases into the subject of us by asking, "Are you still thinking you might want to check out the Seattle offices?"

"I haven't ruled it out," I say, which, admittedly, is a different tune than I was singing at the beginning of the summer.

"So...Malcolm...?" she says.

I flash a glance up at her from my menu. "Yeah?"

"I saw the TikTok where he fell."

"I figured you might have."

"You wanna say more?"

I sigh and push the menu aside. I get the same thing every time I'm here anyway. "He's a risk," I say.

"You hate those," is her soft reply.

"I don't hate *him*, though."

"No, it didn't look like it."

"Look, in my defense, I thought he hit his head."

"He did hit his head. On the floor."

"The thing is he's had this girlfriend since high school, and she's been out of town. They were serious about each other."

"And now?"

"I really wanted to move on from this," I say, defeated.

Her expression is sympathetic. She reaches across the table to hold my hand. "He's your stepbrother isn't he?"

"Was. He *was* my stepbrother."

"There is something sort of...I don't know. Magic between you."

"Between us, or is it just me being stupid?"

She frowns. "Why stupid?"

I give her a condensed version of our troubled history and she says, "You weren't stupid. And you weren't the asshole."

"He turned me into one, though."

"It sounds more like you turned yourself into one," she

disagrees. "Which is totally understandable defense against how you were treated."

"I just—if it hadn't been so disastrous when it went wrong the first time, it might be easier to trust these feelings."

I'm relieved she doesn't look heartbroken. Maybe she saw me as a long shot, too, or maybe I misread the whole situation with her in general. Who the fuck knows? I'm not exactly a genius at knowing when someone likes me, much less wants me.

"You're a stronger person now. You have a life you're building. You have a million opportunities. And you're what? Twenty-four?"

I nod.

"That's plenty of time to bounce back if it doesn't work out."

"I've never really been in a relationship before," I admit.

"They definitely have their pros and cons," she says.

"Were you head over heels for your ex when it all started?"

"A hundred percent," she says.

"You think you're more cautious now?" I ask.

"I think I'm just looking for different qualities. He wasn't very nice, my ex. There were red flags."

"Like what?"

"Like he was a terrible tipper."

I laugh. "I agree that's a red flag."

"I didn't expect him to cheat, though. That never occurred to me. So, I admit, that makes me question my judgment a lot more than I used to."

"Sorry," I say.

She shrugs. "I wasn't the one for him. That's how I see it now. There's a man I've been talking to who works a floor down in my building. Also divorced, similar story. Like I feel like I can just tell he would never cheat because he's so—can I say devoted if we've never been on a date?"

"You haven't gone out with him? Has he asked?"

She shakes her head, laughing softly. "No. But he texts me all the time. Random things. Stupid things. Like he's determined to keep my attention."

"Do you like him?" I ask.

She shrugs. "He's growing on me."

"Mal's like an invasive tumor I've had since I was a kid, so I know the feeling. You should ask him out."

"Oh, God…" she says like I asked her to try rock climbing without a harness.

"Wait—before I convince you, show me a picture."

She does, and I determine based on looks and his LinkedIn profile that he's good enough for her. We order our food, and I try to convince Norah to step outside her comfort zone. I promise her she can always run anything potentially shady by me. and I'll keep her from doing something she'll regret later.

She pays the bill after an easy forty-five minute conversation, and we slide out of the booth, ready to put the final touches on her presentation.

Taking my hand again she says, "Thank you."

"For what?" I ask.

She shrugs. "I don't know. Reminding me it's okay to go after what I want."

"You did the same for me." I give her a hug, grateful to her for giving me friendship and hope at a time when I was operating on an extremely shaky foundation.

"You've mellowed out a lot, you know," she says, still in my arms.

I laugh, burying my face in her hair. "I might be happy or something crazy like that."

"Enjoy it, Ryan. You deserve it."

"Thank you," I whisper. "So do you."

When we part, I feel someone brush by me, a shoulder against mine.

The back of Malcolm's head is all I get as he and Bailey walk to a booth in the back of the dining area. Bailey, however, turns to scowl at me.

"Oh shit. It's almost one." Norah says. "We need to get back. I have to add two more slides to my power point."

"One second," I say, walking quickly to catch Mal before he sits down.

He looks at me with wild eyes. "So that's her?"

"I—yeah, but—"

"Classy," he says. "You look great together. A perfect fit."

"Mal—"

"Not now, Ryan. Today's been shitty enough."

"We need to talk," I say.

He looks stricken.

"Not like—"

He shakes his head, and that shuts me up. "I left a bunch of shit at your apartment. I'll be by later."

"What?" I ask. Does that mean he's coming back to take his shit? Or he wants to talk, too?

"If you don't mind," he says, gesturing at his menu. "I'm hungry."

With that, he sits down with Bailey, and I read her angry expression differently now. It's not a how dare you hurt Malcolm look, it's more of a thanks a lot for making me deal with him like this look. Frankly, I'm surprised as hell they're having lunch just the two of them, but I guess we've all bonded.

Moderately reassured that we'll get the chance to clear the air tonight, I tell them I'll see them later and head out with Norah.

I trust Bailey not to let him spiral too hard.

CHAPTER TWENTY-NINE

MALCOLM

"You need to chill the fuck out, dude."

Either I'm not understanding something, or Bailey is fucking *blind*. It took me exactly five minutes after watching Ryan walk off with Norah Butler to put together that she's the woman in Seattle waiting for him to wrap up this internship and return to the Pacific Northwest.

I can't fucking believe how beautiful she is. I mean—I can—Ryan's hot as hell, but I don't know why I pictured her being some mousy finance nerd. Maybe because he hasn't exactly been falling all over himself to text her or call her—there's no pictures of her anywhere. I thought she was a back-up plan—not a fucking *goddess*.

I should have pressed for more information. I should have asked him point bank if he was still planning to move to Seattle. I shouldn't have assumed *anything*.

"I don't think I can do this," I say bluntly.

"Do what?" Bailey asks.

"If you could see inside me right now, you'd run screaming."

"Why? What's inside you?"

Depression. Insanity. Jealousy. Insecurity. Doubt. Fear. No—

it's not fear. It's abject fucking terror that I am way too late and not nearly enough. "Do you think he's straight?"

"Ryan?" she asks.

"Yes," I hiss at her.

"I think he's bi."

"What does that even mean? Is that really a thing?"

She laughs, a loud barking laugh. "Yes, Malcolm. Bisexuality *is* a thing. Did you or did you not just break up with a woman?"

"But I'm *gay*."

She frowns. "So what was that girlfriend of yours? You're gonna tell me you were never attracted to her? You never had sex?"

Kaylin is a sore spot today. Breaking up with her had been awful. She was understanding when I told her about Ryan, but she did cry, which made me cry, and we spent half the evening holding hands and remembering the good times. It was fucking awful. She never said as much, she's too nice, but I feel exactly like I wasted ten years of her life.

"I was confused," I say to Bailey. "That doesn't make me bi."

"Well, I'm gay, and you'd have to pay me a lot of money to have sex with a man."

"Maybe it's different for guys."

"I think it's just you if we're being honest."

"What about *him* though?" I ask, jabbing my thumb over my shoulder at the door where Ryan recently walked out.

"I haven't put much thought into it. Sorry."

"Well, put some thought into it unless you want me to start crying."

Her eyes widen. "What difference does it make how he identifies if you guys are into each other?"

"Did you not see the way they were touching?"

"I mean..." she shrugs and looks down at her menu like she knows exactly what I'm talking about. "Look, I'm not the best person to ask about bisexual people. I get that people can be attracted to a lot of different types, but I find there's usually a clear preference when it comes down to it. But my experience is limited."

"Sounds like you've had bad experiences."

"A lot of girls want to experiment in college. It's fun until it isn't, you know? Anyway, stereotypes happen for a reason, which isn't to say it's not a valid identity, it's just...*I've* had bad experiences."

"Like girls would hook up with you but end up getting serious about a guy?"

"Yeah, something like that."

"I think if I were bi, I would have broken up with Kaylin a while back."

"What makes you say that?" she asks.

"Because I'm not all that attracted to her. It's more like I got used to her."

"But at some point, you were attracted to her."

Do I really want to tell Bailey what led me to pursue Kaylin in the first place? If Ryan hadn't been interested in her, would I have found some other random girl to wave around in front of him to prove I wasn't what I was too afraid to admit I actually am?

I don't think so. She was—God forgive me—*convenient.*

Christ, I fucking hate myself.

Because he *did* like her. He might have accidentally confessed feelings for me, but if that hadn't happened, he probably would have gone on to date Kaylin himself and live a perfectly straight life. That's what he's been doing after all, isn't it? Until I started shamelessly throwing myself at him? "There's no guy you could possibly be attracted to?" I ask Bailey.

She squints at me like she's thinking really, really hard.

"Maybe like…" then she wrinkles her nose and shakes her head. "I can't with penises. Sorry."

"None taken," I say, and she laughs.

"Malcolm. Get it together. He's crazy about you. It's blatantly obvious."

"What if he doesn't want to be? What if he'd rather be crazy about her?"

"Now you're projecting."

"Am I?"

"Yes, because that sounds like exactly what you did. You didn't want to admit you wanted to kiss your stepbrother, and then you found a girl you could tolerate and took your angst out on her. You just happened to like her in the meantime and stuck with it. Maybe you convinced yourself you could keep lying to yourself forever, but that's not him."

"You barely know him," I say, although she's gotten quite the read on *me*.

"I know he's not half as confused as you are."

"I think you're wrong about that," I say with a fair degree of confidence. Ryan might not outwardly be as big of a mess as I am, but he's decently fucked up over what's happening with us. But enough to give up on it?

"I just mean he's crazy about you. And very protective."

Miguel said the same thing. "How do you know that?" I ask.

"Because he told me."

"When?"

She sighs. "Are you okay? Are you going to survive the rest of the day and not spiral into a jealousy vortex?"

"Sure," I tell her. Her tough love isn't going down easy today, and besides, I know what I know, and I saw what I saw. Ryan and Norah looked like endgame, which makes me a fling.

And if that's not the case—if it's just my paranoia making that hug look like more than it was—the doubts I have about him and me are still baked in. All his walls, his boundaries, his restraint—it can only mean one thing. He doesn't want me to get too close. Even the times I thought I was getting closer—breaking through—I might have only been wearing him down. Forcing words from him he didn't mean or wasn't intending to say—all while trying to recreate that one moment I shit all over ten years ago and do things better this time.

But *have* I done better? Have I been clear enough about what he means to me? How important he is? Or have I been too busy trying to get into his pants to say what I'm feeling from the bottom of my heart?

Isla gives me a withering look when I return fifteen minutes late from lunch. I hesitate before sitting down because I just—*can't.*

I can't with this. With her. With this place.

Today sucks, but working with Isla has been a nightmare. I've known for a while this isn't the job for me, and the idea of doing it for one second longer feels impossible. Especially today. Particularly now.

They say there's no time like the present.

Instead of taking my seat or any shit she's about to give me for taking a long lunch, I turn, walk down the hall to Georgie's office, and knock.

"Come in," they call out. When they see me, they grimace. "Can you make this quick? There's a lot going on today."

"I'll make it super fast," I assure them.

Georgie nods and gestures to the chair in front of the desk. "Go ahead."

Without sitting, I put my ID badge on their desk, "Thanks so much for the opportunity, but I don't think this is the place for me. I'm gonna go ahead and quit."

"Oh." I have their full attention now. "Do you need to talk about this?"

I shake my head. I don't. My mind is made up, and I already feel ten pounds lighter.

"Is it Isla?"

"It's more me," I say. "Isla didn't help, but honestly, I'm not a good fit for this kind of work. I'm sorry for wasting your time."

Georgie takes off their glasses and leans back in their chair, regarding me carefully. "You all right?"

"I don't know."

They sigh, a softer look on their face, like they wish they had time to get into this with me now, but I picked a bad day. "Well, touch base with me on Monday. If you have a change of heart, let me know."

"Will do." I appreciate the offer, but this doesn't feel like an impulse. Already I feel slightly more in control of my own destiny. "Thanks, Georgie," I say, and then back out of the office. Without a word to Isla, I gather my things and leave Marks & Baker for good.

It's NOT long before my phone starts blowing up.

RYAN

What the hell did I miss? What happened? Also are you coming over or not?

Ryan's text feels aggressive, but I think that's a me problem. I already feel like a bloody pulp, so anything less than someone tucking me in with the softest blanket would feel like too much.

ME

I quit. It's not a big deal. And I can't make it tonight.

RYAN

Bullshit. Do I need to come to you? We need to talk.

I hate those words. There aren't words for how much I hate those words.

ME

If you want to talk, you can call me.

RYAN

Ffs

My phone rings.

"Hey."

"What is this?" he asks.

I assume he means the fact that I'm in my apartment without him. "This is me taking a minute."

"Why would you quit without saying anything to me first?" he asks.

"You were clearly busy, and it's not like I never told you I hated the job."

"You hate *Isla*—"

"No, Ryan. That's not what I said." I sigh, wishing Stephanie were curled up against me while I lie on the couch. Wishing *he* were. I also wish for different kinds of wishes. Like to be one of those people who thrives on being alone. "I told you it wasn't for me."

"You said you didn't think it would be for you. That it *might not* be. You never said straight up you hated it and you were quitting," he argues.

"Look, I'm not gonna argue semantics with you. Whatever I said—this is what I meant."

"What the fuck are you gonna do now?"

"Look for another job, I guess."

"Mal…"

"What?" I ask, sensing the reason "we need to talk" is coming. I cover my eyes with my hand and do the best I can to prepare myself.

"Why don't you want to come over?" he asks.

"I just a need a minute, okay?"

He makes a noise like whether it's okay or not is debatable. "You haven't told me what happened with Kaylin."

"We broke up."

"Really?" He sounds doubtful.

I frown, genuinely confused. "Yes, really. Why are you asking it like that?"

He sighs heavily. "Listen…when I was over there picking up your badge, I found the engagement ring."

I sit up, arm stiff against the cushion and eyes wide open. "*What?*"

"Yeah, so…I don't know what that was about, but if there's something you wanna tell me…"

"I got that last year," I say immediately. "I never proposed. Obviously."

"Why?" he asks darkly.

"Because, I… I wasn't sure. Like I didn't know if I was just doing it to go with the flow or because I really wanted to marry her, so I figured I'd wait until I knew for sure."

"And?"

Is he serious? "Well, it's not on her finger, is it?"

"It freaked me out," he says.

"Why didn't you say something?" I ask. As I recall, he came home that night and fucked me into the mattress with his clothes on. This *certainly* never came up.

"You told me to trust you," he says.

I don't have anything to say to that, so I go quiet. So does he.

It gets darker in the living room. I never bothered to turn on the lights when I got home.

Eventually he says, "So you're not avoiding me because you're engaged to Kaylin."

"I'm not...avoiding you." My hesitation doesn't exactly sell the lie, but it's the best I can do.

"And you didn't quit the internship to avoid me?"

I wouldn't call what I'm doing right now *avoiding Ryan,* but again, semantics.

"You looked really good with that woman today," I say. "Norah."

"Mal..."

"Seeing you together was actually the first time I ever believed you were serious when you told me you were straight."

"Didn't we just talk about this?" he asks.

I can't really remember what we talked about or when and where. I mostly remember how I felt around him. Good or bad. Elated or twisted with jealousy. Having him or missing him. But I'm fairly sure we haven't directly addressed the issue that was so in my face today at Big Bites. "About whether you'd rather be with a woman than with me? No, we really haven't."

He dodges the question in that way he often does when he still has points he wants to make. "I talked about you with her today, you know? Specifically about how you bore easily."

I shake the phone, half wishing it were his neck. "I don't bore easily," I snap. "I just don't keep doing shit I'm not interested in."

"So what's your usual timeline on that?" he asks. "Two months? Three? A few weeks? What?"

"Fuck you, Ryan."

"I only ask because you were with Kaylin for a *decade.*"

Goddamnit. "You're never gonna get over that are you?" I ask because I think that's what this all comes down to. My one unforgivable mistake. Lying. Pretending to be someone I wasn't because I was too afraid to admit I wanted to be with him.

He makes a frustrated noise, and I can picture him pacing his rug, his turns getting sharper the faster he goes. "I have to, don't I?"

"Not if you want to end things."

"Why the fuck would I want to do that?" he nearly yells.

I used to think I was really easy going as a boyfriend, but it turns out, I'm not. Not even a little. I'm high maintenance as fuck. I can't think of a single reason why Ryan would want to be with me—not if he could have a woman like Norah. Shit, he'd be better off with Miguel. This train of thought leads me to ask the most pathetic question I've ever asked in my life. "How could you possibly want me?"

"Malcolm. I swear to God, don't make me come over there. You know I hate that place."

"Maybe we should take a break," I say.

He sighs heavily.

"I'm spiraling, Ryan."

"No shit."

"So, I think I need a break."

"Where have I heard that before..." he mutters.

"I don't mean it like—"

But before I can finish the sentence, he hangs up on me.

I sit on the couch for another three or four minutes while I absorb what just happened. I gulp back a strong swell of emotion before pushing my ass up off the couch. I know I fucked up. Again. And I can't just sit around and do nothing all night.

It's Friday, and we're supposed to film another episode tomorrow, so I guess I'll see him then if he doesn't kick me off the team in the meantime. He might have to now that I'm not in the internship.

And then what would I have? This apartment. That's what. This shitty, depressing apartment. No girlfriend, no dog, no podcast, no job, no friends, no Ryan.

Damn.

I don't regret quitting Marks & Baker, but I don't think I realized until now that, in doing so, I was setting fire to every pillar that holds up what I call a life. Ryan understood though. He was trying to help me.

I've been in therapy long enough to know when I need help. Am I great about asking for it? No. But in light of the current circumstances, I make the bare minimum effort. I text Andrea.

ME

Quit the internship. Me and Ryan might be on the outs. I'm not suicidal. No rush.

Once that's sent, I take a shower, hoping by the time I come out, she'll have replied. If not, then I probably won't hear from her until tomorrow.

Once I'm clean, I have a few texts from Bailey I ignore but nothing from Andrea, and that's when I consider—really consider—going to Ryan's to clean up my mess. I need to, so I get dressed, pocket my phone and wallet, and head out. However, when I get into the Uber, I'm no more clear on what I want to say to him than I was when I had him on the phone. I should have used different verbiage than "take a break." I realize that now. Maybe I should have called a time out.

The last thing I want to do is break things off with him. I'll be wrecked if he does, but I guess I'd understand. I haven't done nearly enough to keep him.

He doesn't see me as a safe bet, and I can hardly blame him. But since when does he have to play everything so safe? Has he always been like this, or is this another byproduct of the way I tormented him?

I shouldn't need his reassurance the way I do. He's been straightforward enough. He's not a man of many words, but the ones he's said have meant something. To me anyway. Probably to him, too.

I know Ryan well enough to know I need to let him breathe for a minute, so I give the Uber driver a different address.

Miguel answers his door in a pair of gray sweats and nothing else. His hair isn't in the usual bun. It's down, and it's longer than I would have guessed, falling just past his shoulders. He's not a large guy, he's probably 5'9 and a buck forty, but what there is of him is sleek and fit.

"I love your hair like that," I say.

"Malcolm," he says warily. "What are you doing here?"

"Oh. Right. Can we talk?"

He glances over his shoulder like I might be asking someone else, then he looks at me again and nods, stepping aside to let me in.

I start talking immediately. "So, I'm having a misunderstanding or something with Ryan, and I don't know how to fix it."

"I'd suggest showing up randomly at *his* apartment. You want a drink?"

"No, I don't want to bug you." I sit down on his couch.

He stops by his kitchen, pours himself a glass of red wine from an open bottle and walks over to sit with me. "What's the misunderstanding?"

"I got really, really jealous of him hugging a woman he was thinking about starting a relationship with today, and I kind of lost it."

"A woman who *what*?"

I do my best to explain what little I know about Norah while Miguel gets up and pours a glass of wine for me, too. Once I think I've got Miguel on the same page, I take a sip, tell him it's great wine, and ramble on. "The thing is, I've been with the same girl since I was fourteen years old. We officially broke up yesterday."

"Oh. Sorry, Mal—"

"Thank you. It sucked. I mean, it was long overdue. I wasted a lot of her time, and she lowkey wants to kill me, but I think we'll probably stay friends. We were already on a break."

"Hm?"

"This summer. She's been in Europe, and we were on a break, so it's not like I was cheating on her."

"But Ryan knows about her," Miguel says with the look of someone trying to connect the dots.

"Yes. That's what I'm getting at. Without going into the whole history—which isn't irrelevant, but I don't want to waste your time either—Ryan found an engagement ring I bought last year when he was grabbing some stuff from my apartment the other day."

"Oh..." Miguel nods. "Got it."

"What?" I ask, feeling like he's made some sort of connection I haven't.

"Nothing, go on."

I open my mouth to press him further on the point but startle when a hulking shadow passes over the wall behind him.

Miguel sighs and turns around as Nathan—bare ass naked—appears in the hallway and sees me.

His eyes open comically wide before he dashes back into Miguel's bedroom.

"What the *fuck*?" I ask.

Miguel puts a hand on my knee and leans in. "This is why we text first, honey."

"Holy shit, I'm so sorry. Should I go?"

I mean, of course I *should* go—but I'm secretly praying he

won't make me. Now that I've started talking, I really need to get the rest out.

"It's fine," Miguel says. "He didn't text first either. So. Engagement ring."

I give him the abbreviated version of why I bought but never gave Kaylin the ring, and he listens attentively. Nathan reappears fully clothed and goes into the kitchen like nothing is amiss.

His skulking around would be sort of a power move if I were trying to seduce Miguel, but it comes off a little ridiculous, and the first thing I want to do is tell Ryan about it. Then Bailey. Because it's quite obvious Nathan's not the one in charge here, despite the impressive size difference. I don't love continuing this talk in front of him, but he's not giving me a choice.

"It's a trust issue, I think," I tell Miguel, trying not to name names or use pronouns. Not because I care if Nathan knows I'm gay, but because it'd be too obvious that I'm talking about Ryan, who—at least until the other day—wanted to keep our relationship quiet.

"I can understand that," Miguel says, sliding a meaningful look Nathan's way. Nathan who hooks up with women all the time. Including in the unisex with my mentor. There's some definite subtext I'm picking up on, but since Miguel seems fine with whatever's happening, I'll save my questions about him and Nathan for later.

"How do we get past it?" I ask instead.

"Sounds like you *both* have trust issues."

"But I'm a psycho," I say. "Like batshit. Crazy in love— emphasis on crazy."

Miguel laughs, and I think I hear Nathan making an amused noise, too.

"Ha ha, yeah, I know. It's not attractive."

"It's adorable, Mal. In small doses."

"Right, well...it's kind of an all day every day thing with me. I feel like I need to let him breathe."

Miguel gives me a dubious look. "Did he ask for that?"

"No. He said we 'needed to talk,'" I say with air quotes.

"Sometimes that means exactly what it sounds like."

"It *sounds like* he wants to tell me this has been fun and all, but his future's with Norah in Seattle. Not on some stupid podcast with me."

"Are you talking about Ryan?" Nathan asks.

Fuck. I glare at him. "I just saw you coming out of Miguel's bedroom naked. As a reminder."

"I noticed that," he says. "I also feel like y'all are talking about me, too, so pardon me for taking an interest."

Miguel cuts him a look, and Nathan raises his brows like he's daring Miguel to tell him he's wrong.

"So you think you're smothering him or something?" Miguel asks me.

I do my best to ignore Nathan's persistent presence. "Something. I have no chill when it comes to him. Norah was like—chill personified."

Miguel drains his wine and nods. "Look. Here's what I wanna say. Ryan is upfront. He says what he means, and from what I can tell, he means what he says. If he said it's you—it's you. And it sounds like he wanted to talk because he's worried about you. Everybody was shocked in debrief when you weren't there and Georgie broke the news. I don't think he wants to break up with you. Not at all. I can't even imagine that. In terms of what to do about the ex girlfriend? Just reassure him. That and time. Being consistent. Showing up. Trying not to broadcast all your crazy at once."

Nathan looks like he's taking mental notes while he goes through the motions of making a sandwich.

"That's it?" I ask.

"Men aren't that complicated," Miguel says.

"So, in terms of breathing room?" I ask.

"Let me put it this way. Do you really want to let him sleep on this mess with that woman in town?"

I startle. "No," I say. I definitely do *not* want that.

Miguel sets his empty wineglass on the coffee table. "This is the one exception where you should just show up."

"Show up," I repeat. "You get all that, Nathan?"

"Don't you have some place you need to be, Malcolm?"

I turn back to Miguel. "Thank you. Hopefully I'll see you tomorrow."

He walks me to the door, and before I leave, he gives me a hug. It's a good one. Not as good as Ryan's, but very welcome. "You'll be fine," he tells me. "I promise that boy's just as crazy about you."

I appreciate him saying that, but truthfully, given the way I feel about Ryan—there's literally no way that's possible.

CHAPTER THIRTY

RYAN

Calyx checked on me via text because I skipped the gym again today, but now he's at my apartment, commiserating about how hard it is to trust people and how much they suck in general.

"Does this dude have any hobbies that don't include hurting you?" he asks from my bed while I slump in my desk chair and pick at a rubber band ball I've had since I was in undergrad.

"Making me happy," I mumble.

"Ugh. Gross. But I guess you have been happier. It's disgusting. Is he that good in bed?"

"It's not that—but yes—he doesn't do anything halfway. He commits, you know? Until he doesn't."

"That makes no sense," Calyx says, and I can't disagree.

"I was ready to give him a chance. I was gonna tell him I want to find my own place here in San Francisco and clear out a space in the closet and empty a drawer for him and shit."

"And now?"

"I guess we're on a break. I can't believe he just quit."

"You or the job?" Calyx asks.

Both? "The job," I say. "Like is he stable?"

Calyx lies down on his side and makes himself comfortable. "I don't want it to sound like I'm defending him, because I'm definitely not, but maybe he's just trying to find himself. Not all of us know what we're meant to do the second we crack open the right book or whatever. It's not like he's flailing at forty. He's our age. I change my mind and take breaks from shit all the time."

"Is that why you've been in town almost all summer?" I ask.

"Burnout's no joke."

"How long *have* you been modeling?"

"Since I was five."

"Is there something else you'd rather be doing?" I ask.

He shrugs. "Dunno. But I reserve my right to do something different."

Calyx is making a good point. There's just the one big flaw. "How do you explain him being with the same person for ten years if he didn't want to be with her."

He gives me a slow blink like my ignorance stuns him. "You think being with someone for ten years automatically means you'll want to be with them forever?"

"No, but—"

"People grow apart. They were together in high school. I imagine a few things have changed. I know I've changed in the last ten years. If you want to tell me you haven't, I might have a trophy made for you. For being really fucking boring."

"You're a mean little thing."

He gives me a harsh look. "You made me skip my workout."

"I didn't make you do—" I shut up when I see my bedroom door open. "Hey," I say to Deacon.

"You have a visitor."

Calyx sits up and runs a hand through his hair. My heart thuds in anticipation of Malcolm. But Bailey slides past Deacon and comes in. She looks from Calyx to me, then at the empty beanbag. "Maybe we should send out a search party."

"What?" I ask, trying to school my breathing rate back to normal.

"I was hoping Mal would be here, but if he's not, and he's not at his place—"

"He's not?" I ask.

She shakes her head and walks over to Calyx with her hand outstretched. "I'm Bailey."

"I figured," he says. "Calyx."

"Oh, I know. Is that your given name?"

"No," he says, and they shake hands.

"It's not?" I ask.

He shakes his head.

"What is?"

He laughs. "Like I'd ever tell."

Bailey asks, "Is it that bad?"

"In my opinion, yes."

"Well Calyx was a good choice," Bailey says. "Definitely suits you."

"Thanks."

"Anyway," I cut in. "Malcolm. Have you talked to him at least?"

"I texted, but he didn't text back," Bailey says.

"He's probably with Kaylin," I say. The thought is a huge blow, but it's logical. In theory, it's possible he's out with his guy friends getting drunk or something, but as pathetic as he sounded on the phone earlier, I can't picture it. It makes more sense that he'd go to her—his safe place or whatever.

Yes. It pisses me off. I will kill the fuck out of him if they get back together—provided he was honest about them breaking up in the first place.

But Bailey dismisses my statement. "No way."

"How would you know?"

"Because I was the one with him at lunch today while you were playing kissy face with that hottie."

"Excuse me—I did not *kiss* her. Are you sure he wasn't home? Maybe he just didn't want to come to the door."

"I wasn't subtle," she says. "One of the neighbors told me to leave or he'd call the police."

Calyx snorts a laugh. "I like her," he says to me.

"Already? I think of her more like an acquired taste."

Bailey plops onto the beanbag with her phone in hand, thumbs tapping the screen. I get a ping from the group text, and I check it. She wrote: *Checking in for tomorrow night. Can I get RSVPs for 6pm?*

She looks at me expectantly.

"I'll be there," I tell her.

"Put it in writing. Do you want to make sure he's okay or not?"

I sigh, typing out my response.

ME

I'll be there

MIGUEL

All set for 6

BAILEY

Mal??

MALCOLM

Am I still invited?

She and I both let out simultaneous breaths. She's the one who responds, though I wonder if it should be me to do it.

BAILEY

No rules, right? We can't do it without you.

I like her response, both on the inside and with a virtual heart in the group text. The bedroom door opens again, and this time, it *is* Malcolm. I stand immediately and try not to rush him. It's only when I finally see him that I realize how much I needed to.

I take a few steps toward him as he examines the room full of people, narrowing his eyes at Calyx. "You have a lot of company," he says.

"I texted you. And called. And went by your apartment," Bailey says to him.

"Sorry, I was—" Mal glances at me. "At Miguel's."

"Why?" I ask cautiously.

"I figured someone needed to talk some sense into me."

Bailey is still ensconced in the beanbag. "And did he?"

"I'm *here*," he says, matching her snark.

I turn to my surprise guests. To Calyx, I say, "I'll see you at noon tomorrow." And then Bailey. "Six. I'll be there."

She's assessing Calyx. "Wanna get a drink with me?" she asks him.

He lights up. "Yeah!"

"Awesome." She rocks herself up to standing. To me she says, "We need to get a dog."

I glance at Mal, and he looks slightly pained at those particular words. I had a feeling he was more attached to Stephanie than he'd admit. I kind of was, too. Even Bud is currently sniffing the air for his tiny canine friend as he winds himself around Malcolm's annoyingly bare ankles.

Calyx, as he's leaving, drapes an arm around me, planting a kiss on my cheek. I'm pretty sure he's meeting Malcolm's eyes when he does it given the way Mal's nostrils flare. "Noon, or I'll be knocking down the door again."

I gently push him off me, and stare at Malcolm until we're alone in the room with the door closed.

"Is the break over already?" I ask him.

He shoves his hands into his shorts pockets and presses his lips into a line. "Poor choice of words. Didn't realize they were a trigger."

"Me neither. But it turns out..." I trail off. I want to hug him, but I'm afraid he'll turn any physical contact into a reason not to talk to me, and there are still things that need sorting out. The "break" being the main thing.

"I'm ready to talk," he says.

I nod, still frozen in place.

"What we have—no wait—I shouldn't say that," he stammers. "What I feel for you isn't anything close to what I felt for Kaylin. Even in the beginning. What I want with you and me is different, too."

"How do you know?" I ask.

He sighs. "That's not where I wanna start. Can we sit?"

I gesture to the bed, and he sits on the end of the mattress. I stick with my desk chair but roll it closer to face him.

He continues with his gaze on his folded hands. "I knew the job wasn't for me by the end of the first week. I knew I hated basketball after two practices. I knew I wasn't in love with Kaylin and never would be the first time she said the words to me. I might not always know what I want, but I can tell pretty quick when something's not for me."

I'm listening. I nod for him to go on.

"So that's the timeline you asked about," he says.

"If I hadn't showed up when I did, would you have eventually married her?" I ask.

He counters with, "Would you have given a shit if I did?"

Of course I would have. It wouldn't have hurt the way his initial rejection did, but it wouldn't have felt good. "Yeah, but I wouldn't have been surprised."

"How'd you feel when you saw the ring?" he asks quietly.

I lean back and rub my mouth. "Scared." It comes out as a whisper.

"But you trusted me?"

"It wasn't easy," I admit.

"But you did."

"I wanna say I did a better job trusting you than you did trusting me today."

"It's not exactly a trust thing for me," he says. "It's more like insecurity. You don't say a lot, Ryan, and when you do talk, I wonder sometimes if you're just being nice."

"Why would I do that?"

"Be nice to me?" he asks.

"No—just—blow smoke up your ass."

He shrugs. "I don't know. I told you—I'm insecure when it comes to you. And I know it shows, and I guess I just wonder how long you'll want to put up with it."

"I've put up with worse from you," I remind him.

"That's not helpful," he says.

"There's nothing you could ever do to me that I wouldn't forgive you for," I tell him. "That's what 'I love you' means when I say it to you." I pause and consider him. The totality of him. All the things I know now, and what we've shared. "But maybe you need to hear something different."

"Yeah," he sighs, sounding utterly defeated. "I need to hear that you're not planning to leave for Seattle at the end of the summer."

That's what he's afraid of? After all the kisses, all the showers? The confessions under streetlights? This man will never cease to surprise me. "Look at me, will you?" I ask.

He does, lifting his gorgeous eyes to meet mine. "I don't think that's what you need to hear. I think you need me to tell you I *like* you."

He blinks and swallows, the truth evident on his beautiful, expressive face. "Do you?"

I nod.

"Why?"

I roll my eyes. "I don't know. Jesus. I could ask you the same thing about me. I like hanging out with you. You're fun."

"Fun?"

"Entertaining," I try again. Fuck, I'm terrible at this.

"Like...a clown?"

I laugh. "Fuck, no, not like a clown. Christ. More like a good video game."

He gives me a watered-down grin. "What about with my clothes on?"

I nudge his knee with mine. "Jackass, I wasn't talking about sex."

"But the sex is good, right?" he asks.

"I don't know how you can ask that."

He sighs this huge, exhausted sigh. "I don't know how you can avoid answering half the questions I *do* ask. It's like I need a fucking bulldozer with you."

"A what?"

He gestures at me vaguely. "The walls, Ryan. When the fuck are you gonna let me in?"

I stare at him in surprise. "You feel like I haven't?" Because it feels to me like the exact opposite. Like I've dissected myself and shown him all my soft insides.

"Is the sex good for you?" he asks again.

"Yeah," I say softly. "Yes. The best."

"And are you planning to stay in San Francisco once the internship is over?"

"If we're still together, and you want me to, then yes."

He nods. "I guess that's the best I can ask for."

No. I can do better, so I keep talking. "If we keep doing the YouTube and the podcast, we'd have to be here, right? I know Bailey doesn't want to stop once the challenge is over, and Miguel seems pretty invested, too. It's been this total pain in the ass that it turns out I look forward to more than just about anything. And we're making a ton of money."

"It is pretty cool that we were able to do that," he says. "I don't want to quit that either."

"That's saying something," I say, half as a joke. He pretends to glare at me. I ask him something else. "What did Miguel say that calmed you down?"

"He said a lot of things, but mostly what I took away from it was that you wouldn't say something if you didn't mean it, and I realized that as long as I've known you that's more or less true. And I love that about you. You mean what you say."

I nod.

He goes on. "But that's not nearly the only thing I love about you."

My heart thuds. I'm so used to reassuring him that when he turns the tables on me, I always feel the need to brace myself for fear of being swept away.

"You probably already know you ground me," he says. "You're my history. My heartbeat. My first fucking love. My brother, my partner. My best friend. Somehow you get me—you always have, and I think it's because you've got the best heart of anyone I've ever met. I want to deserve you. I want to have the only key to everything you've kept locked inside. I want the chance to love *all* of you. Because I know I will."

Is this what it means to feel seen?

I'm much too far away from him. I lean forward and ease his

back to the bed, climbing on top of him before putting my arms around him and positioning us on our sides.

He presses his mouth to mine, and I part my lips to let him in. Our tongues brush lightly, and I take a deep breath. "You scared me today."

"You scared me, too." He slots all his limbs into place, finding our familiar tangle with ease. *Getting comfy.*

"Not talking to you last night was stupid," I admit.

"Agreed," he says. "You don't get to do that again."

"Did you need me?" I ask.

He nods.

I slide my leg over his to lock us in place. "I'm sorry," I tell him. "Is Kaylin okay?"

"She will be, I think."

"And you?" I ask.

He holds me tight. "You make everything better."

"Be patient with me, okay?" I ask him. "I'm learning as I go. I've only ever been in love with you, so I have limited experience expressing myself."

"I've only ever been in love with you, too."

"It's not a competition," I tell him.

"It's pathetic is what it is," he says.

I laugh. "Maybe. So, what do you think? Are we on the same page?"

Mal smooths some hair off my forehead and looks into my eyes. "You tell me. Have I done enough? Have I convinced you you're it for me?"

"Yeah," I tell him. "You finally did."

"*Finally*," he repeats in a whisper like he loves the sound of that.

Nudging his nose with mine, I align our mouths and kiss him again. His hand moves down my chest, and we sigh against each other. "I'm glad you're here."

"Me, too," he says.

"Don't go, okay?" I ask.

"Really? You wanna run that by your roommate first?"

"Not particularly."

"Because I mean, I'm clingy as fuck. I'll totally overstay my welcome."

I grab his ass and squeeze. "I'm counting on it."

CHAPTER THIRTY-ONE

RYAN

We've made it to the last week of the internship with only two drop-outs—Malcolm and Jia, who left almost the instant she heard Malcolm did. She and I text, which is how I know she already has a new job up the street—a real job, not an internship—with a wealth management firm. It's only been three weeks since she left, but she's happier already and glad to be away from all the office drama.

I'm not sure how they did it, but Nathan, Lisette and Piper managed to stick together as a team to finish the challenge. Debrief started early today so that we could present our results. Bailey is foaming at the mouth to go first.

Georgie calls on her to step up and present.

It's clear from the pinched look on Piper's face that she knows we came out on top, but if she's annoyed now, she'll be super irritated when she finds out by how much.

Bailey's prepared a power point. The first slide is titled *Finance Bros: A Scaleable Social Media Venture.* It's not what I would have called it, but she insisted on putting the presentation together herself.

Miguel and I stand behind and to the left of her while she begins her prepared remarks.

"Let's face it—these days—the best way to make a quick buck is either to try your luck in Vegas or go viral. One might cost you your shirt, but the other—well, there's no risk, but the reward can be high." She looks pointedly at Piper. "Very, very high. Even negative attention is attention, and that's the goal—to get people to fork over their most valuable commodity—attention."

I shove my hands in my pockets and try not to blush as she goes on about all the market research she did on pets and thirst traps as content that often goes viral. "Our first investment was a fifty-one dollar consultation with an experienced influencer. He in turn gave us some ideas about how to leverage trending hashtags and some of TikTok's features, like the stitch feature."

The next slide is of Malcolm, shirtless, leaning against a wall, holding Stephanie. "The wall lean is trending. Stephanie's cute and a total character, and Malcolm has an aesthetically pleasing upper body."

I press my lips together so I don't laugh. Spoken like someone who is absolutely not attracted to Malcolm.

"But what's better than a little competition?" A slide flashes of me and Bud—it's a screenshot with my @billiondollarblackcat handle. "Opposites attract—not just each other, but users, too. After only a few stitches, we started to notice people choosing sides. Team Just the Tip and Team Black Cat. Within a week of starting the stitches per our consultants advice, our engagement increased by two thousand percent by playing off the competing advice."

She clicks into a slide of the Patreon.

"Our plan from the beginning was to transition to a subscription model. The platforms for crowdfunding are already out there.

GoFundMe, Kickstarter, but Patreon suited our needs best and fostered community. We were able to interact directly with subscribers and determine what kind of content would keep their interest. By soliciting feedback and adding some more personal touches—" She changes the slide. "A Discord." Another slide change. "And some behind the scenes footage enabled us to garner the level of engagement that fosters long term relationships."

I have to admire all the keywords she's throwing in. I couldn't have done this presentation better.

"By the time we debuted on YouTube, we had a built-in audience." She talks about the extended subscriber-only content and how we shifted our tone for "our" audience, tailoring the episodes to who was watching. And then she moves into numbers.

"Our first week following the launch of the Patreon yielded over three thousand subscribers—converting about a tenth of our TikTok followers. All told, we spent about two-hundred and seventy-five on equipment and consultations before we started earning. Our primary investment was time. Time to research and time to interact and make engaging content. Our income came from subscriptions, and more recently, sponsorships and advertising. All told, when we teamed up, we started with two-hundred-ninety-five dollars. As of yesterday..." She pauses dramatically.

"Our net yield for the challenge is nine-hundred seventy-six thousand dollars. And counting. Any questions?"

There's a stunned silence, which leads me to believe the other group got nowhere close.

Nathan raises his hand.

We spend the next few minutes discussing everyone's individual contributions and how we made decisions on how to distribute the workload. We field a few questions as to what our major roadblocks were and how we felt we worked together as a team, mostly by Jonathan and Georgie.

Once we're done, we have a seat, and Jonathan looks to Piper. "Your turn."

What follows causes me to nearly piss my pants to keep from laughing. Piper, Nathan, and Lisette describe nearly word for word the ChatGPT vintage t-shirt scheme. It starts with flipping t-shirts, then moves into electronics purchased from the profits off the overpriced shirts. It escalates to concert ticket scalping and then follows with sales of "trending items" like smart watches and *limited edition sneakers.*

Granted, it's a lot of work, so the fact they were able to pull it off is impressive in a way. Their profit, however, is not. Twelve grand, and I'm rounding up.

Bailey asks the first question. "Where'd you come up with that idea?"

Piper glares furiously at her. "It was entirely collaborative."

Bailey with her shit-eating grin responds with a cheerful, "Uh-huh."

Wrapping up, Jonathan declares our team, "The clear winner," and gives Bailey praise on an excellent presentation. She'll get a job here for sure.

I can't wait to text Mal, but Bailey stops me. "Let me come over and tell him with you."

"Me, too!" Miguel pipes up.

So, after work, we walk together to my apartment. It's impossible to entirely resist the urge to laugh at Piper, but I try to keep it civil since Nathan and Miguel have whatever they have going on. Whatever it is, it's obviously not affecting Miguel the same way it's changing Nathan.

Put it this way—I've heard zero sex happening in the unisex over the last few weeks. The most interesting work gossip is that

Isla might be seeing someone seriously based on her easy smiles and her increased productivity.

I happen to know it's Charlie, but he asked me not to say anything about it.

Bailey, Miguel and I come home to a party.

I mean—it's not a rager or anything, but Calyx and Deacon are here. So are Charlie and Isla. Miguel's and Bailey's mentors are also here, and, of course, Malcolm.

Underneath the congratulations banner and the gold balloons, I walk into his open arms. He hugs me tightly and kisses me hard on the cheek.

"You never know," I tell him. "They could have been striking it rich with midnight dog walking."

He laughs, the warm sound hitting my ear just right—just enough to send chills down my back. "But they didn't."

"No," I say. "They certainly did not. Vintage t-shirts."

"You're shitting me."

I laugh so hard, tears fall, but there's a lot of relief, too. Not because we won, and the challenge and presentation are done, but because *he's* still here. He's the best prize of all time.

He holds me through my laughter and plants a softer kiss on my face.

"Watermelon margs!" Bailey shouts. "Mal! You shouldn't have."

"You really shouldn't have," I tell him.

"Deac made regular ones too."

"Deacon gives a shit about me."

He grabs my head with the hand not in a cast, obviously about to give me a real kiss, but Miguel pulls us apart. "Not now, lovebirds. Crawl out of each other's asses and mingle."

Reluctantly, I do, taking a hug from Calyx while Mal keeps his hand on my lower back. "So, are you guys gonna keep doing the show, or is this it?" Calyx asks. "Because Bails and I are just getting started.

"I don't plan on quitting," I say, looking at Mal.

My boyfriend shrugs. "It's pretty much my only source of income, so I'm stuck with it."

"Yeah," Calyx laughs. "You seem super devastated."

"You said you'd be traveling this fall," I say. "Is that still happening?"

He wrinkles his pretty nose. "I might go to New York for fashion week, but that's it. Is finance a good major or what?"

I raise my eyebrows. "You wanna go to school?"

He makes another face. "Not really. I don't know. Honestly I'd teach yoga for a living if it paid the bills."

"Do YouTube yoga," Mal suggests.

Calyx grunts. "I need another drink."

Deacon and Mal have been working hard today. The living room is set up like an actual gathering space instead of a gym, and decorations are everywhere. We've never had this many people in the apartment at once, and if someone told me at the beginning of the summer this was how it'd end up, I wouldn't have believed them. It's a testament to how much I've changed that I wouldn't have today end any other way.

Maybe *one* other way, but the night is young.

Deacon's food is a huge hit, and soon enough Isla's working the karaoke machine she brought over. Nathan shows up at some point to keep an eye on Miguel who lets his hair down literally and murders 'We Are the Champions" in an ear-grating but ultimately hilarious fashion.

I have two margaritas, refuse to sing, and while I love most of the people here, the one I love the very most just keeps getting sexier, making me increasingly horny and ready to wrap this party up.

He's a vicious tease in his open-collared white button down

and ass-hugging slacks. Every time he catches me looking at him he'll do something like brush his thumb across his mouth or unbutton a button. At one point, he reaches into his half-open shirt and rubs his fucking nipple.

With the party in full swing, and no one even close to moving toward the door, I remember I have a bedroom with a door that locks and a beanbag chair that would look amazing with a half-naked Malcolm on his hands and knees.

Knowing he'll follow me because he is, in fact, clingy as fuck, I excuse myself from my conversation with Charlie and go into my room.

By the time Mal comes in, I've got the lube and a flesh light on the beanbag and a dick so hard, I had to open my pants.

"For the record," he says, "You barely beat me back here. You look so fucking hot when you're mingling."

"Shut the fuck up and get over here."

He glances at the beanbag. "Is that for me?"

"Hope you don't mind getting fucked to karaoke."

He untucks his shirt and finishes unbuttoning it. "Always been a fantasy of mine."

"I missed you today," I tell him.

"You say that every day."

That's probably true, but today I actually mean something more by it. "Do you think if we both did the show full-time we'd get a book offer or something?" I ask.

He stops with his shirt halfway down his arms. "Are you proposing...a partnership?"

I grin at him. "Something like that."

His brows lift. "Then I have a proposal for *you*. Bailey told me she knows of someone in her complex who's moving out next month. She said she could get us an early look."

"Whoa—what?"

He shrugs and removes his shirt. "We can talk about it later."

Malcolm knows exactly how much I like Bailey's apartment complex, and while Deacon's great, and I know he and Malcolm are becoming friends, the idea of having a place of our own—a *perfect* place... Okay, now I really need inside him. He's gotten really good over the last few weeks at speaking my love language.

Now he's not getting naked fast enough. I walk over to him and get started on his pants, tugging him in the direction of the beanbag at the same time.

He unbuttons my shirt as we move. When we make it the short distance, I kiss him and slide my hands down the back of his slacks. "Holy—" I pull my mouth away from his and meet his eyes, unable to keep from squeezing the silky fabric I just discovered encasing his ass.

"What's happening here?" I ask.

"See for yourself," he says, all slut and shining eyes.

I push his pants down to reveal the satin undies he's sporting. They're black with lace insets on the hips. They also have a slit in front that his erection has made its way through, and my brain melts down. "Man panties?" I say.

"They feel amazing on my skin," he says, voice low and sexy.

"They're obscene."

"Mmhm."

"Is there...?" My fingers slide through another open seam in the back and my dick throbs hard. "Where the fuck did you find these?"

"The Castro," he says.

"You fucking slut." Those are the only words I manage before I'm all over him, kissing him and fondling his hole and grinding my cock against his.

He shoves his free hand into my hair and wraps his casted arm around my back. He's got a plug in, and I remove that, tossing it away while he gasps into my open mouth.

"I was planning to pound your ass, but now I need to look at you."

"I love you," he whispers.

"Lie down."

The beanbag might as well be a sex chair for all the things we can do with it. The versatile piece accommodates every sexual position we've been able to dream up. He fluffs it around a little before climbing in, legs spread. I get undressed quick, but leave my socks on, impatient to be on him. *In him.*

"Legs up," I demand.

He obeys, sliding his forearms beneath his thighs and hiking his long legs back. His stretched hole shines with leftover lube from the plug, and it's my mouth's first stop.

"Fuck, *Ry*," he groans as I kneel to lick his rim and suck at his opening. The black satin against my cheeks is such a turn on, I'm leaking everywhere. I want to ask him what gave him the idea to wear something like these, but my mouth is busy with higher pursuits. Moving up, I suck his balls into my mouth before taking a turn with his cock.

The sweet taste of his precum explodes on my tongue, and I groan around him.

"Babe—oh my God."

The way he verbalizes literally everything never, ever gets old.

"You feel so good," he goes on, whimpering. "I love your fucking mouth. I love you so much."

I love him, too. He's precious and irreplaceable. He's everything, and he's mine. I know because I've claimed him repeatedly, and I'm about to do it again.

Sliding my mouth off his cock, I sit back on my knees and lube up. He watches with a glaze of lust in his eyes as my hand moves up and down my shaft. I spit onto his hole, and he jerks, shuddering when my aim is perfect.

Three things get Mal off best. One is being treated like a whore while everyone gets into position, the second is being treated like my greatest treasure once I'm inside him. The third and final thing is a deep, thorough fuck where I do whatever he tells me to.

With my hands holding his legs, I enter him on a slow, hot slide, eyes on his face while his neck arches, and his eyes flutter shut. His lips part as he pants and stretches to accommodate me. "*Fffuuucckkk yes...*"

"Tell me you bought more of these. In every color," I say, caressing the satin covering his ass cheeks.

"I can. If you like them."

"I love them. You've got the prettiest pussy I've ever seen."

"*Mmmph*...thanks," he says, voice strained. "I was hoping you'd say that."

"Yeah? Well, it's the only one I want," I add, just to make sure he doesn't misunderstand. *Actual* pussy is the furthest thing from my mind tonight. I've wanted nothing but this from the first time we kissed.

"I love you, Ryan," he says again.

I bend over him, wrapping my hands beneath his neck. I kiss his mouth and stroke my cock slowly inside him.

Distantly, I hear Nathan on the mic singing "Killing Me Softly," and it's not bad. Better than the Skid Row ballad I've had running on a loop in my head for two straight days.

Malcolm's body is warm and tight, giving feedback all over the place, from the tightening of his thighs around my back to the press of his fingertips on my waist. The pace of his breaths. The rhythmic clench of his hole. The chaotic mess of his kiss.

His cock throbs between our abs, and I go a little rougher. I keep kissing him to stop him from making too much noise, but I'm feeling pretty good too, so the grunts are coming from both of us.

"Fuck, I'm gonna come," he says.

"Prove it."

I kiss his neck and thrust faster, increasing the friction on his dick and chasing the release zapping up and down my legs and spine. He grabs for my ass and holds me deep, working himself against me until he bursts with a cry and a full body spasm. "*Ryan—Jesus.*"

I grunt. "*Mmph*—fuck yeah, baby, I love that so much." The way his orgasm feels on my cock is goddamn heaven, and I bite his shoulder as I come with a growl, my load shooting in hot spurts as my dick jerks inside his tight, clenched channel. My breath escapes me in jagged gasps while his chest heaves against mine.

His limbs are all around me. I couldn't move if I tried, and I don't want to. Burrowing my face between his neck and shoulder, I soak in his warmth. The words:

"I love you so much."

"I love you more," I whisper, knowing no matter what, it'll always be true.

"Should we get back to the party?" he asks.

"No," I say. "They're fine. I want to be right here."

"*And* work with me every day?"

"If I can manage to keep my hands off you."

"I'm sure you'll be fine," he says, annoyed.

It's allowed. I'm still pretty good at finishing my homework before I take my treat, so to speak.

"What about the apartment?" he asks.

"*Very* interested," I tell him.

"Yeah?"

"Why do you sound surprised?"

His hands move up and down my slightly sweaty back. "That's a lot of *me* time."

"You've been here twenty-five days in a row. Do you hear me complaining?"

"You get a break when you go to work, though."

"I don't need a break from you," I tell him. I can't get enough. I'm not sure I ever will.

"Even *I* need breaks from me," he says.

"Well, you don't get the amazing view."

He laughs quietly and gives my ass a soft slap. "I'm pretty happy with the view from here."

"I'm glad you're happy," I tell him.

"It's more than that," he says.

I move slightly so I can see him. "Care to share?"

"I would if there was a word I knew for it."

"Try. You can even use sentences."

"Okay." He takes a deep breath, and there's something softly shy in his gaze that I love. "It's like belonging, sort of? Like I belong here with you. This is *right*, Ryan. Don't you think?"

"Yeah, I do. And you *do* belong with me, dumbass. You always did. I tried to tell you."

He closes his eyes and leans his forehead against mine. "I told you I'm not as smart as you."

"You're fucking perfect," I say. "Infuriatingly perfect."

"Emphasis on infuriating?"

I kiss him before saying, "Depends on the day."

His arms and legs loosen, and I shift, my softened dick sliding out of him. We turn onto our sides and, ignoring the mess between us, cuddle close, like we always used to, but better.

Bailey belts out "Africa" from the living room, and I smile, my thumb moving back and forth over Mal's sexy nipple. "What are you thinking about?" I ask.

Running his hand through my hair, he sighs and says, "I'm thinking...best summer ever."

EPILOGUE

Malcolm

Four Summers Later

I find Ryan sitting on the floor of our bedroom beside an open moving box while he flips through a book. "And I thought my ADD was bad." I sit next to him and take the book from his hand.

"Hey," he objects mildly, but he leans on me, shoulder to shoulder as I look down at the page he was reading. It's our book. The one we wrote together. It came out last year, hit the New York Times Bestseller list, and kicked off a three-month book tour where we traveled to thirteen states and spoke to packed auditoriums, signing and smiling until our hands and faces cramped.

He was reading the foreword Bailey wrote. In it, she tells the story of the internship and the hundred dollar challenge in the wry, funny way only she could. It ends with her, Ryan, and Miguel all being offered jobs with Marks & Baker, and Ryan turning it down to go into business with me. It's not a love story or anything, but you wouldn't know it from the sentimental way Ryan gazes down at the words.

I get it, though. It was the beginning of us, of who we became —who we're still becoming. Slowly, I close the book, waiting for him to object, and place it in the box with the others when he doesn't. He sighs, picks up the roll of packing tape and seals the box shut.

I put my arm around him and check in. "You hanging in there?"

"I'll miss this place," he says.

"Me too. Good thing it's not really going anywhere," I remind him.

We've been in our condo for more than four years now. The first year, Bailey stayed in the complex until she was rolling in money both from her job at Marks & Baker and revenue from our show. She bought her own place—a dream house near the Painted Ladies in Alamo Square Park.

We're not following her—we're really not. Except that when one of the actual Ladies went up for sale, Ryan and I couldn't resist snapping it up. The chance to live in a historical landmark was too tempting—too perfect. The previous tenant was an old man who passed away. His kids wanted to make a quick few million. The house needs work, but one of the casual benefits of working from home is that we'll be able to oversee all the projects.

We already have our studio set up on the top floor, ready to start filming as soon as we move in. But this apartment in the Castro holds a lot of memories. Mostly amazing ones. Since we didn't *have* to sell it, we aren't, and the next residents will be a lesbian couple who will fit right into the eclectic vibe of the complex.

Ryan and I aren't billionaires, not yet, but between the two of us, we've made great investments as we've grown our brand. Those, along with the best-selling book, mean we can do virtually anything we want.

We had to learn a lot as we went in terms of being "finance bros." Without actual jobs in finance, we were just a couple of former grad students spouting off on YouTube. That's changed. Our side hustle—if you want to call it that—is a sort of boutique investment firm, run by him and me, where we've taken on a handful of clients and put our knowledge to work, gaining experience with investments and yes—risk analysis. We've made mistakes. We've lost money, we've made money, but it turns out, we do know what we're talking about. Now more than ever.

Ryan is intuitively brilliant with the markets, and it turns out, I don't suck at risk assessments. They're actually right up my alley since I have such a long history of taking risks, I guess. It's much more interesting when I'm dealing with someone else's livelihood than my own. I also hate the thought of someone not trusting me, and between those contradictions, I hit my stride and found the right balance.

All that to say, Ryan and I make a great team, which has surprised no one more than him.

"I was thinking about your birthday party when Bailey brought that stoner who made those gummy cookies in the kitchen," he says.

I laugh. That girl had been so weird. I've never seen anyone more focused, slicing marijuana gummies into tiny pieces—totally taking over our kitchen for an hour and a half while everyone else at the party, including Bailey watched me open my presents—all of which were more appropriate for a bridal shower than a birthday. Sex toys and lingerie. In my defense, it was all male-appropriate lingerie, but obviously Ryan said something to someone. There was a clear theme.

All the gifts went to good use, except the corset Miguel gave me. I tried it on and everything—in private when Ryan wasn't home. It wasn't me. I'm a pretty undies and maybe a garter man. Like I'll wear stockings but not heels. Thongs, not bras. Ryan likes my nipples too much to cover them up.

"What about when Jill and my dad spent the week?" I ask.

"Jesus—why'd you have to bring that up?"

It had been a memorable time and not planned at all. Long story short, Ryan and I are stepbrothers again, and, as that's a relatively recent development, neither one of us is quite sure how to feel about it.

One thing I know for sure is how I feel about him. "Even memory lane has potholes," I tell him.

He turns in my embrace, burying his face in my neck. Heather's managed to find me, and she's stumbling her way over my thigh to get on my lap. Reflexively, I help her up. She's even tinier than Stephanie was—and she's one of my favorite earlier memories of living here.

Ryan got her for me about a week after we moved in. She's another Yorkshire Terrier, and we've had her since she was weaned. I'd been so determined not to let her bond too strongly to Bud, I didn't put her down for weeks and forced her to sleep in bed next to me every night. I mean, she still sleeps there, but I don't have to force her anymore. It's her expectation.

Bud's protective of her, though. He's got a hell of a paternal instinct for a stray tomcat.

Also, I think he missed having Stephanie around as much as I did. Heather is her own person, though. She's less needy than Kaylin's dog—she's more demanding. Ryan calls it entitled, but I say she just knows what she wants and has high standards.

He pets her now, even though she's in my lap, and his knuckles keep grazing my cock.

"It's the end of an era," he says.

"Nothing's ending, gorgeous. We're just getting a better view."

"It's a good investment," he says, like he's trying to reassure himself.

I grin into his hair. "Oh, absolutely. The remodel will add a ton of value."

"Yeah," he sighs, his hand moving off Heather and onto my inner thigh. "A smart real estate move is always a good idea."

He's talking like we're planning to flip the house, but he and I both knew when we stepped inside for the first time—it's a forever home—like it was for the previous owner. I literally pictured actual kids—grandkids—who will be obligated in our will to keep the house in the family—sitting in the breakfast nook, taking first steps in the bright front rooms, doing homework in front of one of the bay windows, sitting around a huge Christmas dinner in the spacious dining room.

Our friends, our family, our pets, making themselves at home.

"It's a great idea," I say, meaning the house, meaning his hand on my leg, meaning staying together forever.

"I have another idea," Ryan says, his mouth finding the spot beneath my ear that never fails to send chills racing down my spine and harden my dick.

"Tell me about it," I say, sliding my hand beneath the hem of his shirt to touch his warm, smooth skin.

"We should have some people over in a few weeks."

"A party?"

"More like—a reception."

My heart thuds. If our chests were touching, he'd be able to feel it. "Keep talking."

"There'd be cake and champagne."

"Aren't you skipping a few steps?" I ask.

"Like what?" He kisses my neck. "Invitations?" Another kiss. "Decorations?" Another.

My fingertips press into his lower back, and I use my grip on him to leverage myself from sitting with a dog on my lap to straddling his. It's such a smooth move, Heather doesn't know what hit her, and she lets out a huff. But I'm not done yet. With my hands now on Ryan's shoulders, I push him until he's on his back, and I'm lying on top of him.

His eyes sparkle in the late afternoon light as he gives me a smart ass grin. "It was just a thought," he says.

"Oh, is that what that was?"

"Yeah, but now I can't think."

If he's referring to the way I'm slowly rubbing our crotches together, I can understand why. Our chemistry tends to burn off any reasoning trying to get in its way.

His hands are down the back of my pants now, exploring my bare ass cheeks and the satin strip dividing my cheeks. Do I always wear fancy underwear? Yeah.

Sue me. I love a silky thong almost as much as he does.

"You were talking about cake..."

"Right... Anyway, we can talk about it later?" he asks. "Maybe at dinner?"

"You gonna take me out?" I ask.

"Well, I'm not cooking."

We're gonna need to hire a chef. We only get home-cooked food when Deacon drops some off for us, which is about once a week if not twice. It's the way he pays us for managing his finances. Plus, he's a good friend in general.

"Should I dress up?" I ask.

"I have something picked out for you to wear," he says, and if it's possible, my heart races even faster.

"Sounds like an occasion."

"Depends on you," he tells me, grabbing me by the face and bringing me in for a kiss.

"Oh, I'm a sure thing, baby. You should know that by now."

"Maybe I need to lock this supposedly sure thing down."

I kiss him for that, knowing what's coming and barely able to wait to shout my *yes* from the rooftop or wherever he proposes. I had a terrible thought that he was going to wait eleven years— one year longer than I was with Kaylin just to be sure I wasn't going anywhere, but I guess signing a lease, being in business together, co-authoring a book, and in general sharing every part of our lives has proven I can be trusted to stick around.

"Should I stop?" I ask, about to hit the point where my need to come will overwhelm my ability to quit dry humping him.

"Why would you ever want to stop?"

Lube for one thing, I think, but kiss him again anyway, my grind against him more purposeful. We're both wearing sweats, so the chafing won't be that bad, but, as always, the idea of having him inside me is infinitely more appealing.

"If we're going out, I could use a shower," I tell him.

"A shower sounds fucking great."

We make it there in record time after a mad scramble from the floor and a short chase. Soon enough, we're chest to chest, my heart still pounding madly against my ribs while he uses my entire body as friction. His mouth seals to mine, and our tongues engage in their familiar but never boring dance. Kissing him always excites me, and it's not just the mechanics of it—which are technically outstanding —it's the feeling and intention behind it. He's *like—completely in love with me*, and there's no way I ever feel his love better than in his kiss.

But I am one horny motherfucker, and the need to get him somewhere inside me has me whining and begging.

He takes me against the shower wall, my back to the tile and my ass gripped in his strong arms. With my legs around him and my mouth never far from his, he fucks me until I'm coming untouched, shooting onto my chest and whimpering down his throat.

When my aftershocks start contracting through me, he shoves in deep and spills with a sharp cry. Cradling me in his arms, he kisses me breathless while we both come down from the high of quick, hot shower sex.

"Mal, I love you so fucking much."

He's rarely the first to say it—even now—so when he does, I reward him by saying something like, "I'm all yours," which is what I say now because if he's planning what I think he's planning, I don't want him going into it with any doubt.

"I hope so," he whispers with a light kiss on my cheek as he helps me lower my feet to the floor.

His proposal at the rooftop restaurant with a view of the bay and the Golden Gate bridge is met with a resounding yes from me. In his dress shirt with the sleeves rolled up, his hair blowing softly across his face in the breeze, and his expression all vulnerable and open wide, it's the easiest commitment I'll ever make.

"Did it go the way you wanted?" I ask after the waiter drops off a bottle of champagne.

"You said yes, so..."

"I mean—did it go to plan? Was it everything you pictured?"

"Not gonna lie, I was waiting for a clear night. I had to pay extra to get a table when I saw the weather would stay nice."

He still hasn't answered my question. "And was it worth it?"

We're holding hands across the table, a thin platinum band on my ring finger gleaming in the real candlelight from the hurricane lamp to the left of our arms. "As long as you weren't agreeing to be agreeable in public, then yes. Totally worth it."

"Can I ask you something else?"

He gives my hand a squeeze. "Sure."

"Was it hard?"

His expression falters, and his rough swallow is visible. There's a lot of emotion on his face and in the grip he's got on my hand. "Yeah," he whispers.

It occurred to me when he was down on his knee looking up at me, that he was putting himself out there in a way he hasn't since we were falling in love. And before that—his first confession when we were fourteen.

We take each other for granted a lot. It's easy when you live and work with someone all day every day. When you share all the same friends, and pets and parents and life. It gets comfortable. While I know every I love you is the truth, the words do lose a little meaning over the years.

Ryan's proposal was an act of faith. In me. In us. In the future we're planning. One we begin again every day.

"You did amazing," I tell him.

"Are you happy?" he asks.

I am fucking *over the moon*, but Ryan responds better to simpler sentiments. Being extra in bed is one thing, but being my effusive lovesick self out in the real world usually ends up getting me a flat stare and an eye roll. I try to save that shit for when I'm talking about him with other people. "Very," I say with enough sincerity to equal the amount of joy exploding in my chest. "What about you?"

"I mean...you're the love of my life, so..."

"Ryan," I whisper.

He smiles at me, a definite shimmer of unshed tears in his eyes. He was *nervous*. Like *really* nervous.

"Yeah," he says. "I'm happy."

"Then I think we should take that champagne back to the old place and give it a good send off," I say.

He sighs. "You're just worried about Heather."

"She's not used to being alone."

He stands and pulls me up with him. With his other hand on

my cheek, he gives me a kiss that I can't help but melt into. I love her, but I couldn't care less about Heather right now. This is the most romantic night of my life, and I don't want an inch between us for the rest of it.

"You're shaking," he says softly.

"Sorry," I breathe. "It's a lot."

He does the perfect thing. He wraps his arms around me and folds me into a tight, warm hug that's as familiar as breathing and as necessary as air. But it's something else, too. It's *us* in our original formation. It's our connection manifest. Our love complete. It's what we always come back to.

And always will.

THE END

ACKNOWLEDGMENTS

It's a whole new world!

When I started writing this book, I fully intended it to be a one-off. This was one of those books fully conceived based around a title, and then I took literally all of my favorite tropes and started writing.

I've been writing romance a long, long, long time. My MM work is only a couple of years old, but I come from the world of contemporary romance and trying to make it big with romcoms. Turns out my style isn't quite what's required to "make it big" in trad publishing, but I've definitely made my peace with that.

All that to say, *Finance Bros* truly represents a marriage of the big, ensemble cast romances I used to write with the intimacy of my MM work. And because of that ensemble casting, voilà—a new Bay Area world was created, and I couldn't stop at just one. Therefore, look forward to *Gym Bros* and *Tech Bros*.

Anyway, I hope you liked it.

Thanks a million to the ARC readers who took an early look at Finance Bros and left reviews or made amazing edits. Each and every one means so much to me. Thanks to The Author Agency for doing all the hard parts for me and enabling me to focus on the book itself. Highly, highly recommend.

An extremely special thanks to Cara (@spicyreadsandheas) for alpha reading and being an early cheerleader for Ryan and Mal. You really did convince me the book wasn't trash and encouraged me to keep going whether you believe that or not. And I am so extremely excited to work with you to bring the book to people's ears this fall!!! Yes, that's right. I've now produced my first audiobook with Cara, and it is an immense privilege to be able to work with someone with the kind of experience and care she brings to all her audio projects. It's available now!

To my beta readers, Dee (@thatswhatdeeread), Amanda (@amandagetslit), Kelly (@book_ishkelly), and Terri Lee for the early feedback to help me fine-tune this book and make it the best it can be. I appreciate all of you more than you know.

Thank you Eva Scalzo (my amazing agent.) Having a pro beta reader is the very best, and while your lack of emojis in text messages often makes me doubt your enthusiasm, it makes it all the more special when you eventually add an exclamation point. Thanks also for your input on the cover. RavenRed Designs is in your debt. It's such a privilege to know you and have you in my corner. Eva also gets full credit for the *Gym Bros* and *Tech Bros* titles and therefore the continuation of the series.

I want to thank David and Marta DaSilva (@pro_art_digital) for the illustrative work I commissioned at literally the last second. I am in awe of your talent and extremely grateful for your willingness to fit me into your busy schedule. I will be back for more! Their accounts are absolutely worth a follow because the processing reels are utterly mesmerizing if you're into that kind of thing. I loved watching Mal and Ryan come to life with your digital pen!

Thank you to Harley Chase and Brandon Francis for working with me and Cara on this indie audiobook. Both of you are TOP TIER and the book is incredible because of it. Thank you for the way you brought my guys to life.

Special thanks to my husband Robert for his incredibly annoying knowledge of Chat GPT. Yes, no matter how you ask it, the vintage t-shirt scheme really is something Chat GPT is proud of. But I promise, AI was only used for research purposes in that we were researching how someone would use AI to complete a one hundred dollar challenge. We're currently in the process of teaching Robert that he doesn't need AI to survive. If he weren't already a teacher, he'd definitely be a tech bro.

I genuinely couldn't ask for a more supportive partner who truly celebrates the indie publishing process and the whole world of indie romance, including my little niche inside it. Thanks, honey for all you've done and everything you're still doing for me and other indie romance authors.

Finally, a huge enormous thank you to YOU, the reader who made it through this book and who's read or will read or listen to anything else I've written. With your enthusiasm and support, I've been able to dedicate more time to writing and publishing even more books, which, in my opinion, is the best job in the world. I can't wait for you to read what comes next.

Until then, all my love.

xoxo,

August

ABOUT THE AUTHOR

August Jones is an author of queer erotic romance and a voracious reader of smut. She resides in Texas with her family, pets, and her electronic devices.

Her love language is words of affirmation.

Feel free to reach out to her on Instagram, Threads, TikTok, or check out her website https://augustjonesbooks.com where you'll find a link to subscribe to her mailing list. Join August Jones Spice Squad on Facebook! Secrets will be spilled.

WHERE TO FIND ME

If you liked this story, come hang out in my quiet corner of the internet. I'm on all the major channels, and I also have a newsletter that only shows up when there's something worth sharing: new releases, bonus scenes, and all that fun stuff.

I also have a **Patreon: August Jones Author.** If you subscribe, you'll get first look at literally EVERYTHING, a direct line to me and Calleigh, and lots of other fun goodies including art, discounts, and ARCs.

Sign up for my newsletter

Follow @authoraugustjones on Instagram & Threads & TikTok

Join the Spice Squad reader group on Facebook.

For signed copies and special editions visit my website. Store only opens when stocked, so be sure you're signed up for the newsletter or you follow me somewhere!

https://augustjonesbooks.com

ALSO BY AUGUST JONES

Manhandled Series

(MM/MMM/Erotic)

The Handler

The Baller

The Director (MMM)

The Influencer

Audiobooks available on Audible. Manhandled is also on Hoopla.

Special Edition of The Handler

(contains exclusive bonus epilogue)

Doormen of the Upper East Side

(MM/Erotic Romance)

The Heir's Disgrace

The Muse's Undoing

The Sinner's Sanctuary

The Liar's Reckoning

Bay Area Bros

Finance Bros

Gym Bros

Tech Bros

www.ingramcontent.com/pod-product-compliance
Lightning Source LLC
Chambersburg PA
CBHW032013110726
47901CB00004B/1068